PRAISE FOR THE
GHOSTWALKER NOVELS

"I cannot wait to see where Ms. Feehan takes us next."
—Fresh Fiction

"Packed with adventure . . . Not only is this a thriller, the sensual scenes rival the steaming bayou. A perfect 10."
—Romance Reviews Today

"Daring . . . Fresh . . . Who knows what the next book will bring?"
—HeroesandHeartbreakers.com

"Explosive! The sexual chemistry is literally a scorcher."
—Fallen Angel Reviews

"The fastest-paced, most action-packed, gut-wrenching, adrenaline-driven ride I've ever experienced."
—Romance Junkies

"Wow! . . . Made me hungry for more."
—The Best Reviews

"Sultry and suspenseful . . . swift-moving and sexually charged . . . In short, it is an electrifying read."
—*Publishers Weekly*

"Brilliant. The sexual energy . . . is electrifying. If you enjoy paranormal romances, this is a must-read."
—Romance at Heart Magazine

"Intense, sensual and mesmerizing."   —*Library Journal*

"[An] erotically charged romance."   —*Booklist*

D0044306

Titles by Christine Feehan

SPIDER GAME   PREDATORY GAME
VIPER GAME   DEADLY GAME
SAMURAI GAME   CONSPIRACY GAME
RUTHLESS GAME   NIGHT GAME
STREET GAME   MIND GAME
MURDER GAME   SHADOW GAME

HIDDEN CURRENTS   DANGEROUS TIDES
TURBULENT SEA   OCEANS OF FIRE
SAFE HARBOR

WILD CAT   WILD FIRE
CAT'S LAIR   BURNING WILD
LEOPARD'S PREY   WILD RAIN
SAVAGE NATURE

EARTH BOUND
AIR BOUND
SPIRIT BOUND
WATER BOUND

DARK GHOST   DARK SECRET
DARK BLOOD   DARK DESTINY
DARK WOLF   DARK MELODY
DARK LYCAN   DARK SYMPHONY
DARK STORM   DARK GUARDIAN
DARK PREDATOR   DARK LEGEND
DARK PERIL   DARK FIRE
DARK SLAYER   DARK CHALLENGE
DARK CURSE   DARK MAGIC
DARK HUNGER   DARK GOLD
DARK POSSESSION   DARK DESIRE
DARK CELEBRATION   DARK PRINCE
DARK DEMON

SPIDER GAME

CHRISTINE FEEHAN

JOVE BOOKS, NEW YORK

JOVE

**An imprint of Penguin Random House LLC
375 Hudson Street, New York, New York 10014**

SPIDER GAME

A Jove Book / published by arrangement with the author

ISBN: 978-0-515-15610-2

PUBLISHING HISTORY
Jove mass-market edition / February 2016

PRINTED IN THE UNITED STATES OF AMERICA

10 9 8 7 6 5 4 3 2 1

Cover art by Dan O'Leary.
Cover design by George Long.

Penguin
Random
House

For Manuela Barth, for all the help you give me with my community welcoming new members and answering questions when I'm so immersed in my writing, I forget everything else. I appreciate you more than words can say!

For My Readers

Be sure to go to christinefeehan.com/members/ to sign up for my PRIVATE book announcement list and download the FREE ebook of *Dark Desserts*. Join my community and get firsthand news, enter the book discussions, ask your questions and chat with me. Please feel free to email me at Christine@christinefeehan.com. I would love to hear from you. Each year, the last weekend of February, I would love for you to join me at my annual FAN event, an exclusive weekend with an intimate number of readers for lots of fun, fabulous gifts and a wonderful time. Look for more information at fanconvention.net.

Acknowledgments

With any book there are many people to thank.

In this case, the usual suspects: Domini, for her research and help; my power hours group, who always make certain I'm up at the crack of dawn working; and of course Brian Feehan, who I can call anytime and brainstorm with so I don't lose a single hour. I absolutely need to give a shout-out of thanks to Neil Benson, owner of Pearl River Eco Swamp Tours. He graciously took me out into the swamp several times on both day and night tours and patiently answered every question I asked. I've been to New Orleans many, many times and learned more from him than I had in all my other visits put together. I will be using his information in many upcoming works.

The GhostWalker Symbol Details

SIGNIFIES
shadow

SIGNIFIES
protection against
evil forces

SIGNIFIES
the Greek letter *psi,* which is
used by parapsychology
researchers to signify ESP or
other psychic abilities

SIGNIFIES
qualities of a knight—
loyalty, generosity,
courage and honor

SIGNIFIES
shadow knights who protect
against evil forces using
psychic powers, courage
and honor

nox noctis est nostri

The GhostWalker Creed

We are the GhostWalkers, we live in the shadows
The sea, the earth, and the air are our domain
No fallen comrade will be left behind
We are loyalty and honor bound
We are invisible to our enemies
and we destroy them where we find them
We believe in justice and we protect our country
and those unable to protect themselves
What goes unseen, unheard, and unknown
are GhostWalkers
There is honor in the shadows and it is us
We move in complete silence whether
in jungle or desert
We walk among our enemy unseen and unheard
Striking without sound and scatter to the winds
before they have knowledge of our existence
We gather information and wait with endless patience
for that perfect moment to deliver swift justice
We are both merciful and merciless
We are relentless and implacable in our resolve
We are the GhostWalkers and the night is ours

CHAPTER 1

———— ⟿ ————

Trap Dawkins sighed as he tilted his chair on two legs, automatically calculating the precise angle and vector he could tip before he fell over. He was bored out of his fucking mind. This was the fifth night in a row he'd come to the Huracan Club, a Cajun bar out in the middle of the fucking swamp, for God's sake. Peanut husks covered the bar and round, handmade wooden tables with a crude variety of chairs covered the floor. The bar was constructed of simple planks of wood set on sawhorses surrounded by high stools also hand carved.

To the left of the bar was a shiny, beautifully kept baby grand piano. In the bar that was mostly a shack out in the middle of nowhere, the piano looked totally out of place. The lid was open and there wasn't a dust spot—or a scratch—on the instrument. It was also completely in tune. The piano sat on a raised dais with two long steps made of hardwood leading up to it. There were no peanut husks on the platform or on the stairs. Everyone who frequented the bar knew not to touch the piano unless they really knew how to play. No one would dare. The piano had gone unscathed through hundreds of bar fights that included knives and broken bottles.

Trap glanced at the piano. He supposed he could play. Sometimes that helped his mind stay calm when it needed action. He couldn't take sitting for hours doing nothing. How did these people do it? That question had occupied his brain for all of two minutes. He didn't really care why they did it, or how, it was just plain a waste of time. He wasn't certain he could take much more of this, but on the other hand, what alternative was there?

He'd come looking for *her*. Cayenne. In spite of the fact that no one could accurately describe her, Trap knew she frequented the bar. This was where she chose her victims. The robberies in the swamp were only rumors, whispers, the men too embarrassed to say much. They were always drunk. Always on their way home. They were men with bad reputations, men others steered clear of. She would choose those men and they wouldn't be able to resist her. Not her looks. Not her voice. Not the lure she used.

He sighed again and glanced toward the bar, wishing he had another beer, but seriously, it was nearly one in the morning. She wasn't coming. He would have to endure this nightmare again.

"Fuck," he whispered crudely, under his breath. He had discipline and control in abundance. But he couldn't stop himself from the destructive path he was set on. He *had* to find her, and that meant coming to this hellhole every night until he did.

"How you doin', Trap?" Wyatt Fontenot asked, as he put a fresh bottle of beer on the very rickety table in front of his fellow GhostWalker and toed a chair out so he could straddle it. "You ready to leave? You're lookin' like you might be startin' a fight any minute."

Trap would never, under any circumstances *start* a fight. But he'd finish it, and he'd do that in a very permanent way. That was why half their team came to the bar with him.

"Can't leave," Trap said. Low. Decisive.

Not that he didn't want to leave, Wyatt noted. Trap said *can't*. There was a big difference. He'd told Wyatt he was looking for Cayenne, the woman he'd rescued from certain death, but knowing Trap, that was so far out of his reality that Wyatt hadn't really believed him. But now . . .

"Trap." Wyatt kept his voice low. Steady. His gaze on one of his closest friends.

Trap was a very dangerous man. He didn't look it, sitting there, legs sprawled out in front of him, his chair tipped back and his eyes half closed, but there was ice water running in his veins. More, he had a brain that worked overtime, calculating everything even as he observed the minutest detail of his surroundings.

He had a steady hand and the eyes of an eagle. He was silent and deadly when he stalked an enemy, and he was known to go into an enemy camp alone, death drifting in and the reaper drifting back out. He killed without a sound and thoroughly, taking out the enemy without raising an alarm. When he returned, he was the same exact man—cool and remote, his brain already moving on to solve another problem.

Trap raised those piercing glacier-cold eyes to his. An icy shiver crept down Wyatt's spine.

"I've known you for years," Wyatt continued. "You get caught up in problems, Trap. Problems that need solvin'. Your brain just won' let it go. This woman is a problem. That's what this is."

Trap sighed. "You know better. You, of all people, know better."

"You don' become obsessed with women. Hell, Trap, you hook up for an hour or two and then you walk. Not a night. An hour or two at the most."

Trap didn't deny it. "I fuck 'em and then walk away because I don't need the entanglement but I need the release." He stated the fact mildly. Unashamed. Uncaring.

"This woman is a *problem* to solve to you. That's all she

is. This has nothin' to do with the woman herself, just the mystery of her. You have to know that." Wyatt's Cajun accent was becoming more noticeable, the only thing that betrayed his wariness.

Trap's expression didn't change. His icy gaze didn't leave Wyatt's face as he took a long pull on the beer and set it down. "You grew up in that family of yours, Wyatt. You got your grandmother. Sweet and kind. You had all this." He gestured toward the swamp where Wyatt had grown up. "Running wild. Living a life. Having a *family*. You know what that's like."

Wyatt remained silent. Trap never talked about his past. Not ever. They'd met in college when they were both still teens and worked together on numerous projects that made both of them very wealthy. Wyatt had joined the service, and ultimately the GhostWalker psychically enhanced Special Forces unit. Trap had followed.

In the years they'd known each other, Trap had never once alluded to his past. He sounded like he was gearing up to do just that, and Wyatt wasn't about to blow the opportunity to learn more about what had made his friend as cold as ice. He simply nodded, keeping his gaze just as steady on Trap's, mesmerized by the blue flame that burned ice-cold under the glacier.

"I had two sisters and a brother. Did I ever tell you that?" Trap's fist tightened around the neck of the beer bottle, but he didn't lift it to his mouth. "My name wasn't Dawkins back then when I had them. It was Johansson." He said the name like there was a bad taste in his mouth. "Changed it legally in order to keep that shit out of the spotlight. To keep my enemies from finding me. Didn't work with the enemies, but it did with the press."

Had. Wyatt's heart clenched hard in his chest. He regarded Trap as a brother. He had for years. He shook his head slowly. What kid had enemies they had to hide from? Enemies so dangerous they needed a name change? Wyatt remained silent. Waiting. Letting Trap take his time.

"My brother, Brad, and my sister Linnie were younger than me by a couple of years. Drusilla was older by a couple of years. Dru took care of us while our mother worked. She worked because our father didn't." He raised the bottle to his mouth and took a long pull. Through it, his eyes didn't leave Wyatt's.

Dread built. This was going to be bad. Really bad. Many of the GhostWalkers had difficult lives, which was probably why they made the military their home, but Wyatt knew the hell that was there under all that ice, those blue flames that burned white-hot and glacier-cold, meant whatever had happened to Trap was going to be bad.

He felt movement behind him and knew Mordichai, another GhostWalker and member of their team, was coming up behind him. He dropped his hand low, down by the side of the chair and waved him off, counting on Mordichai to understand—to know not to come near the table or allow anyone else to.

"My father despised me. I was different, even then, even as a child. He wasn't in the least bit logical and half the time he didn't make sense. He hated the very sight of me, and Dru took to stepping in front of me when he was around, because the moment he laid eyes on me, he had to beat the holy hell out of me."

Trap shrugged, the movement casual. "I didn't understand what I did wrong, and poor Dru tried her best to shield me. I was so young, but already too old in my mind."

Wyatt understood that. Trap rivaled some of the greatest IQs in history. Wyatt was intelligent, but like many others he was especially gifted in certain areas. Trap was just plain gifted at everything. Along with the brains, he had the fast reflexes and superb body of a warrior.

"My father wasn't proud of me for being gifted. If anything, he took it as an affront. Dru always said he felt threatened by me, but I was a little kid and I didn't see how I was a threat to him."

Wyatt didn't make the mistake of letting compassion or anger show in his expression. Trap would close down immediately. Trap kept his emotions under tight control and Wyatt realized why. There was rage coiled deep. So deep that it was never—ever—going to be purged.

"We never told Mom about the beatings, but one day she saw the bruises and the swelling. He'd broken my arm and a couple of ribs. She took me to the hospital, and he was arrested. While he was in jail, she packed us up and moved us out of the city. I was eight. Dru, ten. We went clear across the country. His family bailed him out. He had two brothers, both as worthless and as vicious as he was."

The chair never moved, remaining balanced on two legs as Trap took another long pull of his beer. He put the bottle down with deceptive gentleness on the table. The movement was precise and deliberate. Just like Trap. Just like everything Trap did.

"They found us when I was nine. My father came into the house late at night while his two brothers poured gasoline up and down the walls inside and outside the little house we rented. He dragged my mother out of bed, down to the room where my little brother and sister slept. He shot them both and then shot Mom in the head."

Trap's expression didn't change. His tone didn't change. He might have been reciting a story he'd read in the papers. Wyatt's fist clenched beneath the rickety table, but he didn't allow his expression to change either.

"Dru and I were talking together in our secret hideaway. When we first moved in, we found a closet that was really shallow and after Mom went to bed, we'd sometimes get up and read or discuss something interesting we'd learned that day. We heard the shots and we went to find Mom, to see what was going on. Dru threw herself in front of me when he came at us. He shot her twice and her body landed on top of me. I could see her eyes, Wyatt. Wide open. Blank. She had beautiful eyes, but all of sudden, there was no light. No brilliance. My beautiful sister, so smart, so funny, the only one who could relate to me, who really saw me, saw into me, was dead. Gone. Just like that."

"Fuck, Trap," Wyatt said softly. What else was there to say? This was far worse than anything he had imagined.

"He should have just shot me," Trap said softly, almost as if he was talking to himself. "If he had any intelligence at all, he would have just shot me like he did Dru. She was so smart, Wyatt. A gift to the world. She could have done things, but he took her life for no reason other than he was a fucked-up asshole."

Still, even with the language, there was no change in Trap's voice. None. That rage was buried so deep, so much a part of him, Wyatt doubted he actually knew it was there anymore. He held up two fingers, knowing Mordichai was watching them closely. Most likely the other members of his team were doing the same, not knowing what was going on, but willing to help in any way they could.

The GhostWalkers who had come with them were spread throughout the bar, one sitting on a barstool, one lounging by the famous piano the owner of the Huracan Club, Delmar Thibodeaux, guarded with a baseball bat, and a couple of others sitting at table across the room. All would be watching Trap's and Wyatt's backs, and at the same time appearing as if they had no cares in the world.

Neither man spoke until Mordichai plopped two icy cold bottles of beer on the table and sauntered away, pretending like all the team members were that he had no clue Trap and Wyatt were in a nightmarish discussion.

"How'd you stay alive?"

"He dragged me out from under Dru. I think he wanted to beat me before he shot me, but as I came up I rammed my head into his groin and twisted the gun from his hand as he went down. I'd already calc ated the odds of success and knew I had a good chance. I hot him twice before he was on me. He had a knife in his boot."

Wyatt had seen the wicked scar that seemed to take up half of Trap's belly. He'd been what? Nine, he'd said. His own father had wiped out his family, killing his mother and brother and sisters. Wyatt pushed down the rage swirling deep in his gut. He drew in a deep breath to keep from annihilating the room. The peanut husks on the floor jumped several times like popcorn in a popper and the walls of the bar shimmered and breathed in and out. He took several breaths to get himself under control.

"He stabbed me twice. Once in my belly and again in my thigh. I hung on to that gun, but I went down in all the blood. That's when my uncles came in. They came at me, but I lifted the gun and both backed off fast. I guess they were either cowards or they knew my father was done for, because they left him there bleeding out, threw gasoline all over the floor, lit a match and told me to burn in hell. They got out. I crawled out. Still got the scars on my legs and feet from the burns."

Wyatt clenched his teeth and then carefully brought the bottle to his mouth. He needed action. Something. He almost wished a fight would break out as they habitually did in the bar. When he was younger, he often came there to drink, fight and find a woman, just like most of the other men in the swamp and bayou did. Now he came to drink and fight. He had a woman waiting for him at home.

"I had one living relative, my mother's sister. She was fifteen years younger than Mom, barely twenty-three, and single, but she came and got me and I lived with her. We changed our names, moved and thought we were going to be all right. At twelve I founded my first company after selling two of my patents. We lived good for a while."

For the first time something moved in his cold, piercing eyes. Trap raked his hand through his blond hair, hair that definitely identified him as an outsider there in Cajun country. Had he not been with Wyatt, he would have been the first target chosen for anyone looking for a fight. The fight wouldn't have ended well. Trap wasn't a man who enjoyed a good friendly brawl. You didn't put your hands on him. You didn't threaten him. Even there in the Huracan Club with his team around him, he kept to himself. Wyatt could see the name Johansson suited Trap far better than Dawkins. Trap definitely had some Swede in him, with his build and blond hair.

Wyatt didn't want to hear what happened to Trap's aunt, but he had to know. There were too many flames burning icy hot behind the blue glacier of Trap's eyes.

"For a while?" he prompted.

"Yeah. For a while. I made a lot of money, even through my early teenage years. Went to school, could have taught most of the professors. Did a lot of research in pharmaceuticals, and we both know you can make a fortune there. I just kept making money." He made small circles on the table with the edge of the beer bottle. His gaze once again held Wyatt's. "You know that money didn't mean a fucking thing to me, Wyatt. Not one damned thing. I can't help the way my mind works. The money made it easy to get the lab I wanted and the equipment, but that was all. I live simply. I don't use it."

Wyatt frowned at him. "Trap, I've known you for years. We went to school together. We were both younger than everyone else and yeah, smarter, so we naturally gravitated toward each another. We went into business together. You don' have to convince me you aren' into money."

"She was kidnapped. They took her right out of the house when I was working in the laboratory. She would always come and get me for dinner. I could skip other meals, but not dinner. She didn't come. When I went into the house, the place was a wreck. She fought them, and I hadn't heard a fucking thing."

Wyatt listened to Trap's voice, but he couldn't hear any expression at all. Just the soft monotone Trap often used.

"I paid the ransom, of course. Millions, enough to set them up for life in another country where they could change identities and live life large. I paid it immediately. They returned her body to me on my front porch. She was dead.

They'd used her." Trap's blue eyes went so cold the temperature in the room actually dropped. "Hard. They made certain there was plenty of evidence so I would see that. They hurt her in every way possible before they killed her. They left me a note. Quoted an eye for an eye. They made it very plain that any woman I was with would suffer the same fate."

Trap took another long swig of beer. "I knew it was my uncles. I pointed the cops at them. I hired detectives. They disappeared. Their tracks were so well-covered that I knew they had changed identities. Even bribing the best in the business, I didn't find out who they'd become. All that money I'd made wasn't worth shit, Wyatt. It didn't buy her back for me, and it didn't find her killers."

Wyatt sank back in the chair and regarded his friend. He understood Trap's antisocial behavior much better. He had buried himself in work, cut himself off from everyone, making certain he had few ties. He hadn't blindly followed Wyatt into the GhostWalker unit, he wanted the skills. He hadn't given up on finding the men who murdered his aunt. He would never give up. He didn't tie himself to a woman or let himself feel affection for one. He used his work to keep him apart, to keep his mind occupied so there would be no chance that he would ever put another woman in jeopardy.

"Trap," he cautioned softly.

"She isn't a problem," Trap said just as softly. "Cayenne. She isn't a problem. Fucking Whitney paired us together. I don't ever think about a woman, not even after I've fucked her. Not ever. I go to my lab, and I work until there isn't a trace of her left. This woman I let out of a cage, not knowing if she's going to try to kill me. I just see her a couple of times and I can't get her out of my head. I can't, Wyatt. She's no problem to solve. He fucking paired us together."

Both men fell silent. Dr. Peter Whitney had been the brains behind the GhostWalker program. He'd sold his experimental ideas to the military. They'd tested psychic ability. Those accepted into the program had to test off the charts for various abilities as well as have the personality and physical abilities to withstand Special Forces training. Once accepted into the program, they were enhanced and then trained in every type of combat situation conceivable.

There were four teams, and each had been enhanced not only psychically—as they'd agreed to be—but physically as well—which they hadn't agreed to be. The first team had many problems and a couple of their men had died— succumbing to brain bleeds. Whitney got better after that, improving with each new team, but it became obvious he had used animal DNA to make his superior soldiers.

It came to light that long before he had worked on adult men he had first begun his experiments on female children he had taken from orphanages from around the world— disposable children. He believed they could be sacrificed for the greater good. If his experiments worked on them, only then did he try to duplicate them in the soldiers.

He kept the women prisoners in various facilities scattered around the United States as well as in some foreign countries. He went underground once his experiments had come under scrutiny, but he had friends in high places. They not only shielded him, but believed in what he was doing, so they aided him.

One of his experiments was to pair a male soldier with one of his female experiments, using pheromones to entice them to each other. No one knew how he did it, nor was there a way to undo what he'd done, so when the male soldier came across the female, and she him, they were so attracted, it was impossible for one to walk away from the other. What Whitney hadn't counted on was the emotional attachment the pair formed. Or the camaraderie of all GhostWalkers.

They were not only elite, they were also different from every other human on earth. Some couldn't be in society without an anchor—another GhostWalker who could draw psychic energy away from them. The four teams had formed into a single unit looking out for one another. They trusted no one else and depended on one another. When one soldier found the woman he was paired with, she was protected by all of them—after all, Whitney had performed the same experiments on the women.

Each of the women was combat-trained and enhanced both psychically and physically. Some of them had been used for cancer research. Others had been forced into his "breeding" program. Wyatt had three daughters, little trip-lets, all of whom had snake DNA and were venomous. Trap had come to the bayou to help him find a way to keep them from hurting anyone if they accidentally bit while they were frightened or teething.

"How long have you known?" Wyatt asked. He wasn't going to argue. Trap wasn't a man given to fantasies, and the last thing he would welcome into his life was a woman—especially one he was paired with. One he couldn't ignore and set aside after he'd had her body.

"She bothered me on a level she shouldn't have from the moment I laid eyes on her. I thought—I hoped—it was because she was an experiment gone wrong and they issued a termination order on her. Maybe I could figure out what went wrong and I could fix her. My brain was already trying to assess her the moment I saw her and heard her voice, analyzing what her psychic abilities were and what DNA she might have been enhanced with."

"That makes sense." Wyatt wanted to pounce on that. Trap was holding himself together, but the rage deep inside was close—too close. He didn't dare set Trap off with so many innocents around. He felt the other members of their team moving into positions closer to them. Just in case. That meant they noticed the tension mounting as well. No one really knew Trap's full abilities, but it was generally considered that along with Ezekiel and Gino he was one of the most lethal men on the team—when it came to psychic enhancements.

Wyatt didn't want the building to shake apart and come down on half the men with families living there around the swamp and bayou.

"I tried to make it that, Wyatt," Trap said. "But she didn't let go. I think about her when I'm in the lab working on how to come up with a vaccine that will stay in the system for snakebite. Not once, in my entire life, have I ever been distracted from my work. I dream of her at night, and I have always commanded my own dreams. Not just any dreams, erotic fantasies, and I'm not prone to those, not even when I've gone a while without a woman. When I consider finding another woman to get relief, the idea is not only repugnant, but it's absolutely abhorrent."

"Fuck." Wyatt almost spat the word. "I see why you're putting yourself in this position now. It didn't make sense. You're the last person in the world to go to a bar every night. We've come here now for the last five nights. I thought maybe you wanted to get in better with the locals."

A faint gleam of humor moved through the ice in Trap's startling blue eyes. "Hardly. I did take your advice and hire a few of them to help with the renovations once escrow closed and the land and building became mine, but hanging out with them in a bar is going beyond the call of duty."

"How are the renovations coming?"

The humor deepened. "We're about finished. I know she's living there. No one has seen her, but things go missing, and all of a sudden the men are leery of working there, especially after dark. The workers think the place is haunted. Word leaked out that Wilson Plastics might have been a front for government experiments. I didn't let anyone go down into the lower region where the cells and the crematoria were until we'd gotten rid of all the evidence. Now, it's a beautiful apartment I designed for her. Still, word got out, and the men who really need or want the work show up, but they work in pairs and they won't stay late at all. I think she started the rumors and is sitting back laughing her pretty little ass off. Seriously, I only have a few odds and ends left anyway."

"Did you try to find her there? You hate coming here, that might be a better alternative."

"It's not going to happen. She's got her webs everywhere. The moment I come near there, she's gone. I don't want to risk driving her away."

Wyatt wished he'd had more than a glimpse of the woman Trap had rescued from those cells. Wilson Plastics had been a cover for a dangerous experimental laboratory and termination center for the experiments deemed gone wrong. His three little girls and the woman Trap was certain he had been paired with had been down in those cells, waiting to be killed and then cremated, their ashes taken out to sea so no one could ever know of their existence.

Prior to being Wilson Plastics, the land had been owned by Dr. Whitney. The huge building had been a sanitarium. Whitney had conducted his experiments on the orphans he "rescued" from around the world. The sanitarium had burned to the ground. Whitney's company had sold it, and Wilson Plastics bought the land. Wyatt's GhostWalker team had exposed the company for what it really was, and when the land came up for sale, Trap bought it.

Their pararescue team had decided to make a fortress together right there in the swamp. Wyatt's little girls and his wife couldn't possibly leave the swamp, not until Wyatt and Trap came up with the vaccine that would stay in the system without daily injections. They also had to either remove the venom sacs or find a way to keep the girls from accidentally biting while they grew up. In any case, Whitney was trying to reacquire them, and that meant they needed protection at all times.

"So you think your girl is a squatter, living on your property."

Trap nodded slowly, the humor still in his eyes. "Yeah. She's there. And she's the reason we hear rumors about drunk men being robbed on their way home."

"Those men aren't the best of the bayou, Trap," Wyatt pointed out. "If she's the one doin' the robbin' she's pickin' the men who are particularly nasty to rob."

Trap shrugged. "Doesn't matter. That's not okay, and she knows it."

"She's got to eat."

The humor faded from Trap's eyes. "Seriously, Wyatt, if I'm feeling this way, can you tell me she isn't? She could come to me. If not me, then you. She knows we're GhostWalkers, the same as she is. She could come to us. She doesn't need to rob anyone and put herself in danger like that."

There was an edge to Trap's voice, and a faint shimmer moved through the room. The opaque disturbance made Wyatt uneasy. He glanced across the room to Mordichai, who had a frown on his face. He felt it too. Trap had an energy about him now, one that was distinctly lethal.

"She doesn' think she's the same as we are, Trap. She was listed for termination. She considers herself flawed, just as Pepper always did. Not one of us, but a throwaway. She isn't goin' to come to us. She figures we'll look down on her. That we'll judge her in the way they did. It's possible she doesn't trust herself to be around us."

"She doesn't trust us," Trap corrected. "I can't say as I blame her, but she feels it, the same as me, that pull between us, or she'd be long gone. You know it's true. She had no reason to stick around here. She has no place to stay, no money, nothing. No clothes. She's staying for me."

"She's a GhostWalker, Trap. By now she has all those things," Wyatt persisted. "She can slip in and out of any store or home without ever being seen. If she's the one robbing the drunks, then she's got money. You said yourself you're certain she's setting up her home there in the buildin' you just bought."

"I'm positive," Trap said. "So much so that I'll be moving there soon. I've nearly got the laboratory all set up. Most of my equipment is in. We've got a big workspace, and I can protect it easier than the one we set up in your garage."

"I don' know if I like you livin' there alone right now, Trap, especially if she's there. We don' know how dangerous she is. I know you're close to finishing the renovations, but Whitney could hit us any time. The boys haven't had enough time to set up all your security."

"She's there," Trap insisted. "If I'm there alone, she won't be able to resist coming to me. I'd never be able to resist going to her if I wasn't afraid of scaring her off. She won't hurt me."

Wyatt sighed. There was no arguing with Trap when he made up his mind. "If you're determined to do that, why are we here?"

"I need to see her in action. All of you have asked around. You know she's been here. She's gorgeous. Alluring. Almost as sexy as Pepper. You think these boys are going to forget her? Not be able to describe her? She does something to mute that either while she's here or when she's leaving. I believe it's when she's leaving. She'd want them attracted. She's looking for a type. Someone she believes deserves being robbed. A criminal. That tells me she's got a moral code of some kind."

Wyatt flashed a grin. "They couldn't have decided to terminate her because she's a straight-up killer."

"A black widow? She's that. She carries venom for certain. She can throw webs out. And there's her voice. She can lure with her tone and that damn French accent that's sexy as hell." Trap's body shuddered at the memory of her voice seeping into his body through his pores. The feel of silk on his skin. Her long, thick hair that was so unusual. Black with red highlights right down the center. She had an hourglass figure—high, firm breasts, a small waist and flared hips. Even with her curvy figure she was small, slight even, so she could fit into places few others could get in and out of.

He was a big man. Solid. All muscle without an ounce of fat. He'd been with his fair share of women. He knew he was attractive physically and he was highly intelligent. But most of all he was rich. Not just rich. He was in *Forbes* magazine as one of the richest men in the world, yet he was in the military. He was a prize catch, and women pursued him. He didn't do the pursuing. He had never wanted to take a chance that his uncles would rape, torture and kill another person he loved.

His brain needed to work. He had no choice, not if he was going to remain sane. He couldn't work as long as he was obsessed with Cayenne—and he was obsessed. His body needed relief, and soon. Right now his brain was occupied with fantasies of her and her body. Of the way she felt when she was up against him. Of the way she smelled, that faintly elusive and mysterious mixture of storms and fresh rain. Sometimes he woke up with her scent in his lungs and he wondered if she'd been in his room. He was fairly certain it wasn't possible—he was staying with Wyatt and the rest of the team at Wyatt's grandmother's house and security was ultra-tight. Still, he wondered.

When he woke in the middle of the night, his heart beat too fast and his body was hard and tight and her scent was everywhere. Once he swore it was on the pillow next to him. He didn't sleep much. Sometimes he went days without sleep when he was on the trail of something he was developing for his pharmaceutical company. When he did regularly go to bed, he slept no more than four or five hours and not all at once.

Often Trap got up to read or work out elusive problems. His scribbled formulas were on just about every scrap of paper in the room and a few had been written on the wall. Sometimes he was certain those papers weren't in the same exact spot. He considered that he might be losing his mind. The last few weeks he'd been acting totally out of character, and that's what convinced him he needed to find her. To put a stop to whatever was happening.

If Whitney manufactured their attraction to each other, he should be able to find a way to undo it. Come up with an antidote. Cayenne would stay safe that way. It was the only way he could ensure no one would ever get their hands on her again. He would have to give her up before the attraction grew to the point neither would be able to resist.

Wyatt sighed. "You're going to move to that building before we have it ready, aren't you, Trap?"

Trap nodded slowly. "I can take care of myself."

"Yeah, under most circumstances, but if you're wrong about her, this woman could kill you, Trap. I couldn't harm Pepper. I doubt you could hurt Cayenne."

Trap's gaze turned glacier. "You've always been sensitive, Wyatt. You don't like anyone pointing that out because you think that makes you feminine." He spoke entirely dispassionately, no judgment or expression in his voice. "That's what makes you such a good man. You care about people. You always have. I stopped when my own flesh and blood murdered my family. I couldn't allow myself to feel. If I did, I wouldn't survive. If this woman who is supposed to be *my* woman decides to kill me, she's an enemy. She isn't mine."

"She's scared, Trap."

He nodded. "I know that. I know she'll fight the attraction— and me. That isn't the same as wanting to kill me."

"When a wild animal is threatened—cornered—they often strike out. She's never known freedom or kindness. She has no idea how to live in the world. She's been locked up, experimented on, which means needles and God knows what else. She's never had anyone give her compliments or romance her. She knows nothing but enemies."

"I have a brain, Wyatt," Trap said. For the first time impatience crept into his voice. "I've had a lot of time to think this through."

"I don' want you to do something you'll regret—or worse, not do somethin', which will get you killed."

The ice blue flame in Trap's eyes deepened. Nearly glowed. "She's *mine*," he said softly. This time there was a wealth of expression in his voice. Possession. An underlying anger. That strange shimmer slid into the room again, filling the space where air had been, completely at odds with his intention to reverse whatever Whitney had done to tie Cayenne to him.

"Doesn' seem to me that you're so willin' to sacrifice your own happiness, or hers, to keep those uncles of yours in the shadows. Maybe you ought to consider courting her publicly. Get yourself in the tabloids, let the paparazzi take a gazillion photos of the two of you. That would bring them straight here. Right into a team of GhostWalkers waitin' for them." Wyatt flashed a cocky grin, knowing Trap was the most camera-shy man he'd ever encountered. "Whitney already knows where she is. It isn't like he'd suddenly find her."

Trap looked thoughtful as he took another pull on his beer. "That's not a bad idea. She isn't so easily compromised either. They try to tangle with her, she'll kill them in a heartbeat. I've been trying to find them for years."

"Maybe they're dead."

Trap shook his head. "Not a chance. They're out there, living the good life. Once I find them, I'm going to kill them."

Again his voice lacked expression. Still, that shimmer hung in the air. Trap took another drink and glanced toward the piano. If he played, it would get him through the last couple of hours before Thibodeaux shut the place down.

The door opened, and the night breeze drifted in. Along with it came the scent of rain. Of storms. Of her. Of Cayenne. She was there. At last. He lifted his gaze and for one moment, indulged his need to drink her in.

CHAPTER 2

Cayenne was even more beautiful than Trap remembered. Truthfully, she took his breath away, although he knew Wyatt was watching him closely, so he refused to allow any expression to show on his face. Still, he couldn't just look away quickly as he should have. She moved into the room with such fluid grace it was impossible for any man not to look at her. Every man in the bar turned, and for a moment there was silence as they watched her pause just inside the door. She was all woman, soft curves and wholly feminine. A lethal weapon even without the enhancements she possessed.

Trap thought she was stamped so hard into his memory that she was in his very bones, but still, he'd forgotten the long thick mass of dark shining hair, so black under light it gleamed almost a dark blue. Straight down the middle of the back of her scalp, almost in the shape of an hourglass, the color changed to a beautiful, dark rich red. The effect should have been shocking, but instead, it was intriguing. The difference only made a man want to sift his fingers through those red strands, tunnel deep to see just how far that red went inside that black mass.

Her face was an oval, high cheekbones, a wide, generous mouth with lips that took a man's breath away and gave him way too many fantasies. Her eyes were large, a deep green framed with long, thick black lashes. The dark lashes served to play up the brilliant green color of her eyes so that all a man could think about was staring into them when he was deep inside of her, watching her as he gave her orgasm after orgasm.

Stop. One hand went to the wall beside the door.

The word was whispered in his mind. Sultry. Sexy. A wisp of sound like butterfly wings fluttering gently against the walls of his mind. The sensation didn't stop there, it floated through his body—such a light touch—but it brought every nerve ending possible alive in his body. He was wholly aware of her. Every detail. Trap was watching closely, so he noted the slight trembling. She wasn't nearly as confident as she appeared.

He'd also been broadcasting his thoughts to her. Mind to mind. A detail that vaguely shocked him.

She wore soft vintage blue jeans, worn, as if she'd had them for years when he knew very well she hadn't. They clung lovingly to her hips and framed her ass like a caressing hand. Her camisole was a deeper blue with a light blue contrast—the ribbons binding her breasts behind the material, so that all he could think about was loosening the tie to help himself to those soft, inviting curves. He wanted to see her creamy breasts spilling free for him, with all that dark blue material tight around her rib cage and impossibly small waist framing them.

I mean it, stop right now, Trap.

She might have meant it in her mind, but her body didn't mean it. He could see the faint change in her breathing. For that moment, her green eyes clung to his, and he saw beyond the mask she wore, just as he was certain she could see the real Trap Dawkins. That wasn't a good thing. Not by a long shot. He wasn't a nice man. He was rough. Rude. Insisted on his own way in nearly everything. He had been dead inside until he laid eyes on her, and he blamed her for pouring life into him. Definitely not a good thing.

Cayenne forced her face to remain exactly the way she wanted. Soft. Confident. Interested in everything and everybody. She wasn't any of those things. She was exhausted, starved, light-headed from being so hungry and bordering on desperation. More than anything else, she was terrified. She often came to the Huracan Club. They had free peanuts, and she'd been surviving on them for the last three months. The money she stole she left as payback for the clothes and then the shoes she'd stolen. A few times over the last four months she'd bought burgers right there at the Huracan Club.

She kept air moving through her lungs as she paused just inside the door. *He* was there. Trap Dawkins. She had avoided coming for the last five days, but she didn't dare go without eating much longer. She was too weak and she needed the protein the peanuts provided to keep going. Once she had a little money, she could buy another one of Delmar's burgers.

Her gaze immediately went to Trap as if he were a magnet. There was no pretending he wasn't there. He dominated the room. He was just . . . big. Tall, very wide shoulders, a thick chest, all muscle. He looked intimidating, and he was. Yet, he was the only human being on the face of the earth that had showed her any kindness. He had looked at her and saw a human, not a monster.

Cayenne pushed a shaky hand against the wall, her knees threatening to give out. She'd lived her entire life in a very small cell. They'd allowed her a toilet, a bed, books and a computer. And their fear. For as long as she could remember she felt their fear. She could look into a person and see inside of them—their goodness or their cruelty. Every man who came near her during her childhood had that streak of evil in them, whether too much greed, the desire for power, or their need to hurt others. If they were afraid of her—what did that say about her?

Time seemed to stand still. It tunneled, the walls of her mind curving until there was only Trap there. The way he'd been when he'd come into her cell. She had been moved to the basement cell for termination. They would kill her and cremate her before taking her ashes out to sea. She'd been created in vitro and held in a laboratory all her life. No one would ever know she existed. Or care. Until Trap.

He was a miracle. So gorgeous. A beautiful man. One moment she'd been alone without hope and the next, there he was. He'd appeared as if he'd come right through the wall. He'd slid down to the floor just outside of her cell—the cell with triple locks that were impossible to open. He'd sat there a moment, and then he'd opened his eyes. The impact had been physical, like a wicked punch to her stomach.

His eyes were a vibrant blue. He looked terrifying. All that muscle, those wide shoulders, the strength of him, even his piercing gaze that seemed to go straight to her heart. She hadn't moved. She couldn't. Her heart pounded, and she'd waited, because when she didn't feel the cruelty in him, she'd been so stunned she couldn't think properly. He *looked* scary and *felt* dangerous, yet deep inside, she knew he wasn't a cruel man.

He felt like all kinds of other things, things that confused her. They still confused her. Trap Dawkins was the reason she hadn't fled the area the moment she was free of her prison. He'd let her loose on the world. He'd opened the impossible locks and allowed her freedom. She had no idea what to do with freedom. She had knowledge of the world, but no experience.

She had no money, no food, no shelter. She had no idea how to interact with normal people. She didn't know what normal actually was. She could kill. She'd been trained to kill, and she was good at it, but she had no idea how to fit in with people or interact with them. Even when eventually, driven by need, she carefully chose her targets to rob, choosing men who were violent and cruel, she couldn't enter a store and purchase the items she needed because she didn't know how. Just the thought of that terrified her.

The clothes she wore were stolen. She felt terrible about that. There were very few women her size in the area, at least that she'd seen. The clothes had belonged to a young teenage girl. The family didn't have much, and that made it worse. She'd gone back a few weeks later and left money, but she didn't know what the clothes were worth so she had no idea if she'd given them a fair exchange. Instead, just to be sure, she left money twice. She had two pairs of jeans and two camisoles. No sweater. No jacket. The shoes were too big and she'd stuffed paper in them to keep from hurting her feet when she walked.

Sometimes she stole food as well. She always left money when she did, but she didn't like to steal and knew she couldn't do it that often. So she went without several days a week. Now, the scent of Delmar's burgers made her feel weaker than ever.

She took a deep breath and inhaled Trap. She'd been like a moth drawn to the inevitable flame, unable to stay away from him. She'd stayed close, going back to the old building where she'd been held prisoner, making a lair for herself down in the basement. He'd bought the building and workers had torn it apart, completely renovating it. She'd been forced to stay in the vents and outside until they would leave at night. She'd hated that, but still, she couldn't leave him. And she had nowhere to go.

Something was between them, she just didn't know what. Whatever it was, there was no escaping it. The thread between them was impossible to snap. She found herself sneaking past the guards at the Fontenot home in the middle of the night just so she could be in the same room with him. She *had* to be with him. She knew it was the same for him, but she'd remained deliberately elusive, terrified of what he would want from her.

She had the illusion, the fantasy of him as long as there was no real interaction. The moment, a week earlier, she'd entered the Huracan Club, her chosen hunting ground, she'd scented him. He was actively searching for her. She knew that the moment she became aware of his presence at the club. He wasn't a man to frequent clubs. *She* was the reason he'd come. She'd stayed away until hunger drove her out of her safety zone and straight into the line of fire.

He hadn't come alone either. He'd brought several of his friends. All were combat trained. She recognized the danger in them. Two of the three Fortunes brothers, Malichai and Mordichai. Their brother Ezekiel was most likely at home protecting Wyatt's children. But Malichai and Mordichai presented enough of a threat.

She spotted Draden Freeman. He often ran mornings and evenings. He was a question mark to her. She'd studied all of them and wished she still had access to the laboratory's computer, but when Trap had the building renovated, all computers had been removed and new ones installed. She'd tried them all, but the passcodes, so far, had been impossible to break.

Wyatt Fontenot was there, looking right at home, casual even, when there was nothing casual about him. He was a good man. She could tell that the moment she was anywhere near him, and she liked that he seemed to be protective of Trap.

The fifth man accompanying Trap to the bar was one of those ghosts she rarely saw, so she made certain, even though he stayed in the shadows, that she studied him. She didn't have the best eyesight, probably a by-product of the spider DNA Whitney or Braden, whichever, gave her in a test tube. Still, she had skulked around the Fontenot home enough to know that he had arrived a month earlier and was part of their team.

They called him Gino. When he was still, he was impossible to spot, and twice she'd nearly run right into him. It was fortunate she often used trees to move in, and she'd clung to the trunk to prevent dropping right on his head. She didn't know his last name, but she could see that he was a man without an ounce of fat, cool, nearly black eyes and wide shoulders. He looked just as dangerous as the rest of the team.

She was too weak to fight them all off if they made a move on her. She could only trust that Trap would know she would fight to the death to prevent them from putting her back in a cell. She had gone back to the building's basement, although that was completely changed as well now, but that was of her own free will, not someone forcing her. She would never be forced again. Never.

Trap watched as Cayenne took a slow look around the room, noting the position of every member of his Ghost-Walker team. She made each and every one of them, and she made a show of it, letting them know. She turned back to Trap and raised her eyebrow before sauntering across the room to the bar. She had a great ass and it swayed invitingly as she moved with a silent, fluid grace to lean against the makeshift bar, right beside the two most belligerent men in the place. At once they split up, one moving to her other side so that she was wedged between them. She sent both a smile that jerked their heads up, and one inched a little closer to her as she reached for the peanuts.

Trap realized she'd already marked him as her next victim if he fell for the bait. "Who are they?" Wyatt knew everyone in the area. He'd grown up there, hunted and fished and basically lived off the land during his childhood. He knew these men and he knew their reputations.

"She's causin' quite a stir. Funny that when she leaves no one remembers what she looks like, only that she's been here," Wyatt observed.

"Who are they?" Trap repeated, a slight edge to his voice. Wyatt sighed. "The taller of the two is named Pascal

Comeaux. That family has a feud goin' with mine datin' back to high school. The Comeaux brothers—and there are five of them. *Were* five of them," he corrected. He lowered his voice. "Their brother Vicq was involved in a sex trade ring. The Comeaux brothers like to beat the hell out of women. Vicq went far beyond that. He's dead now. Pascal has a bad reputation. He's married, and his wife is never without bruises all over her. His kids too."

"He's married?" Trap echoed.

"That doesn' slow him down. He's after every woman he sees. Visits Chantelle's place regularly and beats up every woman he pays to sleep with. He's bad news. The Comeaux boys avoid us because we're the only ones that can take 'em in a fight. You notice no one else messes with them. He's got money though. The entire family has money, and that's more than most in the swamp, so they always have women lookin' at them like they might be able to change them."

"So the other one on the other side of her?"

"Is his brother Blaise. Not married. Mean as a snake. She knows how to pick them."

Cayenne's soft laughter drifted through the noise of the bar. Trap reached inside his jacket for his notebook. He'd already begun the equations he needed to keep him working and from killing someone. The next couple of hours were going to be even longer, and he needed something—anything—to occupy his mind and get him through until closing time. He took out a pen and wrote on the notepaper. P = #AR. HYP

Wyatt shook his head and slid out of his chair so he could keep his muscles loose. There was going to be one hell of a fight before the night was through if he wasn't mistaken. He moved around the table to stand to one side of Trap and study the formula he was scribbling in the pages of the small notebook he'd pulled out of his pocket.

He frowned. "*P* is for peanuts and *AR HYP* is what?"

Trap didn't look up. "Arachis hypogaea, you cretin. You went to the same university I did. That's the biological/

Linnaean classification for peanut, and you should know that."

"I don' store useless information in my head, Trap. It's filled with other much more interestin' things. Who cares what the biological/Linnaean classification is. Call it a fuckin' peanut."

"When doing something such as calculating the amount of peanut husks on the floor in this idiotic place you call a bar, you need to be *precise*. I'm estimating the square footage to be five hundred feet minus the dais the piano sits on and behind the bar." Trap pushed a napkin toward Wyatt. "You can do your own calculations."

"Not happenin,' brother. I'm about to get into a major fight with the Comeaux brothers, and my head can' be clouded by numbers. I don' think knowin' how many peanut shells are on the floor is goin' to help me when they pull knives out."

Trap didn't look up from the paper, pencil still moving across the surface. "I don't fight for fun, Wyatt. These boys pull a knife and they're going down."

He scribbled out more on a precise line.

Wyatt was always astonished that Trap could use such a mild, obviously half-listening voice, and yet sound menacing. Not sound. *Feel*. Trap always felt dangerous. Scary. Now Wyatt knew why. A boy couldn't go through the things Trap had without shutting his emotions down in order to survive. He didn't let people in. In fact, Trap pushed others away from him using his abrupt, rude antisocial behavior. Everyone had put it down to his tremendous IQ, believing it was difficult for him to relate to others.

Wyatt had never understood how Trap could be a solid member of their team, treating the other men with obvious affection. He was still a little apart, but he joked and he had their backs always. He cared about them, and it showed. If he could do that, put aside his rudeness for them, he could do it with everyone. He *chose* to push people away.

Trap gave extravagant gifts to the women he slept with,

but he always made it clear he wasn't in the market for a relationship. None of them believed him and they always tried to go back for more, but he never gave any of them false hope. Wyatt realized it was Trap's way of protecting them. He didn't want his uncles to ever think he was falling in love or cared about any of the women he took to his bed.

Wyatt reached for a handful of peanuts, noticing that Trap had cracked several open and thrown the husks to the floor without eating the peanuts. "What's all this?" he asked as he broke one open.

"I had to figure out the percentage of people eating peanuts," Trap said absently, scribbling more equations, but pausing long enough to point out to Wyatt the letter E that apparently represented the percent of people eating peanuts. Beside the letter E he had written two standard deviations runs from 65.0% to 83.6% with a mean of 74.3%.

"The letter F represents the *frequency* per minute of peanut eating," Trap explained, as if it were the most natural thing in the world to want to know how many peanut husks were on the floor of the bar.

Wyatt rudely spun the paper around to stare at it. Trap had written two standard deviations runs from .5 to 3 peanuts per minute with a mean standard of 1.75 peanuts per minute.

"You're really doin' it? Calculatin' how many husks are on the floor?" He gave a hoot of laughter and threw a peanut into the air to capture it in his open mouth. "Did you add that into your equations? My amazin' ability to catch anythin' I'm eatin' in my mouth? That's gonna wreck your minute-eating ratio."

Malichai Fortunes drifted over, followed by his brother Mordichai, drawn by Wyatt's laugher. They stood behind Trap's chair and peered down at the notepaper. Draden Freeman took a position to Trap's right.

"What's he doing now, Wyatt?" Malichai asked.

"Looks like he's figuring out how many shells are on the floor of the bar," Mordichai announced, reaching over Trap's shoulder to grab a fistful of peanuts.

"He's got himself some cryptic notes, N for the number of people in the bar on a weekday." He leaned closer to read the scribbled equation. "Two standard deviations (95% of all possibilities) runs from 15 to 20 people, with a mean of 17.5 people. You counting us as the *mean* people, Trap. That just plain hurts my feelings."

"He thinks most people eat .5 to 3 peanuts per minute," Wyatt pointed out. "Since I've got to toss them in the air and catch 'em before I eat them, I think I might take longer. What if I miss? What about you? You think you can eat faster than 3 peanuts per minute?"

"Go to hell," Trap snarled. "Seriously. You all are worthless." He pulled his paper closer to the edge of the table and wrapped his arm around it as if he could shelter his beloved calculations from them.

"Can he really do that, Wyatt," Mordichai asked, "or is he full of shit?" He looked at the peanut husks covering the floor.

"You could if you estimated the total number of peanut husks on the entire bar floor each weekday, each weekend day and each week by estimatin' peanut-eatin' rates, lengths of bar, that sort of thing," Wyatt said.

"Why would you want to?" Malichai demanded. "That's insane. How would you even know the square footage available without measuring?"

Wyatt laughed. "Trap's always been able to look at anything and tell you the square footage within minutes. We used to make bets back when we were at the university together with other students. We always won."

Trap made a sound of sheer annoyance. "Did you even go to school, Malichai?" Trap was very aware that Whitney wouldn't look at any candidate for the GhostWalker program unless they had above average intelligence, let alone allow them in. One of the things he was most grateful for was that in spite of the fact that he held himself aloof a lot of the time, they shared their humor with him and he could occasionally find that he could actually joke back.

"Not if I could help it," Malichai admitted. "Ezekiel beat the crap out of me when I didn't go, but it was worth it. Well, except in tenth grade. I didn't miss a single day of tenth grade. Miss Conrad taught that year and she was *hot*. She wore tight sweaters, clingy skirts and sweet fuck-me heels. I still dream about those heels wrapped around me." He nudged Trap. "If you got your head out of your ass and stopped doing shit like this, you might find yourself with some sweet fuck-me heels wrapped around you."

"Isn't that what we're doin' here?" Wyatt demanded, as he dropped back into a chair. "He's all hot and bothered thinking about the woman that got away from him. Trap's a ladies' man. Never knew him to miss out on a score, but she just up and scuttled away without even lookin' back."

"She looked," Trap objected, glaring at Wyatt.

"She's not lookin' now," Wyatt pointed out, and the men erupted into laughter.

Trap turned his attention to his notes. "Mb is the maximum number of peanuts per person sitting at the bar." He added onto his note. Two standard deviations runs from 90 peanuts to 130 peanuts with a mean of 110 peanuts.

Wyatt tipped his chair back. "I could take off my shoe, dump shells into my shoe and count them. We could calculate the size of my shoe . . ."

Trap hooked the toe of his boot around Wyatt's chair and dumped him on the floor without looking up. "You're an ass," he muttered. "Mr is the maximum number of peanuts per person sitting at a table." He added to his notes. Two standard deviations runs from 40 peanuts to 75 peanuts with a mean of 58 peanuts.

Draden frowned. "You're assuming for your model all random variables have normal distributions."

Trap nodded as Wyatt, laughing, got off the floor and righted his chair. "He confirmed this by plotting the curves based on all days of observation, collecting data points, and seeing the resulting probability curve that did follow the normal bell curve distribution. He does shit like this while we have to sit around drinking beer and waiting for his woman to show up."

"Have to drink beer?" Trap snorted derisively. "You practically begged to come along."

"Only to protect the locals from your mean ass," Wyatt said.

"What were the numbers you used?" Draden asked curiously.

"I figured, based on my observations, that during the weekday anywhere from fifteen to twenty people come to the bar, but that number triples on the weekends. For the model I'm using, a key distinction is whether a person stays for a short versus a long time. I observed repeatedly that the two cases split fairly evenly, meaning one out of every two people stays just for a drink or two and one out every two stays for several drinks and to chat with their friends."

Laughter burst from the bar. Melodic. Beautiful. The notes filled the air, and Trap tapped his pen on the tabletop repeatedly. He breathed deep as a small, vaporous cloud snaked into the air surrounding the table. Instantly both Draden and Mordichai clapped a hand on Trap's shoulder. He took a deep breath.

"What about the bar sitters versus table sitters?" Malichai asked, clearly wanting to distract him.

Wyatt bent over the paper, reading Trap's equations while Trap continued to stare at the bar. "Bar sitters who stay a short time, 1.5 hours or less, are modeled by the frequency of their peanut eating, while those who stay longer than 1.5 hours are modeled by their peanut-eating capacity."

Trap forced his gaze away from Cayenne. He looked up at Malichai. "That's you, a bar sitter, and you machine-gun them. Wyatt's a table sitter because he likes to have food."

"Delmar can serve up a damn good burger," Wyatt defended himself.

"The average length of a short stay for a table sitter, not

Wyatt, is about an hour. The bar is open on four weekdays and two weekend days with the average number of people tripling on the weekends. One out of every three people sits at a table whereas two out of every three people sit at the bar," Trap explained.

"To be closer to the liquor," Malichai pointed out, nudging his brother.

"There is that," Wyatt said. "I often am conflicted about where to sit. Mordichai doesn't sit. He wanders. Did you figure him into your calculations?"

"What's the ratio of bar sitters to table sitters weekdays to weekends?" Draden asked.

Trap took another deep breath and let it out, clearly trying to get his mind right. He took the notepaper with his calculations written out in his precise, neat hand and began to make seemingly random folds to the sheet of paper right along the various lines of formula.

"It remains the same. On weekends the bar puts out six tables rather than four. By the time I finished it all, I came up with the total number of husks on the floor per week as thirteen thousand, two hundred and ten." His gaze moved past Wyatt, who had inched his chair around just a little more to try to keep Trap from staring at Cayenne as she leaned against the bar.

Pascal Comeaux swept his hand down her hair, fingers lingering for a moment. Cayenne caught his hand, pulled it from her hair and indicated his wedding ring. Trap clenched his teeth. Around them, the air thickened until it was dense—so dense that a heavy opaque gray slipped around them like a veil. Mordichai coughed. Draden cleared his throat. The air was difficult to breathe into their lungs.

"Trap," Wyatt cautioned softly. "You've got to hold it together. We're all watchin' her. Nothin's goin' to happen."

"I was right, damn it," Trap hissed. "She's fuckin' robbin' them. First she flirts her cute little ass off with them. What the hell? Does she go home with them?" The moment he said it, the walls of the room creaked. Expanded and contracted. Overhead the roof creaked, the sound like tree branches scraping against tin.

"You know she isn't goin' home with them, Trap," Wyatt said. "Don' be an ass. And don' take down my favorite waterin' hole."

Cayenne's soft laughter drifted toward them again, and Trap's head came up, rage churning deep inside, right beneath that thick blue ice. He'd had enough, and this time, he was going to put a stop to her shit.

"Uh-oh," Wyatt whispered softly under his breath.

Trap's eyes narrowed. *Stop flirting with them before someone gets hurt.*

There was silence. Outraged silence. Her breath hissed out between her teeth, but only Trap heard it. She turned her back to the bar, leaning on her elbows, which thrust her breasts out toward him. For one moment her jeweled eyes touched his and then skittered away defiantly.

You don't own me. You have no right to tell me whether or not I can flirt.

You want to flirt, you can damn well flirt with me. You want to get laid, I'm your man. You're going to get someone killed.

Her eyes came back to his face. Drifted over the angles and planes. Touched on the shadow on his jaw. *Trap, you know what we're feeling isn't real.*

It's real enough for me, baby. Those two men are brutes. I'll take my time with you. I'll make you feel better than you've ever felt in your life. His velvet voice stroked her skin, deliberately fed her need of him.

Her breath caught in her throat, and she abruptly spun around again. *Get out of my head. I've been a prisoner all my life and no one is going to cage me.*

He refused to leave her head now that he was firmly entrenched in it. He stroked her again. Gently. Intimately. *When I'm inside you, baby, you're going to fly. No cage for either of us. Ever. You're mine, and no matter who comes at you, I'll fucking kill them before they get to you. That's a promise. Now get away from those two.*

There was a small silence again. Trap made himself breathe. She needed to come to him. If he tried to force her, she'd be in the wind again.

This isn't what it looks like. Just business.

She was trying to appease him, but that just pissed him way the fuck off. *I know what you're doing. I don't like it, and you have to stop before someone else figures it out.*

You don't know what I'm doing.

Her voice was always sultry. Sexy. An invitation, but delivered telepathically, mind to mind, so intimate, his body's response was low and wicked, a hard punch he didn't expect. It actually took effort to keep his expression the same.

You're testing them to see if they meet your personal criteria for setting them up to be robbed.

Again there was a small silence. She turned her head to give Pascal another smile. The man reached over and slid his hand down her spine to the curve of her ass. She moved away instantly, saying something low to him. His brother boxed her in, forcing her body back toward Pascal.

Trap stood instantly. The room pulsed with tension. That shimmer moved from their table through the air, thickening more, making it difficult to breathe. Several men coughed. The other GhostWalkers stood as well. Cayenne turned immediately still, sandwiched in between the brothers. She flashed a smile at Trap, ready to defuse the situation. She could see the intent in his eyes, feel the danger pouring from his body. The icy rage pulsed in the air.

She continued to smile at Trap as if they were old friends. "I didn't see you sitting there in the dark. Want a beer?"

Pascal leaned down and said something in her ear. She shrugged, snagged two bottles of icy beer that Delmar put on the wooden plank in front of her and slipped out from between the Comeaux brothers. Pascal let out a snarling curse and caught her long hair in his hand, jerking her back toward his body.

Trap got there first, but every team member had his back. All five of them. Men with cool, dangerous eyes that had seen more combat than Pascal could possibly imagine in spite of his years of growing up fighting.

"Let her go," Trap said softly. Too softly. "She's mine. You touch her again and you're a dead man." He meant it. He let Pascal see that he meant it.

Pascal was mean and he liked to hurt others, but he wasn't stupid. He was a cunning, cruel man who ruled his world with an iron fist. He knew death when he saw it. He knew a situation he couldn't win. He shoved Cayenne at Trap.

Trap's hands were gentle as he caught her to him, trusting the others to keep the Comeaux brothers off of him.

What are you doing? I can't combat this, even with my voice. I could have made him stop. You know that. He's very susceptible to my voice. Trap, I can't make him forget this and he'll come after you. He's a coward and he'll sneak.

He comes after me, he'll die. You should have just come to my table. He pulled her front to his side, clamped her there with one arm tight around her and walked her back to the table in the shadows where he'd waited for her. He kept his eye on the Comeaux brothers as he did so. Both turned to watch her progress across the room. Then again, he noted, most of the men watched the sway of her beautiful ass. Pascal caught his eyes and drew a line across his own throat. If that worked to intimidate others, it didn't Trap.

Trap halted at the table, curled his hand around the nape of Cayenne's neck and drew her to him. She was significantly shorter than him. Touching her bare skin sent tiny electrical charges firing through his bloodstream in a rush of heat. He took the beer bottles from her with one large hand and set them on the table.

She frowned as he drew her right up against him. Both hands framed her face, tipping it up toward his, holding it still as his head came down. His mouth moved over hers. Gently. Seductively. Coaxing her. Her lashes fluttered. Covered the brilliant, shocked green of her eyes. Her lips parted on a gasp of protest. He took full advantage, his tongue sweeping into that heated moist paradise. Tasting her. Taking her inside where he needed her. Stepping back into the shadows, taking her with him now that he'd made his statement to the other men in the bar, sheltering her from the room with his much larger body.

He kissed her thoroughly, starting out gentle and sliding right past gentle to savage. Claiming her. He kissed her like he meant it—and he did. He caught fire, and she ignited right with him. He knew she wasn't experienced because her response was tentative at first, but then the heat rushed through her, the same current of electricity, and instantly her mouth moved under his.

He poured himself into her, kissing her hard. Wet. Long. Her body melted into his and against his chest, he felt her nipples harden into tight, inviting peaks.

Are your panties wet yet? You're so fucking beautiful and you taste so good I want to spend all night eating you.

You have to stop. I can't do this with you. But she didn't pull away. One hand crept into his hair, her fingers twisting deep.

We're in the shadows. We're both GhostWalkers, baby, and we can hide when we want to. None of them get to share our moment.

One moment. That's all we get. Then we're done, Trap. You have to leave me alone. I mean it. You don't and it's going to be war.

She still kissed him back. Feeding his hunger. Feeding her own. Once they started they couldn't get enough of each other. That had never, not once in his life, ever happened to Trap. He didn't lose himself in a woman. He found release, but just kissing her—her mouth moving under his—was better than whatever any other woman had given him.

Because Cayenne gave herself to him. Completely. Holding nothing back in that moment. She wanted him to have this with her. To remember it. She wanted to have him like this, hot and wild and belonging only to her. She stored every second in her mind to take out over and over because she didn't believe for a moment she would ever have it again.

CHAPTER 3

Trap raised his head, breathing hard. Breathing for both of them. He waited until Cayenne's long lashes fluttered and then lifted. Her eyes were a little dazed, and the sight sent blood pounding through his cock. He smoothed one hand gently over her cheek. Her skin was softer than anything he'd ever felt.

"Don't ever tell me you don't belong to me, Cayenne, because you do. You know you do." He knew better than to claim a woman for his own, but there was no denying the pull between them. It wasn't just strong. It was savage. Relentless. He didn't even care that it wasn't logical, when he was a man all about logic. He was cynical and believed in nothing but his team—and the fact that Cayenne was meant to be his.

Her gaze searched his. She swallowed. "Trap. You don't know me. You don't know anything about me. There's a reason I was in that cell where you found me. I would have killed you if I had to in order to get out of there. This stops here."

He heard the brutal honesty in her voice. She was trying

to save him from himself. From her. From whatever it was between them. "Sit down for a minute. Drink the beer. We'll talk. *Talk*. That's all." He had to find a way to reach her. She had become the most important person in his world. He didn't care why. He just knew that if he couldn't have her, he'd never have anyone. Whatever that relentless pull was, it had a hold on him and would never let him go. He would never again be able to be with another woman without wishing she were Cayenne. Without thinking of her, or fantasizing about her.

She shook her head, but she couldn't tear herself away from him. Cayenne put trembling fingers to her lips—lips that looked as if they'd been thoroughly kissed. Trap slid his hand from her neck, down her arm to capture her wrist. He kept the movement gentle, knowing she was like a wild animal, trapped in a corner and ready to run.

"Come on, baby. Just sit a minute. I want to fill you in on a few things going on you may not be aware of," he coaxed. He had to spend more time with her, get her to see things his way. She couldn't be robbing people to find the money for food and clothes. He could easily provide for her if she'd let him. She was afraid. He didn't blame her for that, but she had to get over it. "Just sit down, Cayenne. I'm asking for a minute."

"It's a bad idea."

Her voice was beautiful. Soft. Melodious. Even though it was low and soft, her tone felt like velvet brushing over his skin. He knew her voice carried power. That exact pitch could slip inside a man and influence him to do all sorts of things. He was one of the few that could fight the pull of her compulsions, but it was difficult. Like others, he was susceptible. He just had to keep the logical part of his brain uppermost and he'd manage to escape her influence.

"Maybe," he agreed. "Maybe it is a bad idea. But let's do it anyway."

Cayenne pressed her lips together, but she allowed him to hold out a chair for her, hesitating only a moment before she slipped into it, mostly, he was sure, because he made certain her back was to the wall. He toed his chair closer to hers on the pretense of not wanting to be overheard. He knew he could keep their conversation private, but he wanted his thigh pressed tight against hers.

He needed to touch her. That need was on a primal level and impossible to ignore whether it bothered him or not—and it bothered him. He never allowed himself to *need* anything or anyone. Up close, her fragrance teased his senses, inflamed them until every nerve ending in his body came alive.

She picked up her beer and took a small sip. Not enjoying it. She didn't like the taste. Her expression didn't change, but he knew. He saw her. Or maybe he was locked somewhere inside her mind, because when they spoke telepathically, a part of him had remained in her. More than likely, when he'd rescued her from her locked cell, he'd been nearly as vulnerable as she was. Going through walls, changing molecular structure left him weak and shaky. He'd already done it several times, rescuing Wyatt's little girls before he'd gotten to Cayenne.

He removed the beer from her hand. "What would you prefer to drink?"

Her eyelashes fluttered. "Trap," she protested, glancing around the room at the others drinking the brew. She reached for the beer.

He held the bottle out of reach, an easy feat since he had long arms. "What do you prefer to drink?"

She pressed her lips together and gave in. "Water."

"The entire point of freedom is to do whatever the hell you want. You don't like beer, Cayenne, then you don't drink it."

"I'm fitting in," she hissed.

She didn't sound nearly as annoyed as she wanted. He was looking into her eyes and there was just the smallest hint of fear, as if he could take her hard-won confidence and destroy it. And she did appear confident, breezing into the room and flirting outrageously, aware the men were leering at her. *Because her poise was an act.* The knowledge clicked into place.

"When did they start caging you?" he asked gently, needing to know more. He was fumbling around in the dark when it came to him. If he was going to convince her she belonged to him and needed to trust him, he had to know as much about her as possible. "You've had combat training. You're fast and smart. You know what you're doing. When did they decide you were too flawed to live?" He couldn't keep the edge from his voice or the opaque shimmer from the air.

Long dark lashes drifted down, veiling the expression in her eyes for a brief moment. Hiding from him. Sexy, but still hiding from him. She swallowed, and he watched the motion at her throat. Even that was sexy. His cock jerked hard, straining against his jeans. He nearly dropped his hand into his lap to try to give himself a little relief. Up so close and after kissing her, with the taste of her still in his mouth and her elusive scent in his lungs, blood pounded through his veins, rushing to collect in his groin.

He had a powerful sex drive and was not in the least modest, but he had to go slow with Cayenne. Careful. She was skittish. He had no idea what she did or didn't know. She appeared confident. She was beautiful and sexy, but up close, he got the feeling that she wasn't nearly as experienced or self-assured as she portrayed.

Her tongue touched her lips, drawing attention to that perfect bow. She had red lips naturally, no makeup at all. With every breath she drew, her breasts rose and fell. He remained silent, willing her to tell him. He didn't push, giving her the time needed to make up her mind. Her gaze searched his for a long moment while he heard the clock tick and his heart beat. He was an observant man. The minutest detail didn't escape him, and he noted the fingers twisting in her lap beneath the table where she thought he couldn't see. There was a slight trembling to her lips and shadows in the green of her eyes. She didn't know it, but when she was afraid, her eyes changed. The brilliant green became multifaceted. Just like now.

Cayenne took a deep breath and pushed back the dark mass of hair spilling around her face. Instantly Trap reached over and tucked strands behind her ear. His touch was light, but she felt it all the way to her toes. He was so *large*. A giant of a man and far too gorgeous to resist.

She loved everything about him. His rugged face, all man, the darker shadow along his jaw, blond like that thick mess of longish hair. His eyes, so blue they took her breath. The confidence. The aura of danger surrounding him as if he could explode into violence in a heartbeat. Yet under all that, he had something much deeper she couldn't resist. That man who had done her that first kindness.

She had been so terrified, and she hadn't been nice. At all. That hadn't mattered to him. She'd threatened to kill him and still, he'd given her freedom. When she was close to him like this she felt vulnerable and exposed. Raw. If she gave him what he wanted, she would be completely stripped bare.

He remained silent, and she knew she would give him exactly what he wanted. That compulsion was there. So strong. There was no resisting no matter how terrified she was. She took a breath, again dropped her hands into her lap where he couldn't see them and closed her fists until her knuckles were white.

"I was a test-tube baby. I think they were terrified of me almost from the moment I was born. I've never really been out of a cell. Most of my schooling was done with me in a cell and teachers outside a thick sheet of glass. Or computer screens, simulators and books. When they did remove me from my cell, they darted me first to transport me. My combat experience was usually in the form of fighting for my life."

She did her best to sound matter-of-fact, not at all like telling him about how much her life hurt. It did hurt, and that was unexpected. She hated telling him the truth because she didn't want him looking at her as if she was less than human. He never had, yet knowing her handlers were terrified of her had to make him think exactly what she did—if they were monsters, what was she? She might be beautiful on the outside, and she was very practical about her looks, she could see that she had an impact on people, even when she was in her cell, but inside she was murderous, and she didn't trust herself.

When she was frightened—and Trap scared the crap out of her—she was at her most lethal. She shouldn't be anywhere near him, but she couldn't stop herself. He knew it. She saw the knowledge in his eyes. and that scared her even more. He had power over her. She didn't like that *at all*. Still, even knowing it, she had gone to the Fontenot home and stayed in his bedroom while he slept. She moved through the building he'd renovated and familiarized herself with it, knowing she was going to stay in the same place because she *had* to be close to him.

It didn't make sense that she wanted to be there with him when he was the very person who had disturbed her home— essentially taken it from her. He wouldn't see it that way, but she knew she had no rights. She wasn't even a person. She had no birth certificate or identity outside her cell. She knew that, because growing up, she'd been taunted with that fact often.

"Baby."

Trap's voice was soft. Gentle. She shook her head, afraid something inside her was breaking at the sound of his voice. She couldn't take it. Not when she'd revealed so much of herself in that brief summary of her life. She kept her gaze fixed on the table, on the origami crane folded so perfectly and set in the center of the table.

"Cayenne," he said again. "Look at me, baby."

She didn't want to, because if she did and he saw her the way others did, she wouldn't be able to live with herself. There was no refusing him. She didn't know why she couldn't when her entire life had been devoted to refusing orders. Reluctantly she lifted her gaze to his.

Those beautiful blue eyes stared back at her—caught and held her gaze, refusing to allow her to look away. He didn't look the least bit as if he wanted to "squash her like the bug she was," a familiar taunt she'd come to despise. Instead, she could see a blue flame burning beneath the glacier-cold of his eyes. As if he was enraged on her behalf.

"What do you mean, you had to fight for your life?"

She shook her head. She didn't want to tell him that either. She'd *killed* men. She remembered the feel of their bullets striking with such force her body flew backward. The pain spread through her like wildfire. That feeling was still so vivid it woke her at night. She clenched her fist and pressed it between her breasts where the majority of the time the bullets struck.

"I would wake up inside a maze and have to work my way out. There were no advantages for me, no vents, no place I could fit myself into to hide. Men hunted me. Men like you." Her gaze swept the room, and her chin indicated the other GhostWalkers. "Like them." Her eyes came back to his because he had that much power over her. She couldn't help herself. It was a compulsion to do the things he wanted and she had to fight hard to keep herself from letting him have everything.

He leaned closer. So close she breathed him into her lungs on her next inhale. It felt too intimate, but still, she couldn't pull away.

"Are you telling me those fuckers pitted you against an entire *team* of Whitney's supersoldiers?"

"They were enhanced, if that's what you mean. And each time I came out the victor, they would enhance others using the knowledge they'd acquired of their weaknesses in the battle."

Trap shook his head. "A team? As in how many?"

"Each time there were five."

There was silence. She swore the walls of the room contracted and the ceiling creaked. Around them, the air grew dense and difficult to breathe in. The temperature definitely dropped a couple of degrees. She knew because she didn't have a sweater or jacket and her arms and body chilled.

"*Each* time," he snarled. "How many times did they do that shit to you?"

"Trap," she protested. "It's in the past. It isn't like this just happened to me. Why are you getting upset?" She glanced around the table, and put a hand to her mouth and nose. "The air gets very thick when you're upset. I can not only visibly see and smell your rage, but I can feel it too. Yet you look as cool as ice."

"I'm not as cool as ice, baby, so answer the fucking question." He leaned so close he nearly touched her lips with his. "How many times did they do that shit to you? How many teams were you pitted against?"

Cayenne pressed her fist tight into the valley between her breasts without noticing that she did it, but Trap noticed. He scowled. "Fucking answer me."

"Seven times. Okay? If you have to know, I wiped out seven teams of men."

She pulled back in her chair and lifted her gaze to his. She didn't have a clue that she looked agonized, not defiant. He wanted to hold her. To pull her into his arms and shelter her there.

Her lashes fluttered. She took a breath, steeling herself. He saw that too. "Trap, I could smell their fear. In that maze, all of them were afraid of me."

Trap swore he could feel Cayenne's fingers trailing over his skin with just the sound of her voice. She was very petite, but perfectly proportioned with an hourglass figure. Her size and shape made him aware of being a man, physically stronger, supposedly giving him an advantage. They had forced her to fight men larger and stronger than she was, yet somehow, she'd come out victorious. That should tell him something, but all it did was make him want to strangle Whitney with his bare hands and wish Braden were still alive so he could kill him all over again.

She leaned close to him. "You should be afraid of me too."

"Why would that be?"

"I don't like anything that threatens me."

"I haven't threatened you."

"You're the biggest threat of all, and don't pretend you don't know it. I react badly to threats of any kind."

"You didn't act so badass when fucking Pascal Comeaux put his hand on your ass." He leaned very close to her, stared straight into her eyes so she could see the flame that burned icy hot under all the blue. "The ass, by the way, that is *mine*. No one else puts their fucking hand on your body."

She didn't flinch away from him.

"And don't think I don't know you've been coming into my room at night." He took a shot in the dark. If she was really coming into his room and he wasn't insane, that meant she got through their security and quieted the hunting dogs Nonny kept in a kennel and running yard. If Cayenne could get into the house, someone else could.

She didn't deny it. Instead she shrugged. "I had to let Comeaux make his move. Just to make certain I wasn't making a mistake."

"Why'd you come into my room?" he persisted.

She looked shaken—confused, a frown moving over her face. "I-I don't know. I couldn't help myself. The first time, I just wanted to make sure you were all right and then . . ." She trailed off.

He nodded, knowing exactly why she'd risked coming to Wyatt's compound when an entire team of GhostWalkers was staying there. She hadn't raised a single alarm. He didn't ask her yet how she got in, but he didn't want her to do it again. Sooner or later someone would spot her. They were the type of men who shot first and asked questions later. Eventually he would have to know to protect the household, but asking now would only spook her, so he backed off.

"Wyatt has his three daughters there, Cayenne. No one is taking chances that someone might try to harm the girls. It isn't safe for you there. Not until everyone gets to know you. I bought the building where they were holding you and I'm renovating it. I started with the laboratory."

She narrowed her eyes at him. "I knew you bought the property and brought all those workmen there so they could tramp through it, making it look . . ."

"Like a home? Yeah, baby, that's me. Why? Are you staying there?" He flashed a small smirk at her. "I knew you were there. You give yourself away with all those spider-webs." Now they were sparring, doing the dance he knew would come eventually when she tried to push him away.

She pressed her lips together and turned her face away from him. "Stay away from there, Trap."

"I'm moving in tomorrow. You want to see me, you come there."

"I'm not playing around," she hissed at him again. "You take too many chances. You act like you don't care whether you live or die."

"Been alone most of my life, baby. It gets fucking lonely. Got a couple of men on my trail who want to kill anything that matters to me, so I don't let anything matter." His eyes bored into hers. "Until you. You matter, Cayenne, whether it makes sense or not, so if you want to kill me for giving a damn about you, make your try."

She sat back in the chair and ducked her head. Clouds of dark hair fell around her face, hiding her expression from his sight. Moodily his gaze drifted over her. Possessively. He *felt* possessive. He felt rage at what had been done to her simmering just below the surface. He was a man of discipline and control and yet he was close to losing both.

Wyatt, will you get a bottle of cold water for her?

You goin' to cut me up I come near your woman? Wyatt was already at the bar talking to Delmar and keeping a wary eye on the Comeaux brothers.

Why the hell would you think that?

Because you've surrounded the table with shadows and that shimmer shit no one can breathe. I don' want to choke to death and leave Pepper with our three girls to raise all alone. She might not take kindly to that.

Trap glanced across the bar to see Wyatt grinning as he reached for the bottle of water Delmar handed to him. Wyatt wasn't wrong. Trap had enclosed them in shadows and a protective ring that would keep anyone else away. He forced himself to relax and breathe. He hadn't made a mistake like that in years. Hearing what her life had been like, just the small bit she'd revealed, had thrown him.

Wyatt handed him the bottle of water, sent Cayenne a cocky grin and made his way to the table where Mordichai sat with his brother Malichai. Trap twisted off the cap and gave Cayenne the bottle.

"Drink water when you prefer it and the hell with everyone else, baby," he advised. "Live free. I don't give a damn what anyone else thinks of me. I care about my team and Wyatt's family and now you. That's it. Everyone else can go to hell."

"Not me." She shook her head decisively. "You can't trust me, Trap. Don't for one minute think you can."

Her fingers moved on the table, a small drumming pattern, not loud, but definitely hypnotic. He put his hand over hers. She gasped as if he'd burned her and nearly pulled her hand back at the contact.

"Be still. Breathe."

She left her hand under his, but her green eyes moved over him broodingly. "I can't breathe. If I do, you're inside me. I feel you there in my lungs, moving through my body. You're a liability. You'd better hear me this time. When I get cornered"—she leaned close—"I'm lethal."

"We all are, baby. Every one of us. Look around you. You see them. You feel them. Every last one of us is enhanced, just like you."

"You aren't flawed. You weren't scheduled for termination."

"Fuck that reasoning, Cayenne. You're intelligent. Because you scare the hell out of them doesn't mean they're right to terminate you. Why would you accept any judgment they pass on you? Whitney and this man who had you in his lab, Braden, are megalomaniacs, believing they have the right to take *children*, *infants* . . ." For a moment a deep well of rage showed in his eyes, burning blue behind the ice.

He took a breath and flicked a glance at the shimmer surrounding them. It took effort, but he breathed away the evidence of that fury.

"To make his superior soldiers as well as the elite Ghost-Walkers, Whitney first experimented on little kids. God knows how many children he killed because they weren't to his liking. He put men like Braden in place, scattering them in various countries in labs to do his dirty work. Wyatt's brother Gator is a GhostWalker. His woman was repeatedly given cancer by Whitney when she was a child. He had another girl living in a sanitarium, training, running missions from right here in the swamp. She was forced to return here. The tract of land and the building I just bought? Whitney owned that. He had the sanitarium there, and it was burned to the ground because he suddenly decided the girl he'd forced to live there was expendable and he sent a hit squad after her. That's the kind of man who decided you had to be terminated. Seriously, baby, get that *flawed* crap out of your head."

She sat back and slowly pulled her hand out from under his. Her lashes fluttered, and he felt that small movement as if she'd fluttered them against his skin. Up close she was potent. He could see every breath she drew. The creamy swell of her breasts lifted when she drew in air. The temptation to tug at the ribbons of her camisole and open that crisscross of blue was difficult to resist. She was very lucky they were in a public place.

"Tell me about Wyatt's daughters."

It didn't surprise him that she knew all about Wyatt and his daughters. She'd been rescued when their GhostWalker team had gone to rescue the toddlers from termination. When the soldiers had come in an effort to try to reacquire them, Cayenne had aided the GhostWalker team in protecting them. The triplets were not yet two and all three of them injected venom if they bit anyone. Wyatt and Trap had been trying to find a way to prevent that from happening.

"They're happy. Nonny, Wyatt's grandmother, is an amazing woman. She's in her eighties, but she goes out in the swamp and transplants flowers and shrubs to keep her pharmaceutical bed alive and thriving. She adores those girls and treats all of us like family."

"What's that like?"

He raised an eyebrow at her.

"Being a family."

Such a simple question, but it fed the rage building beneath the ice. He had to work at controlling the shimmer. Around him the faint, nearly transparent veil thickened, taking the air out of the room. Several men coughed.

Take a breath, Wyatt advised.

This is fucked up, Wyatt. But he took the breath. Killing everyone around him wasn't going to help her. He made himself breathe. Deep and even. Finding a rhythm. Letting the ice inside consume him. He knew he was broken on the inside. He'd accepted that premise a long time ago and then used it as his strength. Cayenne hadn't had a chance. Living in a fucking lab. What the hell was that? Who would do that to a child?

"Were there other women?" he prompted. "Like Pepper, Wyatt's wife. Did you get to see them? Talk to them?"

She shook her head and rubbed her hands up and down her arms as if she were cold.

Trap took the jacket from where it was hanging on the back of his chair and wrapped it around her. She looked startled. Looked as if she might protest. She didn't. She slipped her arms into the sleeves and held it close to her. It was his favorite jacket. He wore it a lot. That meant his scent was all over it. Now his scent surrounded her. There was a certain satisfaction in that.

Trap never thought that he'd ever be in this position. He had accepted that he wouldn't have a woman of his own. He wasn't that boy anymore. He had made himself into something dangerous. Something lethal. He knew some of the GhostWalkers were concerned with the experiments done on them with the DNA of animals, but he was stronger and faster, and he'd always been strong and fast. Now he was a predator, and he needed to be. He was actively hunting his uncles. His friends were like him. They were building fortresses in order to survive any attack on them or their families. Let his uncles come for the woman that meant something. He would be ready for them.

He'd been prepared to send Cayenne away. To find a way to reverse what Whitney had done, but the moment she'd stepped through the door of the bar, he knew he wouldn't do that. He didn't have anything or anyone who mattered to him other than his teammates. Unexpectedly, Cayenne was very important to him, and the more he learned about her life, the more he was determined to make the rest of it something else altogether.

He wasn't certain why she would be paired with him, but there was one thing all the GhostWalkers were certain of—the pairings worked. The couples worked as a team in the field. They were extremely physically compatible, and all of them had developed incredibly strong emotional attachments.

Trap hadn't thought himself capable of emotional attachments for a long time—until he met Wyatt at the university and then his GhostWalker team. He had chosen to follow Wyatt into the military because he wanted the psychic enhancements. He was grateful for the physical as well. He was determined to find his uncles and kill them. He would hunt them until the day he died. That had been his reason— to turn himself into a weapon—even more of one than he'd already made himself.

"Trap." She said his name low. Her voice a caress. A soothing rasp of velvet over his skin. *Trap.* She moved inside his mind much more intimately. "What is it? What is making you so upset?"

He stared at her in astonishment. He hadn't changed expression. He'd been extremely careful that the cloud around them stayed thin. Nothing should have betrayed his emotions. How had she known?

Deliberately he ignored her question. "You wanted to know what a family is like. Wyatt's grandmother always has something on the stove cooking. She has music playing in the house and she dances with the girls. Pepper, Wyatt's wife, dances now as well. The house always feels welcoming . . ."

Cayenne shook her head. "Not Wyatt's family, Trap. Yours. What is your family like?"

His heart jerked hard in his chest. He didn't want to lie to her. Or scare her. He'd shot his own father. Deliberately. He'd been nine years old, and he would have killed his uncles if he could have as well. What did he tell her? His woman. She had a right to know the danger she faced when gave herself to him—and she was going to give herself to him. He would accept nothing less.

"My family is Wyatt and the team, Cayenne. I don't have anyone else."

"But you did," she persisted. "You were born into a family, not taken from an orphanage and put in a lab or, like me, made in a test tube."

He sighed. "I tell you this, baby, and you're going to run for the hills. I don't want you to do that. How about I promise I tell you after the first time you let me have you. Once I've been inside you, once I've claimed you for my own, it will give me a fighting chance that you'll stay with me."

There was a short silence. "You know about my child-hood. It's only fair to tell me about yours."

"I'll give you this, Cayenne, you'll know the worst of me, what I'm capable of, what I was born capable of doing, not what anyone shaped me into."

She reached out, and this time, she was the one who took his hand. "Tell me."

He shook his head. "I'm not sharing that fucked-up shit with you before you commit to me." He had to change the subject and turned the spotlight back on her. "Coming here, choosing victims and robbing them is not okay. You know that, and you can't keep doing it. These men may not be enhanced, but sooner or later, you're going to slip up and you'll make a mistake. Then you'll have to kill an innocent to defend yourself or they'll kill you."

"I have to eat," she whispered. "Do you think I *want* to rob people? I make certain whoever I choose is someone who deserves a little payback."

"If you want to eat, you come to Wyatt's. His grand-mother would welcome you. If you don't want to do that, come to me. Tell me what you need."

Her green eyes flashed bright, anger stirring. Pride. "I don't need your charity, Trap. I don't want it." She picked up the origami crane he'd made from the paper he'd scrib-bled formulas on.

"It isn't charity," he hissed. "Why are you being so damned stubborn? I'm not going to hurt you."

"No, but I could hurt you." She glanced down at the crane, started to say something and then noticed the writing along the wing. "P = #AR. HYP." She didn't ask a question, but she repeated it softly as if musing out loud. Very care-fully she unfolded the crane, revealing Trap's formula and his assessment.

She glanced up at him. "You used the difficult way. You built a temporal model, didn't you? I can see your equations."

She smoothed the paper, running her gaze over the formulas. "I worked this out last week using a spatial model. The peanut husks are concentrated under the bar stools, and I counted around one and multiplied, and around the tables, especially during the first three days after Delmar sweeps. If you notice, almost all the husks around the round tables form a donut ring that runs about one foot under the table to about twice the radius of the table."

Trap stared at her, his heart stuttering in his chest. For the first time, he actually was completely shocked, but he shouldn't have been.

"I just counted the husks around one chair at the four-chair table and multiplied by four to get a pretty good estimate of the total husks associated with the table."

He leaned close. "You took the easy way out. And it isn't very accurate."

She raised her chin. "I did not. I did it the *intelligent* way."

"Over a week's accumulation the peanut husks turn to mulch and can't be counted. They get kicked around . . ."

"I factored in the ones that fall beneath the bar and get kicked back where Delmar works. I came up with thirteen thousand, two hundred and sixty per week." She sent him her first real smile. The kind that made a man's cock hard. Made his heart jerk and happiness spill through his bloodstream like sunshine. She raised her green gaze to his. "Nice. You've got a brain."

Hell, yeah, he had a brain. Excitement burst through Trap. He'd wondered why Whitney had paired him with Cayenne. Now he knew. She could satisfy his mind along with his body. She would be a complement to him in every way, not just in the field or in bed. She would stimulate his mind. Understand him. And he would do the same for her.

Movement had her standing, and he turned his head to see the two Comeaux brothers exiting the bar. "That's my cue to leave. I don't want to see you around, Trap. You stay away from me. I mean it. This is the last time we're going to be friendly." She moved around the far side of the table when he stood also, shaking his head.

"Damn it, Cayenne. Don't make us enemies."

"That's what we are," she whispered. "That's the way it has to be. You don't know the worst in me, and I don't want you ever to know. Or to see. Or to experience."

She hurried across the room to the door, taking his favorite jacket with her. She turned at the last minute and sent a whisper into the air. "See but not see. Hear but don't hear."

Instantly he felt that pull in her voice, the one he felt when he'd gone into her cell to rescue her and she'd called him to her. He was much more resistant than the others, because he didn't allow emotions too close to the surface and her voice seemed to tap into an emotional stream. Now he knew how she kept the men in the bar from describing her.

He signaled to Wyatt and the others, although he didn't need to. They were already disposing of their beer bottles and making for the door.

"I'll meet you back at home," Trap told them. "I've got a couple of things I have to do."

Wyatt smirked at him. "Yeah, I'll bet you do. The boys will take the airboat home and I'll go with you in the *Pepper*. I'm thinkin' you need a babysitter."

He wasn't going to stand around arguing, and when Wyatt put that smirk on his face, he was as stubborn as hell. Trap nodded and hurried out.

CHAPTER 4

The night air felt cool on Trap's face as they hurried out of the Huracan Club and down the steps onto the dirt that fronted the building. Humidity often kept the air a little muggy, a little sultry, and the perfumes of the swamp could be cloying. The brief rain left the trees and shrubbery glistening from the half-moon's beams. Water along the river sparkled liked diamonds.

Trap and Wyatt stayed in the shadows, holding perfectly still. Motion drew the eye and out of habit, neither moved a muscle while they carefully checked the area around them. They had enemies far worse than the Comeaux brothers and never lost their vigilance. As if by mutual consent, without a word, Trap stayed in the shadows covering Wyatt while the Cajun sauntered to the boat. The smaller boat was lightweight and fast, able to move easily through shallow water and speed through the deeper channels.

Wyatt was at home in the swamp and bayous. Born and raised there, he'd spent his youth hunting and fishing throughout the entire area. His home had been built from the cypress trees growing on their property—trees that withstood the water and the insects far better than anything else. The other GhostWalkers were just beginning to know their way around the waterway. Trap didn't mind in the least sitting back and letting Wyatt take the lead.

"She warned me off, Wyatt," Trap announced, with a small sigh.

"She kissed the heck out of you," Wyatt pointed out.

"*I* kissed *her*," Trap corrected.

"She kissed you back, and that kiss didn't seem like a warnin' to me." Wyatt sent him another cocky grin. "Seems to me that was a 'hello handsome' kinda kiss. You probably didn't recognize it, not bein' Cajun and all."

Trap shook his head. "She's going to know we're following her if you keep yapping."

"Trap, that woman wouldn' have stood for you puttin' your hands on her like that if she didn' want to kiss you. She was armed. She's got to be venomous like Pepper and the girls. You took your life in your hands gettin' that kiss, and she knew it and knew you knew it. She rewarded you with that kiss for your bravery."

Trap sent Wyatt a quelling look. "Shut the hell up. You're so full of shit."

Wyatt laughed softly and turned his attention to maneuvering the waterway. He knew the route the Comeaux brothers would take home. They weren't subtle or cagey. They knew no one would ever dare follow them for any reason. The Comeaux family had a reputation in the bayou. They were hard drinking and mean. More than anything else, if you tangled with one, you tangled with the entire family. They had a lot of cousins, most every bit as mean as the brothers.

"I'm not certain how she thinks she can lure them off their boat to shore," Trap mused aloud. He didn't care whether Wyatt heard him or not. He was trying to figure out exactly what Cayenne would do. He had to get ahead of her. His brain came up with one too many ideas. The idea of her standing naked on the shore of the island rose all too vivid in his mind to torture him.

"Trap." Wyatt's voice was pitched low. Very low. Edgy.

Irritated at the interruption, but recognizing the warning in Wyatt's voice, Trap swung his head around to glare at his teammate.

"Let it go, you're rockin' the boat and you've got the water churnin'. Seriously, man, get it under control."

No one in his life had ever told him that other than his older sister, Dru. He could almost hear her, there in the quiet of the swamp, laughter surrounding him, telling him to "get it under control." She didn't mean the same thing, but still, it was a good memory. One he cherished. She always laughed when he annoyed every other person around him. His mother loved him, but she mostly had no idea what to do with him. Dru had a mind like his and a sense of humor that got both of them through the first part of their childhood with a drunken father and an absent mother.

He forced himself to nod. To breathe. The volcano of rage inside of him subsided and became buried under the glacier of ice he had painstakingly built to protect himself and the rest of the world from what he knew he'd become. He sank onto the bench, turning his back once again on Wyatt. What was he doing? He had to think it through. Nothing disturbed him. He didn't allow it. He sure as hell had never experienced jealousy, especially jealousy brought on by his own imagination.

Ever since he'd laid eyes on Cayenne he'd been intrigued. He had gone with his team members to rescue two of Wyatt's little daughters. They were locked in cells, scheduled for termination in Whitney's facility there in the swamp. He had gotten them out and then gone to the other side of what essentially was a jail to find Cayenne.

She'd taken his breath away, but more importantly, she'd taken something else from him, some part of him he knew he was never going to get back. It was hers now. Each time he saw her, the longing in him for a home of his own, one like Wyatt had, filled with love and laughter and warmth, grew in him. With all that, just what was he doing? What did he expect? The woman had spent her entire life in a laboratory. She'd been *used* as a lab rat. She'd never tasted freedom and had no idea what to do with it.

Trap was certain she was making the building where she'd been scheduled for termination her home, and she'd practically admitted it to him. She hadn't left the swamp when she could have. She should have. She was trained as a soldier—all the children Whitney had taken from orphanages around the world had intense combat training as well as combat experience. She might not have practical experience, but she'd had the training. If they were skilled as assassins, he always made certain they were tested in the field, just as he'd tested Cayenne by putting her in the maze with a team of supersoldiers.

Pepper, Wyatt's wife, was a seductress, able to kill with one bite, but they lost control of her, not factoring in that she might be too stubborn, abhor violence and be too moral to control. She had a code, and that code didn't include killing innocents. Trap hadn't been able to read the file on Cayenne. When they'd rescued the children, Wyatt had removed as much as he could from the labs, but Cayenne's file was corrupted. All he knew was that she was deemed too dangerous for anyone to handle her. Every single handler apparently was too terrified to work with her. He had a couple of experts working to recover the data, but it was going to take time.

So how would she get the two brothers off the waterway where she could more easily rob them? And why wouldn't they remember she had been the one to take their wallets? She had to either cloak herself—and that made no sense when she had to lure them to her—or she had a way of completely wiping their memories. In the bar, she'd used her voice to dull the memory of her presence, but what if she could actually wipe out incidents entirely? That was the scariest answer to him because he never wanted her to try that shit with him.

"She's ahead of them, Wyatt. She has to pick her victim weeks in advance and then figure out a route they're going to take to get home," Trap said. That had to be how she did it and why she didn't rob often in spite of her need for money. She set everything up far in advance, including her own escape route. She was a GhostWalker, and GhostWalkers always prepared for everything to go south.

"She somehow gets ahead of them and her boat 'breaks' down," he continued. "She plays the damsel in distress. She was in that cage, and she used her voice to draw me in. She whispered to come closer. She's good at what she does, but she doesn't want to make a mistake. That's why she didn't hang with them longer. She'd already chosen the brothers and was just making certain she'd been right about them being slime buckets."

"So I need to figure where she's going to draw them to the bank and stop before they hear the boat." Wyatt frowned. "Best place would be right before they turn into the canal heading to their homes. The Comeaux brothers all built next to one another, just off of Honey Island. You have to turn off the main canal right where it gets extremely shallow, and there's a narrow canal that leads back to their homes. No one uses that canal but them, so she wouldn't have any business there. I'm betting she gets herself hung up in the shallows on purpose so they have to help her."

"Would they? They don't seem like good Samaritans to me."

"A woman alone at night? Hell yeah, they're going to stop. No one around. They figure they can do anything they want to her and she won' say a word because she'll be too afraid of them. They'd tell each other she had it comin'. She flirted with them. She wanted it. Whatever it takes to make them live with themselves. Who knows? Maybe they just get off on hurtin' a woman. Their brother Vicq certainly did."

There was not only distaste in Wyatt's voice, but an edge of anger.

Trap turned on the bench seat. "You never talked much about that, Wyatt. He had your girlfriend . . ." He trailed off, giving Wyatt the option to tell him or not.

Wyatt shook his head. "I went to school with her. She was beautiful to me. I put her up on a pedestal and didn' see what she was really like. She had a singin' voice that was so amazin', everyone would stop whatever they were doin' and listen. She refused to go out with me in school. I was younger than her because I'd skipped a couple of grades. She didn' think I'd amount to much . . ."

"Are you shitting me?" Trap couldn't believe what he was hearing. Wyatt was brilliant. How could a woman get it in her head he wouldn't amount to much?

Wyatt shrugged. "I went off to the university and came back a doctor. I came back. To the swamp. To the bayou. She didn' like that. She thought I should be a big city doctor. Make the bucks. She still wouldn' go out with me. Then Vicq and his buddies got ahold of her. My brother and his wife rescued her, and I guess she wanted company. She strung me along for a while. I didn' touch her because she was so fragile. I just wanted to take care of her after what they did to her. That lasted until I found out she was sleepin' with a big city boy with tons of money."

"Women fuck up a man's life," Trap said.

"I thought so until Pepper came along. She suits me in every way. I'm a wild man and I belong here. I'm stayin' here and raisin' my family. I love Nonny, and Pepper does too. Joy didn' like *ma grand-mere* at all. She pretended to, and of course our families were friends, but she didn't like that Nonny smoked a pipe and generally didn't have the manners Joy thought she should. Pepper doesn' mind my team runnin' in and out of the house. Joy would have despised that. She would never, under any circumstances, have taken in my daughters. I'm well shed of her."

Wyatt slowed the boat as they turned off the river into a narrow canal. Saw grass rose up on either side of the boat and both men were careful not to touch the tall long leaves of the shrub. Razor-sharp, the leaves could easily slice a hand or arm. The boat barely moved through the water, and Trap could see fallen trees beneath the surface Wyatt had to maneuver around. The water was extremely shallow. Because of the constant erosion, the path boats took through the water was continually changing.

Wyatt lowered his voice. "All kiddin' aside, Trap. I have to ask you this question, and you have to really think about it before you do this. You certain you know what you're doin'? You take on this woman, you can' just walk away from her when the goin' gets rough or you're caught up in the lab workin' on some project that takes over your mind. She's real and human and will need help adjustin' to life outside a lab. She'll have gaps in her knowledge you won' think about. Pepper still has to fight feelin' inferior because of what they did to her. As her partner, you're goin' to have to give her that confidence and protect her from outsiders."

Trap sighed. He couldn't blame Wyatt for asking. He was asking himself the same thing over and over. He had his uncles somewhere out there, and he knew they would try to kill Cayenne. He knew that with every certainty. If he were at all a decent man, he'd turn away from her. He also knew he wasn't nearly as easygoing as everyone thought him. He knew he wouldn't be the least bit laid-back with her. Not when he hadn't had anyone of his own since his aunt had been taken from him.

It didn't matter that he had all the money in the world, not when he didn't have anyone to share his life with. Cayenne was his chance. His only chance. She was lethal. His uncles came at her, they'd be in for a nasty surprise. More, they had no idea what he'd become. He could protect his own now. He wasn't the boy who had picked up a gun and shot his own father, but was too weak to follow up. This time, no matter what shape he was in, he could take them. He was a GhostWalker, and even running on empty, he could continue with his mission. He knew, he'd been practicing for a while now.

"I'm not giving her up, Wyatt," Trap said. "I go back and forth in my mind, but seeing her, kissing her, looking into her mind and her eyes, she's worth whatever it takes."

"It's not goin' to be easy." Wyatt stilled the engine, stepped into the shallow water and dragged the boat to the edge. "She'll probably fight you every step of the way. Pepper did a lot of runnin' before she settled down and committed to me. Your woman's likely to do more than run, you scare her too much."

Trap found himself grinning for no reason. "Maybe the crazy Cajun is rubbing off on me. We've been friends for so long I guess I started thinking I've got Cajun in my blood. I don't think a shy, retiring kind of woman would suit me, although I have to admit, I do insist on what I like in my bed. I like that she's got skills, though, and that she's dangerous. I wouldn't take the chance otherwise. Not to mention, I find that dangerous side of her sexy."

Wyatt shot him a grin right back. "Yeah. You've got Cajun in you, bro. Gator's woman has this knife she put right to his throat when he stole her motorcycle. He thought that knife was the hottest thing and once she showed it to him, seriously, she was done for. Pepper had one as well, not to mention she's got that bite of hers. Makes things interestin'."

"I thought both of you were crazy until I met Cayenne," Trap agreed. "She used her voice on me, and I knew I was up for the challenge. Admittedly, I fought it, but sometimes I woke up and smelled her scent in my room . . ."

"You what?" Wyatt, already on land, spun around and faced him. "And you didn't tell us? We have holes in our security if she's slippin' through. We can't risk that. Whitney has his own army of supersoldiers, Trap. We don' know their abilities, but you can bet, since Whitney knows ours, when he decides to come after the girls, he'll know what kind of enhanced soldier to send."

Trap stepped out onto the spongy ground. He knew to follow in Wyatt's footsteps to minimize the risk of discovery as well as to keep from falling through if the ground wasn't completely firm. He paused and rubbed the bridge of his nose. "I wasn't certain whether I dreamt about her or if it was real. Not until tonight."

Wyatt's eyebrow shot up. "I don' believe a word you're sayin', and if you believe it, you're foolin' yourself. This woman has you actin' out of character, and you and I both know that will get someone killed—her included. One of the boys will take her out if she comes sneakin' around."

Trap swore under his breath. Wyatt was right. He'd known. He hadn't wanted her to stop coming. He liked that she needed to be near to him. Yeah, he'd been vulnerable with her coming in while he slept. He'd never slept when someone was near. Not ever. Not since his father murdered his entire family. When he worked out in his lab before he'd joined the GhostWalker unit, he had all kinds of hidden sensors scattered throughout his house and the laboratory to warn him if anyone came near. He knew it was insanity to allow her into his room, but still, he hadn't stopped her.

"I'm moving to my new home tomorrow," he informed Wyatt, not apologizing. "After tonight, she's going to be so angry with me for interfering with her business that she won't come calling again."

"If she doesn't decide to kill you." Wyatt swung around and began walking, staying to a narrow path just behind the brush and trees.

Trap smirked. "She'll probably consider it, but she won't do it. She couldn't kill me anymore than I could kill her."

"You're bettin' your life, Trap," Wyatt said, holding his hand up for silence. They were both speaking softly, but they needed to cease talking altogether. Sound carried at night, and they were closing in on the canal leading to the Comeaux properties.

Yeah. Trap knew he was betting his life, but he was fairly certain the end result would be worth it. He had calculated the odds, because that was what he did. He ran the data through his brain and knew if he couldn't stop thinking about her—if he couldn't harm her—she couldn't stop thinking about him and she wouldn't want him permanently removed from her no matter what she said. She was fighting the pull between them, the same as he was.

Cayenne was a beautiful woman. Other men were going to try to court her. Maybe most men would run for the hills when they discovered she was dangerous. She would never reveal her enhanced abilities, but she wouldn't be able to help showing her character. They'd be jealous and possessive, the exact same as he felt and they wouldn't be able to handle her. But they were in Cajun country. If Gator and Wyatt Fontenot were anything to go by, Cajun men liked strong women. They liked a little wild in them.

Trap wasn't taking any chances that another man might slip in there and try to claim her. He didn't want to kill anyone over her, and he was fairly certain it could happen. He studied their surroundings as they made their way in absolute quiet, muting their footfalls as they moved. He needed to take his mind off the thought that another man might touch her—or kiss her. Or in any way draw her interest.

Trap, Wyatt hissed.

Trap glanced out into the water. Cypress trees grew along the bank, their knobby knees spread wide to make certain of survival. Gum trees grew higher on land. Brush and plants filled in between the trees, lending the island an unkempt appearance. This was the place of legends. The shimmer floating out over the water would add to that if anyone saw it. If Cayenne saw it, she would know he was close—and following her.

He took a deep breath. Where was the ice water running

in his veins? His team referred to him as the iceman for a good reason. He was the one who went into the hottest spots and pulled out the soldiers torn and bleeding while the others covered him. He faced every dangerous situation without flinching. Over the years, he had forced himself to become the man he was—the man able to protect his family if his uncles—or anyone else—threatened.

Wyatt held up his closed fist, and Trap instantly went still. He opened his psychic senses to the night. Instantly he heard voices. Two men and a woman. His heart thudded in his chest and then settled into a normal rhythm as his training took over. They moved closer, and Wyatt went up a tree to cover him as he approached the trio.

Trap stayed as close to the tree line as possible, wanting the concealment so Cayenne couldn't spot him. She looked very small next to the two Cajuns. She gestured toward her boat with a smile.

"Thanks. I can't believe I ran right onto the bar. I would have gotten it off eventually but I probably would have been here most of the night." Her voice was soft. Whisper soft. Compelling. Like silk. Her French accent was thick. Sexy.

She was throwing out a lure without even knowing it. Trap could tell she was giving them one more chance to walk away.

Pascal Comeaux stepped right up to her. "Maybe you should find a way to thank us."

Trap clenched his teeth as Blaise Comeaux caged her in on the other side, much like they'd done at the bar.

She raised a hand and swept it over her hair in a long, sexy slide. The action called attention to her high, full breasts. He nearly groaned aloud. *Everything* she did was sexy. The way she moved. Her voice. That accent. Her body standing between the two large men. He let out his breath.

Pascal caught her around the waist and pulled her front to his easily. His brother moved in behind her, arms around her as well. She didn't make a sound, but she pressed her head to

Pascal, just for a moment. He yelped and stepped back, nearly letting her go, his face dark and red with sudden anger. One hand balled into a fist, the other stayed firmly around her back.

Cayenne didn't look at him again. She leaned down and bit his brother's forearm. His cry was higher. Longer. She just watched him impassively as he jumped away from her. Staggered. Pascal's hand dragged her closer, and she turned back to him. His fist went back, fury gathering in his eyes.

Trap was there before him, catching his arm, holding back the punch. His piercing blue gaze met Cayenne's. They stared at each another while Pascal's body shuddered and slowly began to crumple. Trap let his arm go so that he fell in a heap very close to his brother. Both had their eyes wide open, but neither could move.

"What are you doing here?" Cayenne demanded, her hands on her hips.

"Saving your pretty little ass."

Her chin went up. Her eyes narrowed. That only brought his attention to the beautiful green surrounded by all those thick, luxurious lashes. He really wanted her eyes open when he was moving inside of her.

She toed Pascal. "I didn't need help."

"I wasn't saving your ass from *them*." There was contempt in his voice.

Pascal's eyes blinked. The fury should have set the island on fire.

Trap switched to telepathy, a much more intimate form of speech. Even if Pascal and his brother had their memories removed, he didn't want even a residue of his conversation with Cayenne in their minds. *I was saving you from yourself. Go home. I'll be there tomorrow. Make a list of whatever you need and I'll get it for you. You want money or need it, you're a GhostWalker. The money will be put into an account for you. We have a collective one, and each Ghost-Walker has received compensation. Whitney's daughter sets up an account for each of us through a trust.*

Something moved in her eyes. Something that made his heart jerk hard in his chest. Her chin lifted, but she followed his lead. *For the perfect ones, not the flawed ones. I'm supposed to be terminated, not compensated.*

Damn it, Cayenne.

I make my own way.

By robbing? Do you get some kind of thrill from it? This is fucking bullshit and you know it. Go home. I'll meet you there tomorrow.

It's my home. You stay away. She sounded stubborn. She *looked* stubborn.

I bought it. I renovated it. You know it belonged to Whitney, and he set up Braden there to finish his dirty work. He had all kinds of ways in and out built into the place. He had passageways in the walls. I took out the crematorium and the cells below and added in stairways to the lower level. The place is my home, and it can be your home as well, but no more of this bullshit, Cayenne. Sooner or later the cops will get involved, or worse, the military. If they send an investigator, you're in trouble.

She toed Pascal. *They never remember.*

There are already rumors. Why do you think I spent the last few days sitting in that fucking place counting peanut husks on the floor? He snapped it at her, rather shocked that he was losing patience. He always stayed cool. She just got under his skin with the vulnerable expression she didn't even know she wore.

She stepped right up to him and put both hands flat on his chest, staring up into his eyes. Her voice dropped low. Intimate. Sliding under his skin and traveling like a fireball, rushing through his bloodstream to settle in his groin.

There's no need to worry about me, cher, *I can take care of myself.* She lifted her face to his.

There was no denying her. Her mouth was pure heaven. He already had the taste of her there. His hands framed her face, and he bent and took possession of her mouth. She melted into him. Her mouth moved under his, her tongue sliding and then dancing along his, sending spirals of heat through his body. He wanted her with every breath he took.

He had to breathe for both of them, unable to stop kissing her. She tasted exotic and rare, like a flower he'd stumbled across. Storms. Moody. The taste of a wild wind, elusive and spinning out of control. He drew her closer, locking her to him, uncaring that the Comeaux brothers lay at his feet, unable to move, paralyzed by something she'd injected into them through a bite.

Her mouth was paradise and he could kiss her forever. No one had ever made him feel the way she did—the ferocious burn in his belly and the fire rolling through his veins with a vengeance. He knew she felt it too. The moment his mouth had come down on hers, she'd ignited as if he'd lit a match to a stick of dynamite.

His hand moved down her spine to the curve of her ass. He had to admit, she had the most beautiful body he'd ever seen. He half lifted her against his heavy erection.

Trap. She murmured his name softly. Intimately. Into his mind. *You didn't come alone, did you?*

She would have to be the voice of reason. Even if Pascal and Blaise didn't remember what had taken place, Wyatt was out there too. He couldn't very well take her like some crazy animal in the middle of the swamp. She deserved so much more.

He came up for air and rubbed his face in the soft silk of her hair. He wasn't certain that helped him gain control. Her hair felt sensual moving over his skin.

Baby, we need a bed and hours and hours to be alone.

I agree. She nuzzled his neck. His throat. Blazed a trail of fire from his throat to his chest. *Who is with you?*

Wyatt. And he isn't happy about your visits. He's afraid someone will shoot you accidentally, just the way I am. I'll be moving in by tomorrow night. As much as I want to be

*with you, don't make the mistake of coming to Wyatt's house
again without first meeting everyone.*

You take a lot for granted, don't you?

Her mouth felt so good against his bare skin. Her hands
had unbuttoned his shirt, fingers sweeping over the muscles
on his chest.

*I don't take you for granted, Cayenne. You're a fucking
miracle to me. No one has ever made me feel like this. I haven't
had a home or a family of my own, not in a very long while. I
never wanted a woman for my own until I laid eyes on you.*

He knew it was too much to give her—to admit. It made
him vulnerable to her, but she needed to know he was playing this for keeps. He'd thought about it. Weighed it in his
mind. Analyzed it from every angle. That was what he did,
even when it came to his emotions—especially when it came
to his emotions. She was worth it; he would never find
another woman to suit his needs.

She hesitated, her ear against his heart. Her hands
smoothed over his chest. *Don't say things like that, Trap.
You don't know me. You don't know what I am. I have no
past. I have no future. You can't tie yourself to me, not even
in your mind.*

*I'm in your mind, baby. I see you. What's inside of you.
The enhanced you matches the enhanced me. Your mind
can give mine the challenge I need. You're going to be wild
in bed. I need wild. I need you. You're in my mind. You tell
me you don't think I suit you. That I don't belong to you.*

He wanted to kiss her again and his hands framed her
face, but she didn't move, pressing herself tightly against
his chest, burying her face against him this time. He swore
he felt tears on his skin.

Are you crying? His hand came up to the back of her head.
He soothed her with gentle caressing strokes down that wild
streak of red. *I'm taking this too fast for you. You have to be
overwhelmed just getting out of that cage. Being free. It takes*

getting used to, not having that structure, but I swear to you, baby, I'll teach you all about living free. Doing what you want to do. Living the way you want to live. You aren't that creature in the cage they were all afraid of. You're a beautiful woman, and I can give you that. Let me teach you how to live. Let me give you the things you deserve.

Stop, Trap. You have to stop. She sounded desperate.

Her breath caught in her throat, and he felt the bite—painful as the venom went in. He kept his arms around her, still smoothing the caresses over her hair while she held him tight. He analyzed the effects of the poison as it entered his system. Clearly her bite injected neurotoxins that affected the nervous system.

I'm sorry, she whispered intimately into his mind. *You have to stay away from me. You have to. I'm terrified of you. Nothing—no one else terrifies me, only you. I can deal with everything else. Everyone is an enemy. I'm on my own and no one can hurt me. But you—you can, and I don't dare let you close. I'll protect myself from you. I will, Trap. Please leave me alone.*

The toxin was fast acting. He would have gone down hard had she not been supporting his weight. He was a big man and heavy, all muscle and solid. As small as she was, she was strong. She lowered him very gently to the ground.

Wyatt, I'm okay, let her go. His first thought was to save her ass from his friend, who would be tempted to blow her head off, seeing him go down.

Wyatt's got to be close, she continued. *I'll fade into the swamp and watch over you until he comes for you. Please listen to me this time. You can't follow me. You can't tempt me. I know you don't want to hurt me, but eventually you would. I can't take that kind of hurt. I just can't.*

She smoothed back his too-long hair. He had a lot of it, thick and unruly. He never took the time for haircuts and right then he was glad. Her fingers tunneled deep, felt good on his scalp as she stroked caresses through his hair, almost as if she were helpless to do anything else.

I wish my voice would work on you, Trap, so you could forget all about me. I've never had anything good in my life. Nothing at all. I wouldn't know the first thing about making you happy, and I refuse to be taken care of. I have to feel like an equal, and I don't know how to give anything back to you. She bent over him and brushed kisses over his mouth.

His heart stuttered. He might be unable to move, but his brain worked, and she was giving him more of herself than she realized.

Very reluctantly she lifted her head and dashed at her face with her fingers, as if brushing away tears. *You remember what I said, Trap. All of it. I will protect myself. I didn't inject you with very much toxin, any more than these two idiots. At least I hope not. I was . . . disturbed. And just so you feel better about what I do, I don't kill them. And I watch over them until they get on their feet. I just move my boat and then lie low until they're safe. None of them ever learn their lesson. They aren't very good men.*

He knew that. It did make him feel better that she watched over her victims to ensure nothing happened to them until they were back up and functioning again. Still, he wasn't going to let her have this one ever again. He was already breaking down the properties in his body, analyzing every reaction he had. He needed to get to his lab fast. Very fast, before the toxin disappeared.

Cayenne brushed another kiss over his mouth and stood, her eyes moving over his face, and this time he knew for certain there were tears shimmering in her eyes. He *hated* that she was close to crying. That she thought it was over between them. That he'd just give her up because she could inject toxin with a bite. He was highly intelligent. He had been certain all along that she could paralyze. He was also absolutely positive that if she wanted to, she could kill with a bite.

Pepper, Wyatt's wife, could. Clearly Whitney had performed experiments in the hopes of coming up with the perfect assassin. A little thing like that wasn't going to deter him.

His eyes followed Cayenne as she removed wallets, took out the cash and shoved the wallets back in pockets. She crouched over the Comeaux brothers, whispering softly. He found, just as the first time he'd ever met her, and then in the bar, that her voice definitely had a compulsion buried in it. Beautiful, perfectly pitched tones. Sensual. Her voice slipped into a man's mind and took control.

Trap wasn't entirely immune, but he had strong barriers. He was psychic as well, and he worked at creating barriers in his mind. His filters, like those of the others experimented on, had been removed in order to allow their psychic abilities to expand. Without filters, they were wide open to all kinds of assault.

Peter Whitney had begun his experiments on children, little girls he'd taken from orphanages, throwaways he called them. The first team of GhostWalkers had the most problems. With each group, Whitney had learned, and he'd continued to try for the perfect soldier. Team Four had the benefit of the doctor correcting his mistakes, but they still needed to build those shields to help with the continual assault on their brains.

"You won't remember me. Or that you still had cash. You drank a lot tonight and when you wake fully, you'll just feel very, very drunk," she whispered to the Comeaux brothers. "You won't remember that Trap or Wyatt were here either."

With one last remorseful glance, she looked at Trap. Then she stepped into the water and onto her boat. He couldn't turn his head to watch her go. He listened for the sound of the engine as it moved away from him.

Footsteps. Wyatt was there immediately, crouching beside him, reaching down to take his pulse. "Well, now, bro. That didn' go so well for you, did it? I thought that woman was goin' to strip you nekkid and have her wicked way with you or I would have moseyed on over sooner."

Shut up. You're enjoying this.

Wyatt laughed and reached down, shoulder to Trap's belly. His eyes weren't laughing. He heaved him up and started back in the direction of his boat. "I've already alerted the boys. They're waiting on the pier to greet you and welcome you home."

You would do that. You couldn't just keep this between us?

"Hell no. And by that, I mean *hell* no." Wyatt moved easily, as if Trap didn't weigh anything. "The great Trap Dawkins bested by a little bitty woman. She took you down so fast, so easily. It was a thing of beauty. I did record it, just so the others could see it."

This toxin is going to wear off and then I'm going to shoot you.

"Yeah, but in the meantime, I get to tell everyone about this. I think the other teams ought to know as well. They all revere you. This is going to show them you're human just like the rest of us."

Take me to the lab and draw blood. I'm going to find a vaccine. Or an antidote. I want it in my bloodstream so the next time she thinks she has me at her mercy, she's going to get a surprise.

Wyatt put him carefully in the bottom of the boat and studied him. "I'm thinking we need to make this more comfortable for you." He reached down and crossed Trap's arms over his chest and stepped back in the rocking boat to survey his handiwork. "Much better. The boys are goin' to think you look like Sleepin' Beauty. Maybe Malichai or Mordichai will give you a little kiss."

Stop amusing yourself and get me to the lab. I need the toxins to be concentrated in my body so I can figure out a way to counteract this. And if any of them kisses me, just let them know I'm going to be injecting them with something very unpleasant while they sleep.

Wyatt threw back his head, laughing, as he started the boat. *I trust your woman is going to watch over the Comeaux brothers. If an alligator got to them, they'd probably poison the poor creatures.*

My woman is going to find out messing with her man isn't the brightest thing to do. And yes, she's watching out for them. Get us out of here. I don't want to give this toxin a chance to get out of my system. It must leave fairly quickly or she wouldn't have the time to stick around and guard her victims.

Victims. I like that. Trap Dawkins, a victim of his own woman. She totally scored on you. Kicked your butt thoroughly.

Trap wished his facial muscles worked so he could scowl at Wyatt, who was still laughing like a hyena, the sound floating out over the top of the motor.

CHAPTER 5

Wyatt whistled low, a two-beat note that traveled over the water. They were being followed. He was all about sound, and as much as Cayenne tried to muffle the engine on her boat, he could not only hear it, but feel the vibration in the air. She stayed well back, but she was definitely following.

Your woman is behind us. She stopped just at the entrance to the canal. She tied up so she's determined to make an approach by land.

Trap swore to himself. The woman was going to get herself killed if she kept encroaching on GhostWalker territory. The men were building a fortress with the idea that they could keep out Whitney's private army of supersoldiers. Every single one of them was determined to protect Wyatt's family. For them, Wyatt's family was their family, and they'd move heaven and earth to protect them.

Gino, circle around and get in behind her. Don't engage, Wyatt cautioned, *but make certain you're in position if her intentions are anythin' but lookin' out for Trap. I don' think she's here to cause harm, so it's just a precaution.*

Fuck that, Wyatt, Trap snapped.

I've got three little girls, Trap, Wyatt reminded.

Pepper and Wyatt's three daughters needed the relative isolation of the swamp. The GhostWalkers realized that in order to provide what the children needed to survive and thrive, they would have to band together to protect them, and that meant buying up all the land around Wyatt as well as most of the land they could acquire along the way to Trap's chosen location.

Fortunately, they had a good amount of money to put into their joint venture. The plan was that eventually each of the men would build a home for himself and his family. Each home would be protected, but in the end, should there be trouble, Trap's much larger place would be their ultimate fortress. Right now, it was Wyatt's home they protected. That meant Cayenne wasn't safe sneaking in.

What does she want, Trap? Wyatt understood Trap being upset, but he had to know security was going to be taken seriously.

Trap didn't know what Cayenne was doing following them. Cayenne was impossible to predict, mainly, he knew, because she didn't have a clue what she wanted. She was lost. Confused with her emotions regarding him. More, she'd lived her entire life in a cage. She really had no clue about life outside that environment. She had to be scared. Cayenne scared was dangerous.

Baby. He reached out to her. Sending telepathy over a distance was tricky. Sometimes it worked, sometimes it didn't. He was a strong telepath. Their connection was strong and growing all the time. That alone made her uneasy.

There was a long silence. Trap felt his brothers—his teammates—moving through the darkness, spreading out to cover their butts. Gino was a ghost in the swamp and would do exactly as Wyatt cautioned. Two would go high to the roof. He managed to swallow his fear. Ezekiel, Malichai and Mordichai were brothers and extremely close. They all had the same rough features. Scars. Longish hair. Cool, steady eyes and hands that never shook, not in the worst situations. Ezekiel and Malichai would lay up on the roof with sniper rifles, and Mordichai would go hunting on the ground. What Mordichai hunted, he found.

Malichai, Ezekiel, don't shoot her. You get her in your sights, you don't pull that trigger. She's mine. Ezekiel and Malichai never missed what they aimed at either.

What the hell happened to Trap, Wyatt? That was Malichai, ignoring his order as if he hadn't heard. Ezekiel didn't say a word. He didn't make an inquiry. He didn't flinch or hesitate, and that told Trap Cayenne was in trouble. More trouble than she'd ever been in, and he was lying paralyzed in the bottom of a boat.

You fucking heard me, Malichai, Trap snapped.

You got your head so far up your own ass, you're not making any sense. Chasing that woman, thinking with your dick. She hurt him, Wyatt?

Trap's heart stuttered. He knew. He felt her now. Close. She'd already made her way through the swamp, up the canal. Ezekiel had her in his sights, and Ezekiel never missed. Never. He had so many kills, impossible shots. Trap felt something close to terror.

Baby, for God's sake, get the hell out of here. They've made you. Whatever you were thinking of doing here, go.

There was a small silence. *I'm just making certain you're okay. You should be recovering. I might have injected a little too much venom because I was . . . excited. I'd never experienced anything like that.* There was anxiety in her voice. *When you kissed me, Trap. I was scared and confused and feeling too much.* Her admission was raw. Honest. Terrified for him.

Instantly he felt settled. *She's worried about me. That's all, Wyatt. Tell the others to stand down.*

Wyatt tossed the rope to Draden. Draden was known in their team as Sandman because he didn't sleep much, and he often put enemies to sleep. He had the looks of a male model—had in fact been very successful in his modeling career before joining the GhostWalkers. He stayed close to Trap, clearly understanding something in Trap most of the others didn't. He ran often and for long distances, mostly, they were all certain, to keep his demons at bay.

Draden would protect Trap with his life, the same as Wyatt. The same as the rest of their team. Wyatt put both hands on his hips and smirked at Draden. "Take a good look at the ladies' man there."

"He sandbagging it?" Draden asked, putting one foot on the boat and peering down at Trap.

"Nope. He tried cuddlin' up to that woman of his. Kissin' her. Probably tryin' to cop a feel and she took exception to his roamin' hands. She don' need a knife to keep her man in line." He burst out laughing. "Give me a hand. I've got to lug his lazy ass to the lab. He wants a few blood samples. Figures we need to get them before this paralysis wears off."

Draden's eyebrow shot up. "He thinks he can come up with some kind of vaccine? Something to keep this from happening the next time she decides she doesn't want lover boy to use his hands on her?"

Wyatt's grin widened. "Yep. That's about it. He thinks he'll fight a little fire with fire." Wyatt stood over Trap's body, one foot planted on either side of his legs. He whipped out his cell phone. "Need to get me a few shots of this. No one will believe she got the drop on him."

Put that away, Wyatt, Trap demanded. He sent a scowl toward the swamp—toward Cayenne. *I'm never going to live this down. He takes those pictures and the boys will have a field day. You didn't have to bite me.*

I had to bite you.

I didn't mind the bite. I'll take the bite if you like that sort of thing. It was kind of sexy, but lose the venom next time. I can't satisfy your needs, baby, if I can't move.

Draden pulled out his own cell phone. "I think it best if

more than one of us has the proof. He's not above destroying evidence."

Wyatt slipped his phone back into his pocket, reached down and heaved Trap's weight over his shoulder while Draden steadied the boat. Trap hung helplessly down his back, arms dangling free. Mordichai came out of the darkness. He reached Trap, caught his longish blond hair in his fist and lifted Trap's head to peer into his eyes.

"She fucked you up royally," he observed. He dropped Trap's head with a grin and pulled out his own phone. "I'll have to email these to the boys so they don't miss out on the fun. Hang tight, Wyatt, let me get a few shots."

I'm fucking going to kill every one of you, Trap snapped.

"Not if that woman of yours gets ahold of you. We won't have to worry about a thing," Draden said.

Wyatt glanced into the swamp. Straight at Cayenne, as if he could actually see her crouched there in the trees and brush. He raised his voice and gave her a little salute. "Thanks, lady. We don' often get Trap over a barrel. We can have months of fun with this. Don' you worry, we'll take care of him for you. Go on home where you'll be out of harm's way. He's safe with us."

There was a small silence. Cayenne emerged from the swamp right out into the open, knowing she was exposing herself to real danger. She looked very small and lost. Wyatt stood sideways so Trap could see her there, risking getting shot. Knowing she stood right there visible to Ezekiel's lethal trigger finger.

"He should be coming out of it by now. The Comeaux brothers both were up and moving within minutes after you were gone." There was worry in her voice. "He shouldn't have any ill effects, but maybe he's allergic."

I'm not allergic. You just injected a little too much venom. It's already wearing off. Go home. I'll be seeing you sooner than you think. Trap made it an order. She wasn't good at taking orders, but she was anxious about him, and he was just as anxious about her. If his teammates perceived anything wrong with a single movement, if they thought her a threat, something bad could happen. He didn't want to have to kill anyone he loved.

She hesitated, and then she looked up toward the roof. She knew exactly where both Ezekiel and Malichai were—something most others would never be able to pinpoint. Cayenne faded into the shrubs, and that told him she didn't have a clue about Gino or his whereabouts. Wyatt turned toward the lab.

"We don' have much time, Draden. He wants as much toxin in his blood as possible to work with. Mordichai, get the door open and get us the blood draw kit. I'll want a lot of tubes," Wyatt said. "This is funny as hell, but he's still our brother and we've got to take his back. The next time she thinks she has him at her mercy, she's going to have a very big surprise."

Mordichai had already punched in codes and yanked the door open. Wyatt took Trap through to the long padded table where he placed the limp body gently. "When we develop this vaccine, Trap, and I have no doubt we will, make certain that it will guard against a lethal dose, accidental or not, just like we did with Pepper and the girls."

Wyatt pulled Trap's arm straight, found a vein and inserted the needle Draden handed him, his movements quick and sure. Pushing the first tube into position with his thumb, he watched the blood fill it. He filled five tubes. During that short amount of time it took to do so, he noticed Trap could move his head around.

"It's wearin' off. If she's still close, reach out and tell her," Wyatt suggested.

She doesn't deserve to know after exposing me to the crap I'm going to get from all of you. She can get her beautiful ass home and stay up all night worrying about me.

"Before you start work, you're going to have to let me check you out. You'll need food, something to drink and a few hours of rest. I know you. You're going to work day and night until you find what you're lookin' for. I'll work with you, but you've got to follow my advice on this, Trap. We don't know if there are any long-term effects yet."

It might take me much longer, and I want to spend tomorrow night in my own home.

"You'll do what I say. I'll help, that will cut down the time. We're already way ahead of the game because we've got the breakdown of Pepper's and the girls' venom. We know what we're doin' now and what to look for. I know you want to get into your home and be with her, but one or two more nights will help with gettin' that woman nervous and anxious over you as well. She told you to leave her alone. Wait it out. She won't be so quick to bite you when you show up."

That made sense. Cayenne had it in her head that she wasn't going to be his woman. She didn't trust the connection. He had no idea how much she knew of Whitney's experiments, but he paired his subjects using a combination of pheromones and something else no one had identified yet. She might not know that, and she'd be even more confused than he was about overwhelming emotions.

Trap didn't give a damn if he had been paired with Cayenne by a psycho mad scientist or not—not when he knew it was more than physical attraction. He could have walked away from that, or had really great sex a lot, but there was much more than his body involved in the way he felt around Cayenne. He didn't know if it was the same for her. Giving her a few days without him, to think it over, to miss him and worry about him was a good idea.

She should have left the area, hell, even the state, the moment she was freed from her cell. He knew that had been her intention, but she hadn't gone. She'd stayed right there in the swamp with no home, no money, nothing at all but her connection to Trap. She'd stayed for him whether she would admit it to herself or not. She'd stayed because she couldn't leave him any more than he could leave her.

His first reaction, when he realized they'd been paired

together, was to let her go free. Not to go near her. Not to give that attraction a chance to grow, because he knew that was his only means to keep her safe. His attempt to be a decent man hadn't lasted very long at all. Maybe she was still struggling with the idea of them together, but she'd get there eventually.

Truthfully, none of them were ever truly safe. Whitney was still after her. Cayenne was still under termination orders, and if Whitney sent a supersoldier after her, that soldier would have orders to kill on sight. At least with Trap and his team to protect her, she had a much better chance. If his uncles came after her, he'd be ready. *They'd* be ready.

Cayenne was no young child like his sisters and brother had been. She was no helpless woman like his aunt had been. She would fight and she would have her own arsenal, without even being armed with a gun. He was more than certain Cayenne had been trained to use a gun, a knife and every other weapon known to man. She probably could put together and take apart a bomb using an ink pen. She might not have had the practical experience, but Whitney believed in every soldier or assassin being trained and he wouldn't have made exceptions—even if they kept her in a cage.

Trap nodded his agreement to Wyatt. His body was beginning to sweat. Little beads formed on his forehead and dripped down his face into his hair. He still couldn't sit up, but his muscles were finally beginning to receive messages from his brain. Tremors started. Small ones. Hands first. His foot twitched. The woman had a lot to answer for.

He recognized that Draden, Mordichai and Wyatt were keeping a close watch on him in spite of nudging one another and poking fun at him.

Wyatt casually took his pulse. "Your heart rate's up, Trap. Not a lot, because you've got that ice water flowing in your veins, but still, for you, it's up."

Trap worked his jaw. *Doesn't surprise me. She put me down hard.*

Wyatt grinned at him. "Sexy as hell, right? Now you get

why that woman of mine is so damned special. She makes me hard every time I piss her off."

"You two like to live on the edge," Mordichai observed. "Me, I'm going to get me a little yes-woman who wants to cook like Nonny, wash my clothes for me and fuck all night."

"What does she get out of it?" Draden asked.

Mordichai looked shocked. "I told you. I'll fuck her all night."

Wyatt and Draden burst out laughing. Even Trap's mouth quirked, although it wasn't a bad plan.

"You think a lot of your skills," Wyatt observed.

"'Cuz I'm that good," Mordichai said.

Behind him, Malichai snorted as he walked in. "He giving you his life's bullshit plan for a woman?"

"Just because you didn't think of it first," Mordichai snapped, "doesn't mean it isn't perfection. She'll keep the fridge stocked with ice-cold beer for me."

"She goin' fan you when it gets hot?" Wyatt asked.

"Sure. Why not?"

Trap struggled into a sitting position. He was weak. Wyatt was right. He needed water and food and a few hours of rest. Bed sounded good. Too good. Coming up with a vaccine to protect not only him, but all of them, just as he'd done with Pepper and the girls, was going to take time. He needed his entire brain working, and right now, he was too weak to stand long, let alone think clearly.

"I don' think Trap's woman is goin' to be fannin' him," Wyatt said, toeing the leg of the table. "She's goin' to be the one callin' the shots. He went to the bar how many days in a row lookin' for her like some lovesick calf?"

The good-natured ribbing had turned from Mordichai right back to him. He couldn't deny he'd gone to the Huracan Club day after day looking for her.

"I was right," he managed to croak. "She came, didn't she?"

"And kicked your ass," Draden pointed out. "Big badass Trap, the iceman. She *kicked* your ass."

Yeah, he wasn't living this one down for a while. He sighed. "Help me into the house. We've got the blood, store it for me, Wyatt. I'm all for resting."

"Can't wait to hear what Nonny has to say about you getting your ass handed to you by a girl," Mordichai said, smirking. The smirk faded. "Of course, I'm not using the word *ass* or she might try to wash out my mouth with soap."

"You know Nonny would do more than try, Mordichai," Wyatt said.

They all burst into laughter. Draden and Mordichai both swept arms around Trap and helped him to his feet. He staggered and nearly went down as his legs gave way, but they held him up. Wyatt locked the laboratory after them. Ezekiel came down from the roof and joined them as they took Trap into the house. Gino came in from the swamp, silent as always, looking as if he'd been on a Sunday stroll.

Cayenne paced up and down the floor. Her bare feet sank into a soft, thick carpet, a luxury she'd never imagined in her life. The entire basement of the enormous building she now called home had been transformed. At first, when the workers had arrived to tear apart the upstairs, she was certain they would leave the basement area intact. Weeks had gone by, enough time for her to realize most of the houses in New Orleans and the surrounding areas were built up high and few or none had basements.

The long, two-story building had been designed so that any prisoners in the cells below the main floor would die if there was flooding and the water somehow breached the thick concrete and steel walls. She was certain the new owner—before she figured out it was Trap—would just leave the lower floor alone. She'd *hoped* he would.

She'd had to move out when they'd come to tear out everything and redesign it. She'd spent a very uncomfortable time in the swamp, creeping back to her building only at night. At first she'd messed with the workers, making them believe some swamp creature or ghost was around, but then she realized the renovations would just take that much longer. She let them get on with them.

Cayenne watched them, observing all the security measures being put into the building. Several times she saw Trap come in, and with him were blueprints he laid out on a table and showed his workers. She'd gotten ahold of the blueprints and saw that he was changing all the entrances to the tunnels and reinforcing all doors. He replaced the long rows of concrete with banks of windows up high, giving her views that took her breath away.

She had to admit, she had never once considered that terrible place could be transformed into a beautiful home. She loved the upstairs, not to live in, but the design of it all—the spacious rooms and views. The apartment downstairs was far too big for her. She had never really lived outside her cell and freedom was overwhelming. The wide-open spaces made her feel exposed. Because she'd lived most of her life in that small cell, having so much open space terrified her. She would never admit it to anyone, but she couldn't sleep and ended up dividing the room into sections with silken webs. That helped.

She paced more and restlessly jumped up onto the low-slung couch, standing on the cushions, biting her thumbnail. She never bit her fingernails, but she couldn't help herself. She shouldn't have left Trap when she had. His friends had surrounded him protectively, and she could feel waves of both humor and anger radiating out toward her. They wanted to think it was a good joke, but they wouldn't really find it funny until he was fully recovered.

She had never seen camaraderie like that before. She'd heard of it and read about it, but she'd never actually witnessed it. Certainly not among Braden or Whitney's supersoldiers. She'd studied all the GhostWalkers from a distance, and sometimes at night while they slept. Wyatt's home was filled with warmth. The moment she slipped in through the tiny little chimney stack on the roof that no longer was used, she felt the warmth surrounding her.

She'd been careful, staying in the corners, up high on the ceiling, trying to feel what it was like to have a home and family. Again, she'd read of such things, but she had no idea of what one was supposed to be like. The older woman, the one all of them called Nonny, was small and frail. She slept in a bed that seemed too big for her and twice she nearly caught Cayenne, waking when curiosity had gotten the better of Cayenne and she'd slipped down the wall to the floor in order to examine the old photographs lining her walls. Nonny had them everywhere throughout the house.

Cayenne was fascinated by the photographs of four little boys in the process of growing and what those pictures represented. Wyatt and presumably his brothers had grown up in that house. The progression of their aging along with the differences in the house itself kept her coming back to Nonny's room time and time again. Other than being with Trap, she found she loved that room the most. If there was a scent and a feel to home, it was there in Nonny's room.

The other place that had absolutely drawn her was Trap's room. She could sit there for hours watching him while he slept. He never wore clothes to bed. Never. His body captivated her, held her spellbound so that once she was in his room her entire attention was so riveted on his physique that she wasn't certain she could describe the actual contents of the room, not like she could in Nonny's.

She was absolutely fascinated with his body. He was a big man, tall, with lots of muscle, miles of it, it seemed. Even in his sleep, there it was, all beautifully covered by his skin. He had scars. She recognized bullet wounds and several stab wounds and that set her heart pounding, that something could happen to him in his line of work. The worst wound was across his stomach, and it had been deep. There was a second high up on his thigh where the blade had been twisted as it was pulled free, creating a crater. He didn't look like any of the lab techs working for Braden—or Whitney.

He was very proportionate to his size. She knew, because she studied him from every angle. He didn't like clothes, and he didn't like to get tangled in the covers. She'd never been close to a man's naked anatomy, although she'd seen plenty of pictures when they insisted on educating her on the subject of murder—and sex. She decided, after studying his penis several times, that he was too large to fit inside a woman. At rest he was too large, so how could he when aroused? More, in the pictures, she thought men's packages were quite ugly. She didn't think that at all about Trap's. She found herself wanting to know it very intimately.

"Stupid," she whispered. "You let him know you were going into the house. You shouldn't have done that. They'll be waiting now."

She shouldn't go. It was insanity. Suicide. But she could barely breathe for the fear moving through her. Her mind felt chaotic. What if she'd given him too much venom? He hadn't responded like Pascal and Blaise Comeaux. They'd come around, disoriented. Sweating. Grouchy as all get-out, nearly picking a fight with each other, but it had only been a couple of minutes before they'd come around.

She could still hear Wyatt's voice when the brothers managed to stand up and wade into the water to step into their boat. Of course, she was listening for his boat. The moment the brothers had cleared the area, she was on the move, rushing to follow Trap and Wyatt back to Wyatt's home.

She leapt from the couch back onto the floor, digging her toes into the thick carpet. She knew she was going to go check on Trap. She had patience, discipline and restraint when it came to any other person or situation, but with Trap she couldn't stop herself. She knew she shouldn't go, that it was far too risky, but there was no staying away from him.

What if he stayed away from her? She'd kissed him. Given

them both that. At first she told herself it was because she was curious, but she knew that wasn't the truth. She *had* to taste him. She had to feel his body against hers. She could lie to him and tell him she wanted him to stay away, but she couldn't lie to herself. She didn't want him to stay away. She craved seeing him. She needed to see him in the same way she needed air to breathe. She couldn't keep away from him. She didn't understand why, with her discipline, she couldn't train her mind away from thinking about him, but it was impossible.

Shivering, she took a deep breath and forced herself to stay calm. If something had happened to Trap the men would be swarming the swamp looking for her. She had silken lines everywhere, so thin most wouldn't notice. They certainly wouldn't care about breaking one as they rushed through the thick brush. She'd be warned. Over the last few weeks, she had set her alarm system wider and wider, around the building, through the trees and even farther into the swamp itself.

Each silken strand was so thin, nearly transparent, that it blended into the surroundings. Dew and rain could cling to the strand, giving it away, but she took care to always make her work look like that of the local spiders. She was good at web art and could reproduce any spiderweb shown to her.

She wandered over to the small dresser in the corner of the room. Sliding through the layer of webs, she ran her finger along the surface. It was silly really, that they'd put a dresser in the small apartment. Trap knew she was staying there and there was no doubt in her mind that he'd done it for her. She didn't have any clothes. Two stolen pairs of jeans. Two camisole tops and a sweater. One shirt she had from before that she didn't wear, but wanted to keep. And his jacket. That was it. That was the extent of her wardrobe. The rest of her own clothes had long since been ruined in the muddy swamp.

People making their homes in the swamp and bayou didn't have tons of money. Stealing from them was not only immoral, but risky. If a woman only had a few clothes, she knew what those precious clothes looked like. Cayenne didn't dare go into town and shop with the money she'd stolen. She was afraid someone would recognize what she was wearing. In any case, the idea terrified her. She wouldn't know how to go into a store or make a transaction like that. She had no experience.

Sighing, she skimmed her finger over the polished wood. Still, she loved the dresser. Carved wood. So beautiful. Heavy. She wished for a little box, just like the one she'd seen on Nonny's dresser. Her hand hovered just above the sturdy piece of furniture, as if she could touch that box. She mimicked opening the lid with her fingers. The box made music, a soft song, the notes filling the air around her when she'd peeked inside. Her heart had stuttered in alarm when the notes drifted into the room.

Hastily, she replaced the lid and thankfully the music had stopped. The woman Trap called Nonny stirred and then rolled over and looked toward the dresser. Cayenne was already up in the corner, clinging to the ceiling, holding her breath and whispering softly for Wyatt's grandmother to go back to sleep. She'd never dared open the box again—but she wanted to. She thought about it a lot.

There was no more stalling. She had to go. She had to see for herself that Trap was all right after she'd stupidly and childishly injected venom into him. He wasn't going to ever kiss her again. Cayenne touched her lips with the pads of her fingers, found them trembling, and hastily leapt up to the vent to exit the building. They'd even done things to the ventilation system, installing doors every so many feet *inside* the pipework. She knew eventually those doors would be locked with a security code. So far, that hadn't been done, but it soon would be, and the ventilation systems were her exits and entrances.

She moved quickly through the narrow shaft to where she emerged just outside the building and very close to the high chain-link fence. At the top was razor wire. She detested that stuff. This exit was the closest to the fence of all the ventilation doors. She could practically leap from the opening and catch the chain, it was that close.

Cayenne went up and over the fence in seconds. She didn't leap over it like she'd seen Trap's team do, but she could go over it just as fast. She knew the way and went unerringly. Trap's workers had opened a trail through the swamp, cleverly concealed, but since she'd watched them, she knew exactly where the faint trail was and she used it, rather than the boat, to make her way to the Fontenot property.

She made certain to come downwind of the dogs so they wouldn't catch her scent. If they did, she was putting out more of a spider vibe than a human one. They might grow restless, but they wouldn't sound the alarm. She studied the seemingly and very deceptively dark home. It looked as if the occupants were all asleep.

No one appeared to be in the laboratory, which Trap and Wyatt often spent many nights in. She didn't bother to enter the house when they were working, and she'd never found an entry point into the lab in order to see what they were doing. She could guess, though. Wyatt's toddlers were cutting their teeth and they all had venom, much like she did, but they were babies and theirs was snake venom.

She studied the house. They were aware that she bypassed their security, and they wouldn't like it. She'd woven a few webs inside the extremely narrow chimney on the roof. She knew men wouldn't consider that a human being could make oneself so small they could fit in such a place. She was also very curvy and men tended to look at her curves, not realizing how limber she was, how her body could flatten itself, her bones soft, allowing her to become so much smaller.

She knew they had someone on the roof. It was a matter of locating him. These men didn't make mistakes. There was no restless movement. No cigarette smoking, or whipping out a cell phone and playing on it. They remained still and silent for hours on end. Normally, she liked the thrill of pitting her skills against theirs. It kept her sharp and she thought of it as a game.

She could move slow or fast, go up impossible angles and extremely high buildings. She possessed the same stillness and patience these men had. It was fun to slip past them and enter the house, knowing she could. They were highly trained and motivated to keep the girls safe. If she was being strictly honest with herself, she identified with everyone in the house—especially those little girls. She watched over them as well, but she would never admit that to anyone.

She went up and over their security fence. It wasn't that difficult. She knew they sometimes ran electricity through it, but never unless they were on high alert. They didn't want stray animals or a neighbor to get hurt. The moment she cleared the fence, she stayed very still, crouching low to the ground. There was a long, open stretch that was the most difficult area to get through leading to the house itself.

Like most places in the swamp or bayou, the Fontenot home was built up to keep from flooding when the river rose. Made entirely of cypress, she knew it would withstand the water and elements for many years. She could see the craftsmanship and the loving hands in the work. Everything about this place appealed to her.

She had nowhere to go. No one to turn to. These people were like her. Different. Pepper and the three little toddlers had spent their lives—like she had—in a laboratory. Although Pepper had a different education and had been allowed out much more, they weren't like other humans, and they never would be. She had never felt that more acutely than she did right then.

She wasn't part of the GhostWalker team, but she was no longer in her cage. She didn't really fit anywhere. She didn't know how to act. She had to watch others and follow their examples. She often made mistakes. Her training helped her to quickly cover those mistakes, but she learned fast to minimize her contact with locals—other than when she went hunting. She had to eat, so she had no choice but to get money someway, although she went hungry for long periods. She wasn't about to sleep with men like the Comeaux brothers for money, and her particular skill sets weren't very marketable. That left robbery.

Trap didn't like it, but he wasn't the one with the empty stomach. She was up near the edge of the roof and she rested her forehead against the eave. Trap. He really detested that she'd robbed others. His disapproval made her feel ashamed and dirty. She didn't like the feeling at all.

Taking a breath, she eased her body up and peeked over the roof. Scanning. She didn't see anyone close, but she *felt* him. She shouldn't do this. It went against her training—against all logic and common sense. She was allowing something she didn't even understand to control her, but she knew it didn't matter. She was compelled to see for herself that Trap was alive and well—that she hadn't harmed him by injecting too much venom. Sliding carefully onto the roof, she flattened her body, maneuvering beyond what anyone would think possible. She knew it would be impossible to spot her when she wasn't moving. She would look part of the roof structure.

Cayenne let the cool breeze drift over her for some time, reaching out into the night for scents and movement, but none came. Whoever was on the roof—and she was certain someone was up there with her, she just couldn't locate him—was every bit as adept at hiding himself as she could be.

If she was going to do this, she had to take the chance of getting caught. The chimney was only a few feet from her. Cayenne began to inch forward. Slow. Barely moving. Making certain not even a whisper of her clothes sliding over the roof gave her away. For the first time, entering the Fontenot compound, her heart was in her throat.

She made it to the small chimney and folded herself inside. Once crammed into the pipe, she felt relief. Someone had definitely been on the roof with her. His energy was low, but very, very dangerous. There was a part of her that suspected he might have known she was there, but let her through anyway. The familiar elation was gone, leaving her anxious and afraid of Trap's rejection. She'd sought that, even demanded it, although she knew it was really the last thing she wanted from him.

Cayenne resisted the urge to slip into Nonny's room. She needed to—for some reason the room comforted her, and more than any other time, she needed comfort. She didn't know anyone who could *give* her comfort—hold her in their arms like she'd seen Wyatt do Pepper. No one cared that much. She needed that more than she needed to stand in a beautiful room pretending.

In Nonny's room she could and often did pretend she had a family and a grandmother who loved her. Someone. Anyone. She swallowed hard and made her way through the house. She might have had the chance with Trap if she hadn't been so afraid and sent him away. Worse, if she hadn't embarrassed him in front of his friends and maybe actually harmed him.

CHAPTER 6

Cayenne made her way down the stairs like a human being, not a spider. She shouldn't do that either, but she often did when she was in the house, because it made her feel as if she could belong. Walking like a human rather than clinging to the ceiling and making her way was dangerous because she was so much easier to spot, but tonight—tonight she needed to be real. A human being. Someone else. Someone not her.

Deep inside her, something was building—something big and terrible. With every step she took she felt the heavy weight of that dark force gathering. Her breath hitched and her chest felt tight. Tremors racked her body, so much so that she knew if one of the GhostWalkers found her, she wouldn't be able to fight her way free. She kept walking toward him—toward Trap—because she *had* to.

She knew the way to his room, but even if she hadn't, she would have been able to find him. The pull was so strong in her that she always knew where he was. The thought that she could have caused him real harm stabbed at her heart relentlessly. Her stomach knotted. She pressed a hand over her churning belly, over those tight knots, took a deep breath and put her hand on his door.

Trap. She whispered his name. Her nemesis. The man who made her want to be human. The man she wanted more than anything in the world but knew she couldn't have. She didn't dare have him. She wouldn't know what to do with him, and when she was overwhelmed and scared, she could easily make a mistake.

She half turned away, her breathing ragged, coming in little hitches. She didn't know what that was either, only that it was uncomfortable and totally unfamiliar. She needed someone. *Needed* them. Not just someone, she needed the man she'd injected with toxins. The man she'd told to go away and stay away.

She hesitated and pressed her forehead against the door and slid her hand high, to the height his head would be, as if she could touch him. She pushed her body against the door as if his arms were around her and she could feel his body against hers. She tried to pretend that he was holding her, but there was no way to make that real for herself. No way.

She had rarely been out of her cell. She had despised her captors, and yet, if they were still alive, still around, she would have gone back because life outside that cell was *terrifying.* She had not wanted to believe them, that she wasn't fit to walk around with everyone else, especially when she saw inside of them, saw how ugly and cruel they were, but they were right.

She was different. Not human. Not salvageable. She had all the knowledge in the world inside her mind, but not a single bit of practical experience. She didn't know how to do anything but kill. The only person who had shown her any kindness, she'd struck out at and harmed.

Her heart pounded so hard it hurt, but she remained there, pressed tight against the door for a short while, trying to will everything to go the way she wanted. The problem was she was so confused she had no idea what she wanted. She wished . . . She stepped back from the door and dropped her hand to the knob resolutely.

She didn't have to open the door more than a crack to slip inside. Instantly, she inhaled. Deep. There he was, and the terrible churning in her stomach settled. The knots were still there, but the relentless coiling ceased. He was wide awake, head turned toward her, his gaze on her. She froze a foot from him. His hands were linked behind his head, and his eyes were as cold as ice. A blue flame burned beneath that ice. Once his gaze locked with hers, she couldn't look away. She was his captive as sure as if he had put her in shackles.

Every nerve ending in her body came alive. Her heart pounded and her stomach fluttered. Deep inside, something hot and wild moved. Persisted. She recognized that now, because every time she was near Trap, it was there, smoldering like a red-hot ember, ready to burst into flame at the slightest provocation.

Right then, even that flame didn't matter, because the terrible, vicious storm that had been building with every step she'd taken to get to him was close—too close and that terrified her. She couldn't catch her breath. Her eyes burned like fire. Hot and uncomfortable and there was no way to stop it. No way to shove away the force that had to find a way out before she shattered into a million pieces.

"Ezekiel spotted you, Cayenne," he said.

Cayenne. Not baby. His voice was neutral, not soft and caressing. She'd really blown it. She needed him. At least she needed the fantasy of him. She just *needed*, and this was the only human being she trusted enough to go to for . . . what? What did she expect from him? She didn't even know, yet she'd come for something. Something she was desperate to have. His eyes were arctic cold. So cold she found herself shivering.

She shrugged as if it didn't matter. Maybe it didn't. If she didn't have him . . . If she didn't have *this* . . . What was there for her? She may as well have been terminated there in that cold, dark basement. She couldn't look away from his eyes. Those eyes that saw everything, saw right past her armor. Right past her fight. Right into the heart of her, where she was most vulnerable. He *saw* her. He had to know what she was—not human. Made for one purpose—to murder. That alone should have had her running, or killing him.

She did neither. She stared at him while her vision blurred and the burning in her eyes worsened. Her throat clogged until she was fighting for air. She pressed a hand to her knotted stomach.

"Come here, Cayenne."

There was hard authority in Trap's voice. She didn't accept authority. Not from anyone. People manipulated and corrupted. She didn't trust anyone enough to recognize them as an authority. She had vowed she'd never do anything anyone said. She'd been five years old and so tired of the needles and the fear and the punishments when she had first made that vow.

Her captors didn't like her. She was nothing but a specimen. Not human. Nothing. A throwaway. They made certain she knew it, and she despised them all. And herself. She despised that she couldn't get away from them, that they'd taken all her power from her and made her helpless. She'd vowed never to be helpless again. But here she was. In Trap's room. The last place she should have gone. Feeling helpless. Lost. Completely lost and very vulnerable.

"Baby, just come to me. Two steps. I'll do the rest, but you have to take those two steps."

There was no give in his voice—or his eyes. He was implacable, and she had no idea what would happen when she did what he said and took those two steps toward him. Still, she obeyed the command in his voice, in his eyes, moving toward the side of the bed, not looking away from him, but no longer seeing him. Not when her vision was totally blurred. She felt a trickle of wetness making its way down her cheek.

She felt as if she were giving herself to him with every step she took. Letting him take the last little part of herself that she guarded so carefully. Her throat closed, but she forced her body to move, because if she didn't, she would lose everything. She would have nothing. She couldn't live like that anymore, believing she was worthless. That child in the laboratory, in a tiny little cell with eyes staring at her all the time. She had to be more, and she had to have someone see that she was more. That someone had to be this man.

Trap's fingers shackled her wrist as she lifted her hand to wipe at the drops. He tugged until she was forced to put a knee on the bed. Then she was up on the bed with him. She couldn't breathe. Couldn't catch air. Her throat was too clogged, and her eyes burned like hell.

"Don't, baby," he whispered.

There it was. That voice. His beautiful, sensual voice that caressed her skin, but more, slid deep inside to caress her empty heart. He could fill her with just his voice. Give her an anchor, something to hold on to when she was being tossed around in the wind like so much silk. Instinctively, she knew he didn't use that tone on anyone else. Just her.

"I could have really hurt you," she confessed, a hitch in her voice. Her throat was so tight she could barely squeeze words out.

"You didn't," he assured, dragging her down over his chest, pressing her face into his neck. Showing no fear in spite of the fact that she'd bitten him. Injected venom. She couldn't detect the least bit of fear. None.

Everyone was afraid of her. She couldn't remember a time that anyone came near her without elevated heart rates and weapons close. Even when she'd been a child. She had often watched every member of the Fontenot household— even the scariest of them—cuddling the triplets. Holding them close, just as Trap was holding her.

Her body lay curled over his chest. Her front to his front. She straddled him, her legs on either side of him, pressed tight to his ribs. She took up his entire chest, her face in his neck, breathing him in, pulling him straight into her lungs. Her heart pounded harder than ever and blood roared in her ears, but she didn't move, because the storm kept building and she knew it was going to be terrible.

She held herself very still. Fight or flee? She didn't know what to do. He was warm and his hand was soothing in her hair. He was comforting, like Nonny's room, only better. His arms went around her, holding her close, not demanding anything from her. Not speaking, but he began to hum softly. Like Nonny's music box, only better. He had a beautiful pitch to his voice. She'd never really heard anything that beautiful in person before and she knew it was only for her.

Cayenne loved his speaking tone, but found his music voice even better. She closed her eyes because she couldn't help herself. She was completely vulnerable to him in that moment and she knew it. She just didn't care. All the fight was out of her. She just needed. Trap. She needed Trap. She was giving herself to him and she knew it, and she was acutely aware that he knew it as well. She allowed the last bit of feral spider in her to move aside enough to let the soft notes Trap hummed to penetrate until she stopped shivering.

The storm broke, wild and uninhibited, yet quietly, sobs welling up uncontrollably, terrible, from her heart. From her soul. Her fingers curled into his shoulders and she pressed her face tighter against his neck while the storm took her.

Her eyes leaked tears and she wasn't certain why, only that she felt safe enough in his arms, there in the dark, to shed them. She had years of tears stored up, so she was very happy when the humming turned to words and he sang softly to her, stroking soothing caresses through her hair and down her back. She could spend a lifetime right there, letting the tears flow, listening to his voice and feeling the warmth of his body against hers while his hands moved through her hair and massaged the nape of her neck.

Trap held Cayenne as close to him as humanly possible

and just let her cry. He'd never held a weeping woman in his life, but from the moment he'd touched his mind to hers, outside in the hallway, when he'd heard the first hesitant *Trap*, he'd known she needed him with the same intensity as he needed her. Maybe it was for different reasons, but he wasn't alone in this and that was all he needed to know.

This wasn't just about the explosive chemistry between them. Right in that moment, the only thing in his mind was to hold and comfort her. To find ways to show her what life with him was going to be. He wanted to give her everything he could possibly give her. She deserved that. She'd never had anything and she would never expect anything from him.

He knew what greed was. He had far too much money pouring into his accounts every minute of every day. He'd worked for it, but still, thanks to the magazines making him one of the most eligible bachelors in the world, the write-ups on him, the disclosure that he was a billionaire several times over, women threw themselves at him.

Trap was often rude. Beyond rude. He'd developed that as a form of protection and now it was ingrained in him. He was demanding in bed because he knew he could be, and then he kicked the women out, refusing to allow any woman to sleep in the same bed with him. He never took them home with him. Never. None of the women had any idea who he was, or even cared to know. They knew about his bank account and that was enough for them.

Cayenne had no idea about bank accounts and whether or not he had money. She could care less. She was alone. Afraid. Different. A throwaway. He'd been thrown away by his father and uncles. He had trust issues and recognized that Cayenne had those same issues deeply ingrained in her.

He hated that she was weeping as if her heart had broken, but he was grateful she'd come to him. That she'd given him that. She had handed him something precious. He knew he was a bull in a china shop when it came to relationships, but he read books and he observed carefully. No detail got past him. And he had instincts. He had always relied on his instincts.

Cayenne was vulnerable to him—and only him. She would never show this side of herself to any of the other men no matter how much she was hurt. He had that from her. That raw honesty. That soft spot. The truth that was her heart, and he would protect it with everything in him.

"All right, baby," he crooned. "You're going to make yourself sick. If Nonny wakes up and hears you crying, she'll be in here like a shot. She'll box my ears and take you under her wing. I like holding you when you need it, so I don't want that to happen."

She continued to weep but much more silently.

He smiled at the ceiling and tunneled his fingers in the thick mass of hair. Silky soft just like her skin. A man would get lost in that hair. "I'll admit asking for that might be a little selfish. I want to be the man you turn to when things get all out of whack for you. I want you to feel safe with me and not anyone else."

Her hand moved. She'd laid on him without moving a single muscle, almost as if her body had melted into his. Now, her hand stroked down his shoulder, over his biceps. He felt that touch burn through sinew into bone.

"I don't know where to go, Trap. I know that's your home, not mine. But I don't know where to go," she whispered, choking out the admission.

His hold tightened on her and he found himself frowning. "Is that what this storm is all about? Baby, I had that apartment built for you. I chose every piece of furniture down there. For you. It belongs to you."

He heard—and felt—her breath hitch. Very slowly she lifted her head, her tear-drenched green eyes searching his blue ones. "Trap." She whispered his name. Disbelieving. "You did?"

"What the hell am I going to do with all that girlie shit, baby? I knew you were using the basement. I don't like you in it, but I reinforced the walls against flooding just in case. Still, eventually, I hope to lure you upstairs with me. I'm giving you fair warning about that. I want you in my bed, and I'm not going to play bullshit games. Right now, you need your space, and I'm going to give it to you as long as I can. So yeah, that apartment is all yours. I won't go down there unless you invite me."

"Really?"

This time her voice was breathless. The sound shot straight to his cock. He was stark naked and he didn't need that happening. Not now. Not when she needed reassurance and a gentle hand. He wasn't a gentle lover. He was demanding. As bossy and as abrupt in bed as he was outside of it. He didn't want to scare her away.

"I just said it. I don't like bullshit, Cayenne. When you want or need something, you have to come out and tell me. I'll do the same. I don't want you robbing people. I want you safe, with a roof over your head. I want you warm with food in your belly. I don't have a clue what women need in the clothes department, so I'm setting up a little safe in the kitchen. It'll always have cash in it. You need something, either put it on a list and I'll do my best, or take the cash and buy what you need."

She moistened her lips with the tip of her tongue. Her eyes were red and swollen from crying. Her cheeks were wet and splotchy. He thought she was beautiful. He had to fight the urge to kiss her.

"I don't know how to do that. Or where to go to do it. I've never left the swamp," she confessed. "I stole these clothes off a line, and I'm always afraid I'll run into the woman and she'll know I took them even though I left her money twice."

She sounded ashamed. He had hoped he could get her to see that stealing was wrong. He realized she knew stealing was wrong, but she'd been desperate. He didn't like her feeling ashamed.

"Don't worry, honey, we'll go into town together and get you clothes. You're a fast learner and I have no doubt you'll learn all about shopping."

She blinked rapidly, her dark lashes fluttering, drawing his attention to their length. Beautiful. He loved her face. He could look at it forever. Perfect symmetry. High cheekbones. Oval shape. That generous, generous mouth with her bowed lips. Small straight nose. Her large, fuck-me-all-night eyes surrounded by long, feathery lashes.

"I don't like to go where there are a lot of people. That's why I chose the Huracan Club to hunt—that and they have peanuts for free and he sells burgers. There weren't a lot of people to choose from to rob, but I can't control or manipulate a large group of people with my voice and I didn't feel safe out in the open. The club was deep in the swamp."

"We'll get you past that, Cayenne. That's one thing we're going to do. Make certain you feel safe. You'll have to know what's coming at you now."

She blinked again. "Coming at me?"

"You're mine. You gave yourself to me, and I'll be damned if I let you take that gift back. You can have time, baby, but you don't have a *lot* of time. I told you I'd tell you about my life when you're lying next to me in bed, and I will. But you have to know now that I have enemies and they'll come after you to hurt me. Caring about you makes me vulnerable. I haven't been vulnerable in a long time, not since they murdered my aunt when I was very young."

"Why do you care about me?"

He should have known she would dismiss the danger. Cayenne wasn't afraid. She had all the confidence in the world as a warrior. She didn't have confidence in herself as a woman—a human woman.

His fingers tightened in her hair. Fisted. Forced her head back exactly where he wanted it, his eyes boring into hers. Claiming her. Possessive. She needed to see that about him. He didn't let many people into his life, but he was utterly loyal to those he did. He had never claimed a woman for his own, had never wanted one enough to risk her or to fight for her, but all that had changed.

He was fierce in battle. Ice-cold, but ferocious and relentless. He'd learned every skill he could so he was always prepared for anything. Prepared for this moment. This claiming. His woman. The woman he never believed he'd have.

"I'll never let you go, Cayenne. You'll be as much a prisoner with me as you were in that cell. I can teach you to live life large. To live it free. But I won't let you go. We have trouble, you don't like something, baby, you'll have to learn to talk to me. I'll do everything in my power to make you happy, but you're mine, you stay mine."

She frowned. She didn't look afraid of him, but then, she was a spider, a woman who could slip in and out of places and she didn't realize he wasn't talking about physical captivity. He knew her mind would go there first.

Trap shook his head. "I'm not talking about locking you up, baby. I'm talking about keeping your heart. Holding you close to me always. Never giving you back your heart. Never. You give me that, I'll keep it safe, but I won't return it."

She laid her head back down on his shoulder, turning her face into his neck. He felt her breath. He lost her eyes, but her body had once again melted into his. Her tongue tasted his skin right under his jaw. A tentative touch, but that told him she was curious. More than curious. She had a need just the same as his.

He had to be patient. He had to let that need build until she came to him. He couldn't take it from her. Too much had already been taken. He needed to be the one that gave her whatever she needed or wanted. Give her everything she could want or need until she understood that she was safe with him and that he was real and his caring was real.

"I don't think that's such a bad thing, Trap," she whispered against his jaw. Softly. Clearly trying to puzzle out what could be the deception—the con—he was running on her.

She was in his mind. He felt her there, a soft little presence, clinging when she didn't notice that she was. It was intense to have someone sharing one's mind. To feel them gently pouring into every shadow, those dark places where insanity lurked. He knew she couldn't help but feel his sincerity—or hear the honesty in his voice. She didn't trust it, and he didn't blame her. He had to earn that.

"I want to show you what it's like to have a family. To live in a house and laugh and love. I want that for you. I didn't have it very long, but I did have it. I want the chance to make that happen for you. I started with the apartment because I want you to feel you always have your own space. Even when we're together, when you're living with me and sleeping in my bed, when you need it, that apartment will be there."

He turned his head and brushed her forehead with his mouth. "Just remember, baby, once you share my bed, that's where you'll sleep. Right beside me."

She was very still, stroking his arm, her fingers absently tracing little patterns over his muscles there. "Why? Why would you want that?"

"I want to be able to hold you just like this. You have a bad day, I need to be there for you. I have one, I want your arms around me." His hand shaped the nape of her neck. Slid down her spine to the curve of her bottom. "I want to reach for you in the middle of the night. It takes a lot to keep my cock happy, baby, and I'm fairly certain with you there, ready for me, for the first time in my life, I won't be thinking about fucking every minute of the day because you will have satisfied me. I swear, Cayenne, I'll do everything in my power to keep you satisfied."

She was silent, absorbing the information. Still unsure of him. Still nervous about giving herself to him, but knowing she already had. He felt that. He knew she wasn't rescinding, only feeling her way.

"Everything is new to me, Trap," she confessed. "I lived in a cell and had minimum contact with people. All my training was done in closed environments because they were afraid I'd escape and be let loose on the world. They were right to be afraid, I would have. But just like now, I wouldn't have known what to do. I might have even gone back. I don't understand about family or relationships. I don't know the first thing about a home or how to make one or be in one. I don't know how to support myself or anyone else. I don't know how to please you that way at all."

He groaned softly. "Baby, you kiss like sin. That's a good thing. Hot and wild, just like I need. You light up for me. Catch fire. That's all you. Everything else, I can teach you. I know what I'm doing. I want that chance as well. You've got instincts, Cayenne, good ones. You burn for me when you get close. I have no doubt you'll please me and I'll please you. I tend to be very good at giving instructions and telling a woman what I want from them. I'll want you to do the same."

She turned her face into the hollow of his shoulder and bit down gently. "I don't like that."

He held himself still. He didn't want her agitated where she might really bite him again before he had the chance to build enough antibodies in his system against her particular type of toxin. He was absolutely certain he could find a way to do that.

"Don't like what?" he murmured, keeping his voice gentle.

"The idea of other women with you." She lifted her head again, her green gaze searching his blue one. "Why is that? I mean, I *really* don't like it. My stomach just got tight and I felt the venom wanting to be released. Also, the thought kind of hurts."

He wanted to smile at her voice. That thoughtful, interested tone, with just a small note of annoyance. "Of course you wouldn't like the idea of me with other women. I don't like the idea of you being close to other men. Didn't you notice I was really upset when Pascal put his hand on your ass?"

She nodded, not taking her eyes from his. Not blinking. Looking for the information she needed and trying to understand. "Yes, I knew that upset you, but I didn't know why. When you got all snarly with me, I tried to figure it out, but nothing made sense to me."

"Men and women often have multiple sex partners, but not when they make a commitment to each other." He searched for the right words. "You belong to me, and I belong to you. That's the commitment. The promise we give each other. That means, I don't fuck other women and you sure as hell don't fuck other men." He couldn't keep the growl out of his voice. He had animal DNA and he was an alpha. The idea of another man putting his cock in her was more than he could take.

She nodded her head but she was frowning almost in confusion. It was a point he didn't want there to be any confusion over. None.

"Do you understand what I'm saying to you, Cayenne? Because had you let Pascal kiss you, touch your body or fuck you, there would have been hell to pay. I have control, but just like you have triggers that can be dangerous, I do as well. I would have killed him."

She sighed and pressed her forehead to his shoulder. "I guess I have a lot of things to learn. I don't know if I'll ever get everything straight. I have to get out of here before your friend on the roof decides I've done something to you."

"He knows you're just visiting with me. We can talk telepathically to one another, and we do often to keep our skill level up."

"Like you do with me."

"Not exactly. It's much more intimate with you." Trap couldn't tell her what the difference was. She would have to feel it. He poured himself into her mind in the same way she did his, filling her with him. He wanted to be there with her, surrounding her and caring for her.

"Are you a white knight?"

Her voice was accusatory, almost as if she was getting angry with him. She started to shift her weight. The movement was subtle, so subtle he nearly didn't feel it even though her body was soft and pliant against his. She felt boneless, all silk. He didn't allow that deception either. He tightened his arms, using his strength to hold her when she would have slipped away.

"Don't," he cautioned. It was a command, nothing less.

Cayenne went still, her gaze drifting over his face, this time wary. Lost. Confused. Fearful. A touch of something else. She didn't struggle, but she was poised to flee.

"What do you mean by white knight?" he asked softly.

"I don't need rescuing."

He stared up at her face. A slow smile curved his mouth and touched his eyes. "Baby." He whispered the endearment softly. "If there's anyone on this fucking earth that needs to be rescued, it's you." He kept his arms steel bands around her, preventing movement. "That's lucky for me."

She shook her head, and for a moment her eyes went wet again. Tiny drops of shimmering opaque tears caught in her long eyelashes. His hand slid into her hair, fisted there and pulled her head down to his. His mouth claimed her tears, brushing her eyes and lashes, down the sweet curve of her face to her mouth.

"I need rescuing too, Cayenne. I've been alone too damn long and I want my own woman. I want a home. One that's yours, mine. You're going to make that monstrosity a home for me."

He allowed her to raise her head, nuzzling her face as she lifted it, with his nose. Silken strands of her dark hair caught on his shadowed jaw. He liked that. He liked any tie between them, no matter how small.

"I don't know how, Trap. I go through this house and I recognize what it is. All the warmth. The laughter. The beautiful things. They weren't made with money, they were made with hands. I don't know how to do any of that."

She sounded sorrowful. So sad it tore at his heart. She looked crushed. He pushed the hair from her face, tucking it behind her ear.

"You aren't supposed to know how, Cayenne. We're going to learn that together. We're going to live life our way, not how others live their lives. We'll find our way."

"I've never cooked anything in my life. What if you want to eat and you're sick or something and can't cook?"

He laughed softly at the sheer desperation in her voice. "We'll cross that bridge when we come to it. Honey, we're not even in the same house and you're already trying to find things to keep us apart. Don't make shit up. There will be plenty of things about me that will piss you off. We can have a cook if you want one, but since I intend to fuck you every chance I get, anywhere we are in that house, it might get a little embarrassing. I've imagined you spread out in front of me like a feast on that dining room table. I chose the table just for that reason."

Soft color crept up her neck and into her face. Her lashes fluttered, and she pressed her lips together and rubbed them back and forth. "You're very sexual, aren't you?"

"That bother you?" His gut tightened. He didn't mind that she was inexperienced—in fact just the opposite, he fucking loved that she was just his. But he was sexual. He *needed* sex. He came off a marathon research project and he was exhilarated, as high as a kite, and always his cock was as hard as a rock and even after hours of sex, he often wasn't in the least sated.

She swallowed hard. "I don't know. I don't know what it's like. What if I don't like having sex?"

A slow smile eased the tight knots in his belly. "You'll like it, because I'll make certain you do. Trust me to make sure. We could start now if you wanted." He put a little hope in his voice.

She looked horrified. "Are you crazy?" Her hands went to his shoulders and she pushed, trying to get space between them. "I can't stay. Really. And if your friend comes in here to check on you and sees you like . . ." She glanced over her shoulder to the long, hard length of his cock, fully erect against his stomach and nudging her rounded ass as she lay on him.

"He'd probably say my woman should take care of me," he said.

She gasped. "That's just . . . He wouldn't really, would he?"

"Sure he would. He's got a cock too. If he was hurting the way I am, he'd want me to tell his woman to get to work, so he'd do the same for me."

She studied his face. "You're teasing me."

He laughed softly, his fingers massaging the nape of her neck. "Yeah, baby, I am. A little bit. I would very much appreciate you taking care of my misbehaving cock, but we're not there yet, so I'm not going to be demanding."

Her eyebrows shot up. "Are you going to be demanding another time?"

"Yes. Very." He was honest. His fingers continued to move on her neck, his gaze on her face. "Right now, with me talking to you this way, are you wet for me? Slick between your legs? Burning?"

She nodded slowly, giving him that. "Yes. I get that way a lot around you."

He loved that she was so honest and matter-of-fact. She wasn't embarrassed about sex itself, it was interesting to her, but she was embarrassed that she didn't know how to have good sex. That was more than a start. She hadn't said no to trying to make his house a home either. Not one single time had she objected to him moving into the house. He'd made more progress than he'd expected.

"Cayenne, I've got a project in the lab that's important. I'll need a couple of days to finish it up."

She didn't like that, he could tell by the stillness in her. By the way her expression shut down. He liked that she didn't like it. Already, she was anticipating him living in the same house with her. It was a monstrosity of a house, but she wanted him there with her.

She was afraid, and he couldn't blame her. If he hadn't been so intent on making certain she wasn't going to run from him, he might have been a little afraid himself at the sheer power of the pull between them. He didn't know the first thing about relationships. He knew he wasn't an easy man and wouldn't ever be. He was too driven to find answers. He'd warned her, and so far she wasn't running.

"I would wait, but this is important," he reiterated gently.

She stuck her thumbnail in her mouth and chewed on it, that little frown he found adorable on her face. "You have a really good lab at the house."

That was true. But she was there, and he knew from the peanut discussion at the Huracan Club that she very well might know exactly what he was up to, and he didn't want that.

"I'm a good two-thirds into the project. Moving everything would set me back. If you need me—or anything at all—just let me know. Give me a couple of days." That wasn't exactly a lie. His work on the triplet's venom was a jumping-off point.

Her chin lifted and she scooted off of him. He couldn't help but notice that her eyes dipped to his engorged cock. Her gaze burned over him, and his cock responded with a hard jerk so that she couldn't look away, clearly fascinated.

"I'm not worried. Do whatever you need to do. I'll be fine. I was doing fine on my own," she pointed out.

He reached out and caught her wrist, drawing her back toward him. Her wrist was very small. He could have wrapped his fingers around it twice. He found it strange that he hadn't noticed that. She was very curvy and those curves were soft and lush, yet when she was close to him, he could see how petite she was. With her curves, it didn't make sense that she could get into small spaces, like the tiny chimney stack Ezekiel had said she'd entered the house through.

"Don't be that way, baby," he said softly. "I'll be home as soon as possible. I'll stock the fridge and bring a few cookbooks. Do you have food to cover the days?"

She nodded immediately, almost defiantly, which sent up red flags. He tugged on her wrist until her gaze met his. "Seriously, Cayenne. I don't want you to go hungry."

"I won't go hungry." She stepped back. "I want to leave now. I don't spend time with people, and this is the longest I've ever really spent with someone. I have a headache."

"From crying."

She scowled at him, clearly not liking the reminder that she'd broken down in front of him. "Maybe. I think more likely that you gave me too much to think about and it made my brain explode."

"That could be as well."

She took a step away from him and then turned back. "Wyatt's grandmother comes to the swamp often and harvests various plants right outside the south side of the fence. Do you know what she's doing?"

"She's created a natural pharmacy there. Wyatt told me she spent a good forty years or more transplanting plants so she could have them in one place. She uses them to help people when they can't go to a doctor."

"Isn't Wyatt a doctor?"

Trap nodded, slowly easing his body into a sitting position. He deliberately didn't cover up because he wanted her to get used to him naked. He liked being naked, and he wanted her to like it as well. "He charges money, babe. That's the way of the world. Of course he takes on patients his grandmother recommends to him and gives away his services if they can't pay. Well, they use the barter system instead of money."

"I'd like to learn about her plants and what each of them does to help sick people," she said, her voice thoughtful. "I'm going to use your computer. I spent a lot of time on computers and found most of the answers I needed. Is there a password?" She didn't sound worried, but there was a challenge in her voice, as if she expected him to say she couldn't have access to it.

"Cayenne, I'm not going to keep you off the computers. I don't like my things touched in the lab, but I created a workspace for you there as well if you want it. Everything in the house is for your use."

He turned his head toward the door just as she flattened herself against the wall, staying in the darkest corner. Trap reached down and hastily pulled up the sheet. There was a knock. They exchanged a long look, both inhaling the scent of Wyatt's grandmother. She smelled of lilacs and baby powder.

You okay, Cayenne? He knew she was holding her breath, holding herself still, much like a wild animal trapped in a snare. *Grand-mere wouldn't hurt you for anything.*

"Come on in, Nonny," Trap invited aloud, knowing he had to.

I stayed too long. I stayed too long, Cayenne chanted. Both hands went to the wall and she looked as if she would scurry up toward the ceiling.

Breathe for me. You don't want to get so agitated you accidentally hurt her, Trap cautioned. *Stay still and breathe. I'll handle this.*

The door opened and Nonny's head came into the room while her body remained firmly on the other side of the door. "I know you're up a lot at night, Trap," she said softly, her faded but extremely intelligent eyes studiously on his face. She didn't so much as glance around the room. "I wanted you to know I fixed a few things to eat and left them out in case you get hungry in the middle of the night. You don' eat it all, I'll just have to throw it out."

"You didn't have to do that, Nonny." Like she didn't have a houseful of people to feed. She'd fixed that food for one person, and it wasn't him. He smiled at her. He couldn't help it. Nonny had a way of claiming those men who had stayed to help protect Wyatt's daughters from the constant threat of Whitney. She was helping Cayenne because she knew Cayenne belonged to him.

"When you get old, Trap, you'll learn you don' sleep so good. I cook when I can't sleep."

"Thanks."

"You feel like takin' that food with you to the lab, I put out a few bags to makin' the packin' easier. And Flame left some clothes she wanted to donate to the secondhand store. I haven't gotten around to it yet, so I put the things in a couple of bags by the door. Next time you or Wyatt go to town, would you take them for me or find someone who can put them to good use?"

"Sure thing, Nonny, and thanks. I really appreciate it." The woman made him wish he'd known his own grandparents.

Nonny waved and was gone, quietly closing the door behind her.

Cayenne pressed herself tight against the wall. "She did that for me, didn't she? She knew I came here tonight. She's probably been aware when I've come before. I'm so embarrassed. Sometimes I stayed in her room because it felt . . ." She covered her face. "I can't ever face her."

"Babe, just stop. You freak out when people are nice to you."

"I don't know what to do with that."

"You don't have to do anything, just let them be nice." He could see the panic on her face, in her eyes. She edged toward the door, and he knew he had to let her go. She was too upset to soothe. "Take the food and clothes, babe. I'll be there soon," he assured, but she was already slipping out the door.

CHAPTER 7

Trap stood just outside the tall chain-link fence surrounding his home. There was satisfaction in finally getting the renovations finished enough that he could live and work there. The building was massive. He liked space. He needed space. The laboratory was on the same floor as his living quarters. He had a massive recreation room complete with a pool table and big-screen television, because what man would go without those if he could afford it? At least his teammates had insisted he needed the TV so when they came over they could watch it. He wasn't much of a television watcher.

He also had a home theater for movies—at the urging of the team. He wasn't much for movies either. The team members had a lot of input for the space in the old factory, including a bowling alley. He'd vetoed that one, and there had been some sulking on Malichai's part.

His laboratory was first class. Trap never stinted on his work environment. He had the best and the latest equipment and didn't mind spending a fortune on it because his work made him a fortune several times over. Wyatt's lab had been made as good as they could get it, but this gave Trap so much more room for the various machines he needed.

Light spilled through the windows he'd installed, long rows that brightened every room, especially the lab. His bank of computers was in the far corner, away from the various bottles and tubes he needed to conduct his experiments when he was on to something vital.

He had a desk and multiple shelves for his reference books. Hundreds of drawers were clearly labeled with everything he might need for work. He had the money for anything he wanted or needed, and he had a great assistant who personally brought him everything he asked for, anytime, day or night.

His office was large, a polished and wide mahogany desk gleamed, with his personal computer and two laptops waiting. The chair was one he'd chosen personally after sitting in dozens. He'd had a second office built, the desk smaller, but made of beautiful wood. The room was cozier, the shelves filled with every kind of reference book imaginable. He'd included works of fiction, every genre, so if his woman decided to go on a fiction reading spree she had choices.

His kitchen was awesome. He didn't cook much, but he set it up with the best appliances and cookware possible, mainly because he considered he would be living there for years. The kitchen was huge, and it actually was two kitchens: the appliances mirrored one another from opposite walls with a long aisle down the middle. Double rows of pots and pans hung overhead. He wanted to make certain his home could accommodate the entire team and their families if it should be needed.

He added a shelf for cookbooks, because he liked to learn new things and he would be cooking for Cayenne as well. He wanted good, nutritious food for both of them.

In his blueprints, he'd included many bedrooms, telling himself they'd need them if the GhostWalkers and their families had to retreat to a fortress, but that didn't explain the nursery set up right next to the master bedroom, or the reasoning for positioning several bedrooms close, but not so close that his hopefully *great* sex life would ever have the slightest interference.

This would be his home base. He'd changed every entrance leading to the tunnels and to the house itself so Whitney wouldn't have the new specs. That would make it more difficult for his private army to penetrate. The windows not only were bulletproof, he had installed armor-plated screens that came down with the touch of a button. Every door in the house both inside and out was plated as well.

He had stashed weapons throughout the building, in every room and in the tunnels. He had an arsenal, enough for a small army—which his team was—should they need it. He'd had the roof redone in several places, giving them shadows to work with, small places that concealed and protected their bodies should they have to fall back on his home as a fortress. What he didn't think of, the other members of his team had.

There was a helipad outside with a state-of-the-art helicopter, several armored vehicles and a private plane waiting at the small private airstrip he'd purchased. The hangar there housed a small jet as well as the plane.

Security cameras had been installed everywhere throughout the house. He had access to the security screens from his own computers as well as every other device he owned—and he owned a lot of them. He'd done a sweep of the house before he'd moved his things in. The furniture was untouched, but Cayenne had been in the kitchen. She'd been hungry enough to eat the food Nonny had fixed for her.

He'd sent Wyatt over with more groceries when he was working longer than he'd expected. Instead of a couple of days, it had taken four long days and three nights working on an antibody that hopefully would neutralize any toxin she might inject in him. To his shock, he'd worried about Cayenne every moment of that time. That was unheard of.

As a rule, he focused so completely on what he was doing, nothing else entered his mind. He knew the pull between them was strong, but strong enough to disturb him while he worked? That was . . . unsettling. Disturbing. Ominous, when he thought about the days and nights ahead.

She'd eaten some of the groceries he'd sent, mainly the fruit and vegetables. That made him inexplicably happy. It was the first thing she'd taken from him without protest, and he thought it was a good sign that she wouldn't try to kill him for being so late the moment she laid eyes on him.

She was staying in the lower level—the apartment he'd designed. He knew she was because the spiderwebs crept up the stairs and the cameras showed large veils of white silk covering the various rooms. He took it as a good sign that she had made herself at home there, especially after he'd confessed he'd had the apartment built just for her.

The space took up the entire lower story. He could fit two houses in her apartment. Clearly she wasn't used to the space, because she occupied only one room and the adjoining bathroom. She obviously slept behind that heavy veil of silk, and more webbing was strung across the room from wall to wall, but it wasn't dense and allowed her to sit on the cozy furniture.

The bathrooms—and there was a dozen of them—were mostly stark, ready to be decorated, but Nonny had begun to do just that in four of them. His master bedroom had a bath connected to it and there were three in the apartment on the lower story. Nonny had completed one downstairs— the one closest to the bedroom. He hoped Cayenne liked it. The only thing the cameras could see was the draped silk, beautiful masterpieces of silk, hanging everywhere.

From the moment he bought the place, he had suspected she was staying in the building, so he'd asked Wyatt's grandmother to make it especially nice. He'd inspected it and the bathroom had smelled really good and the walls were painted a soothing blue. The claw-foot tub he'd brought in was wide and long and he made certain several hot water heaters had been installed, so there was hot water on demand throughout the entire building. The shower was spacious, and the towels were particularly soft.

He moved with fluid grace to the gate. It was locked. He kept it that way. He could easily go up and over the fence, and he preferred that to bothering with unlocking the lock. He crouched, prepared to leap over it, when he noticed the almost invisible skeins of silk. She wanted to be warned when he moved onto the property.

Yeah, baby, I'm moving in, he whispered softly, intimately, into her mind. He knew the path to her. It was so ingrained in him, almost as if she were already a part of him, that it was easy connecting with her. *I'm home.*

There was silence. That made him smile. She was upset with him for taking so long. A good thing. He took the fence. It was high, but he had no trouble jumping it and landing softly on the other side. He deliberately broke a few of the fine silken threads, letting her know he wasn't going to be careful about it.

This is my home, Cayenne, he said firmly. *Everything in it belongs to me. Including you. I told you that the other night.*

Her breath hissed out. She moved in his mind, a stirring, and for the first time, she felt a little like a spider instead of the sensuous woman he knew her to be. *This is my home. You should have come when you said you would. Now I've claimed it.*

She *was* upset with him. He had taken too long. She'd given herself to him, cried in his arms, and he'd taken too long to get back to her. He had to do damage control, and he had the feeling he was starting all over again.

That's right, baby. And I'm in it, so that means I belong to you. That's the way it works, so get used to the idea.

He unlocked his front door, using the keypad. Just inside the entryway was a second door and his palm was coded in.

Babe, you're going to have to have your palm programmed in. I'll have to do that now that I've activated this. You'll be able to use it at all entrances, including the vents and tunnels you like to travel in.

There was a small silence. *Is he coming after us? Whitney? You said he was the mastermind of the laboratory in France. Do you think he'll come here?* She sounded vulnerable again. She'd met Whitney and she despised him, sensing his madness, and his cruelty. That was before she'd witnessed it firsthand.

He felt a curious melting sensation in the region of his heart. He was a scientist and had never believed in those types of physical responses. He'd had his share of women, and never once did he have the type of emotional feelings that manifested as physical. Cayenne could make his heart stutter and his gut knot up. She could do a lot of things to his body without even trying, but he was beginning to realize it wasn't just his body that was affected by her.

I think he might—eventually. But we'll be ready for him. Wyatt's place is nearly finished. When you feel up to it, I'd like you to help me figure out some of the holes in his security. You got in, that means someone else might, and we have the girls to protect. Deliberately he acted as if he knew she would help them, that it was a fact, a given that she would be part of their team. He knew protecting the girls mattered to her, because already, once, she'd come out of the shadows and risked her life to help them.

What are you doing right now? he asked, as he strode through his home to the master bedroom.

Sitting in the chair looking out the window. I like that I can see out but no one can see in even if I have the lights on. I didn't know that was possible. The windows make me feel as if I can reach out and touch the plants. Have you noticed how beautiful the nights are here? I couldn't see outside from my cell. Not here and not in France.

He felt a surge beneath the ice, the one that told him his

volcano was still present, would always be present and hidden beneath the glacier inside him. *Fuckers,* he whispered softly. *You're free now. And I've got tons of plants up here,* he enticed her. Because he wanted to see her. Even *needed* to see her. Even though he could acknowledge that to himself, it still bothered him, because to need any woman made him vulnerable.

It isn't the same thing as being outside.

That was true, but he didn't want her outside—especially at night. He wanted her there with him. Close. In his bedroom if at all possible. He made a mental note to add an abundance of plants throughout the building. With them came an automatic watering system so they wouldn't die. He'd forget to water. He was like that. He forgot a lot of things when he was working.

What are you wearing? He dropped his voice even lower. He had always been good with women because he had a voice that could seduce or compel as well. *Tell me, baby. I've been working night and day, but I thought of you. So many times. Wondering what you were up to. What you were wearing. Do you wear clothes to bed?*

He could feel her moving in his mind. This time there was no hint of the spider, only the woman. The seductress— that beautiful woman who was just as drawn to him as he was to her. He smiled as he placed his duffel bag on the floor and made his way to the kitchen. He had a few more treasures in store for her.

No. I don't like clothes when I'm sleeping. They twist around my body and wake me up.

His mouth went dry at her declaration. He didn't like wearing clothes at night either, but just the thought of her naked . . . All that silken skin. So close. Out of reach. *Are you wearing clothes right now?*

She'd better be, because if she wasn't, there was no way he was going to get any sleep. He'd spent the last few days and nights working on building a vaccine. He wanted his own body to build antibodies against the neurotoxin. He'd worked nonstop, no food, no rest, making certain he was right. The research he'd been conducting on trying to find a vaccine for the venomous poisons in Wyatt's little girls had actually given him a boost toward his goal, but it had taken much longer than he'd anticipated. He'd left her alone and clearly she felt abandoned.

I don't wear clothes when I'm alone. Too cumbersome. In any case, I don't have that many clothes and I don't want to ruin them. There's no need for clothes when I'm here in the house.

His heart nearly stopped. It definitely stuttered, another physical reaction he would have said was impossible. His mouth went dry. He'd just taken the cap off the milk carton and was raising it toward his face to take a drink. His hand seemed to lose its ability to grip and he nearly dropped the carton. The woman knew how to put images in a man's head. It wasn't just her voice that drew a man, it was the entire package.

For some reason that opened up a small crack in the glacier, just enough to allow a vein of bubbling magna to escape. Fear burst through him. He didn't understand why, but it was brutal. He wasn't a man who ever felt fear, because he had nothing at all to lose. Suddenly she was there. He couldn't allow fear so he covered it, reaching for something else. Something dark and ugly. Something he hadn't known was a part of him.

They put you through seduction training? Did you take off your clothes in front of men so you learned how to strip slow and show off your body? Is that what you do, Cayenne? You seduce them before you kill them?

Pepper, Wyatt's wife had been trained to seduce a man and then assassinate him with one venomous bite. She hadn't cooperated, and she'd landed in the swamp, in the very building he resided in, when there was a crematory set up to get rid of the bodies scheduled for termination.

The idea of Cayenne being taught to use her looks, her

voice, her body to please a man, to entice him so she could bite him, paralyze him or kill him, sickened him. *Sickened* him. He shoved the carton of milk back in the refrigerator and slammed the door shut. She would have been taught by male instructors how to please a man, the best way to seduce him. She'd pressed her body close to his. Kissed him. She was a dynamite kisser. Fourth of July. Fireworks exploding. A taking-a-man-to-heaven kind of kisser. He could still taste her in his mouth. He still had the scent of her in his lungs. He knew neither would ever go away. He pushed away the conversation they'd had about her training. About her being in a cell. She was beautiful. Sexy. Deadly.

Why would you ask me that?

There was hurt in her voice. One small note. He almost missed it. *You kissed me, Cayenne. You kissed me, and I lost a part of myself to you.* He had lost much more than he thought when he kissed her. He'd never felt so exposed before in his life. Need moved through him. Hunger. There was no way to stop it, and the idea of being out of control when he controlled his entire world hit him hard. *I thought you were as into me as I was into you, but then you bit me. Paralyzed me. Left me out in the swamp as alligator bait. All along, while you were kissing me and I was lost in you, you were planning to paralyze me and leave me there in the mud.*

Okay, maybe she hadn't done that. She'd asked him and he'd told her Wyatt was close. But he wasn't anything special to her. She watched over the Comeaux brothers as well. Maybe before he'd arrived she'd been pressing her body up against one of them. He could hear himself ranting like a jealous idiot, but that pressure inside his chest wouldn't let him stop.

You know I didn't do that, she protested, the hurt increasing in her voice. *I was into you. I lost a part of myself there as well.*

That small stream of orange-red lava continued to slip through the ice. *I'll just bet you did, right before you paralyzed me. You're talking about sleeping nude and sitting downstairs right within my reach without a stitch on, putting that image in my head. Seriously? That's not seduction?*

No! She sounded adamant. And maybe close to tears. The hurt was definitely there. *You asked me questions. I have no reason to be deceptive. I just answered you. Was that wrong? Should I have lied? What difference does it make if I wear clothes to bed or sleep without them? Or lounge around in my own space without them? How is that seduction?*

He nearly groaned. How was it not? Her voice rang with truth, but along with that honesty was the soft velvet note that brushed a man's skin and wrapped around his cock like a tight fist. Squeezing. Stroking. Caressing. His cock responded to that. It was impossible to maintain control.

You flirted with Pascal and Blaise. It was no wonder they thought they were going to score the way you were carrying on.

There was another long silence. He felt her frown just as if he was standing in front of her. He knew she had a habit of licking her full bottom lip with the tip of her tongue. He'd seen her do it in the bar when she was sitting there at his table. The only real sign of nerves other than when her fingers twisted together beneath the table. He knew she was doing that right at that moment.

Heat rushed through his veins and blood pooled low and wicked. His erection was painful. Huge. Worse than when he was a fucking teenager. It was impossible to walk around with an enormous hard-on. Cold showers weren't going to take it away. He needed Cayenne. Really needed her.

I don't flirt. I wouldn't even know how to flirt. I haven't been around all that many people.

What the hell was that in the bar? The edge to his voice was now in his mind. He couldn't take a step so he didn't try. He opened the front of his jeans to give himself a little relief. The material couldn't stretch that much. His hand circled his cock, fist closing tight. Why the fuck couldn't he stop being such a bastard? Why were images of her with other men wreaking havoc with his brain?

I think I'm angrier at you over that, putting yourself on display to those two morons, than you betraying me by leading me on with that kiss and then paralyzing me.

He wasn't angry with her for biting him. He actually understood that. She'd been terrified. A part of her was not only protecting herself, but she thought she was protecting him. She could have killed all three men, but she hadn't. She wouldn't have left them lying there for any wild animal to find. She had stayed to watch over them. Every time he thought about her sandwiched between the Comeaux brothers there at the bar with the sound of her laughter floating back to him, now *that* made him angry.

I had to find a way to survive in a world I was totally unfamiliar with. I needed money for food. I needed clothes. I followed various women and observed them and then I acted the way they acted. They appeared friendly. Most were married. When they talked to their friends they laughed. I laughed at the things they said even though, to me, it wasn't funny. I tested them to see what kind of men they were. But I wasn't flirting.

Fuck. Fuck. Fuck. She was crying. Again. *He'd* made her cry. He'd wanted to hurt her because sitting in that damn bar watching her with those two losers, two of the worst men in the swamp, had hurt him. He acknowledged that now. He had to. He had to come to terms that she gotten under his skin.

You fucking know you belong to me, Cayenne, so tell me why we're doing this dance. I don't want you going to a bar and standing close to other men, showing them your body. Letting them touch you.

I didn't let them touch me, she objected.

I didn't see his hand on your ass—the beautiful ass that, by the way, belongs to me? I didn't see that? Is that what you're telling me?

I don't want to talk to you anymore.

I'll just bet you don't. My cock is as hard as a rock. But then you know that, don't you? You make it that way. You sit there naked and tease me with your voice, knowing you shouldn't have allowed that man to touch you like that, not ever. The only man who touches you is me. The only man who kisses that mouth is me. And I'm the only man who is going to be inside of you. So stop fucking around. You need money, I left a cache in the kitchen for you along with plenty of food. Make a list of what you need and I'll bring it home. Figure this out soon, lady, or you're going to find I don't have patience for this dance and I'm going to be coming after you.

I don't understand half of what you're saying to me.

You understand me. You're in my head. You know what I want. You know what we're going to be doing together. I spell it out every time you're in my mind. I want you in my bed. I want you as my partner, including in the lab, because after that peanut comment I know damn well you'll be an asset there. You fucking gave yourself to me four nights ago, and I'll be damned if you take yourself away.

You didn't come. Her voice broke.

He knew he was being a bastard, but he still couldn't get that image of her sandwiched between Pascal and Blaise out of his mind. He couldn't push aside the black jealousy, because if he did, he'd have to face the reason. The real reason he was angry with her. He set his jaw stubbornly. He'd held her. Comforted her. She'd *given* herself to him and there was no going back, he wasn't allowing that.

I want your mouth on my cock and I want to be buried balls-deep inside of you. I want to tie you up and take my time, making you scream with pleasure. I like playing, baby, and I want to spend the rest of my life knowing you'll let me do that. That you'll enjoy it. Not just enjoy it, but crave it. I want you thinking about me day and night, waiting for my touch. For my cock. For anything I want to do to you.

There was another long silence. He thought he'd lost her.

He made it back to the master bedroom, every step painful. He was making his erection worse with every image rising in his mind. He wanted her to know what kind of man he was, what he would demand of her in the bedroom. The kind of complete surrender he would expect. The kind of partner she would be for him.

Cayenne drew her knees up, making herself very small in the chair she nestled in. Trap was angry with her, when he should have been apologizing, or at least comforting her. Instead, he acted as though she was a seductress and had betrayed him in some way. That wasn't logical and it didn't make sense. She'd had four months to study him. He was never out of control. He was often rude to people—even his teammates—but he wasn't out of control.

She pushed aside the things he'd said to her and tried to move deeper into his mind. He hid things from himself. Not things. Emotions. He was jealous, but he used jealousy to cover something else, something much deeper. She was under his skin, there was no doubt about it. His mind was consumed with thoughts of her. Images, most erotic, but many of just holding her. It had meant a lot to him, comforting her the way he had. That she'd come to him.

Trap wasn't used to feeling vulnerable. She was. He always was in control. She'd been powerless in her cell, at the mercy of others. He wasn't equipped to feel the force of their combined pull. All along, because he knew about families and relationships, because he'd lived in the world and she hadn't, she thought he had the upper hand. She realized he didn't. He cared for her. *Really* cared for her. She mattered to him. He seemed to be experiencing that for the first time, and it didn't sit well with him.

She rubbed her chin along the top of her knees trying to figure out what to do. Trap was a difficult, complicated man. Granted, she didn't know about relationships, but she could feel how much he wanted her. Not just wanted, although there was a part of him that wished that what he felt for her was just physical, but it wasn't. She knew that. She was in his mind and she caught glimpses of his vulnerability. He felt exposed. Raw. *Afraid*. Of what she wasn't certain, but to protect himself, he allowed jealousy to rule.

The tip of her tongue moistened her bottom lip. For the first time in her life, she knew she could make a decision that was hers alone. Trap couldn't force her to do anything. It was her choice to stay with him or to go. It was her choice to figure out what bothered him so much that a man as strong as he was couldn't face it, or to walk away from him.

The thing was, she wanted him to belong to her. If that meant it would take some work on her part to understand him, she was going to do it. She didn't sense cruelty in him the way she had in others. He was a man of strength, but he didn't hurt others on purpose. He actually was quite kind in his heart, and that made him vulnerable. He hid that kindness, didn't want anyone to see it, but she did.

Trap Dawkins was going to be her choice. She was going to learn how to have a relationship from him. She was going to learn how best to please him. And she was going to learn how to handle things when he lost his mind and struck out using one emotion to cover another. Because that was *her* choice. She found herself smiling, feeling empowered. Determined. Her man was going to teach her things about sex, but again, on her terms. He needed to learn who she was, just as she had to figure him out.

Trap stripped and headed for the shower. The cool water did nothing to cool his body or the images running around in his head. He took care of his cock, but it didn't seem to help. In the end he lay in his bed—the bed that was finally big enough to accommodate his size—and stared up at the ceiling. He had a fan, but he didn't use it. The room was cool enough, his body temperature was just too high because the molten lava still moved slow and hot through his veins.

He'd never wanted a woman the way he did Cayenne.

The need was sharp and terrible. His cock refused to soften. His body refused to relax. He couldn't get the images of her wrapping her lips around him and taking him in her mouth out of his head.

He fisted his shaft with his hand, made small circles, pumped, but he did so almost absently. The hand job in the shower hadn't worked, so he knew he was in for a long night and he was damned tired. He'd been up for days. He let his lashes drift down and almost immediately smelled her unique fragrance. He stayed still, forcing himself to breath evenly. She was in the room with him. Right there. Close. Close enough to draw the scent of her deep.

He kept his hand moving. Slow. Lazy. A slide. A jerk. Knowing she was watching him. Needing her to watch. Excitement moved through him, a wave of heat. Very slowly he opened his eyes, and there she was. His breath caught in his throat. She was above him, clinging to the ceiling with her hands and toes, body spread out, naked. Her ass was beautiful. The slope of her back, the curve of her hips and the small, tucked-in waist gleamed. Her hair spilled in a dark cloud around her shoulders and cascaded in waves like a dark waterfall flowing from the ceiling. Her green eyes were on his fist. His cock. Watching. Fascinated. Hungry.

Before he could move, silken threads shot out and wrapped his upper body into a snug cocoon. Tying him. Preventing his arms from moving. He tested the silken strands, knowing that spiderwebs woven like this could be stronger than Kevlar. There was no breaking those threads. He lay there, seemingly helpless. At her mercy.

Trap was a man all about control—especially in the bedroom—but there was no denying he found the situation hot. Her body was flawless. Mind-blowing. She dropped from the ceiling, dangling from silken skeins. He could see her full, beautiful breasts, the darker nipples, already peaked for him. She had tiny tight curls of black at the junction between her legs, but there was that red streak right down the center in the shape of an hourglass—directly over the path to her glistening lips. She was already wet for him.

"What the hell do you think you're doing?" he demanded, but he didn't care what she was doing. His voice was hoarse, and lust welled up in a brutal, savage demand. He knew the sight of her dangling over him, stark naked, would be burned in his mind forever. He would always have that erotic picture to take out and examine whenever he wanted.

Her gaze drifted over his body, lingered on the heavy erection he held in his fist. The silken strands held his wrists down, but his cock jutted out right below the webbing. His cock, and one fist. The other hand was trapped on his chest. Again he tested the bindings with a burst of strength. They held.

The tip of her tongue came out to lick at her full bottom lip. His gaze jumped to her mouth. She had full lips. A bow of ruby red. Not pink. Red. Like the hourglass made up of tight red curls. Beautiful. Unbelievable. The things he wanted to do to her filled his mind.

"Let me up, baby. I can make you feel really good, you let me up."

Cayenne shook her head slowly, her body settling on the end of his bed. Her gaze remained fixed on his cock. She wet her lips entirely. His cock jerked hard in his hand. Pulsed with life. She was on her hands and knees, but low, as if she might spring away any moment, or crawl to him. He preferred she crawl to him. The idea was so erotic, his cock pulsed again, and this time, tiny droplets appeared.

"Let me up," he said again. Demanded.

Her gaze jumped to his face. Faint amusement crept into her eyes. "I decided to try some of those things you have in mind, Trap. Tying you up sounded really good to me. I don't have to worry about anything you'll do that I don't understand. I can work it all out for myself. I like experiments. And I like to learn new things. Sex has always sounded interesting, but I never wanted it before."

"You let me up and I'll teach you just how good it can be," he offered.

She shook her head. "You said this was important to you. I need to find out if I can give you the things you need."

He groaned. "You missed the point, baby. I can give them to *you*. Make it so good for you, you'll need to come back over and over."

She moved. Placed one hand on the mattress toward him. One knee. Her body undulated, sexy as all get-out. Clouds of hair, shiny as a raven's wing, slid over his ankle. The sensation burned up his leg, teased his thigh like a thousand fingers, slid deep into his balls, burning a fire until it settled in his cock. Throbbing there. Staying there.

He was her captive. He'd never been in the position before and everything in him screamed at him to turn the tables on her, to tie her up and show her what sex with him would be. He didn't move. Didn't test the strength of all that silk again. She looked too hot, creeping slowly toward him like a wary, wild creature. Her eyes were enormous and such a startling emerald color. He could almost see the facets in the gems pressed into her face and surrounded by feathery black lashes.

When she moved, muscles rippled beneath the silk of her skin. Her long hair brushed along the mattress and over his bare feet and ankles. He could see the tiny red hourglass nestled in the tight black curls shimmering seductively as she inched toward him.

It wasn't entirely because she looked hot that he stopped fighting the silk—she looked frightened. He didn't want her afraid of him, and not because he feared her bite, but because she was his. His woman. However, she needed to learn that truth, whatever it took to let the knowledge sink into her mind and body, he was willing to give her. Even this. When it killed him to keep his hands off of her.

She circled his ankle with her hand. Her touch was light, but it seemed to burn right through his skin. Her gaze clung to his almost as if asking his permission when she had him trussed up like a turkey.

Cayenne shook her head. "Not like a turkey. Like the image you had of me tied to your bed."

His cock jerked hard as that particular vision filled his mind. Cayenne, sprawled out on his bed. Her legs spread wide, silken ties at her ankles, keeping her open for his pleasure. Her arms above her head, lifting her breasts to him like a beautiful offering, her wrists bound with those same silks, anchored to the headboard he'd carefully chosen and then reinforced.

"I think I'd do the ties a little differently, but yes, you have the general idea." Deliberately he added to the erotic picture in his head. Taking her hips into his hands, slowly bending his head to the feast in front of him so that her hips bucked wildly and small, panting gasps escaped. Her eyes went wide with shock—with the desire to know what it was like. Seduction came in all kinds of forms. His woman liked knowledge. All kinds of knowledge. He was going to be the man to fill in all those gaps, and he was going to show her exactly what he liked in the process.

"Does this mean you get your way and then I get mine?" He kept his voice low and intimate, using his ability to stroke caresses with his tone shamelessly.

There was no doubt in his mind that he got to her—that she was as affected as he was. A flush stole over her body. Her breasts rose and fell and her fingers stroked up his shin and then began a slow massage into muscles and tight sinew already strained from just that little contact with her. Wanting. Needing. The hunger building out of control just as he would do with her if he had silken ties.

Her fingers moved up his body, stroking along the muscles, teasing his body with a promise of things to come. Fingers of desire caressed his thighs, dancing over them, kneading and massaging deep into his flesh and then brushing streaks of fire over the nerve endings as she lightened her touch. For a woman who didn't know what she was doing, she certainly found a way to inflame him further.

Maybe it was the thought of being so helpless, at her mercy, in the way he fantasized and intended she would be at his. Her mouth followed her fingers, a mere brush, a whisper of a touch, her tongue tasting the defined muscle along his calf, her lips following the path of his shins. It was exquisite and yet not enough, not even close.

Trap had never considered that a woman's touch could be so carnal when she wasn't touching his cock. She turned his long legs erogenous—trigger points for licking flames as if her tongue stroked tiny embers up and down his nerve endings. He hadn't been aware of nerve endings in his legs— not like this. Not this unceasing, relentless burn that moved up his thighs straight to his groin.

In his hand, his cock thickened more. He was a big man and she had him nearly bursting right through his fist. He could feel his pulse pounding, the blood so hot, engorging his erection until he pulsed and throbbed with need. He wanted, even needed her mouth on him, but as she moved up his body, she ignored that raging part of him. His fist continued to pump, but the rhythm changed so that it wasn't at all lazy as it had been.

She crawled up his body, sliding her naked limbs over him, clearly feeling much braver with him bundled tight in all that silk. The junction of her legs left a hot damp trail over his thighs as she moved up him. Her breasts felt soft and inviting, her nipples twin points that seared him right through the ropes of silk as she inched up him.

"You're nice and wet for me, baby," he managed to get out, as the heat between her legs bathed him in liquid moisture. He'd never felt anything sexier in his life. He'd certainly never seen anything more sensual than the way she moved up his body. "I can make you feel really good. Untie me."

"I'm feeling really good already," she whispered, her gaze dropping to his mouth. Her hands skimmed his chest right through the silken bonds. "Next time, I'm going to tie you like you want to tie me. I see the advantage of it now. I improvised, but it doesn't give me full access to your body, and I want to explore every inch of you."

His cock jumped in his fist. The blood pounded there and roared in his ears. Little jackhammers began to trip in his head. "You untie me, I'll let you explore."

Her green eyes drifted over his face, studying his expression, committing the angles and planes to memory. He knew what she saw. Face darkened with desire. Hooded eyes filled with lust. With hunger. He knew before she shook her head that she wasn't going to untie him. She didn't feel safe.

"I need to do this. You'd take over."

He would. He couldn't deny that. "Baby, even if I do, you'll feel good in the end, I promise. I can show you things . . ."

She shook her head. "I learn things for myself. But first"—her fingers moved through his hair—"I want to kiss you again. I can't stop thinking about the way you kissed me. It was unlike anything I ever imagined, and I thought about kissing a lot."

"Have at it, baby. I don't want you to think I'd ever deprive you of that," he said. His cock was on fire. She was beautiful with that waterfall of hair and amazing green eyes. She wanted him. Her body was as hot as hell. The junction between her legs left a scorching slide of need along his chest and burned like an inferno right through the silk. He was afraid she was so hot she might melt those threads, but then he'd be free to do whatever he wanted to her.

Watching his expression, slowly, inch by slow inch, she lowered her head to his. Her mouth skimmed. Gently. A whisper of touch. Featherlight. Back and forth over his lips. Unexpectedly, she brushed a kiss over each of his eyes and trailed more along his cheekbone, and then used the tip of her tongue, as if tasting his skin. He had no idea why that moved him, but he felt those little touches, not in his burning cock, but in the region of his heart.

Before he could say anything, her mouth settled over his. He gave her that first press of her tongue into his mouth. His heart jerked hard in his chest. *That* touch he felt in his cock. The feel of her lips, the small, moist invasion, stroking along his tongue, so tentative. He swore her mouth was a match and she just lit a powder keg.

He couldn't wrap his arms around her, but he took over the kiss and she let him. He liked kissing her. No, he actually loved kissing her. She gave herself to him, pouring her taste and need right down his throat. He took everything she gave and demanded more. He wanted her as hot for him as he was for her.

I am. There was a little sobbing note in her voice. *I want you, but I'm not coming to you until I'm not so scared. I have to trust you, and I don't know how to trust.*

That little admission tore him up. *It's all right, baby, you take what you need from me. I have patience. Just know that a little fear can add to the excitement of what we're doing here.* He gave her that because it was necessary to soothe her some way and he couldn't hold her in his arms to give her reassurance. Cayenne deserved comfort. He couldn't imagine how afraid she must have been every day of her life in that laboratory with guards surrounding her and men's fear of her beating at her.

You aren't afraid of me. I paralyzed you. I would do it again if you scared me too much. She lifted her head reluctantly as she made the admission, her green gaze moving over his face broodingly, as if she couldn't quite believe he wasn't afraid and she was looking for the truth.

He realized *she* was afraid of herself, of what she might do, and he needed to give her the confidence to keep going, to claim his body for her own. She didn't know she was claiming his heart. She needed to learn to trust herself much more than she needed to trust him at this point. He could give her that as well.

CHAPTER 8

Trap held Cayenne's gaze. She was definitely affected by his kisses. Her breasts rose and fell fast now, her breath coming in ragged gasps. He was fairly certain if she didn't move, the spot where the junction of her legs rested on his chest really was going to melt right through the silken ties.

Baby, you're my woman. That means I'm your man. No matter how afraid you get, you're not really going to harm me. I could never hurt you. Not for any reason, although— deliberately he narrowed his eyes—*I intend to retaliate over that bite. My woman doesn't paralyze me and then leave me for Wyatt and the boys to tease mercilessly. You just left me there alone.*

You weren't alone, and I checked on you.

I told you not to come to Wyatt's home. You could have been shot. That had scared him when he realized she'd come back to the Fontenot home after he'd warned her away. He'd reached out to Ezekiel and warned him, asking him to allow her through.

Trap had sensed her need, a terrible, dark need welling

up so strong that in the end she'd awakened not only Nonny, but Wyatt and the other team members as well. She hadn't known she was broadcasting such distress because they stayed away and allowed him to comfort her on his own, but they knew and it upset all of them on her behalf.

"Touch yourself."

Her long lashes fluttered. She sank back on his chest, straddling him, her knees on either side of his ribs, her green gaze on his face. He could see she was tempted to follow his instructions, but he realized if she did it, she'd comply because he asked her, not because she realized how it would make her body feel.

"Cup your breasts, baby." He kept his voice low. Gentle. Seductive. His heart pounded while he waited for her to make up her mind.

Very slowly she brought her palms up under her breasts. His breath left his body in a rush. Just that action sent damp heat spilling from between her legs to moisten the silk and his chest where her sex was pressed to him.

"That's beautiful, Cayenne. See how beautiful you are? Tug on your nipples. Stroke them. Pull. Imagine my hands on you. That's what I'm doing. My hands are big. I can be a little rough. Do you like it rough or gentle? Which makes your body come alive? Are your breasts sensitive?"

She followed his instructions to the letter, her fingers gentle, then rougher. Pinching. Tugging. Rolling. It was so hot watching her he was afraid his cock would explode. He followed the movement with his fist wrapped tightly around his thick shaft. Her breath came in ragged gasps, and she threw her head back.

"Feel good, baby? That's what I'd do to you, but more. Now lean toward me. Feed me your right breast, but keep working on your left nipple."

She didn't stop what she was doing, but she hesitated before she again did as he asked, scooting up his chest, dragging her hot entrance over him, leaving a trail of moist heat in her wake. A moan slipped up her throat as the silk massaged her sex, adding to the burn building in her. She leaned slowly toward him, watching his face as if mesmerized by the dark lust she saw there. Her nipple teased his closed lips, sliding along the seam. Watching her closely, he opened his mouth and curled his tongue around the offering.

Her breath slammed out of her body, her fingers pinching her other nipple hard. She was more than sensitive. He swore he could feel a spasm between her legs through the silk holding him captive. He drew her breast into his mouth, his teeth tugging on her nipple, and then he flattened his tongue and drove it to the roof of his mouth. Before she could catch her breath, he suckled hard. Deep. Using teeth, tongue and the heated moist interior of his mouth, he drove her up fast.

She cried out, a small sound somewhere between fear and need. Instantly he pulled back, licking her nipple lightly, his mouth wandering over the soft mound, occasionally stopping to suck on her soft skin, raising bright red brands.

She smoothed back his hair, breathing hard. "Is it always like that?"

"It gets better, baby. This is just a small taste of what it will be like when you're in my bed."

Her eyes were enormous. Shocked. Hungry. Definitely wanting more.

"Tell me what you're feeling? Do you like this?"

She nodded slowly, her eyes so green they gleamed at him. She looked sexy, so hot he could barely breathe looking at her. She didn't have any inhibitions. She didn't make judgments about right and wrong. She was afraid, but it was all new, and she had trust issues. He had to give this to her. Let her feel in control.

"This is amazing. It is better when your mouth is on me," she admitted. "But it's scary at the same time."

"Doesn't that add to the excitement? To what you're feeling?"

She didn't take her gaze from his when she nodded.

"Untie me, baby. Let me show you what you really need."

She thought it over. He could see how much she wanted to, but she just couldn't. There was too much fear of the unknown—of him. He was incredibly strong, and he had his own talents. Just the difference in their sizes gave him all the advantages. He saw the regret in her eyes.

"You could do something to me I didn't like." *You could hurt me.*

He felt the echo of her fear in his gut. She really was terrified of him—of more than what he could do to her physically. And that made her terrified *for* him. She still thought of herself as a monster. If she were hurt, she would strike out.

"It's all right, Cayenne," he assured her gently. "This works for me, but you need to know, something doesn't work when you're in my bed, you just tell me, we'll stop immediately. Always. If you're just afraid because you don't know what is coming, we'll stop and talk about it. When you're in my bed, I want only pleasure for you—for us. So if you need this time to explore and feel in control, take it."

"You're not upset with me?"

"Baby." He said it softly. "How can I be upset with you? Look at you, you're absolutely beautiful and so sexy I can't believe what a lucky man I am. Of course I want my hands on you. And my mouth. I want my cock inside of you. I want to make you scream with pleasure."

She blinked. Her lashes fluttered and her face flushed. Her hands crept up to her breasts involuntarily. "You can do that?" Her voice came out breathy. Excited. Shocked.

"Yeah, baby, I can do that. Slide your hand down your body, Cayenne, but do it slow. Feel that glide of your palm. Over your belly. Down lower. In those tight curls. Stroke the hourglass with your fingers." He wanted to stroke that hourglass. His fingers itched to do so. His mouth salivated, needing to trace that red outline with his tongue.

She took a breath and then complied, following the image of his hand as it slid down her body from her breasts to her belly button.

"I'll be spending some time getting acquainted with your body, Cayenne," he said softly, his own breath hitching, becoming labored. She was more than sensual. Her fingers sliding down along the path in his mind. He couldn't feel the soft silk of her skin, but watching was hot.

"See all those drops of cream caught there? I'd use my tongue to get every last one. Curl your fingers inside where I want to touch. Feel all that sweet, spicy honey? That's mine. That's for me. I want that. I can't get it myself so you'll have to do it for me."

She gasped as her fingers disappeared inside. His breath slammed right out of his lungs, leaving him burning.

"Fuck, baby, that's the hottest thing I've ever seen in my life. Feed it to me. I need that right now. Bring your fingers out coated with my honey and feed it to me." His voice was hoarse. His fist pumped harder.

She withdrew her fingers and held them out to him. He opened his mouth, without leaning toward her, forcing her to lean into him, burning his chest with her sex as she pushed her fingers gently into his mouth. He closed his lips around them, his tongue curling and stroking to get off every last drop of honey.

"That's not enough, baby," he said softly. "I need more. You can't just give me a taste and then take that away. It's mine, and now I'm starving for it. Crawl up here. Close. You'll be in control so don't be scared. I can't hold you down like I want to and eat you until you're screaming for mercy, but I can show you a little of what it can be like."

"I don't understand." But she was already moving her body toward his face, caught up in the sexual spell woven so tight between them—the temptation to know more drawing her to him.

"Open your knees wide, Cayenne. Scoot a little more

until your thighs are on either side of my face." He breathed the wild, exotic scent of her into his lungs. Need was so strong he found himself shaking. He didn't do that. Ever.

He had never once, in all the fantasies he'd had, all the times he took a woman, envisioned this. Unable to use his hands. One fist tight around his throbbing, pulsing cock, so engorged his skin felt as if it might burst. If someone had asked, he would have said he would hate it, but now, he'd never burned hotter.

"If you get too scared, you can just inch away. But let me have this. You know it's mine. You know you are. Your body is. Push forward, baby and keep your knees wide. Put one hand on the mattress beside my head. Remember, you're in control. You need to grind down, do it. You need to move your hips, do it."

"I don't want to hurt you." The fear was pressing in on her again, but the lure of knowing more, receiving more pleasure—pleasure she'd never known in her life—sharing this with *him*, was even stronger.

Her gaze remained steady on his. "No one's ever given me the things you have, Trap. It's terrifying and exhilarating at the same time. I dream of you. Usually when I dream, well—things aren't nice. But when you're there, you change everything. I didn't know I could feel like this. Physically or emotionally."

That was his woman, honest no matter what. She had no idea how to lie to him, and he loved that. He needed it. In his own way, the ride was both terrifying and exhilarating to him. He was taking his one shot at the dream of having someone of his own. Someone who really cared about him, not his money or prestige. Not the awards he'd gotten for his research or getting her picture in magazines or on television because she was on his arm. Never once, with all the times he'd been with a woman had his emotions been just as strong as his physical reaction, and with Cayenne, he found both were off the Richter scale.

"Neither did I," he admitted. For her. Because she deserved to know.

"Trap." She leaned down, right over the top of his face, creating a cocoon with her body, showing him just how flexible she really was. "I wouldn't *want* to share this kind of pleasure with another man." Her voice was a soft whisper, but the words penetrated deep, wrapped around his heart and squeezed like a vise at the admission.

"Baby," he said softly. "You're killing me. You have no idea what I want to do to you right now. It's a fucking good thing you've got me tied up in all your silk. Lean over me, one hand by my head. I want to eat all that honey. I'm starving for it."

He sounded starving for it, his voice hoarse with need. His mouth watered. She smelled like honeysuckle. Jasmine. A wild storm building.

She did exactly as he instructed, her eyes on his face as she pressed her hand into the mattress on one side of his head.

"Work your breast, Cayenne," he instructed. "Tilt into me."

Then his tongue was there. Right where he wanted. Needed even. That first taste sent a shudder of pleasure through his body, and she jerked, gasped, a small cry escaping.

Yeah, baby, it's that good. This is what I can do to you. Take you all the way with my mouth. It's even better with my fingers. And when I get my cock inside you, you're going to be screaming for me.

I'm already going to be screaming. This is even more terrifying. But good. So good.

He wished he had his hands to hold her in place. Knees wide. Her body trembled continually, and her breath came in ragged pants as he stroked long, deep caresses, drawing out the honey and taking it into his mouth—taking *her* into his mouth. She tasted like heaven. Like his. He used his tongue like the weapon of seduction it was, pulling out every stop. Giving this time to her. Making it all about her.

Her little sobbing gasps began to rise from silent to a musical symphony he was fast becoming as addicted to as he was to her taste. When he began to gently suckle on her clit she jerked away from his assault.

No, no, baby. Let yourself go. Give yourself to me.

It's too much. I can't stand it. I can't.

Take a deep breath and relax. Let go. I swear to you, I've got you. I can't force you to do anything you don't want, Cayenne. This is all you, honey. You like this, right?

Too much. I like you too much.

There it was. Her fear that if she let go, she was giving herself fully to him. He couldn't combat that because it was the truth. He'd tried sweet and gentle. He tried going along with her to give her the confidence to come to him. He wanted this for her. He wanted her to know just how good it could be. It was time to take a different route, see if commanding her worked, because he wasn't getting anywhere with coaxing her.

Damn it, Cayenne. You fucking know you belong to me. You know it. Stop playing games in your head and just do what the fuck I tell you to do. I can't touch you and comfort you because you're the one dictating the terms here. You've handicapped me. Completely. This is it, all I can give you, so get your sweet little body where it belongs and let me give this to you.

Her eyes moved over his face. He kept his gaze on all that startling green. The facets were back, very much in evidence. She was trembling, but his demand worked. She swallowed hard and moved back over his face, closing her eyes.

No, baby, look at me. He gentled his voice. She was so beautiful. So vulnerable. He wanted her to come apart for him. For her. So she knew pleasure. He wanted to be the one who gave her pleasure. *I want you to see me when I give this to you. You need to understand what's happening here. I want your acknowledgment that you do. I need to see that in your eyes.*

He waited. He could feel her heartbeat, the pulse of life, of fear right there in the heart of sex. The scent of all that sweet, spicy honey waiting for him to collect called to him, but he held on, not moving. Waiting. She took a deep breath and lifted those long feathery lashes. Giving him that. Giving him her.

He settled his mouth over her and took what belonged to him. Nothing in his life had ever been as good as this moment. He took her back up slow. Leisurely. Talking to her softly. Intimately. Mind to mind. Whispering how beautiful she was. How brave. How lucky he was that she was his. To let go. Relax. Take the chance. With him. Trust him. He'd catch her. He'd be there for her. He made that vow. He would be there for her.

He knew she would capitulate, because if there was one thing for certain he knew about Cayenne, she didn't lack courage. She might be terrified, but she faced the unknown, head-on. Her breathing changed. The music started again. The ragged hitches in her breathing.

That's my girl. Let yourself go. Move your hips, baby. That's it. Don't stop, just let go. Grind down. Let go.

He stared into her green eyes. Saw shock. Saw dazed wonder. Saw the exact moment when she became his. Her mouth formed his name. He became her talisman. Her sword. Her shield. Her everything. She became his. His heart went crazy. That look pierced deeper even than his heart. He took her down gently, his tongue lapping. Tenderly. Wanting to hold her. Needing to hold her.

Baby, let me free now. You need my arms around you. My body sheltering yours. Come on, you can't still be afraid of me.

Her lashes fluttered. She took another breath, still trying to draw enough air into her lungs to stop the burning. She shook her head and moved back away from him, to stare down at his face. He smiled at her, trying to be encouraging.

"I've got you all over my face."

He did. She was everywhere. Just the scent of her was enough, but giving her that first orgasm had nearly sent him over the edge. Knowing he'd put that look on her face gave him more satisfaction than anything else. Deliberately he licked his lips, taking in the sensual treat.

"Babe. Let me loose."

She moved, that sensuous slide of her body back down over his to the end of the bed where she crouched, watching him. He'd never seen anything as beautiful as her naked body, the fluid way she moved, muscles rippling beneath all that soft, inviting skin. Her breasts were marked with his possession. Strawberries covering them. Red. Swollen. Her nipples tight.

"You take my breath away," he admitted. "So damned beautiful, Cayenne. Come on, baby. You had your fun. Untie me."

She shook her head, her gaze dropping to his cock. "I'm not finished. I want more. I need more, Trap."

His heart began to pound all over again. Hunger was stark and naked in her eyes. With her flushed body and her breasts swaying with every ragged breath, he nearly lost control right then, spilling more of his seed onto the throbbing, jerking head of his cock.

"I don't know if I can take much more," he said softly.

"You gave me such a gift, Trap. I need to know I can do the same for you."

He groaned, his cock swelling in his fist. Aching like a bear. He tried to be as gentle as possible, talking to her as honestly as possible. "Baby," Trap said softly. "I'm trying to give you everything you need. I want that for you. I want to *be* that for you, but you're killing me here. I don't know how much more I can take."

Cayenne's lashes fluttered. Her palm shaped his ankle,

fingers settling around on either side as if she had to hold on to anchor herself. "I'm not certain what you mean."

He tried to stifle another groan escaping in his spite of his resolve. "I don't want to come on my gut, honey. I prefer your body or your mouth. I don't want to be acting like some teenage boy with no control. That's not going to make much of an impression on you, now is it?"

She swallowed, and the action of her throat sent another groan rumbling up his chest. It wasn't a big jump to imagine his cock there, her swallowing as he pumped into her mouth. In his fist, he nearly exploded, pulsing, leaking so much that his shaft was slick from the movement of his thumb swiping and drawing the liquid down to coat the spiked steel in his palm.

"You're making an impression, Trap," she said softly. "I like the images in your head. Seeing what you're seeing and sharing the feeling makes my body feel hotter and more out of control. My breasts ache, and inside, something is coiling tight and burning me so that I feel restless and needy just like when you were eating me."

"That's exactly how you're supposed to feel, Cayenne. See? You're not going to have any problem with this. Untie me now, baby, and let me show you just how good this is."

She pressed her lips together and then resolutely shook her head. His breath left his lungs in an explosive roar of protest. He almost blew it by moving *through* the silk. He could move through walls. To rescue her, he'd done that. Silk would be easier, but Cayenne needed to feel in control. Trap imposed a rigid discipline, clenched his teeth and forced himself to remain still, not taking control from her, although he had known all along he could have. This night was hers. Whatever she needed—even if it killed him—and it might.

She moved again, one hand, one knee. Slow. He wasn't certain his heart could take the way her body undulated, fluid and sexy as she crawled toward him again from the end of the bed. She wedged her knee between his legs. He should have felt vulnerable, but he was a GhostWalker and he had enhancements she wouldn't know or consider. Or if she did, she didn't realize just what he could do. Her concentration was fully on his erect cock. Jackhammers tripped in his head. His blood thundered in his ears and rushed through his veins with the force of a fireball. He liked that she was watching so intently. His fist tightened around his shaft. He pumped. Up. Down. A lazy slide, when there was nothing lazy in his mind.

Her other knee joined the one between his legs and he shifted to accommodate her, spreading wider. "What do you plan to do now, baby?"

His voice had gone low. Enticing. Smoldering. She was over the top of his thighs now, her face so close to his cock. Her lips just out of reach. There was no thrusting up, filling her mouth. She was in control, not him. His thighs were spread wide enough to allow her body between his legs. Her hair fell over his skin like a dark waterfall. He swore a thousand fingers danced over his thighs and brushed along his heavy sac.

"I want to taste you. Feel what it's like to have you in my mouth."

"You don't have to take that, Cayenne. I'll give that to you. But I need to touch you. Get this silk off me."

She shook her head without looking up. "You want your cock in my mouth. I see it in your mind. You want me sucking you. My hands on you. I'll give you that, but my way— not yours. I don't want to be afraid of you, Trap, or of any of the things you want to do to me."

"So this is an experiment?"

"It's how I have to learn."

Another groan escaped, this one deep and hungry. He had to give her this no matter the cost to him. "No biting, babe," he cautioned, his cock jerking hard in his fist at the thought.

Her gaze jumped back to his cock. A slow smile curved her mouth and lit the green of her eyes. "A little fear can add to the excitement of what we're doing here."

She quoted him nearly word for word—threw his words back in his face and left him wondering if she intended to bite him.

"You bite me and there's going to be all sorts of trouble. I love your ass. I really do. That sweet curve would look good with my handprints on it, all warmed up and nerve endings screaming for more. You'd be so wet for me, baby. Let me up. Let me make you feel good."

"If that's supposed to be a deterrent, or a punishment, I have to tell you, Trap, it doesn't sound like one." She said it with a small smile on her face, once again leaving him wondering if she intended to bite him.

Yeah. Okay. That made him hotter. That thrill of the unknown. That bite of trepidation. Being at her mercy. He squeezed his fist hard around his cock, needing to feel a bite of his own. He was going to explode without her mouth if she didn't hurry.

She shook her head, and her palms slid tentatively up his thigh as she settled back on her ankles. Her breasts swayed invitingly. She moved her hands over his muscles slowly. Too slowly. His cock jumped in his fist and spilled more pearly drops. She leaned closer to him, lowering her head until he felt her breath.

"All right, you're in control, but at least open your thighs so I can see how wet you are for me. I need to know you're loving what you're doing."

She stayed still for a minute and then slowly complied, sitting back on her ankles, allowing her knees to fall apart so he could see the tangle of curls at the junction between her legs, the little dewdrops on the red hourglass.

"Beautiful," he whispered.

Without warning, more silk spun around his wrist and pulled his hand sideways, away from his cock, pinning his arm tighter to the mattress. He swore as her fist replaced his. Her hand was much smaller and her palm barely curled around him.

She smiled at him. "Don't you like this?"

Her hands slid up his thighs, moved around to the inside, kneading and stroking. Her mouth followed, small kisses. Licks. He felt her tongue sliding along his inner thigh, and his balls went tight. Hard as twin rocks. She licked her way up to his scrotum. The breath left his throat and his hips moved restlessly. Very gently she cupped his balls, swept her palm over them lightly and then rolled them boldly. Her mouth moved over them, her tongue licking and stroking, making little circles that went straight to his brain—short-circuiting what was left of his ability to think clearly. Sensations shot straight up his spine. He wasn't paralyzed under all that silk, and he couldn't stop the shifting of his legs or the lifting of his hips. Another groan escaped, husky and needy.

Her smile went wider. "Yeah, Trap. I think you like this a lot."

She studied his face, the desire there carved deep for her to see. The lust gathering in his eyes, dark with sensuality, lashes heavy and hooded. There was no hiding it from her, and he didn't try. He bucked his hips at her. Demanding. He kept his gaze on her face. She was so beautiful, and he wanted to witness that moment when her lips surrounded his cock and she drew him into her mouth.

The thought was so sensual more droplets leaked, this time onto his flat, very hard belly. Her breath caught in her throat. Her green eyes instantly were riveted to his cock. She wrapped her fingers around his shaft one by one again, testing, pressing harder.

"I had no idea a man could be this big. How do you fit inside me?"

"I'll fit," he assured her with confidence. She was killing him, but he was going to die happy so he just watched her. She wanted to explore, hell yeah, he was up for that, at least until he couldn't take it anymore. He allowed his muscles to expand and contract as if testing the bonds holding him again. "You were made for me. You're already so slick and ready. Let me show you how good it can be. What I gave you before is nothing compared to what you'll feel."

She ignored his enticement. "I need you to show me what to do with my mouth. Show me again in your head," she said. It was an order. One he might make. Their roles were definitely reversed.

"I control what goes on in bed," he said.

"Not this time." She gave him a little smirk, but her gaze remained on his cock. Her breath stayed there, warm and enticing, teasing him with anticipation.

She *seemed* to be in power, but he could take some of that back by influencing what she did through the images in his head. He showed her what he needed. What his body was on fire for.

Cayenne leaned closer. The tip of her tongue made a little experimental foray over the velvety crest, catching the droplets. Tasting him. Her tongue slid around her lips as if savoring his flavor and then dipped down to follow the wet path on his belly to catch every drop.

So that's what you taste like. Mmm. Good. I like it. I wanted to like this because I could see how much you needed your woman to like doing this to you. I need to know I will be able to give you whatever is important to you.

The most important thing of all to me, babe, is that you want to give me this kind of pleasure and that you enjoy doing it. That will get me off every time.

She tasted again, savoring this time, real enjoyment in her eyes. He fucking loved that—that pleasing him meant something to her.

I do want to, Trap. I just don't know how. There was demand in her voice. In her mind. She wanted instructions.

Use your mouth, baby. Tight. Like a fist. Suck hard and keep your tongue moving. You want the shaft nice and wet. Remember what I was doing with my fist? You want to do that with your mouth. Use your other hand to stroke and caress that soft area just between my anus and balls. Cup

*my balls, roll them gently. You have lots to play with. Take
your time, and don't do anything you don't enjoy.*

She didn't hesitate, following the image in his mind and
his intimate instructions. She wrapped her lips around him
and swallowed him down. He'd never seen anything more
beautiful. Sensations tore through him and he shared them
with her. Letting her feel what she was doing to him. Her
fingers moved against him and he lifted his hips, driving
deeper into her mouth.

Heaven. Paradise. She sucked hard, her tongue sliding
under the flared head to find that sweet spot in his mind.
Her free hand continued to stimulate and caress until he was
on fire. Her tongue felt like a flame stroking his shaft and
then licking up and down until her saliva coated his cock
and she had about half of him in her mouth.

"Look at me. I want to see your eyes." He poured command into his voice, trying in vain to keep his gaze on the
junction between her legs. With her kneeling between his
legs, her thighs spread wide, he wanted to see if fresh liquid
gathered at his hard authority.

Are you wet for me? Burning for me?

Yes. She answered without hesitation.

*Even when I talk to you like that? When I tell you what
to do?* He *had* to know. He was demanding in bed.

When you use that voice, the burn gets hotter.

Satisfaction moved through him. Relief. There was no
doubt in his mind that she would suit his every need. At
once her lashes lifted and he could see that wide expanse
of green. Definitely enjoying herself. That was what he
needed to see. She liked giving him pleasure, and she liked
learning. She even liked him making demands.

I love how you taste. Is it always like this?

"Just with me," he growled. "*Only* me. That's it, baby.
Suck harder. A little deeper. Son of a bitch, Cayenne, that's
fucking beautiful. Breathe through your nose, and you'll
have to control your gag reflex. Breathe, honey."

His own breath came in a ragged gasp and in another minute he would have to resort to telepathy because there was no way he was going to be able to talk. Not with her mouth sucking him hard and then switching abruptly to gentle. Not with her tongue wrapping itself around him, doing little circles and then suddenly fluttering like butterfly wings.

"Baby, I'm getting close. Most women don't want to finish it in their mouths."

What do you like?

She sucked him deeper and he felt the burst of heat rocketing through his body. His hips bucked, pushing even deeper. Her tongue pressed tight against the sweet spot just beneath the crest of his cock and that sent flames rushing through his veins.

I want your mouth sucking me dry. There was no way to talk. No way to do anything but let her mouth take him.

He drove into her helplessly, and she didn't pull away from him or fight. In return, he didn't break the silken bonds. He gave her this moment because she was determined to give him paradise.

The explosion was unlike anything he'd ever had in his life. He felt the fire moving up his legs, along the path her fingers had taken. Everything in him, every sensitive nerve ending fired and sped toward his groin. Her mouth was hot and moist and she suckled hard, greedy, kept him deep, pulling every drop out of him, milking him with her mouth. He felt the tight squeeze of her throat and mouth as his cock swelled and pumped. Once. Twice.

He shouted hoarsely, the cry torn from him as his seed rocketed out of him, driving down her throat while he was thrown into a place he'd never been. She'd taken him there. He floated for long, blissful moments. Her mouth stayed on him, surrounding him with scalding heat. Gentle. Careful. Her tongue curled around him as if guarding him while he stayed in that place of absolute beauty in his mind. A gift he'd never expected from anyone, let alone a woman. Absolute beauty. Absolute peace. She'd taken him there.

He'd never felt truly sated in his life. He could take a woman all night and still be semihard. In his mind the act had never been enough to satisfy him. It relieved the terrible ache, but it didn't satisfy. Until now. Until Cayenne, and he couldn't even touch her hair falling around his hips and thighs with his fingertips.

You have no way of knowing just what you've given me. He whispered the admission in his mind. Intimate. It was all he could give her, and he knew it made him vulnerable. Maybe too vulnerable. She had to see what her gift meant to him, she'd shared his mind. Shared that amazing, beautiful experience.

Cayenne sat up slowly, licked her lips, her gaze somewhat dazed. Her lips swollen. She looked almost as sated as he felt. "The silk will loosen in a few minutes, Trap. Don't come down to my lair. I have to think about things."

"Baby." His voice was hoarse. It broke on a groan. "I need to hold you. To touch you. You just gave me something beautiful. I'm not so selfish that I don't want to give you something back."

"You already did."

"More, I want to give you more. At least take off the wraps and let me hold you."

She shook her head slowly and backed away from him. "I can't. Not yet."

He could see she was afraid. Afraid that she'd gotten in over her head. The gift she'd given him had meant something to her as well. It had tied them closer together. He took a breath, let it out and nodded.

He forced air through his lungs, afraid he'd never have enough again to breathe right. "Get food and something to drink out of the kitchen. Money's there. Tomorrow we'll put your prints into the security system. I wrote the code for you. More than anything right now, Cayenne, I want to hold you. I want you in my bed sleeping next to me. I've never slept in the same bed with a woman. I've fucked them, but I didn't trust any more than you do. I want that for us. That intimacy. You. In my bed."

"I want that too, Trap, but I really have to think about this. You have the house and the money and all the knowledge. I've got nothing at all to give to you. I don't know how to walk into a store and buy groceries for us, let alone how to cook them. I need to know I'm bringing you something as well. Something valuable."

"We talked about this. I want it all with you, Cayenne. A home. A wife. Children. I want a partner in the lab. You calculated the amount of peanut shells on the floor of the bar . . ."

"I was bored out of my mind," she said. "Not every man going into a bar is a rat. I wasn't going to rob just anyone. I had to do something. Not only was I bored, but I was terrified—and hungry. Some days I only had those peanuts to eat. Most of the time, I gave the money to the families I took clothes from."

He detested that. "Those days are over. Just the fact that you could calculate the number of husks means intellectually we're a good fit. I need that. I can't be bored by my partner. You like knowledge."

"It's more than liking," she confessed in a rush. "I have to keep my mind occupied or I go a little crazy. I have to keep learning."

He smiled at her, wanting to touch her. Needing it. "Come here, baby. Free my hands so I can at least touch you. And before you leave this room, I need you to kiss me again. I promise you, you're safe. I won't take anything from you but a kiss."

"You're very tempting right now and I'm . . ." She broke off.

Clearly the things she'd done to him had aroused her again, and this time, there'd been no relief. None. Her nipples were hard little points, and between her legs he could see the evidence of her desire. She still had a flush to her skin and her eyes were a little dazed. Her breath came in rapid little pants.

"Give me my hands or let me use my mouth again if you don't want my cock right now, Cayenne. You know I can take care of you. Taking me like that made you needy all over again. Let me help you with that." He was thrilled that the act of giving him so much pleasure had made her burn for him.

She stepped away from the bed. Not stepped. There was movement but no noise. She walked in absolute silence. Like a spider. He couldn't help but be amazed as she glanced upward toward the ceiling, one hand going up. Immediately there was a silken cord hanging and she was already making her way upward. When she stirred, her movements were very spider-like, and yet at the same time, she was a beautiful, sensuous woman.

Trap stayed very still, watching her as she scurried to the corner across the ceiling to the vent. She turned her head, looking over her shoulder, long dark hair falling in clouds around her. "You promised me that you wouldn't come downstairs, Trap. I'm holding you to that promise. I have to think about this. I hope I can get where you want me to be, but I'm not there yet. You have to let me do this my way."

Then she was gone.

CHAPTER 9

———————⌗———————

Trap woke up to the sound of a fire alarm going off and the scent of burned bacon permeating his room. He leapt out of bed and ran toward the sound. The master suite was a distance from the kitchen and he cursed living in such a huge space as he sprinted, naked and barefoot, through the old factory and then skidded to a halt just inside the door.

Cayenne stood beneath the fire alarm, glaring at it, hands on her hips, her hair and clothes covered in flour, or what could possibly be egg and batter. White clouds of powder floated in the air and lay strewn across the floor in sweeping patterns like sand.

Trap pressed his lips together to keep from laughing, stalked through the gray-white room, and stepped behind her, close, his body touching hers, to reach up and turn off the blaring alarm. She froze. He was significantly taller than she was, and with his arms around her, she was mostly caged in. He completed the circle, his arms becoming steel bonds as he leaned his chin down and nuzzled her neck.

"Good morning, Cayenne. I see you're busy." There was no possible way to keep the humor out of his voice.

She turned in his arms to face him because he didn't give her much choice, annoyance on her flour-smeared face. "Don't you dare laugh."

He took her mouth, flour and all. That beautiful, adorable mouth, with her full red lips that had stretched around his cock and brought him a piece of heaven only the night before. She kissed like an angel and used her mouth like a sinful temptress. The moment he kissed her, she melted into him. Flour and all. Her arms slid around his neck, fingers curling into his hair. That felt good. It felt better than the time he became one of the youngest doctors to win the Nobel Prize in Medicine for his leading research in adaptive immunity in subset B&T memory cells. He didn't give a damn about prizes, only the research, but he did give a damn about the woman in his arms.

Cayenne had no last name. She had no birth certificate. She had no identity. But she was going to be his wife. She would have an identity to the rest of the world, because it was going to be very public when he took a wife. One of the world's most eligible bachelors getting married wasn't going to fly without notice. He wasn't going to scare the crap out of her by telling her that just yet, but he was *never* giving up that mouth. She could kiss and she didn't have a clue yet how. Still, it was the best kiss, hands down, he'd ever had.

He lifted his head slowly and brushed his hand down the red hourglass in her hair. "Fuck, baby, you kiss like an angel."

The way she stared up at him, as if he was the only man in the world, as if he could walk on water, took his breath. He touched his forehead to hers, in an effort to keep it together. She didn't need him attacking her, laying her out like a feast on the kitchen table just the way he fantasized the moment he saw the damn thing.

"What are you doing?"

Her lashes fluttered. She had a light dusting of white powder on the tips. That made him want to kiss her all over again.

"I was cooking you breakfast." Cayenne sounded annoyed and frustrated all rolled into one. "They have cooking videos on the Internet and I was following the steps, but somehow things didn't go right. They make it look so easy, Trap. I wanted to make this for you but . . ."

She turned in his arms and surveyed the chaos along the counter, the still smoking mess that looked to him like it could have been a pancake at one time, and sighed.

"Clearly I did something wrong."

"Well, babe, first thing to know, when you cook you need to wear an apron. Just that. Nothing else. I've got one hanging on the little hook in the pantry here."

Keeping a straight, serious expression, he walked across the flour-covered floor, leaving footprints behind him. He held up the little black and white apron he'd spotted in one of the online toy stores he'd been looking in right before he'd found her. The apron was lacy and short, very short, with ties in the back and nothing else. The front would cover her breasts, but just barely, and had open French lace so her nipples would peek out at him as she worked.

Cayenne studied the little apron and then her green gaze went to his face. "That's what I'm supposed to wear when I cook for you?"

"Yes." He nodded his head. "Exactly."

"That's the secret to cooking you something great?"

He nodded again and crossed back to her, thrusting the apron into her hands. "I'll start the cleanup, and you go put that on. We can cook together and see if that helps."

"Trap." She shook her head, half smiling, not really believing him but a little uncertain if he was teasing her or telling the truth. "I've never been in a kitchen in my life. Especially when someone was cooking. The food I ate was always the same, some kind of rations, not anything like they have on the Internet. The first time I ate a burger at the

Huracan Club, I threw up. The same with the fries. I don't know anything about this, and I'm trying to learn so I can give you that home you want. I have to rely on you to tell me the truth. None of those people cooking on the videos were wearing a little apron."

"They aren't in *our* kitchen," he said. "They don't know what works for us."

A slow smile curved her mouth, making him want to taste her all over again. There was nothing stopping him so he did, reaching with one hand to curl his fingers around the nape of her neck and pull her to him. Using his thumb under her chin, he tilted her face up and took her mouth. He wasn't sweet and gentle about it because he didn't feel sweet and gentle, he felt a little savage. Taking her on the kitchen table was out, not when he felt like this. He wasn't going to do her rough, not when her first time with him was probably not going to be the best for her.

He poured himself into the kiss, taking her mouth with his own. One hand caught hers and he brought her palm down his chest to the massive hard-on he was sporting. Using his own hand to curl her fingers around his shaft, he kept kissing her, squeezing her fist down tight around him.

That's yours, baby. All for you. No one else but you. You wake up needing that, you let me know. I want you sleeping next to me, Cayenne. No more hiding down in that basement behind your silk. You. In the bed. With me.

The entire time he filled her mind with him, with his warmth and strength. With his demand. He kept kissing her. Over and over. Using his mouth and his fingers wrapped around hers, doing a lazy slide and pumping gently with her palm so that lightning streaked through him, his blood pounded through his body and centered in his cock. It was the perfect way to start a morning. Hot kisses and her hand wrapped tight around his heavy shaft.

You going to give me that, Cayenne? You. In my bed?

Very slowly he lifted his head and looked down into her

eyes. He brought up both hands to frame her face. To hold her still, so she had to look at him. "Are you going to give that to me, baby? Did you think about it last night? Alone. There behind your silk."

"Where I'm safe," she said in a small voice.

"Where you're alone. Existing."

"Will I be safe with you, Trap? I don't mean whatever is threatening either of us. Not Whitney. I'm asking will I be safe with *you*?"

She looked so lost. Very vulnerable. How could a woman be such a warrior, taking on *teams* of Whitney's enhanced supersoldiers, yet be so completely defenseless when it came to being a woman? She was beautiful. Seductive. Naturally sensual. She kissed like a dream. She'd given him the best blow job of his life. There was no guile in her. No subterfuge. She wasn't flirting or trying to be cute and adorable, both of which she was.

He bent his head and gently brushed his lips over hers. A barely there touch. "Baby, I'll protect you with my life. I'm not a nice man all the time, and I'll piss you off and maybe even hurt you without thinking when I say or do something stupid. I can be that man, that thoughtless dick sometimes. But I swear to you, on my life, that I'll do everything in my power to make you happy. I'll have your back. I know you'll have mine. If there's one trait I have that runs deep, it's loyalty."

Her lashes fluttered. The green in her eyes went to an amazing emerald. "You really want me to put on this apron while we cook?"

His cock jerked. His heart stuttered in his chest. "Yes, baby. Please. I would very much like you to put on that apron and nothing else."

"Where's your apron?"

He grinned at her. "I got one to match." He bent and did another brush of his mouth across hers and once more walked through the flour to the pantry door. It was a good-sized pantry, just like everything else in the house, the size of a large bedroom. Everything inside was easy to see with the lighting, and the wall facing him as he yanked open the door, deep inside, was false. With a touch of his palm, he could open the hidden tunnel and have an escape route. His apron hung on the hook next to the one that held hers.

He loved that she went along with his sexy teasing, making it easy and fun. He wanted that. He also wanted to know she'd want him with the same urgency he did her. He was going to do his best to keep this morning about fun, learning to cook breakfast together with a dash of spicy sexual play to show her she could be his partner in every way.

"Cayenne," he said softly, as she turned away, presumably to clean up. "Thank you for doing this, for cooking my breakfast for me."

"It was an utter disaster."

"It meant everything to me," he corrected.

Her smile lit her face, made her eyes go a crystalline green and called his attention right back to her full, red lips. "Then I'm glad. I'm going to take a quick shower and I'll be right back." She glanced down ruefully at her clothes. "I'll soak my clothes as well."

"There's a laundry room, Cayenne."

She blinked. Went still. Her smile faded. "I don't know what that is, Trap."

He stepped close and caught her chin in his hand. "I'm definitely teaching you to use the washing machine and dryer, baby, because I despise doing laundry. One summer I didn't wear clothes in the house or lab so I wouldn't have to wash clothes. Then I hired a housekeeper to do it, and I don't like other people around much. My team, you and maybe Nonny, Pepper and the girls. Even with them I'm not the best. Nonny's always threatening to wash my mouth out with soap."

"Why?"

"I swear a lot. She doesn't like it, and she's right. I shouldn't swear around her or the girls."

"Why? Swearing is just words, isn't it?"

"Not-so-nice words, babe," he said. "Don't follow my example. Most of the time I work by myself so it doesn't matter what the fuck I say. Now, around Nonny and Pepper and the girls, I have to watch my mouth."

"But I still don't understand. Why would it bother them for you to be you?"

"I'll be me around you, honey," he promised, knowing she wasn't going to like what he was in every situation. "There's a bathroom just down the hall with a large shower and plenty of towels. It's stocked with shampoo and conditioner for your hair, toothbrushes and hairbrushes. Just about anything you might need. Use that one and save time."

She nodded, and he watched her go. Watched the way her very shapely ass swayed as she moved, tempting him into all sorts of sinful fantasies. He forced his mind back to the kitchen and the mess she'd created. He found himself smiling for no reason at all. If he wasn't already falling for her, this mess definitely turned the tide. She'd tried. For him. She had no clue how to cook, but she'd gotten up early, looked up cooking videos and tried to make him breakfast.

He went back to his room and got his cell phone so he could take pictures. Lots of them. He added a video of the entire room. He wanted to have both to remember this moment. His woman, doing her best, giving him a priceless gift. The question came up in interview after interview: What did one get for the man who had everything and could get anything he wanted? You gave him this. A messy kitchen and burned pots and pans. Flour all over your face and clothes. You gave him something no one else had ever bothered to do or would think of doing. Yeah. He was falling hard. And he was framing the damn pictures and putting them up on his wall.

He got to work. She'd tried pancakes and eggs with some kind of sauce. She hadn't started small, but then she didn't know what was easy or difficult when it came to cooking.

He put on a pot of coffee and then scrubbed the floor and counters. Trap had the space ready for her, although the way he'd designed the kitchen, he had two kitchens, each mirroring the other with a long center aisle dividing them. He figured if the team and their families had to retreat to his fortress for protection, they would have plenty of cooking space. He had this double kitchen, the large kitchen in the downstairs apartment and a third kitchen in the wing of the house where he'd installed another huge suite. The large recreation room divided the space.

The burnt odor had faded by the time she returned. He didn't need to turn around to know she was there. She moved in silence, but she had an addicting scent, the one he recognized now. The storms. The flowers. The scent of his woman.

"Trap?" She came up behind him, her hand sliding up the back of his thigh, over his very cut buttocks. "Is this how I'm supposed to wear this? Does it look right?"

She stepped close to him and he felt her tongue slide over the trail her hand left behind. Just the lightest of touches. It didn't matter how light. He felt it sink into his bones.

He closed his eyes for a moment, savoring the feel of her palm sliding over his bare skin. He loved that she was tactile. Loved it more that she was oral. Loved that she was made for sex and sin. For him. That she had no inhibitions and would welcome the way he liked to play.

He turned slowly, and his breath caught in his throat. "Fuck, baby," he whispered softly, his hand dropping to his cock. Already the loincloth apron was tenting hugely. "You look amazing. So damned sexy I'm not certain I can concentrate."

She looked sexier than any of the pictures he'd seen with a woman demonstrating what the apron looked like. She might be tiny, but she was all there, an hourglass figure, her breasts high and thrusting against the lace, stretching it, pushing out her red nipples, the lacy webbing emphasizing the soft, full curves. The tie showed off her small waist and flaring hips.

The skirt of the apron, short, but pleated and sassy, moved just a bit when she shifted her weight and showed him a peek of her tight black curls and a hint of that red hourglass.

He drew in his breath as he used his finger to indicate for her to turn slowly. She complied. Her long hair fell down her back, silken waves she'd tamed with a dryer, reaching past her waist to skim the sweet curve of her ass. He definitely was fixating on her body. He reached down and cupped both cheeks, kneading with his fingers, sinking deep, claiming that part of her for his own as well.

"I can't imagine that we aren't going to whip up a masterpiece with you in that outfit." His apron wasn't lacy, but the material was white and black checkerboard and when his cock was soft the entire crown peeked out under the apron. When it was hard, his cock nestled in the fabric as if being caressed, pushing against the stretchy material.

"Are you certain about this, Trap?"

"Absolutely. Do you drink coffee?"

She frowned. Shook her head. "It always smelled good when others had it in mugs, but no, I was never given coffee."

"What about chocolate?"

She shook her head again.

"Whipped cream?"

"No."

"Whipped cream is a specialty item, baby. It can be used for all sorts of things. It can go on top of your coffee, a dessert, in a crepe, or all over me or you so the other one can have the fun of licking it off. Then there's chocolate sauce or fudge."

"I'm beginning to see a pattern here, Trap," she said. "Does everything revolve around sex?"

He flashed a grin. "Now you're getting it. Come on. I'll make you some chocolate and you can try that while I whip us up some eggs and potatoes."

"I want to learn, Trap. I spent the night reading articles about families and cooking and making a home. There are magazines online that specialize in things like that. I'm pretty certain I can turn what I read into practical experience." She glanced around the kitchen a little ruefully. "I was thinking about where I went wrong this morning. I tried to do too many things at the same time, didn't I?"

He couldn't help himself. He curled his fingers around the nape of her neck and drew her to him. "What you did was perfect for so many reasons I can't even tell you."

Her eyes went soft. Happy. The tension in her eased. "Even though I totally screwed up, it meant something to you then?"

"Yeah, baby." He pulled her tight against his chest, just holding her there where she couldn't see his face. He was a GhostWalker, and normally he didn't give a damn about anything, so it was easy enough to keep his features a stone wall. There was no hiding what her gesture meant to him. All he could do was hold her tight against him and bury his face in her wealth of hair. He nuzzled the top of the red hourglass nestled in all that black silk. "It meant a fuck of a lot."

She slipped her arms around him and held his back. Melted into him. She felt soft and warm and *his*. Suddenly, it wasn't about sex, and no matter how subconsciously he tried to make it that, he knew he'd slipped past *falling* and right into *gone*. Abruptly he pulled back, caught her around the waist and planted her sweet little ass on the center aisle.

"Sit there and observe your master."

She laughed softly, and the sound felt like music. He glanced sideways at her as he pulled out a mixing bowl, which he filled with cold water and a grater.

"I'm going to put you to work. You can grate the potatoes right into the cold water while I fix the eggs."

"You're removing the starch with the cold water."

He flashed an approving smile over his shoulder as he quickly washed four potatoes at the sink and handed them off to her. "You do have your alarm system spread around the complex outside, right?"

She nodded, frowning as she slowly began to grate the potatoes, finding a quicker rhythm and sticking with it. "Of course. I like to know what's coming at me. I've got feelers outside the fence as well as inside. No one will get close without us knowing. Why, are you worried we'll be attacked?"

He shook his head. "No. I'm worried my team will come check on me, and they don't get to see you looking like this."

"I thought you liked this apron."

He paused in the act of breaking an egg into a mixing bowl, his gaze moving over her as she sat there, grating the potatoes for him. Every moment sent her breasts swaying invitingly beneath the stretchy lace. He set the bowl aside, placed a hand on the island surface on either side of her body and leaned in close. So close it forced her body to tip back. To catch herself she had to put her hands back behind her, thrusting her breasts upward. He took the offering, settling his mouth around her right breast, right through the lace.

The apron and this body are for me. Not for my friends. Not for anyone else. You don't show it to them. You don't share it with them. It's mine. You're mine.

She made a soft sound and caught his head, cradling it to her with one hand as she tipped farther back on the island. He followed her body, leaning over her.

Now you're just making me hungry for all that honey. I could have breakfast a different way, and then go back to your cooking lesson.

Instantly he felt her body go from soft and pliant to tense. He wanted to groan in sheer frustration. Blood pounded through his veins and filled his cock with need.

Baby, your first time with me is going to be in my bed, not in the kitchen, although we're going to be spending a lot of time in here later. Lots of island space, the table, counters.

He trailed kisses from her breast up to her chin. Biting gently, he kissed his way to her mouth and caught her lower lip between his teeth. *Are you going to sleep in my bed tonight? All night?*

There was a small hesitation. His teeth bit down just a little harder. Tugged on her full lower lip. *I want to spend hours making you feel good, baby, and then I want to hold you close while we both fall asleep. Are you going to give me that?*

I'm really afraid.

I know you are, Cayenne. But you have to trust me sometime. I'll take care of you, I promise that. Say you'll spend the night in my bed. I know if you promise you'll keep your word.

What if I'm so scared I bite you?

Then I'll spank your pretty little ass very hard. After, I'll make certain you're feeling good all over again, but you won't bite me again because your hot little bottom will remind you not to.

How can you make everything sound hot? In your mind it even feels hot.

Because whatever I do to you is going to be hot and you're going to like it.

Then it really isn't a punishment, is it? Or a deterrent.

She had a point, but then he didn't care. He was going to make everything hot and pleasurable for her. His teeth tugged harder. *Say it, Cayenne. Tell me you'll be in my bed tonight.*

Yes. Fine. But if I bite you, that's on you, not me. You won't be able to spank me because you'll be paralyzed and at my mercy. That might be disappointing.

He let go of her lip, his tongue sliding over it to soothe the sting. "Maybe, but sooner or later, I'd come out of it and you'd have to face the music." He straightened. "And then, baby, I wouldn't be disappointing you in the least."

He turned resolutely back to their breakfast. She'd given her word and he knew she wouldn't break it, no matter how terrified she was. She had too much courage. "I've been considering this cooking business, Cayenne. Do you really want to learn?"

"I told you I did." Her breath was still a little ragged but she sat up and began grating the last potato.

He couldn't stop looking at her. She looked beautiful with that dazed, shocked look on her face, as if just that little encounter had been a gift from him. He'd made her body sing when he'd put his mark on her breast. She had quite a few of his marks, strawberries covering the soft curves. He wanted them on other, more secret places. He'd taken advantage the night before and put a couple on her inner thigh. He could see them, the little brands that said she was his.

"I didn't realize men weren't all that far from the cave days. Around you, baby, I feel pretty primitive."

She flashed him a smile as she set aside the grater. "I don't mind you being primitive. I kind of like it."

She touched her breast, running her fingertip over the wet lace. The sight set him on fire all over again. It was an innocent gesture. She didn't know how to be a siren, but she was one naturally. He suppressed a groan and forced his mind back to the task at hand. To give himself something to do besides jump her, he took the finished bowl of potatoes, drained the water and replaced it with more cold water.

"Nonny is a great cook. I mean really, really good. Her food isn't the kind you find in a fancy restaurant, but it's the best I've ever had. I think she pours love into everything she cooks."

"The bread and soup, or whatever it was, was very good. I ate all of it. In small doses because when I'm not used to something, it can make me sick."

"Nonny would teach you cooking in a heartbeat, Cayenne. Pepper is learning, from what Wyatt tells me, so you could get in on those lessons and have some girl time."

There was a long silence. He looked up from beating the egg mixture. He already had the potatoes in the pan. She had gone very still. So still, he knew if it was dark and she was pressed against a wall, she'd be next to impossible to see. Like most of the GhostWalkers, she could change her skin color to mirror what was around her. She hadn't done that, but her eyes had gone from a clear vibrant green to multifaceted. He was beginning to recognize her signs of distress.

Immediately he made certain the flame was low enough and turned to her, one hand cupping her face, his thumb sliding under her jaw. "What is it, baby? We talk about things, remember? We have to do that for this to work. It's new territory for both of us."

Her gaze slid away from his. She studied her hands, her fingers twisting together. He put his other hand over hers to still her fingers. His thumb caressed the soft, vulnerable sweep of her jaw.

"Baby," he said softly. There was no response. He kept up the brushing strokes to soothe her. To let her know he had her back. "Cayenne, tell me what's upsetting to you about going to Nonny's and learning from her. I love this, the two of us, but honestly, I have limited knowledge of cooking. You don't have to learn, but if you wanted it, she's there and she would welcome you."

She remained silent for another long moment. Finally, *finally*, she lifted her gaze to his. Her tongue touched her lower lip, leaving a wet gleam that instantly drew his attention.

She sighed. "I can barely force myself to trust you, Trap. This. What we're doing, it terrifies me. I have no idea how to talk to anyone, what's polite and what isn't. I left all the talking to the men in the bar. I just laughed occasionally and murmured a word now and then. They were satisfied with that. It wasn't like with you, where I feel like I can ask you questions and you don't care if I screw everything up."

"Do you think Nonny would form some sort of judgment of you if you made a mistake?"

She shrugged. "It's her home. I wouldn't care, but she means something to you. I can tell she does. Wyatt too. The others. Even Pepper. I feel that in some way, because you are choosing me, I represent you. I don't want to make you look bad or silly or wrong for your choice in front of your friends."

Trap let out his breath slowly. He was putting a lot of pressure on Cayenne without realizing it. She really didn't have any experience with other people. She had no idea how to make small talk. She was good at taking cues from others, because she was extremely observant and she learned quickly, but she had to be a wreck inside.

"Baby, I love that you feel that way. I would never be embarrassed or upset over anything you did in front of my friends. Not ever. Nonny is the last person in the world to ever make a judgment on another human being. She's the perfect woman to help you learn the things you feel are necessary to be with me. I can teach you anything you want in the abstract, or sex, or even in the lab, but I'm not good with niceties. In fact, Draden, a close friend of mine, is always handing me books on manners."

"Really?"

He had no choice, he had to turn back and flip the potatoes and then pour the egg mixture into the skillet. "Yep. All the time. I could give a flying fuck about other people, but those people, Nonny, my team, Pepper and girls, they matter to me. But, Cayenne"—he turned back, looking her straight in the eyes, wanting her to see he meant exactly what he said—"*you're* my family. You're my woman. You're going to be my wife. You'll need to know the things Nonny can teach you, because out in the world, far from here, there are men with cameras and they will be all over us, the moment we step one foot outside the swamp. Sometimes they don't wait for that. Pictures of me command a lot of money and if anyone gets wind of you, that picture will be worth even more."

"I don't understand."

Of course she wouldn't know the first thing about gossip

magazines or the frenzy for stories and pictures on one of the world's most eligible bachelors. The burning question remained, why had he joined the service and why had he put himself in harm's way by training in the Special Forces? That alone was fodder for articles and speculation for months, years even.

"I'm just saying, honey." He pushed the eggs around, making certain to pull the pan before they were entirely cooked. He didn't like undercooked eggs, but he really detested overcooked ones. This method seemed to work. He pushed them around a little more, allowing them to continue to cook without the flame, just from the heat of the pan. "I'm not pushing you, but letting me take you to Nonny is a good idea."

"I'll think about it."

He caught her around her small waist and lifted her to the floor. "Sit at the table. The plates are in the cupboard along the wall there." They were in plain sight, but he wanted to give her a task to take her mind off meeting his friends. He needed a little more time to figure out how best to get her to a place where she felt comfortable with him and then with others. "Silverware is in the top drawer beneath the cupboard where the plates are. Grab a couple of the smaller glasses for orange juice as well."

He watched her moving in silence, her body swaying as she stood on her toes to reach for the plates, stretching all the way out. He nearly went to help her, but he knew that could be dangerous. The sight of her like that, her back to him, long hair swaying, caressing the curve of her shapely ass, her tiny tucked in-waist with just a bow around it, had him as hard as a rock all over again. He had to fight off the hunger in his cock.

She used silk, attaching it to the two plates and drawing them toward her. Her drag lines were strong, he knew that. Spider drag lines could be every bit as strong as the Kevlar used in their vests. She was adept at using silk. She pulled the plates to her, caught them and transferred them to her other hand so she could pull out the silverware. She used the same method to get the small glasses out of the cupboard.

He didn't have fancy. He hadn't thought about fancy. He should have. For her. His dinnerware wasn't fine china, more thick crockery that appealed to the man in him. She didn't seem to mind. She actually ran a finger over the plate a little reverently.

"These are beautiful, Trap. I've never seen anything like this."

He should have known. Fancy was all relative. She'd been fed nutritious rations, probably on a paper plate, nothing she could turn into another weapon. The crockery was stoneware, hand-cast and painted. He had big hands. He needed plates and glasses and mugs that didn't make him feel he would crush them if he wasn't thinking about it every second. "Glad you like them, babe," he said, as he put the eggs and hash browns on their plates. "When we're finished here, I thought we could head into New Orleans and pick you up some clothes. That way, if you want to return those camisoles and jeans you can, although I have to tell you, I like the camisoles."

She glanced up from pouring the orange juice and sent him a little smile. "That's a little scary too, Trap."

"Not when you're with me. You don't have to say or do a thing. We'll look at the clothes. Either of us likes something, you can try it on and we'll buy it."

"I don't have money, and I'm not taking yours." She sat down in her chair, lifting her chin at him, her face set in stubborn lines.

He stared across at her for a moment, and then slowly, his grin came. The smile started around his heart and just continued from there. "Baby, that would sound a lot more intimidating if you weren't so fucking cute sitting there with your chin on the table. You need a booster seat."

She glared at him.

"I'm just stating a fact."

"Very funny." She shifted, drawing her knees under her. "You aren't paying for me, Trap. I've read enough to know that's not how it works, so don't try to convince me otherwise."

He leaned across the table, holding her gaze, wanting her to know this was a point he wouldn't yield on. "I don't give a fuck what other people do in their relationships, Cayenne. *I'm* the man. *I* take care of my woman. I don't care if you make a million bucks spinning webs and selling them, *I* still take care of you. That's who I am. That's the man you're going to spend your life with. I pay. You let me. And you do it graciously."

"What do I give you to make things equal between us?"

His gaze moved over her face with swift impatience. "What you give me is everything I ask of you. Being here with me when you're scared out of your fucking mind. Trying to cook for me when you don't have a clue how. Wearing an apron and nothing else just because I ask you to. Following my commands when I tell you to touch yourself. Letting me leave my mark all over you because you knew it was important to me. Sitting on my face when it was frightening. Giving me the gift of watching you come apart with just my mouth on you. Sucking my cock and swallowing when you didn't have to, just to please me. Having a fucking brain and not being a nitwit so I'm not tempted to tape your mouth closed like I am with nearly every other woman I've . . ."

"I get it, Trap. Stop talking about your other women. I'll go into town with you, and you can buy me my own shoes. The ones I have are too big and I hate them. I have to stuff paper in the toes and they're so uncomfortable."

He scowled. "You should have told me right away."

"It's no big deal, but since you want to buy me something and you're getting all manly and growly and caveman about it, then shoes are what I need." She took a forkful of eggs tentatively. "I like these."

"Try the potatoes. Manly? Growly?" He poured approval into his voice. "Now you get it. That's me, baby, I'm the man and you concede in all things to your man."

She rolled her eyes, and he wondered just where she'd gotten that particular gesture or whether it just came naturally to her. He was fairly certain the eye roll meant she wasn't taking him all that seriously.

CHAPTER 10

⟨~~⟩

Cayenne moved closer to the protection of Trap's body. He was such a big man and fitting under his shoulder the way she did, his arm around her, she all but disappeared as they walked together toward the boutique he'd asked Wyatt about. She was aware of the two men flanking them, trying to give them space, which she was grateful for, but she didn't like that Trap thought they needed them. Draden and the man they called Gino gave her a half salute with their chins and then acted like they were busy noticing the sights.

She felt sick. She bunched her fingers in Trap's shirt with one hand and shoved her fingers into his back pocket with the other.

"You're trembling, baby," he said softly. "We're not going into battle."

"People are staring at us," she pointed out.

"You'll get used to it, Cayenne," he said, his stride even. He didn't look down at her, but he kept his arm tight around her, sheltering her with his body as much as possible.

"Why do we need your friends with us?" she asked.

"We've both got enemies," he said tersely.

She flinched at his tone. Ducked her head. Clearly he didn't want to talk. She hadn't wanted to come, and now he seemed a completely different man, his face an expressionless mask and his answers to any questions abrupt to the point of rudeness.

She sighed. "We don't have to do this, Trap. Really. I don't mind the shoes." She was wearing a pair of Wyatt's sister-in-law's jeans. She had to roll them up and they were a little snug through the hips and very loose around her waist. The top was pretty but again, tight across her breasts and too long for her. She didn't care what she was wearing, but walking even the short distance from the car to the shop she observed other women and they certainly were put together a lot better than she was.

"We have to do this." His eyes didn't meet hers, but instead, scanned the buildings and the rooftops above them.

Cayenne realized that he had her body tucked close to his in order to hide her face from a man across from them who had a camera. He was shielding her. *Shielding* her. From a camera. She also knew he hadn't brought Gino and Draden and any other members of the team to New Orleans because of a camera. That meant he was expecting trouble. She was not the type of woman to cower from danger. She might not like going out in public because she didn't like making mistakes and she hadn't had the time to study others around her to see what they did, but she refused to have Trap shoulder the danger.

She straightened her shoulders, composed her face and let go of the death grip she had on his shirt. If they needed Gino and Draden with them, it was probably for a reason. She inhaled sharply. She didn't have the best vision, that was true, but she had a really good sense of smell. The air brought information to the tiny, microscopic hairs on her body, and her brain processed data quickly.

There were several people on the street in spite of the

fact that it was closing in on four thirty. She realized that Trap had timed their shopping spree for the end of the shopping hours in order to make certain the sun would begin to go down by the time they finished. She recognized more than Draden's and Gino's scents. Malichai was close with his brother Mordichai, and if she wasn't mistaken, Ezekiel was on a roof across from them, probably with a sniper rifle. Trap was definitely expecting trouble.

"Tell me," she murmured. "And don't bother with explaining that you're the man and I'm the woman. I want to know what you think we're going to run into."

His eyes, glacier cold, shifted to her face. His arm tightened around her body, clamping her to his side, and one big hand cupped her face, pressing her head into him. He never missed a stride. Then his eyes were gone and he continued walking toward the row of shops.

You know better than to fuck up a team mission. You may have been trained as an assassin working alone, but Whitney would never neglect your training to that extent.

I had no idea you were running a mission, Cayenne pointed out. *Because you didn't mention it. I thought we were going to shop for shoes.*

He kept his hand on the side of her head, pressing her face into his side. *You don't face that camera. You know it's there, don't pretend you haven't seen it.*

You're worried about a camera?

Among other things. Just keep walking and acting like we're out on a date. We're going shopping for shoes.

She was silent. His voice was brusque, almost to the point of rudeness. There was no emotion. No soft whisper of "baby," no connection of any kind. Trap had shut down emotionally. She couldn't decide between hurt and anger at him. Since hurt was an alien emotion and one she didn't know what to do with, she settled for anger.

I may know better than to fuck up a team mission, but unless I'm told there is a mission, I can't possibly know that's what I'm doing by asking for information. And just so you know, I'm not hiding from cameras. If they get a picture of me, what's the difference? Whitney knows where I am. You wouldn't have brought an entire team in to prevent somebody from taking my picture. The termination order is still out on me. That's why the team is in place, not for some man with a camera who is not military.

Nice to know you have a brain. Try looking up at me and smiling.

Cayenne resisted the urge to just stop right there in the middle of the sidewalk. *Try looking down at me and smiling. You keep this up and I'll be sinking my teeth into your side and you'll go down like a ton of bricks.*

She was looking up at his face, and his lips twitched—the beginnings of a smile—but he got it under control and kept moving both of them until they were at the door of a shoe shop, Gino and Draden closing in behind them. Close. So close she could feel them almost against their backs. They didn't brush up against her, but still, she didn't like their close proximity. She felt trapped. Icy fingers slid down her spine and she felt the venom rising in reaction.

Trap opened the door to the boutique, took her through, and the instant they were inside, she felt the coiled tension in him ease. *Stay away from the windows. Keep to the interior of the shop.*

At last. Trap wanted to let out his breath and all but pushed Cayenne into the store. This was supposed to be his surprise for her. Shopping. Teaching her the thing women seemed to love. He'd wanted to give her that gift. Instead, he was giving her fucking hell. He'd planned to take two bodyguards, Gino and Draden—not for him—but for Cayenne. He knew there was a possibility of an enemy waiting for them. He'd known there was a possibility of a photographer as well. It wasn't as though the leeches didn't ferret out his whereabouts every moment of the day. Still, he thought he could control the situation enough to give his woman a great experience.

Ezekiel had insisted he go into town ahead of them and do recon. He had been assisting Cayenne into the vehicle when word came that a full assassination team seemed to be waiting in town for her to show.

He hadn't been prepared for the emotions choking him. Making it so he couldn't breathe. He couldn't think. He couldn't use his fucking brain. She'd done that to him. She'd shut down his ability to function when she was in danger. That black hole inside him, always at the edge of his vision, yawned wider, threatening to consume him. He was falling in before he knew it.

He'd known fear and anger when his father had shot Dru. He'd known fear when his aunt had been kidnapped and rage when she'd been thrown at his door like so much garbage. He hadn't known terror. He'd had four months of thinking about her night and day and now Cayenne was so far under his skin there was no getting her out and no surviving if something happened to her.

He didn't want her part of the team as the others insisted. He didn't want to take her into town and set her up as the bait so they could destroy Whitney's supersoldiers. He wanted to lock her away somewhere safe, a place where there was only the two of them.

That black hole inside of him was icy cold. It reached out to devour him. Swallow him whole. The roaring in his ears nearly drowned out the sounds around him. He was aware of Cayenne, acutely aware of her. Every movement. He knew he was making this trip a nightmare for her. All he had to do was talk to her. Explain. Say something. Anything.

He couldn't, not without losing himself in that icy black void. He had not allowed himself to live or feel after he'd lost his aunt. He held himself away from everyone so that he couldn't be destroyed, so that his father and his father's family wouldn't win. He felt nothing. He ate, he drank, he fucked and he worked, but he didn't feel—not until he'd gone through a wall and he'd seen a woman caged and under a termination order.

He watched her struggle to survive for four months when both of them knew she could come to him. He'd waited for her, and then finally, because he was obsessed he went after her. She'd given him so much. Coming to him and wrapping him in silk, giving herself to him when she was so afraid. Trying to cook for him. Giving him that as well. He hadn't known she was so deep. So entrenched. He hadn't known a man could feel like this.

He held himself together with a thread. That thread was nowhere near as strong as her silk. He had walked her into a trap. If he told her the truth, he knew what she'd do. He knew it with a certainty that had his belly tied into tight knots and that hellhole of pure cold yawning so wide. Cayenne would ditch them all and try to go after the assassination squad herself. She'd pit herself against them without hesitation, and he couldn't allow that.

Because of him, she was there in town, facing a termination squad. His team surrounded her, but if he made her a part of that, she'd be in even more danger. The photographer might get a picture of her before he was ready, before he had all of her protection in place and then she'd be in even more danger. Because of him. Just like his family.

If his father hadn't hated him so much, maybe they'd all still be alive. If his uncles hadn't hated him, maybe his aunt would be alive. If something happened to Cayenne, because of him, he knew there was no survival. Nothing left for him. He'd taken a chance without even knowing he was going to. He'd gotten in too deep before he'd ever realized he'd opened himself up for that.

He couldn't give her up. If he was any kind of a man, he would, but he couldn't. He didn't have that kind of strength. He could only see this through, this day where everywhere he turned there was danger to Cayenne and he was so paralyzed with fear for her that he couldn't do anything but hold himself together the only way he knew how—distancing himself from every emotion he had.

Cayenne let go of Trap the moment they entered the store, her gaze sweeping around the large room. Shelves of shoes and boots lined the walls. In the middle, dividing the room, were two rows of seats, the rows back to back. A man came out of the back and stopped dead, staring at her. He was significantly shorter than Trap and much more slender. He didn't have those wide shoulders or that thick, muscular chest, but she recognized that some might consider him good-looking. His face was too soft for her to think that, as was his body.

For Cayenne, Trap was the ultimate male and no one else seemed to compare to him. She loved that he towered over her. That his hands were big and his arms and chest were amazing and thick with ropes of muscle. She loved his tapered body where his ribs narrowed into his waist and hips. She loved that he was such a big man but could move in absolute silence and disappear into the dark in the same way a much smaller man could. His hair was amazing, always a bit unruly, thick like a lion's mane, and blond, in direct contrast to the clerk's dark short hair. His hair—and his tag said his name was Alain Daughtry—was spiked with some kind of hair product that made it stand straight up. His choice of hairstyles didn't inspire running one's hands through it, or curling fingers into it when his mouth was . . .

Stop.

A low, burning fury in Trap's mind shook her. She glanced up at his face. Totally expressionless. Eyes so cold they sent a chill through her, yet she could see a blue flame burning beneath the glacier there.

You do not ever picture another man's mouth between your legs. That's mine.

She burst out laughing. She couldn't help it. He sounded like he might throw her over his shoulder and march her right out of the store, as if Alain Daughtry, some clerk with the "ew" factor very much in evidence, could be a threat. She forgot about being angry or hurt and tucked her hand in the crook of his arm. She was beginning to suspect that Trap's bursts of jealousy hid something much deeper.

I was picturing your mouth between my legs and remembering how delicious it felt when I tunneled my fingers in your hair. I'm very fond of your hair.

He stared down at her for what seemed like forever. She couldn't look away, and she had the odd sensation of drowning.

You're seriously going to say something like that to me in the middle of a shoe shop with my boys not two feet away?

Another mistake. She sighed. She had no idea what she'd done wrong *again. Apparently honesty isn't what you're looking for, Trap. Maybe you'd better tell me the rules, because I'm totally lost.*

She brought her hand up to her hair in agitation, running her fingers through the red hourglass that rose and settled back into the thick black. Alain inhaled sharply, drawing her attention. His gaze was on her breasts. He actually licked his lips, and she could smell the testosterone flooding his body. The scent of musk rose, offending her.

She *detested* this trip. There was nothing remotely fun about shopping and if she never did it again, she would be quite happy.

"Can I help you?" Alain asked, hurrying over.

He moved close. Too close. Right into her personal space. She found it difficult to control the venom. She glanced up at Trap for guidance. He didn't look at her, but he caught her arm and pulled her in close, away from the clerk.

"My girl needs shoes. She wears a size five. I'd like to take a look at those ruby boots, the lace-up ones with the heels, those two pairs of heels." He indicated a black pair with red soles and a red pair with black soles. The red pair had a small black bow on the toe and straps that ran up the ankle, the

black peeking around the red. "Also a pair of hiking boots
and walking and running shoes. And"—Trap paused until he
got the clerk's full attention—"you can stop ogling my
woman. You deal with me. You talk only to me, and you don't
touch her. I'll try the shoes on her feet. You got that?"

His voice was low. Dangerous. So dangerous, the tone
sent another shiver down her spine. Still, the venom
retreated. She didn't have to protect herself from a slimy
man who couldn't control his lust when a female customer
came into his store. Alain took one look at Trap's face with
the lines of rough carved deep, then his gaze jumped to the
two men on either side of the door, not hiding what they
were. He nodded over and over and turned to scurry into
the back room.

"Sit there, Cayenne," Trap said. He gestured toward the
seat farthest from the windows and doors.

She sank into the chair and Trap knelt at her feet. He
removed the boot with the paper inside and rubbed his large
hand over her foot.

"You'll need stockings as well."

"I don't need the heels," she whispered, glancing toward
Draden and Gino. "I don't go anywhere I could wear them.
Just the hiking boots and running shoes."

*I like heels, and I'm going to like them on you. You can
wear them for me when we're alone. Later, you'll need them.*

Need them for what? She wasn't going to ask. She was
done asking questions. She didn't understand what he meant,
but it didn't matter, because she was never going to repeat
this experience again if she could help it. She just wanted it
over with. She wasn't going to protest again. In fact, she was
going to sit quietly, endure the torture, and the moment she
was back in her home, she was going to her little cave, surrounded by her webs and curl up and just be alone where
she could breathe. And that would be after she kicked Trap
very hard in the shins.

His hands were warm on her feet, his fingers massaging

her calves and heel while they waited. Trap was such a mixture of contradictions that she felt confused, unable to read him. He looked cold. He *felt* cold. But his touch was completely at odds with both those things.

She didn't look at him. She didn't look at the two men standing on either side of the door. She kept her gaze fixed on the plate glass window, looking across the street to the man fitting a zoom lens to his camera. He seemed excited. Very excited. His gaze hadn't left the shop since they'd gone in it, and she watched him as often as possible.

Alain returned with boxes of shoes and set them down beside Trap. "I didn't realize who you were, Mr. Dawkins. It's an honor to have you in my store."

"*Doctor* Dawkins," Trap corrected, without looking at the man. "And put your cell phone away. You take a picture of my woman or me, one of my men will remove your cell phone from you. If you've already taken a photograph without my consent or knowledge, you'd better delete it now, because if I see that shit on the Internet, or in a magazine, my men will come back to your store and fuck you up. Do we understand each other?" Trap turned his head and met the clerk's eyes.

Alain stumbled back, his face losing color. "You don't understand. You come into my store and I get a photo, I can advertise big with that. Makes me exclusive."

"You snuck a picture from the back room?" Trap's voice was mild. His hands continued to open boxes and pull out heels even as the room seemed to go down in temperature and an icy menace invaded.

He slipped the black heel onto Cayenne's foot, over the small little nylon socks Alain had tossed down with the boxes. The shoe fit like a glove. There was a small silence. The tension in the room increased. Draden stirred, and Alain's gaze jumped to him. Trap put the second shoe on Cayenne and held out his hand as he got to his feet.

Alain whipped out his cell phone. "I only got a picture of your back. It wasn't a good angle," he confessed hastily and showed it to Trap. "I'm deleting it now." He continued to hold out his phone so all three men could see he'd removed the picture.

I take it you're some big deal. Somebody worth photographing. She kept her voice neutral when she felt hurt all over again. He had known she didn't want to shop for shoes or anything else. He also knew it was difficult for her not knowing what to expect. He still hadn't made it easy by disclosing information to her. He hadn't even told her that much—that he was known in the outside world.

She didn't know why she considered the teams invisible for the most part—like she was. People who lived in the shadows. She needed to rethink giving herself to this man. She didn't know him. She'd let herself be carried away by the way he'd treated her, the kindness and of course, the way he made her feel physically and emotionally. No one had ever really seen her until he had, but that didn't mean she knew him. He certainly didn't know her.

Still, she squared her shoulders as she stood up in the high heels; she was a warrior and no one could take that away from her. Not Whitney. Not Trap. Certainly not any enemy. What the hell? The shoes *killed* her sense of balance. She stood still, feeling them out. Finding the perfect way to stack her core over them so she could walk without falling. She let go of Trap's hand, not looking at him. Not wanting to look at him. He'd put her in this position, and for reasons only he knew, he'd abandoned her.

She took a cautious step, trying to look as if she'd been wearing heels all of her life. She had a strong core and a good sense of balance. Once she'd calculated that with the way her foot was tilted, the height of the heel bordered right on the edge of her ability to keep from stumbling, she knew if she walked slow she could pull it off. If the heel had been one inch shorter, it would have been easier. Trap could do the calculations as easy as she could and he would have known that when he chose the heels.

Thankfully she made it across the room, walking to the back shelf rather than toward the windows. When she sat down, again without looking at Trap, he removed the heels, handed Alain both the black and red pairs and proceeded to try the boots on her. Thankfully the heels were lower and much more stable. She liked the way they looked, they were comfortable, but still felt heavy on her feet. She didn't voice her opinion, nor did Trap ask for it. He handed the boots to Alain.

The running shoes were next. Trap put them on her, this time after demanding socks. The shoes were much more comfortable than the heels, although she had to admit, even with the small heel on the boots, she liked them the best. Money exchanged hands. Trap purchased both pairs of heels, the boots, hiking boots, and two pairs of the running shoes along with multiple pairs of socks.

Relieved that it was over, Cayenne didn't say a word as Trap put the shoes on her feet and had Alain put her old boots in with the packages. She watched as Gino went through the door first, did a sweep of the street and then nodded. They followed, Trap's arm around her, clamping her to his side, one hand shielding her face. Draden brought up the rear, packages in one hand.

Instead of turning back toward their SUV, Gino led the way down the street toward more shops.

"What are we doing?" Cayenne asked.

"Shopping." Trap's voice was clipped.

She glanced up at his face. No expression. Eyes as cold as ice. He looked tough. Chiseled. Gorgeous. His blue eyes were so striking and his hair unruly, a darker shadow just beginning to appear along his jaw. There was something about the way he moved, something fluid and catlike that appealed to her. She loved the ripple of muscles beneath his tight tee, the way his shoulders were so wide and his hand, the one covering her face, actually was big enough to shield it.

"You said shoes," she reminded, eyeing the little fancy boutique he was heading for with distaste. She wanted to be back in the swamp where she could breathe, smell information in the air and see what was coming at her. Here, in the city, everything was too close. There were too many cars, too many people, buildings too close together with little alleyways and places an enemy could hide.

She kept her gaze on Trap's face as she made her protest. He didn't so much as glance down at her, not even to show her his mask.

"You said shoes. I said shopping. You need clothes. We're getting them."

His voice was clipped. Almost irritated. Cayenne didn't bother to protest further. It wouldn't get her anywhere, and at least inside the shop, they were off the street and more protected. The man across from them followed, snapping pictures with his camera, clearly elated, and that bothered her more than anything else. She could accept enemies. More than likely, the enemies were hers, not Trap's. But if he was famous, if there was a reason for the camera and he hadn't told her, that was wrong.

Just out of curiosity, are you on some kind of medication? Or maybe you suffer from a disorder such as bipolar? I've read of these things.

Why would you think that?

She knew he was looking down at her, but she refused to look up. *I can't imagine.*

An older woman with glasses hanging around her neck like a necklace hurried over to them the moment they entered the stores. Her high heels were on the very edge of being too high, but she walked without the least bit of a problem, as if she'd been born in them. She looked elegant with her very sophisticated suit. Her skirt was just below the knee and houndstooth with a matching short jacket. She wore a black silk shell beneath the jacket. Her nametag said *Mrs. March* on it, and somehow, even the nametag looked elegant on her.

"Dr. Dawkins, I didn't realize you were in town. Welcome to my store." She beamed at him, not bothering to pretend she didn't know who he was.

"I recently purchased a home here," Trap said easily. "Out near the Fontenots' place. Nonny told me you were the one to come to for help. My fiancée needs clothes, jeans, shirts, sweaters, dresses and underwear."

Mrs. March widened her smile as her gaze swept Cayenne. Trap loosened his hold on her so she could step away from him, squaring her shoulders and lifting her chin, determined to get through this nightmare as well. She had no idea what to do and Trap wasn't giving her guidance, but the woman seemed to know what she was doing.

"You're very small. I've got some things in your size, but a limited variety. I can special order anything you need." Mrs. March spoke directly to Cayenne.

Cayenne took a breath and forced a smile. "Thank you, I appreciate that." Her voice came out low, but it came out. She didn't glance up at Trap. She refused to rely on him for any kind of cues. He wasn't giving them, and Gino and Draden were facing the street, Gino by the door, Draden closer to them. Closer to Trap, she noted, almost as if he were Trap's bodyguard. She knew Mrs. March noted that, and it only served to make Trap more important to her.

The saleswoman bustled around, pulling out soft blue jeans and little camisoles. Sweaters were thinner and softer even than the other jeans. The sweaters were pullover, one that fell off the shoulder and another that clung to her curves. Mrs. March added tank tops and underwear, beautiful little sexy bras and lacy thongs and boy shorts that Trap indicated without consulting Cayenne.

She noted that Mrs. March remained professional at all times. She didn't try to be overly friendly. She didn't fawn on Trap. She didn't even pull out her cell phone and try to get a picture of him. Most of her conversation was directed at Cayenne. Trap did stay close to her, and twice when she couldn't think of an answer to Mrs. March's question, he stepped in smoothly and answered for her, making it seem as though he was just part of the conversation.

The amount of clothing Trap purchased was alarming. She didn't know if she could wear all those clothes, let alone *where* she would wear them. Still, she remained silent, not even protesting telepathically to him. She wanted to go home, to her lair. She needed to be alone and think about this side of Trap. This person who wasn't at all what she thought him to be.

It wasn't that he was cruel, like her guards. He hadn't abandoned her—although it felt a little as if he had. It was his aloofness. He was so withdrawn and emotionally gone. That was it. He was without any emotion whatsoever. He could turn it off so easily, while she struggled with unfamiliar feelings in an unfamiliar setting.

Don't, Cayenne. Let it go until we're home.

Obviously, she'd been broadcasting her distress, and poor him—she was upsetting him. *This was one of the most difficult things I've ever done and you're supposed to have my back. You don't. Not. At. All.*

Damn it, let's get through this and we'll talk at home.

She didn't deign to look at him. She decided if he could show no emotion toward her, or anything else, she could do the same. She was very polite with Mrs. March, mainly because the woman was the consummate professional and made shopping easy. Unlike Alain, she didn't get any perverted vibes off of her at all. Mrs. March liked doing her job. She enjoyed helping others and she knew clothes. She had confidence in her ability to see what would look good on others and she took satisfaction in making others look good.

Mrs. March insisted on her trying on a short dress with a clingy skirt, emphasizing her curves. She felt a little ridiculous coming out of the dressing room, barefoot, no panties, the dress backless so that she felt the swish of her long hair slithering down her back and pooling in the curve of her buttocks. The material and the silk of her hair felt— decadent. Her heart actually pounded when she stepped in front of Trap. Waiting. In spite of everything, hoping, maybe even needing a reaction.

She got none. No heat flaring in his eyes. No warmth pouring into his mind. He was completely removed from her. From the dress that had felt sexy but now fell flat. She wanted it off. She would have turned to rush back to the dressing room, but he stirred, held up a finger and moved it in a circle, indicating she turn around.

"Beautiful." Mrs. March breathed the word. "Truly beautiful. That dress is definitely made for you, Cayenne."

A little bell over the door tinkled, and Gino stepped in front of her before she could see who had walked in. The air in the room thickened. Became almost too dense to breathe. Mrs. March coughed. Trap slid in between Gino and Cayenne, a smooth move, one she barely comprehended. She saw Draden, out of the corner of her eye, move into position on the other side of Trap.

Cayenne didn't like being boxed in. She really didn't like having her sight cut off. She felt the danger in the room. She smelled the man who had entered. Heard his footfalls. Light. A soldier, from his precise, measured steps. She shifted to the right, outside the pocket Trap and Gino had created.

Don't you fucking move. Trap snapped the command.

She ignored him. She wasn't a woman to be bossed around and she didn't accept his authority or his protection. She didn't accept any of this. She was in a stupid dress, hoping to make Trap notice her like some little kid looking for attention. The sight of her hadn't changed that glacier in his eyes, hadn't aroused the least bit of interest, so she'd be damned if she was going to have him look after her.

She ignored his warning and took another step away from him, letting the newcomer see his target. She spotted him instantly because she knew by the vibrations in the room exactly where he was. He was built like a boxer. His face was scarred, his eyes showing nerves, but they locked on her instantly. Flared with excitement. For a moment, she thought he'd draw his weapon. He looked as if he might.

Mrs. March moved, walking right up to him, looking classy in her high heels and her welcoming smile. "May I help you?"

Trap's fingers settled like a shackle around Cayenne's wrist. He jerked her to him so hard she actually stumbled. Already in fight mode, she nearly sank her teeth into his wrist, but she was off balance and his other hand caught her hair in a tight fist, yanking her head back and away from his arm.

Are you fucking nuts? You're going to paralyze me with our enemy a few feet away? He nearly shook her, but instead, he walked her backward, using her hair and his body along with his vise-like grip on her wrist to take her to the dressing room. *Change fast. He's the scout for his team. We aren't going to war in a dress shop, or even here in the city where someone else can get hurt.*

She complied, mostly because she was angry with herself that her first instinct was to bite, to take him down because she was in unfamiliar territory with an enemy who clearly had come to terminate her. She had to get away from Trap and the others. If she did, she could lead the man and his team away from them. Trap would be furious, but she really didn't care. He had set this entire day in motion and clearly knew ahead of time that the threat to her was viable. *He hadn't told her.*

Trap stepped into the dressing room as she slid the dress off her shoulders and allowed it to slither to the floor. She wore nothing under it but her skin. Shocked that he walked in on her, she stepped back because he gave her no choice.

His gaze moved over her, and this time she caught a hint of possession, or arousal, she wasn't certain which or both before it was gone and his eyes were ice again.

He caught up her camisole and thrust it into her hands. *Don't you even think about ditching the team.*

You knew they were waiting for me to show up in town, didn't you? She pulled on her jeans and the camisole without looking at him again. Furious. Spider furious. The venom was close. She actually thought about injecting him, rolling him in silk and leaving him there in the fitting room. His team would never leave him unprotected.

It was logical. They knew you didn't have clothes or food. Sooner or later, they figured you would have to come for supplies. I sent a couple of the boys in earlier to scout around. They spotted John Butler. We all know him. He flunked out of the program right before we all were approved. So yeah, I knew. I also knew you'd want to go after them yourself, and that just isn't going to happen.

She sank down onto the beautifully appointed chair and put on her socks and then her shoes, grateful they weren't the boots that had been too big for her. *You didn't think I had the right to know?*

I don't give a damn whether or not you had the right, Cayenne. You aren't alone in this anymore. You're with me. That means you stay safe and you become part of the team.

She stood up, close to him. Deliberately close. He didn't move back like she expected. Like he should have. The venom was there. So ready. One motion was all it would take, lean into him and bite. She forced air through her lungs, trying to tamp down the hurt that was far more dangerous than the anger.

"But I wasn't made part of the team, was I, Trap? I'm the bait, not a member of your team. You don't accept me, so why would your friends? Move aside. I want to leave, and you don't have the right to stop me."

"Baby." He spoke aloud as well. There was the faintest

humor in his voice. "I know you think you're holding all the cards here, but you're not. That's all the warning I'm going to give you. I'm a GhostWalker, the same as you. I'm enhanced, the same as you. I know what weapons you have. You don't know the first thing about mine."

She studied his face. He wasn't in the least bit afraid of her. He knew she was angry and hurt, but he wasn't worried. "Fine. Let's just get out of here. Don't bother paying for the clothes. I won't need them."

"Stop being angry. You know once we're home we can have this out. Not here. This isn't the time and it isn't the place. I want you alive and I want every member of my team alive."

"I said I'm ready to go." She went to move past him.

His arm blocked her. "There is an assassination squad in town. They have a sniper on the roof."

"No doubt Ezekiel has already lined him up in his sights."

"He might miss."

"Ezekiel doesn't miss," she said. "If he did, you wouldn't have him up on the roof. He's always the backup. Always. He's your go-to man." Even as she let him know she knew what was going on, she still waited for him to step through the door first.

He didn't. Not right away. Instead, he caught her chin in his fingers and forced her head up. "We'll go home and sort this out. You aren't taking off. You gave me your word. Did you forget that?"

She had forgotten, which was shocking to her. She wasn't used to interacting with others and she had committed herself to him. She'd made that her choice. She didn't know the first thing about relationships or men. She only knew what she did and didn't like. She loved the way he treated her when they were alone and detested the cold, remote way he treated her in front of his team. She didn't understand it. When she didn't understand something, she was wary of it.

"I had forgotten," she admitted honestly. "I don't like this, Trap. Not at all."

He was silent, his eyes, still glacier-cold, on her face. Chilling her to the bone. Right through the bone to the marrow. She actually shivered. He was so removed she wasn't certain he was the same man.

"I don't like who you are right now." She had no idea how to soft-soap it. Maybe she didn't even want to. She didn't believe she was striking out at him, although she was hurt, but those were her honest feelings. She *didn't* like who he was.

Something flickered in his eyes. Deep. Beneath the blue glacier. Something she couldn't quite catch but she wished she had. "That's too bad, baby, because this is me. This is how I keep it together when my woman is in danger and I've allowed her to become a target to draw the fuckers out. This is who I am when I'm in public. You can't take that, Cayenne, I guess we need to know that now."

There it was, her out.

He shook his head and caught her chin, forcing up her face, so her eyes met his. "That's not an out. That's we'll fix this when we get home."

Cayenne sighed and held herself silent, instead of telling him to go to hell like she should. She caught a glimpse of something behind the ice in his eyes. More, and she hated to admit it to herself, the pull between them was so strong, even when he was a jerk beyond all comprehension, the fact that he confessed to her in his not-so-nice way that she was his woman and he had to "keep it together" while she was in danger. *That* she could understand. When a person had enhanced physical components that made them lethal, they had to be especially careful when something upset that. More than anyone else, she understood that.

Cayenne nodded her head. "We'll talk about it at the factory," she conceded, not giving him anything else. She couldn't. The hurt ran deep, and she hadn't expected that.

"At *home*." He bit the word out between his immaculate, straight white teeth.

She couldn't look away from the ice in his eyes, afraid if she couldn't pull her gaze away, she'd be frozen from the inside out. Very slowly she nodded her head. "I don't know what a home is, Trap, but yes, there, where we sleep."

The moment she uttered those words, she knew she'd made a mistake. His expression didn't change, but beneath the ice, the same flicker of emotion came and went, but for her, deep inside the very core of her, she remembered the feel of his mouth on her most intimate parts. The feel of his most intimate part deep in her mouth. Her feminine sheath pulsed. Spasmed. Warm liquid heated the junction of her legs. She forced her body to remain absolutely still so the squirm wouldn't give her away.

Trap's eyes moved over her face and again, there was a hint of possession, but something else was there, stroking at her skin. At the hurt. Like a soothing caress. Abruptly he leaned down and scooped up the dress, bunching it in his hands. "Let's go. I have to pay for these."

She opened her mouth to protest, but he shook his head and stepped out of the fitting room, looking around. The store was empty other than his teammates. "You're clear right now. Stay away from the windows."

She stood at the back of the store while he went up front and paid. She watched him the entire time. Not once did his expression change with Mrs. March as she gamely tried to engage him in conversation. He simply didn't answer a single comment, so in the end, the clerk fell silent as well.

Gino faced the front of the store and Draden stayed close to Trap, close enough to protect him if there was trouble. She might be the one a team was sent to terminate, but Trap's team members were determined to keep him alive. That made her feel a little better. She didn't want any of them getting hurt on her behalf.

Once again, as they went to leave the store, Gino stepped out first. Trap moved in close to her and went to circle her waist with his arm. She sidestepped away from him, thinking she was out of reach, but he had long arms and he caught her hip, preventing her from stepping out of the boutique.

Wait for me. Ezekiel and Gino have to clear the streets first.

CHAPTER 11

———❧———

"Where are they going to hit us?" Trap asked, the cell on speaker so they could all hear. "Most likely places."

Not *if*, but *are*. Trap knew the termination squad would try for her. There was no way to get out of the vehicle and lead the men away, but still, maybe Trap would see reason. "Trap," Cayenne began.

He held up his hand for silence, not looking at her. Cayenne sighed and stared out the window. She was either part of his team or she wasn't. It appeared she wasn't. He didn't even want to hear what she had to say. She knew his team went into war zones, the hottest zones possible, but that didn't negate the fact that she'd taken on several of Whitney's teams of supersoldiers. She knew how they thought. What they would try. She was more familiar with them than they were.

"There's a bend about three miles from you, the curve is sharp and the swamp closes in on either side. It's away from traffic and a perfect place to hit you. I'm going to come to you and try to get in behind them with Joe, Diego and Rubin," Wyatt's voice intoned over the cell.

Cayenne didn't know Joe or the others, but she assumed they were more of Trap's team members. She didn't care what Trap said, or how many times he held up his hand for silence. Her heart beat wildly, because she *knew*. She just knew. "You can't do that, Wyatt," she said, unable to help herself. "They'll expect you to come to our aid. I can guarantee they've got at least four, maybe five others ready to hit your house and go after the girls. We won't need help. We've got more manpower than you do."

To her surprise, Trap didn't try to silence her. Mordichai, driving, slowed the vehicle and pulled to the side. Immediately, Gino and Draden climbed out. Gino stood on the side step and hung on to the passenger door. Draden moved to the back and stood on the fender. Ezekiel slipped into the swamp.

"Roger that," Wyatt said. "We'll handle them here."

"They have a kind of armor built into their bodies," Cayenne continued. "Braden and Whitney tried to duplicate the webbing of a spider woven tight and injected it onto their bones. It didn't work, so he used a liquid metal. That gave them an inside armor, but it also somewhat distorted their bodies and they don't live long because he revved up their systems. They run on adrenaline. They're fast, really, really fast. Don't be deceived by their bulk. They'll keep coming at you."

"I've fought them before," Wyatt reminded. "They were difficult to kill."

"I remember. Go for the throat. You have to be precise when you do. There isn't that much on them that's vulnerable. Inside the mouth. The eyes. The throat is the best bet. Do you have a sniper?"

"Diego has one of the longest shots recorded, over a mile in a wind. He'll do," Wyatt said. "He thinks Ezekiel outshoots him, but they're close."

"Ongoing argument," Mordichai said. "Those two don't like it and give us the bird whenever we have it, which makes it all the more fun."

Cayenne instantly recognized the easy camaraderie. She'd never had that. She wished she had, but then, she wasn't certain she'd know what to do with it if she did. Being so close to so many people was difficult for a prolonged period of time, especially in the close confines of the vehicle.

"Make it a throat shot. Sometimes they use guards in their mouths, woven webs that fit in like a mouthpiece. Same with eye covers. If they're wearing that, the throat is your only bet. They tried using shirts and wraps, but they couldn't produce enough silk. Orb spiders working night and day, millions of them, couldn't produce it. Braden and Whitney . . ." She trailed off, one hand going to her own throat in a defensive position.

She became aware of eyes on her. Every man, even those outside the SUV, was watching her. She swallowed hard, trying to push memories away. The door in her mind yawned wide and threatened to pull her into that nightmare.

Baby. Trap said it softly into her mind. Intimately.

There he was when she didn't want him there. Not then. Not when the nightmares were pushing in. He had to stay removed from her. Remote. Not the Trap she knew. The other one. The ice-cold jerk.

Don't. Not now.

She knew she sounded like she was choking, because she was. She couldn't pull her hand from her throat, not even when she knew all of the men with their piercing eyes saw her fingers trembling.

Trap shifted subtly, but his bulk blocked her body from the others. His hand slipped over hers, fingers curling around her throat, over her hand, warm and strong. *Whatever they did to you, baby, know that they can't touch you now. It's over. They won't get their hands on you. You aren't alone this time. You aren't locked up.*

She nodded, forcing air through her lungs. Trying to close the door in her mind that had cracked open so the nightmare could spill out. Trap was intelligent. She could weave silk.

He had to know—or at least guess—what they had tried to take from her. He couldn't know how painful those sessions had been, pinned like an insect to a table, pierced with needles while men laughed cruelly and made fun of her. She let her lashes sweep down to veil her eyes, trying to hide the terror and agony from Trap. She didn't want him to know the things they'd said about her. What she was—not human— a monster.

They always shot her full of a drug so she couldn't move. She could barely breathe, but they kept her aware. Always aware. For a moment she couldn't breathe. Strangely, it was Trap's hand over hers, his large palm completely enveloping hers, so that the pads of his fingers were against her skin, his thumb sliding along her jaw.

"Thanks for the tips, Cayenne," Wyatt said. "I want updates the moment you take out the team," he added to the others.

"We'll need cleaners," Trap reminded. "We can't have bodies lying around in the swamp. Reporter hanging around."

"Has he followed you?"

"That he has. He's hanging back, but he's pulled over. Draden's going to incapacitate him right before we move out again."

Cayenne swung her head around, looking out the back window. She'd missed that. She didn't miss much, but being inside the vehicle surrounded by Trap's team was difficult for her and she hadn't been as alert as she should have been.

Trap swept the pad of his thumb along the vulnerable line of Cayenne's jaw. He leaned close to her, giving her his warmth. His body's shelter and protection. *You okay now, baby?*

He'd seen the door in her mind, that glimpse of hell. He had his own door, his own hell, but the thought of Cayenne's small body pinned to a table, needles holding her down in the way an entomologist would pin an insect, filled his throat with bile. His stomach churned, knotted, a terrifying rage building that needed to be kept under the glacier of ice protecting the world around him from the havoc he could wreak.

Her gaze came back to his. Caught there. He held his breath. She was beautiful. Exotic. He couldn't imagine that other men hadn't seen her the way he did. She might be pint-sized, but she had lush curves perfectly proportioned so that along with the hourglass in her hair and embedded in the tight curls covering her mound, her figure was a perfect little hourglass.

He still had the taste of her on his tongue and he knew that would never go away. Exotic like she was. Ruby lips, full and inviting, it was difficult to keep from taking advantage right there, knowing she was hurting, especially with the taste of her filling his mouth. He wanted this over, wanted her safe. Facing her going into battle with them sickened him, but at least he could control this, be there to look out for her, instead of her trying to do it all herself.

I need to know, Cayenne. We can abort if you aren't ready for this.

She shook her head. He felt her take a breath. Felt it in her throat, the pulse beating there. Her eyes were steady, all that green going multifaceted. He found his mouth curving into a smile in spite of everything. She was ready. His little warrior woman. Still, the knots in his stomach didn't ease and the terror that gripped him below all of his icy resolve was far too close.

"Ezekiel's in position," Gino reported. He slapped the top of the SUV. "Let's get it done."

Mordichai glanced back at Trap. Trap nodded. "Take us close. Gino will give the word."

Draden leapt from the fender and disappeared into the swamp to their right. She lost sight of him almost immediately. Mordichai set the vehicle in motion.

"We're just leaving him?" Cayenne asked, astonished.

Trap shrugged. "He'll catch up. He knows where we'll be, and Draden can flat out run faster than we can travel in this thing through the swamp." He smiled down at her. "He isn't small and compact like you, but he has the heart and muscle and lung capacity to travel at extraordinary speeds for distances too. You wouldn't think anyone with his muscle mass could run like he does, but although he's built like a sprinter and has explosive speed in a sprint, he can cover distances just as fast."

Trap sighed. "Whitney knew what he was doing by the time he created his fourth team. He made far less mistakes as he continued his experiments, learning from each of the teams and members with problems. He corrected most of the problems, but by enhancing them even more physically, he created a few new problems."

Cayenne nodded. "Most of his 'mistakes' were terminated, but not all."

"The men are more violent, which I'm certain Whitney was going for, but taking into account our already aggressive personalities, that was a major mistake. My team tends to keep to themselves and police the more dangerous members ourselves."

"Draden runs because he has to run," Cayenne guessed quietly, accurately. "It takes the edge off. I've seen him out in the swamp. I spin silk. I go into the swamp and create masterpieces. I can lose myself in the art and the work and it helps."

He'd given her pieces of his team, and Cayenne gave him something back. None of them had to be embarrassed, because she understood. She might not be a member of their actual team, but she was a GhostWalker. She understood the differences that set them apart. He hoped she would come to identify with them.

Gino slapped his hand on the roof, and Mordichai instantly pulled the vehicle into the swamp beneath trees. Gino was gone instantly, melting into the thick foliage as if it had devoured him. Trap, the other men and Cayenne slipped out in silence.

I'm better out there. Cayenne indicated the denser woods.

Trap didn't like it. There was saw grass, poisonous snakes, alligators, and on top of that, it could be marshy in places. He reached out before he could stop himself and wrapped his fingers around her upper arm. His fingers met his palm and his heart plunged. She never quite appeared as small as she was. On some level her size added to his need to protect her. Or maybe it had nothing to do with that and everything to do with the emotion tightening his chest.

Cayenne halted and looked up at him. For a moment, Trap swore the entire world faded away. He only saw her face—that beautiful face framed with that waterfall of shiny black hair. He loved the way the red hourglass nestled deep almost unseen and then when she turned her head, the small movement set the red on fire. He drank her in, once more tasting her on his tongue.

Kiss me. If he was going to let her go into battle, he was going to do it knowing she knew she had a reason to come back to him. He'd been a bastard, the one he'd perfected over the years, and she was confused and hurt by his behavior. He couldn't explain, not even to himself, because he didn't dare look too close at what he feared most. But he needed her to kiss him. To give him that.

Her green eyes went darker, even more brilliant and vibrant than they already were. Her gaze shifted to the men disappearing into the brush and trees.

Doesn't matter if they see, Cayenne. You're my woman. You go into battle, you go anywhere away from me, I want you to kiss me.

He needed that from her. He needed to carry her taste with him, her scent, the essence of her so that he could keep her safe in his own way.

She didn't protest. She looked confused and a little vulnerable. He liked the look a lot. He would take that look with him, hold it close, because his woman was adorable. Fucking beautiful. Lethal as hell, and that only made it all the more sweet. He held on to that thought. She was lethal. Dangerous. Capable.

Cayenne stepped close to him, one hand sliding up his chest, her head tipped up. He cupped her face. Pure beauty. All his. His thumb slid over her soft skin. He swore the pad of his thumb melted into her, she was that soft.

Trap didn't waste any more time. He took her mouth. He did it long. Hard. Pouring himself into her. Taking her into him. He used his mouth to tell her the things he couldn't say to her. When he lifted his head and rested his forehead against hers, both of them were breathing ragged.

Stay safe, baby, he whispered.

You too.

Cayenne waited for his fingers to loosen around her arm. She was trying desperately to get her wits about her again. Trap had just kissed her senseless. He was back to calling her "baby" in that soft, caressing voice that felt like a touch on her skin or a brand deep inside of her. He didn't speak to her almost the entire time in town on their shopping expedition, and he'd clamped her to his side like she was some appendage he had to guard. Now, he kissed her good-bye and allowed her to go up against a team of Whitney's supersoldiers. He was the most confusing person she'd ever met.

She hurried into the brush, making herself as small as possible. Her bones weren't like other bones. She knew that. When she was lying pinned to the table, she heard them discussing how her bones were soft and she could flatten herself and twist into impossible positions in order to get into tiny places. Her palms ached and she curled her fingers over the tiny scars in her flesh. In her bones. Where they'd pinned her to the table.

When Whitney had the labyrinths built that she was taken to in order to fight her way out, in the later mazes he had included smaller and smaller spaces for her to fold herself into. She understood they had cameras and filmed her moving through the maze, but the most she could do was destroy the soldiers when she found them. Still, she knew they watched as the supersoldiers tried to kill her and she was forced to defend her own life.

She moved with confidence through the heavy brush. Few branches or leaves touched her skin. When she needed, she drew them away from her with silk so there would be no whisper of movement. The soldiers were enhanced and, aside from their armor that often distorted their bodies, they had similar, and oftentimes, mirrored gifts that GhostWalkers had. She couldn't take a chance that one or more had enhanced hearing.

Cayenne didn't try to find the team of GhostWalkers deploying in the swamp. She knew how to fight the soldiers, and if she could cut down the odds before Trap was in place, she'd be happy. She didn't like that he was so big. He moved in silence, but he presented a large target. She couldn't think about that because it messed her head up. She didn't want to envision him in danger at all. If she did, her heart pounded, her mouth went dry and chaos reigned in her mind.

She began to lay threads of silk through the trees and bushes, thin, so thin they were nearly invisible. The sun had set and without that brightness, her silk blended into the surroundings. Little feelers, ones that would warn her when a soldier was on the move. She kept the strands low, so if broken, they wouldn't be felt.

She moved up into the trees. It was a favorite way for some of the soldiers to travel, and definitely their marksmen would go high in order to try to kill Trap and his team. She would be their first target. They were looking for her to carry out the termination order. If they managed to get any member of Trap's team, that would be a bonus. Whitney probably had cameras on all his soldiers to record the fight. She hoped she could prevent him from seeing a thing.

As Cayenne continued to spin silk through the branches,

she felt the first light tremor on one of her feelers. Instantly she crawled down the tree trunk, headfirst, moving in silence, following the thread back to the danger. In those few moments going down the tree, she pushed all humanity from her mind and became pure spider.

Long ago, when she'd been first pitted against enemies trying to kill her, she realized that allowing the huntress to come to the forefront, to think of herself only as a spider, was the only way she could kill and survive intact. If she thought too much about what she was doing, knowing she was hunting human beings, she couldn't have done it, but they were *enemies*, sent to kill her. That reduced the battle to kill or be killed. *That*, the huntress could cope with.

Her enemies never hesitated. Each and every one of them hunted her through the labyrinth with only one intention. She read people. She felt the cruelty in them, or the indifference—or most especially, revulsion. They were eager to kill her. Every single one of them. She hadn't done anything to them nor did she want to harm them in any way, but if she wanted to live, she had to make the decision to kill. Whitney had forced that on her. That choice. Now he sent another team for the same thing.

She moved through the trees, following the feeler. The closer she got to the soldier, the more she knew about him. Her senses reached out along the silk. He was average height. Not nervous. If anything, he was giving off supremely confident vibrations. That gave her pause and she sank down exactly where she was. Anyone going into battle, even seasoned veterans, were cautious when facing enemies like the pararescue team—all enhanced soldiers. The termination team had to have been briefed on what they were up against. One of them had come into the little boutique and obviously recognized the men inside. They knew. So why would he be so confident?

She wasn't careless and she didn't have anything to prove. She could take her time and assess the situation. The soldier had disturbed the silken thread, but he hadn't moved. *He hadn't moved.* He knew the feeler was there. He had to know. That meant they were looking for her silk. Which meant he was the bait to draw her out. Their sniper had to be in the trees somewhere with a clear line to the soldier's position.

Cayenne began to move again, this time circling around behind the soldier. She couldn't get to the sniper. He could be yards away, but that didn't mean she couldn't take down the bait. There was no whisper of sound as she used a rabbit trail to make her way behind the silk.

She spotted the soldier, his back to her, his automatic weapon in his hands, ready to use. He kept sweeping the area alertly and several times he nodded his head and moved slightly to his left. A footstep, no more. Clearly following instructions. This team had telepathic communication. Not all of Whitney's supersoldiers had been capable of that.

The sniper was lining up his shot for the maximum coverage. The soldier had chosen to disturb a feeler more exposed than the others. They thought she would have to expose herself to a bullet in order to take him down.

She took a deep breath and allowed the vibrations the soldier gave off to swamp her. He was eager for the kill. Eager to be the one who finally was able to kill the poisonous spider they all dreaded so much. She'd killed so many teams, and yet he would have the glory and bragging rights once he drew her out.

She concentrated on his legs, from his knees down. Silk shot out and began to wrap him. Loose at first so he couldn't possibly feel it. The sniper wouldn't be looking at the soldier's legs. Not at first. She wrapped him fast, tightening the threads with a vicious snap. He toppled instantly, going over backward. At once she spun more silk, wrapping his arms and the weapon he held, taking care to clog the trigger to prevent him from firing.

A bullet slammed into the ground six feet behind her. The marksman was firing blind, trying to save his spotter. She didn't even flinch. She kept spinning the silk until the soldier was completely wrapped from head to toe like a mummy. He couldn't move. He could barely breathe. Two more bullets hit in rapid succession, each one closer. The sniper was guessing where she was by the way she'd wrapped her enemy.

Report in. Trap's voice was sharp, pouring into her mind.

Perfectly fine. She delivered her news abruptly, closing down the path between them. She couldn't think like a human. She couldn't be emotional. Trap made her that way. With him, she was all about feeling, and she couldn't risk it.

Cayenne moved then, retaining the strongest line, woven with several strands. As she slipped to her right, in denser cover, she flattened herself behind two larger cypress trees, staying inside the "knees" protruding from the ground all around. At some point the area had been underwater and the tree had grown the knees in order to survive. She was able to fold herself in one of the knobby barrels.

Cayenne was enormously strong, especially for her size. No one would ever attribute that strength to her, but even though she felt the heavy drag of the soldier's weight, she knew, from experience, that she could move him. She yanked hard and the body slid toward her. Not a lot. A few inches. But that was enough, all she needed. Instantly another shot rang out. This one clipped the tree, showering the area with splinters of bark. She already had the soldier where she wanted. His head and neck were in the shadows. In the foliage and behind the ring of cypress knees, she delivered the fatal bite and slipped away, leaving the soldier staring with lifeless eyes up at the sky through the leaves.

Before Trap could make an enquiry, she hastened to assure him. *Still fine.*

The moment she opened the path, she caught a glimpse of the "iceman." She knew his team members often referred to him by that nickname and she knew why. She'd experienced his ice, but that little glimpse enlightened her further. Trap was completely removed from what he was doing. He moved like a wind of sheer death through the trees, taking the hottest location and using a knife, getting in close and going for the throat just as she'd advised.

Her heart stuttered, realizing what he was doing. She didn't like the fact that he put himself in danger without so much as flinching. He simply took point and went after the other soldiers aggressively. She wasn't a woman to swear, but she managed a few curse words as she moved locations, crawling along the ground until she was well back in the cover of the swamp where she could stand and begin to run.

She went on the hunt now. She knew the sniper would have to move, but she had a good sense of where he was. She could determine where he would go. In the distance she heard a gun go off, and her heart nearly stopped and then began to pound.

Trap. She had to know. She had to be human in spite of her resolve, because the thought of him injured was more than she could bear.

Fired at Gino. Missed. Gino was already on top of him. You don't want to miss Gino when he's coming at you. Two down.

Three. I'm going after the one in the trees with a rifle.

Gino says a five-man team hit us. That means with the sniper we've got one other man. Be careful, Cayenne, their focus is on getting you.

She knew that already and she wasn't afraid of them. Spiders didn't have fear, just purpose, and she was hunting now. She ran fast, making no sound, not even allowing a whisper of movement against the brush. Where she could, she used silk to aid her, swinging from branch to branch to cover greater distances above the denser foliage.

When she was close to the tree where the sniper had set up shop, she climbed high, going up the trunk fast, flattening her body against the bark to keep from presenting a target for anyone to see should they be looking. Again, because she was so slight and didn't weigh much, there was no movement of branches or leaves—and that was what saved her.

The breeze was slight and it shifted just enough to warn her. He was still in the same tree. He hadn't moved. She cursed again, silently this time. *Very* silently. The sniper, the moment he knew his spotter was dead and he'd given his location away, should have moved. Would have moved. She'd walked into a second trap. This time the sniper was the bait.

Breathing very slow and evenly, she stayed very still, flattened against the tree trunk, hidden in the crotch of two branches. They were thin, barely there, but large enough to shield her body from view—if she didn't move. Whoever was on the business end of a rifle had a scope and he'd be able to see her quite clearly if she moved. This close, it was a huge risk to reach telepathically to Trap. Sometimes just that psychic energy could draw attention with an enhanced individual.

She closed her eyes and drew in another shaky breath. The sniper was just out of her reach, but so close if he turned his head and looked up he could possibly see her. She could use silk, but even that was risky. The shooter had to be close enough to ensure he wouldn't miss, with a good view of the sniper and tree. The tree didn't have much foliage. The sniper was hidden from view below due to the way the trunk split. He was in the very lowest point, his rifle set up along the thickest branch. He could almost lie down, and clearly he was comfortable.

He wasn't nearly as confident as his first spotter had been. He didn't like being the bait. He was used to lying up somewhere, far removed from hand-to-hand combat, and taking out his enemies from a distance. He certainly wasn't used to being the one drawing out his foe. She smelled sweat on him. Determination and that same revulsion of what she was. He especially disliked her after what she'd done to his spotter.

She had always relied on herself. She went over every move she could make in her mind. She was in sight. The wrong breeze. Her hair moving. Anything at all might draw attention. Just being in such close proximity meant eventually the marksmen would look up and spot her. She practiced jumping on him in her mind. Jumping, biting and rolling off the tree. The problem was, she didn't know which way to roll.

Trap. She touched his mind delicately. It was the only play left to her until she knew where the man with the rifle was. She hoped Trap would understand that ultra-fragile brush in his mind.

At first she thought maybe she hadn't used enough strength to reach him, but their connection was so strong she couldn't imagine that, so she stayed still and waited.

Coordinates.

Just that. His touch was every bit as subtle as hers had been. He knew. He understood she was compromised and he was already coming to her. A part of her didn't like that she'd reached out, asking for help. Not in a combat situation. She always worked alone and that suited her, but she couldn't deny that there were moments she could have used help and it was sheer luck that she survived and not her enemy.

She sent the coordinates and the information that she was pinned down. One sniper in the tree with her and the other focused on the first marksman. She didn't want Trap dead, so that meant risking communicating even more information. She kept her gaze just to the right of the marksman below her. She didn't want a steady gaze to alert him, but she had to see what he was doing at all times.

He lifted his eye from the scope and shook his head. He looked around and then pressed his hand over his ear. He'd caught an echo or backlash of the psychic conversation. She wasn't surprised. She was only a few feet from him. She didn't dare close her eyes, or change her breathing pattern. She kept it slow and even, hoping Trap didn't talk any more to her. She tried to hold the danger in her mind, so if he touched her, he would see it. She *willed* him to see it.

Without warning, the man below her bent to his rifle, a

smile playing around his mouth. "Got you, you big bastard." He sounded elated. He caressed the trigger with his finger and then adjusted something on his rifle.

Her heart skipped a beat. She turned her head slowly to follow where his rifle was aimed. She could see into a tree a distance away. Trap was there, coming up behind the other sniper, the one aiming straight at the tree she occupied. There was no way in hell the marksman below her was going to kill Trap. No way.

She used silk, wrapping it quickly around the rifle, jerking it away from him just as he fired the shot. The rifle banged against the tree just below her, and the other sniper took his shot. She was already in motion, leaping on the man below her, trusting Trap to kill the one already lining up his second shot at her. She put him from her mind as her enemy caught her in big hands and tried to throw her off of him.

She clung to him, refusing to allow it. At once, he wrapped his hand around her throat and began to squeeze. He used his other one to keep her mouth from closing in on him. He didn't seem to need both hands to strangle her. He was strong enough with one. She couldn't reach any part of him with her mouth as long as his hand was around her throat, and worse, she didn't have much time. Already she was seeing spots and the edges of her vision had gone black.

He had armor beneath his skin, but his throat was vulnerable. She retaliated the only way open to her, she wrapped silk around his neck, forming a noose, and pulled it as tight as she could. He was holding her off her feet, so she didn't have leverage, but she managed to plant her feet on the tree trunk and use her strength to lever backward. He was unprepared for that move, distracted by the silk strangling him, and he staggered, loosening his hold on her throat.

She lunged at him, sinking her teeth into his wrist, trying to inject enough venom to paralyze him. His fist caught her hair and yanked her head away from him. He flung her out of the tree by her hair. She turned in midair and landed on her feet in a crouch. She couldn't drag in enough air. Her lungs burned and her throat felt swollen. It was painful to swallow. She kept her eyes on him as she landed.

Smirking, he drew another gun from his boot. She was ready for that. The moment he pulled it out, she sent strands of silk to capture it, wrapping it up and yanking it away from him. The gun went flying out of the tree. He leapt to the ground, following it, landing right in front of her. At the last moment she caught the gleam of a blade as it raced straight at her.

She hated knives. Really hated them. Knives reminded her of the thin needles piercing through her hands and shoulders, through her feet and ankles. So thin, but causing so much pain. The knife went into her abdomen, the tip cutting through her skin. The burn was a bear, but the woven silk stopped the blade from going any farther in spite of the strength behind the stab.

Their bodies were close. She stared up at the triumph in his eyes as she leaned into him and bit his wrist where he held the knife, still certain he could push the blade into her. She was just as certain he couldn't. She didn't feel triumph when she delivered the lethal dose of venom into his veins. She felt nothing at all. She was—empty.

She stood toe to toe with him, the tip of the knife burning through her flesh, watching the venom take him. Time slowed down and for Cayenne, the process seemed to take forever. He reached for her throat again, wrapping his fingers there. He let go of the knife and tried to reach with the other hand, clearly intending to wrench her neck, to break it, knowledge that the knife refused to go any farther into her finally hitting him.

The stunned look she'd seen before. The recognition that it was too late for him. His arms dropped. His knees went to the ground. She stepped aside, her palm cradling the knife. He toppled face-first into the vegetation. She stared down at his body for what seemed an eternity. She was exhausted and wanted to spin a cocoon, crawl into it and sleep for a week.

"Give me the knife, baby," Trap said softly, his arm curling around her waist. "Let me take a look."

She looked up at him—at his gorgeous, tough, all-male features. His beautiful eyes, at times so cold they could freeze a person from the inside out, or, like now, blue flames that spread warmth right through bones. His hand wrapped gently around hers and he took the weapon from her and dropped it on the fallen supersoldier.

Trap frowned as his fingertips moved over her throat, confirming the evidence of her swollen, burning throat was there for all to see.

"The wound is shallow. I injected the venom and he went down." Her voice sounded hoarse and it hurt to get the words out.

"Your throat?"

"Burns, but it will be all right. Was anyone else injured?"

He reached down, one arm sliding behind her knees, the other around her back. He lifted her against his chest, cradling her close. She should have protested. She didn't want to be carried through the swamp for his entire team to see, but his body was warm and she was cold. Shivering. Numb. Empty.

"Let me have this," he coaxed softly, nuzzling the top of her head with his chin. "I had to watch him strangling you. I saw him throw you out of the tree and then go after you with a knife. I need this, baby. Give this to me."

She closed her eyes and laid her head against his chest. He wasn't talking about carrying her back to the SUV. He was talking about something altogether different. She couldn't help herself. He felt strong. Warm. He felt like— hers. *Hers.* She'd never had anything or anyone in her life. Trap Dawkins could be as cold as ice, or he could be this man. Perfect. Gentle. Amazing.

He was both, and accepting one meant accepting the

other. She wanted him to be hers always. Whatever that took, she was willing to try. To have moments like this one, when she was so empty she needed him to fill her.

Her arms went around his neck, the fingers of one hand curling in his unruly hair. The other curved around his neck. Her body melted into his. Boneless. Pliant.

Are you giving this to me?

Her lashes felt too heavy to keep up. Was she? There was no other answer but "yes." None. Because he was hers, and she wanted to keep him. She even needed that.

I feel empty, Trap, used up and cold. I hurt everywhere. I just want to lie down and be warm. My throat is very painful. She gave him the truth. She shared the truth of her condition, made herself completely vulnerable to him. She *felt* completely vulnerable in that moment, giving him the raw, stark truth of what killing did to her.

She didn't feel elated, but she didn't feel remorse. Just empty. Either he could understand or he couldn't. In that moment, she couldn't even muster up enough strength to be alarmed that she'd confessed her darkness to him.

I'll get you home and take care of you, baby. You're safe with me.

CHAPTER 12

Trap took Cayenne straight through the house to the master suite. His bedroom. He'd wanted her in his bed since the first moment when he saw her in that cell. So beautiful. So alone. He was a cynical man. He knew that and accepted it about himself. He was pure logic and operated without nerves or fears—until he saw Cayenne. The ice in his veins had melted, and something so hot he was afraid it would consume them both had taken the place of the ice.

Draden came in behind him and placed the bags of clothing and shoes on the dresser. "She all right? Didn't want to ask in front of the others. Her throat looks bad, bruises and swelling."

"I'm a doctor," Trap reminded, his arms tightening around Cayenne, holding her against his body as if that could somehow undo all the damage done to her. "Same as you." His voice was clipped, and he knew it shouldn't have been. Draden really was concerned for Cayenne.

The others had looked at her, then Trap's face, and no one had said a word. His face said it all. He was furious that she had been nearly killed—furious at himself. Terrified of losing her. Stark, raw terror had been there in his eyes and he didn't want his teammates adding to that fear. He wasn't used to the kind of emotions that tore him apart anymore. He'd been done with all feeling when the last of his family had been ripped away from him.

He wasn't the kind of man to commit to a relationship, to practically force a woman to accept him as a partner—not unless he was in so deep it would kill him to lose it all. He didn't build a home inside a factory or have someone come in to decorate shit to please a woman. He didn't think in terms of pleasing anyone, let alone a woman. He kept his life void of entanglements because he never—ever—wanted to be vulnerable. Yet there he was, his woman in his arms, her throat black and blue and swollen, and he'd watched as the soldier had tried to kill her.

He'd been too far away. He'd killed the other sniper, but even with his speed, he couldn't get to Cayenne, and that left him angry. His gut in tight knots. Bile in his throat. His heart nearly stopping. Physical. Visceral. Raw and primal. He wasn't a man to feel any of those things.

He'd shut down his emotions. He lived the way he wanted, without any entanglements, free of all emotional vulnerabilities. Until the moment he had walked through the cell wall and laid his eyes on her. Her voice, hypnotic and sexy, had washed into his brain and left him wanting. Feeling. Too much. Far too much.

"You need anything, Trap, give a shout-out," Draden said, and backed from the room.

Fuck. Trap didn't want to leave it like that. Draden was a brother. Someone he'd allowed in his life, almost as close as Wyatt. He was friends on his terms, and the others let him get away with it. He didn't even know when it happened. He stayed aloof and he was rude, and went for days without talking, but still they were his friends and they had his back.

"Draden," he said softly, his voice low. Almost wishing

the man wouldn't hear. Of course he did, Draden was a GhostWalker with all the enhancements available to him, including hearing. Draden half turned, looked at him over his shoulder, face impassive. Trap lifted his chin at him in a small salute. "Thanks, man." It was small, but it was enough. Trap saw it in Draden's eyes. Draden merely sent him an identical chin lift and then turned and walked out, leaving Trap alone with Cayenne.

He put a knee to the bed and carefully laid her down on the sheets. He hadn't made the bed that morning. He rarely made his bed. It seemed silly when he was getting into it at night. "Baby, I need to check for broken bones."

Her lashes fluttered. Lifted. He stared down into emerald green. His heart did a curious melting thing that left him speechless. She shook her head, the tip of her tongue touching her lips.

"No broken bones," she managed to croak out.

"I have to make certain," he said gently.

"My bones are too soft to break."

He stared down at her beautiful face. Bruises were coming up around her throat. On her cheek. Her voice sounded raspy, but she seemed certain. He touched his fingers to her swollen throat. "I didn't like seeing him doing this to you, Cayenne. Fucking hated it. I don't think I can go through that again. You might have to wrap yourself in a little cocoon where only I can get to you. I'm going to be having nightmares for weeks. Months maybe." He made the confession in a low, shaky voice.

His voice never shook. She had done something to him, and he didn't know how to undo it. He didn't even want to try. The intellectual part of his brain, which was the largest part of him, continued to tell him he'd been paired with her. That such strong feelings for her were a result of being alone too long. Loneliness. A longing for what Wyatt had. The trouble was, even if all those things were true, he didn't care.

"Baby, I'm going to have to look at your body, see what damage he did. I saw him stick you with a knife."

I need to sleep.

"You can sleep, but don't bite me when I take off your clothes. I'm not going to do anything to you but look after you." His fingers smoothed back her hair, liking the way it made a dark cloud across his pillow. He'd dreamt of that thick mass, shiny black across his pillow, his fingers delving deep to find the source of those beautiful red strands with their unique pattern.

I'm too tired to bite anyone, she whispered into his mind. *But I need to go downstairs. This is too open for me. I need . . . smaller. Protection.*

He looked around his room. It was very large. Huge. He needed space. Lots of it. He liked to see what was coming at him. He had several escape routes scattered through the walls, floor and ceiling.

"I can protect you."

The lashes fluttered. Raised. Her beautiful green eyes sent a wicked punch straight to his gut. *I can't relax like this.*

"Spin your webs around the bed. Make us a veil, baby. I'd like that, a canopy over our bed. Do you have enough strength to do that?"

She studied his face, her eyes brooding. Thoughtful. A little frightened. She knew what he wanted. Her. In his bed. More of a commitment.

"Baby. I need this. You. Here. With me. I need this." He admitted it aloud to her, trying to show her. Trying to give her that vulnerable part of him to make up for being a complete bastard. After watching her nearly die right in front of him, he needed to have her close. "I wouldn't fit in your bed. I'm too tall. Weigh too much. All muscle, babe, which is good part of the time but not so good in that little bed you curl up in."

You put the bed down there.

"My mistake. I didn't think you'd be down there long and

I was trying . . ." He trailed off. He'd tried to duplicate her cell in some ways, in order for her to subconsciously accept the apartment as her home. A good first step in accepting the place as home and then him as belonging to her.

He held her eyes to allow her to see the complete vulnerability in him. The stark, raw need. He knew it showed. There was no hiding that deep of a need. It came from a place of terror, something he hadn't experienced since the first gunshot rang out in his childhood home. That nightmare was far too close, pressing on him, the loss of the ones he loved. He'd let her in. He needed her now.

She nodded slowly. *It will take a few minutes.*

"I'll get ready for bed. Leave a route to the bathroom." If she was feeling better later in the night, they'd need it. He didn't say that, but he turned away from her, not giving her the opportunity to change her mind. He hurried into the bathroom and shed his clothes, took care of business, concentrating on keeping his heartbeat as steady as possible.

He'd planned out his battle strategy, trying to find ways he thought would appeal to Cayenne to lure her into staying during and after renovations of the only building she had been able to call home there in the swamp. His biggest hurdle was gaining her trust. As far as he could see, she'd never had a reason to trust anyone. He could see that in her eyes when she looked at him—her defenses working right behind all that green. Her fear. She was drawn to him, compelled to be close to him, but trusting him was an altogether different proposition. He knew the fact that she wanted to give him that was half the battle. If he could keep his terror—and his reaction to it—under control, he'd have a better chance.

When he walked out from the bathroom, stark naked, his room had been transformed. He stopped, his breath catching in his throat as he stared at the lacy, artistic design shrouding his bed. Floor-to-ceiling silk formed a heavy veil, with feelers running through the room, along the walls and creeping out the door. A web covered the two entrances.

Neither of those was ornate, not like the beautiful one wrapping up his bed. She'd created a tunnel for them between the bathroom and the bed and he stood upright in it. The fact that he could meant she'd calculated the height and width of the passageway so he could walk easily. He loved that she could do that. Fucking *loved* it.

He padded through the tunnel to the bed. She was so small there under his covers, he might have missed her but for the black silk spilling over the pillow. Once again he put his knee on the edge of the bed and leaned so he could pull her smaller body to him.

Cayenne didn't resist. She didn't even move her head, but her lashes fluttered as he flipped back the covers. His breath left his lungs in a rush. She had shed her clothes and was as naked as he was. Her color was better. Her body was as lush or even more so than he remembered from the night before. This time his hands were free. He couldn't help using his finger to trace the little hourglass nestled into the tiny black curls at the junction of her legs as he took in her body. Every inch of it. Looking for injuries. Memorizing the exotic luxury that was Cayenne. That was his.

The knife had gone in low and mean. He could see the cut there, a raw wound that still seeped a little blood. He hated knives. He was adept at using them and often did when he went into an enemy camp and didn't want his presence known, but he knew often, the wound wasn't the problem, infection was.

His fingers probed around the cut. Not deep. In fact, fairly shallow. He didn't see how that was possible when she'd fought off a supersoldier, one with enormous strength. He should have been able to drive the blade deep. Clearly the bite she'd given the soldier had saved her. Very gently Trap cleansed the area around the wound with antiseptic and then placed a triple antibiotic cream over it. He added a bandage. She didn't wince. She didn't move, just kept her eyes on his face.

He used the pads of his fingers to whisper over her skin. Soft. Totally soft. Like silk. Like the silk of her hair. The silk of the webs surrounding their beds. Her lashes fluttered and then covered her eyes.

"Baby, is your skin made up of silk as well?" He couldn't imagine how that would occur in her body, but he knew how strong woven spiderwebs could be—they could stop a bullet better than Kevlar—and he didn't have any other explanation.

I'm so tired, Trap. Really, really tired. Can we talk later? Please?

He wasn't certain she'd get the chance to say much of anything later. He didn't intend to talk with his voice. Still, she'd killed a couple of men. She needed to retreat, to let herself grieve in her own way. Whatever she had to do to process that two human beings had lost their lives.

"You know you had no choice, Cayenne," he offered softly, as he positioned her in the middle of the bed and slid in next to her.

She was on her side, facing away from him, one hand tucked beneath her cheek. Her body was cold. When he turned on his side and curled his body protectively around hers, she made no protest. He tucked her closer, his arm sliding around her waist, dragging her body almost beneath his. Close. So close the silk of her skin melted into the heat of his. He slid one knee in between her legs, and buried his face in her hair.

She felt . . . like heaven. In his wildest imagination—and granted he didn't have much of one, he was all about science—he never once thought a woman could feel like her. He inhaled and took the scent of her into his lungs. Deep. Loving the way her fragrance was exotic, something wild. He knew she had wild in her. Her wild called to him, to the dominant in him.

He knew he wasn't a prize, not unless money, fame or prestige mattered. If she was all about him, she would have to put up with his public image. She had already indicated she detested the way he was.

Trap. Why are you upset?

He should have known she was as tuned to him as he was to her. He sighed into the hourglass of red nestled in the middle of her thick black hair. "I can't change, baby, not even for you. I had to train myself to be a cold and unfeeling bastard, which, quite frankly, wasn't all that difficult. I never had many social skills. I never wanted anything or anyone to matter, to make me vulnerable. Out there, outside the walls of my home or my teammates' homes, I have to be that person in order to survive."

He waited a heartbeat. Two. She didn't say anything, but she pressed closer to him, the smooth rounded buttocks sliding against his heavy erection. She didn't seem to mind that he was as hard as a rock. He knew that later, much later, when she was used to his ways, he would have her take care of that before they went to sleep together. He resisted the urge to slide his hand between her legs to see if she was wet for him. He hoped that just their closeness would do that to her in the way it did for him. He craved her taste. It was there on his tongue. His cock jerked at the memory of the feast he'd had, devouring her sweetness. All that exotic honey his.

I didn't ask you to change.

He forced himself to continue his explanation. He needed her to understand, even though he didn't hold out much hope that she would. "But you didn't like who I was when we went to town, and that's part of who I am. My icy demeanor isn't a façade. My friends say I have ice water in my veins, and maybe I do. I disconnect. I learned not to feel anything when I'm in public. When I'm talking with reporters or making an appearance I don't want to make but is necessary."

Why do reporters want to talk to you?

He hesitated. This was a tough subject. He knew her now.

She wanted to stay in the shadows. Once her face was in a photograph, no shadow would hide her for long. It would be a media frenzy trying to get more.

Why don't you want to tell me?

"Fuck." The word exploded from him. He was going to have to tell her the truth. "Baby, I need more time."

For what?

"To hook you." His arm, the one around her waist, dragged her so close she was nearly pinned beneath him. His hand splayed out, fingers wide, taking in her entire rib cage. His fingertips brushed the underside of her breasts. "I want you so into me that you won't run. I told you, for a woman like you I'm no prize."

There was a small silence. She didn't pull away or grow tense. She lay half under him, his body curved around hers and leaning over top of her, almost, but not quite pinning her down. She stayed relaxed, her eyes closed, her body in no way resistant. That shocked the hell out of him.

A woman like me? What about other women?

"You don't give a damn about money or what I do, Cayenne. Other women aren't necessarily like you. Some want to marry a man for his money. And baby, I have a lot of it. A fuck of a lot of it. Makes me a target for women looking to have what I can give them. It isn't about me. It's about the money." He hesitated. "Or the fame. Some women get off on that shit. Cameras all the time. Photos in magazines. Invited to every event possible. My worst nightmare, and that's what they want. They could care less whether or not I want it."

What do you do that makes people want your picture and, I assume, write articles about you?

"I own several companies and I do a lot of research, mostly medical now, although I've come up with some ideas that made everyday things easier for people and those things made me money as well. Medical research has paid off bigtime. I have money, but still, research is expensive. I need grants and allies. So my public face is important at times."

He hesitated again. "I've won a few major awards and that makes me noticeable sometimes. To the press."

That man with the camera. He wanted your picture for magazines and newspapers because you're famous?

He sighed. Pushed his cock deeper into her, finding a soft, heated spot between her rounded cheeks. She didn't pull away. If anything, she gave him more, pushing back against him so he was nestled deep in that warm cleft. His heart jerked in his chest. Blood pounded in his cock.

There was nothing else for it. "Yeah, baby, I'm famous. Since Wyatt became my full partner in most projects, I've begun shifting some of the promotional work to him. Wyatt's good with people. I'm not. I never will be. I'm not comfortable in the presence of too many people. I lack social skills. That's never mattered until I found you. I deliberately bury myself in work. I need my work. My brain just doesn't let it go. I understand work. I don't understand people."

Why do you think you need to hook me before you tell me this?

He nuzzled the nape of her neck, using his nose to burrow through the mass of hair until he found skin. He licked along the smooth, sweet line and then nipped with his teeth. He felt the answering shiver in her body.

"Because out there, in public, the cameras will never stop going after you once they find out you're my woman. I want to make that legal. We needed to create legal documents for you. A history. Everything has to stand up to any scrutiny, so we needed to go to Flame, Wyatt's sister-in-law. She's amazing with computers. She has a counterpart, another woman who is a GhostWalker, Jaimie Fielding. Between the two of them, you'll be so legit no one will ever suspect where you came from. The point being, Cayenne, that you'll be in the public eye every time you go anywhere. You'll have bodyguards with you every minute."

She moved then, turning her head to look at him over her shoulder. In the darkness, he could see her easily with his acute night vision. She looked so beautiful, her green eyes moving over his face, surrounded by those long, feathery lashes.

Bodyguards? Me? Seriously, Trap, do you even know me? Did you not see me in the swamp? I can take care of myself.

He couldn't stop his hand from moving up to cup her breast. She fit into his palm easily and he surrounded the soft, warm mound with his fingers, his thumb sliding over her nipple gently. Experimenting. She was tired. He could see the drowsiness in her eyes, but still, that small thumb brush got him another full-body shiver. A little press back into his groin. Her buttocks tightened around his cock, sending more hot blood rushing through his veins.

"Bodyguards will deal with any public threat, Cayenne, so you won't have to. In public, we can't ever use our skills. You certainly can't paralyze or wrap someone in silk because they annoy you, as much as I'd like to see you take down a reporter or two."

Her features stilled. Something in her eyes shifted, and he knew instantly his playful banter had hurt. She started to turn her head away from him but he cupped the entire side of her face in his palm, preventing movement.

"Baby," he said softly, gently, shocked at the strange fluttering of his heart and the need to erase that look. "I was teasing you. I know you wouldn't do that. If you were going to bite someone and wrap them in silk it would have been the shoe salesman. He was definitely slimy."

Her gaze moved over his face and he waited for her to read the honesty in his eyes. His thumb slid along her delicate jaw in a little caress. "I know you're smart, Cayenne. I knew it the moment you admitted to using a spatial model for estimating the husks on the floor of the Huracan Club. In order to survive these past few months, you've had to adapt and observe and you've done it at an extraordinary speed. I couldn't admire or respect you more."

He took a breath and then gave it to her. The stark truth.

"To say the least, that shocks me. I don't respect or admire very many women. Or men for that matter. Just listening to their inane chatter sets my teeth on edge. Sitting in that bar for days on end, waiting for you to show, nearly drove me right out of my skull."

He was arrogant. She might as well know that about him as well. He was rude in public for a reason—being there made him feel like he was going a little crazy. Sometimes, if he was with Wyatt, or one of his teammates, he could find humor in the situation, but mostly, he just wanted to get away from everyone.

Her eyes went a vibrant green, gleaming at him. Her lips curved into a small smile. *Sometimes, Trap, for a man who doesn't think he can talk well to others, you can be quite brilliant.*

He dipped his head low to brush a kiss across her perfect bow of a mouth. He really loved her mouth. He was gentle, coaxing a response from her, trying not to devour her when her taste exploded on his tongue, igniting every single cell in his body. There were bruises on her face and throat and more around the stab wound. Exhaustion had settled into the depths of her eyes. He wanted to kiss her because— well—he *needed* to, but he was a man of extraordinary discipline and restraint.

He lifted his head, his gaze moving over her face. "I love looking at you," he admitted. "Every single tiny detail of your face and body is etched into my brain for all time. I want to wake up every morning looking at you and go to sleep at night with you right beside me. When I die, Cayenne, I want you holding me and looking at me, right in my eyes, so I take that last sight of you with me."

He let her go, placing her head gently back on the pillow, so that she faced away from him. He settled around her, his arm once more around her waist, fingers splaying wide over her soft belly. He contented himself with using his thumb to slide over the silk of her skin.

"You really mean the things you say to me, don't you?" Her voice was just above a whisper, husky and hoarse. There was a wonder in it. Wonder and something else that alerted him instantly.

"Are you crying, Cayenne?" He shifted subtly, thinking to turn her face back to his, but she pushed deeper into the pillow. "Baby, why? And don't answer out loud. Save your vocal cords."

There was no sound, but he knew tears trickled down her face. There wasn't even a change in her breathing. Still. She was crying, he knew it.

You make me feel things I've never felt before, Trap, she confessed. *Good things. You make me feel as if I really do belong with you. That you really want me with you.*

"And that makes you cry?"

In a good way, I think, although it also scares me. I never thought I'd have that.

He used his fingers to sift through the dark cloud of hair, rubbing strands between them. "Neither did I, Cayenne. Not ever. I wanted a woman of my own, a family of my own, but I never believed I'd find one who could put up with my shit." He sighed. "About this afternoon, baby. I know you were upset . . ."

You explained that to me, Trap. I get it. I just needed to understand. If we're really going to try this, we have to be able to talk things out. I really would like it if you would tell me what to expect ahead of time. I felt alone. Cut off from you. It wasn't a good feeling. I get it now, but I needed to get it then.

She understood and it was over for her. She didn't need a long, drawn-out apology and he knew she wasn't going to be throwing it in his face every time he acted cold in public. He had panicked. She wasn't going to make him admit that. That terror that still was too close for comfort, now tucked away beneath the glacier in his gut.

"I'll work on my communication skills," he said, knowing that would take some doing, especially in public. He had zero skills and knew even for the people mattering the most to him—like Wyatt and Draden—he hadn't overcome the part of him that cut himself off from everything. It was too ingrained. He knew ice had become his defense mechanism from the time he was very young. Ice and detachment. He was good at both.

"And baby, just so you know, we aren't 'trying' this. There is no 'if.' This is it for both of us. We *are* doing this. The only thing we haven't confirmed is whether or not you can meet my demands in bed, and after last night, I am more than certain you will."

She made a small sound of distress. "Trap."

She went back to whisper and he caught the huskiness that told him her throat hurt like hell. Before she could speak he interrupted her. "Use telepathy, Cayenne. Your throat needs rest."

I don't know the first thing about sex. Only the things I read. Only what you taught me last night.

"Did you enjoy what I did to you?"

Yes. No hesitation.

"Did you enjoy what you did to me?" Just the thought of it, the hot haven of her mouth, the silken glide of her lips, the tight suction and dancing tongue, sent more blood coursing through his cock so that it swelled all over again from a semihard state to an iron spike.

Very much. Again no hesitation. *I thought about it for most of the rest of the night, the way having you in my mouth and watching your face was so exciting. Knowing I could give you that. I dreamt about you. I have nightmares, so it was nice to have something different. When I woke up I felt hot and achy. I knew I needed you and I craved the taste of you. I just don't know what to do about it.* She made her confession in a little rush.

He tugged on her long hair and then took several strands in his mouth to slide through his lips. "Your man knows what to do and I'll be more than happy to help you learn. There's no bullshit with you. Either you like something or you don't. Talking to me, telling me what you're feeling and if it works for you is everything. And you have to trust me. You gave yourself to me, Cayenne. That means you know I'm going to take care of you in *all* ways, including your body."

He felt her tense and knew immediately her independent streak was as strong as his was. "I trust that you'll do the same for me." He meant that. He was giving himself into her keeping and he didn't plan on holding back. He was doing this one time. With one woman. Going all in. He needed her to do the same.

"Sex isn't all about the body, not when it's between two people who care. It starts in your heart, Cayenne, and in your mind. It's about giving and taking."

Like last night.

"Yes. With that, you have to have trust that anything I do to you will end up rocking your world."

I couldn't let you have your hands, Trap, she admitted. *I was too afraid.*

He heard the shame in her voice.

I don't like feeling fear. I especially am uncomfortable when I don't know something. I'm used to having knowledge because anything I read, I retain. Since living outside my cell, I've found that practical experience and book knowledge are two different things. Sex is still an unknown.

"We'll take care of that."

Knowing that doesn't alleviate the fear of the unknown, Trap, she pointed out. *I studied you over the last four months. I've been in your bedroom countless times. You don't sleep with clothes. I knew your body before I ever actually touched you. I wanted you even without ever really talking to you.*

He knew that feeling. It had been the same for him. She'd intrigued him, and few things intrigued him. Fewer women did. The obsession had grown over the weeks until the scent of her in his room and the knowledge that she was close drove him to seek her out. He stayed quiet, willing her to continue. The more he understood, the faster he could make their life together work smoothly.

I don't trust anything I don't understand.

He didn't either. He knew about Whitney's pairing of two enhanced individuals. He wanted to create the perfect soldier. Cayenne matched him intellectually. She didn't have an ounce of bullshit games in her, something very necessary in a woman for him. It was most likely the same for her. Whitney had a knack for finding the right partner, but he obviously felt he couldn't control Cayenne. He didn't like wild cards. He'd demonstrated that over and over, especially with the women. He seemed to easily terminate the women.

Every time I looked at you, my body suddenly wasn't my own. I felt hot and needy and burned inside. I knew what the chemistry was because I'd read about it, but you hadn't even touched me. It didn't make sense.

"And you distrusted it."

Of course I did. I fought your pull, but I couldn't stay away. I was kind of upset that you fought it better than I did. I knew you felt it too.

There was a small silence. He waited. He had known she was there in his bedroom many nights, he just hadn't been able to spot her or prove it. But he'd known and he'd jacked off to the scent of her, wanting her to watch, groaning her name when he came in a white-hot fountain of brutal need.

When you did that, when I watched, it was literally the hottest thing I'd ever seen. I'd watched a few films on the Internet, but they didn't in any way make me feel anything. When I saw and heard you, I wanted to crawl all over you, to put my mouth on your cock and to taste you. I needed to lick you clean. I burned. I burned every night I saw you do that and didn't really know how to make it go away.

It wasn't the best time for her to be telling him this. She needed to sleep, and right now, his cock was so fucking hard he was afraid he would explode, just burst apart. Still, he wanted to hear it. He needed to. She thought she was giving him facts, not realizing she was giving him the world.

No one has ever done any of the things for me that you did. You made me a home. You gave me food. You talked to me like no one else has ever done. You bought me shoes and clothes. I don't know why you want me, Trap, I don't know what I can give you back, but I want this. I just don't understand your life or where I fit into it.

He understood immediately. She was all but asking if she fit into his world there in their home, and in the outside world as well.

"Baby, are you afraid I won't want you outside our home?"

There was a small silence. *I'm afraid either way. I want to share every aspect of your life and feel part of it. I didn't like feeling as if I wasn't in the know with your team, that you all were part of something I wasn't. On the other hand, the thought of learning that side of things, being with your friends, out in public, that absolutely terrifies me. You weren't shielding my face from the camera because of Whitney. You knew he already knew where I was. You didn't want the world to see me.*

"I wanted to protect you from that side of my life as long as possible. You need a chance to get to know me better, to trust that you can follow my lead in public and know that I'll always have your back. I want you comfortable with my friends, with my team and with bodyguards so when you have to face that side of my life, you aren't terrified. I know what I'm asking of you, and you don't yet. It's enormous. You're giving me so much more than what I'm giving you."

That isn't possible. You're giving me . . . life. I existed, Trap, but I wasn't human. No one but you has ever seen me as a woman. As a human being. As someone worthwhile.

"That may be true, baby, but any number of men who aren't arrogant and rude and have the paparazzi hanging around constantly would want to make you feel that. Someone who isn't bringing you into the mess that is their life. You aren't getting a prize. Money, maybe, but no prize life."

She pushed her body back against his. Tight. Melting into him. He felt her soft amusement there in his mind. Filling him. He loved that she made him feel as if he could never be alone because she would always be there, inside of him.

I'm getting the best prize, Trap. You'll always be that for me.

He closed his eyes, knowing he had to let her sleep. He felt her weariness and knew her fatigue was bone deep. Exhaustion had set in and she was already drifting. He hoped he was the best for her because he wasn't going to give her up. He was going to fight for her with every breath in his body.

CHAPTER 13

I'm getting the best prize, Trap. You'll always be that for me.

Cayenne's voice woke Trap from his restless sleep. He was instantly alert. Aware. His body rock hard. Little jackhammers tripped in his head, drilling deep, digging relentlessly at his brain until the pain was brutal.

She was there with him. His body was wrapped possessively around hers, his hands holding her to him, his legs and arms trapping her close. She hadn't moved in her sleep, not even to put an inch between them. He would have known the moment she'd tried.

When I saw and heard you, there in your room all those nights, I wanted to crawl all over you, to put my mouth on your cock and taste you. I needed to lick you clean. I burned. I burned every night after I saw you do that and didn't really know how to make it go away.

He closed his eyes, savoring the sound of her voice, remembering the feel of her sinful mouth on him. So hot.

Burning her brand into him. The jackhammers drilled deeper, insistently, sending shards of glass through his mind. His cock was pure steel, a thick, savage spike as relentless as the spikes pushing into his brain. Pushing against her body, he couldn't control the jerk of need, the throb of hunger, the rush of hot blood centering in his groin in a painful demand.

Trap inhaled, taking her scent deep into his lungs. *Baby. I can't sleep anymore.* It was still dark and he didn't need a clock to tell him it was around three A.M. The webs shrouding their bed added to the sensual, erotic need flooding him. *I can't wait, Cayenne. If I don't fuck you soon, I swear to God, woman, I'm going to come apart.*

He felt her pour inside his mind. Nerves were there, but no resistance. She was a little drowsy, but already, he could feel the same urgent need building in her. Not brutal or primitive like it was in him, but there all the same.

He slid his hand up her belly to cup her breast. *So soft. Nothing like it. You feel like pure silk.* He used his finger and thumb to roll her nipple. To tug gently. An exquisite torture for both of them. He knew from the night before that her breasts were sensitive. He applied a little more pressure, a pinch then a soothing brush. A flash of heat and then another soothing touch.

I want my mouth here. Right now, baby.

His hand urged her to turn slightly so she was on her back. Again she didn't protest. She went onto her back for him, his body tight against hers, his hand still on her breast. He didn't wait for her to settle, he dipped his head and took the offering. His mouth closed over her lush right breast, his hand working her left one. He suckled while his fingers kneaded. He used his teeth and tongue while his fingers rolled and tugged.

He may have started out gently, but with every hitch of her breath, every keening gasp and soft mewling cry, he got a little rougher. He used the edge of his teeth, and heard more sweet music from her. He marked her deliberately, several strawberries over the slope of each breast, suckling strong, branding her. His teeth tugged and his tongue soothed.

She arched into him, giving him more, her arms going around his head to hold him to her. He fucking loved that. No matter how much he took, she offered him more. She responded to his rough play, and when he interspersed harsh with gentle, her body writhed against his, silently begging for more.

He slid his hand down her soft belly to trace the pattern of the hourglass nestled in the center of the black curls. Her curls were silky, the red of the hourglass even silkier if that was possible.

I'm going to get a tattoo of this, he murmured softly into her mind, more of a thought than words. The pads of his fingers brushed through the tight curls. *A spiderweb and a couple of spiders with this beautiful red hourglass.*

You like it? In my hair and also down there? I can't make it go away. She sounded breathless. Shocked. Sensual. As if the thought of a tattoo matching her hourglass meant something to her.

He was absolutely honest with her. *I would be very upset with you if you found a way to make this beautiful hourglass go away. It's part of you. Why would you want to change that?* There was an edge to his voice and in his mind. *I fucking love the hourglass. In your hair. In your curls.* He stroked the design, feeling the soft tiny straight hairs nestled inside the vee of curls.

I look different from other women.

You look like you. I love the way you look, everything about the way you look, especially the hourglass right here and in your hair.

His hand cupped the patch of curls, fingers curling, finding her warm, wet entrance. His thumb brushed across all that damp heat. For him. Satisfaction eased some of the tightness in his gut. In spite of her nerves, she hadn't pulled away, and her body responded to his closeness. More, when he slid a finger into her, her body clamped down hard, trying to hold him inside, trying to take him deeper.

She was tight. Hot and tight. He was big and getting inside her might be a challenge, especially because he didn't want to hurt her. He turned more fully into her, one arm pinning her against him, fastening her there, as if he was afraid she would try to get away. He slid his finger out of her and brought it to his mouth. Her eyes, watching him, went wide and darkened with desire.

You look exotic, Cayenne. Beautiful and exotic. You taste the way you look. I want you until I can't think of much else. I am going to devour you, baby. I've suddenly got a ravenous hunger for your taste.

I would very much like that, Trap.

He heard the *but* in her voice. Felt it in his mind.

He nuzzled her breast again, afraid of losing her to fear. *You're supposed to like it. I want you to love everything I do to you.* He licked along her nipple and then used his teeth to tug, unable to resist. *Are you afraid?*

I'm nervous, she admitted. *Really nervous, but I can feel how much you want this.*

He knew it would be impossible for her not to feel how hard he was. How hot and ready. His cock was pushing hard against her hip, the blood pounding, engorged and hungry for her. He hadn't tried to hide that from her. He wanted her to know what he was like. More, she was in his mind and she couldn't help but feel the jackhammers tripping in his brain and know he *had* to have her.

I want you to want it too, baby. I like sex, Cayenne. I fucking love sex. When I come off a project, that's all I can think about. Now, with you close to me, it's the same way, but far worse, far more urgent and only for you. I want you every minute of the day. I'm walking around with a fucking hard-on and it's damn painful. I'm not going to lie to you. I'm going to want you all the time.

She didn't tense up at his warning—and it was a warning. He wanted her with every cell in his body. He knew once he had her, it wouldn't be enough. He'd want more. All the time. Just her scent called to him. When her body was close, it was impossible to ignore his body's reaction to her.

You have to be certain, Cayenne. This is about both of us, not just me and what I want. You have to want and need this every bit as much as I do.

I think you can tell I want it too.

He pressed his mouth to her silken skin. He loved the feel of her against him. There was nothing like warm silk. He couldn't help wondering if she would feel like silk inside her tight, feminine sheath, surrounding him, massaging his hard cock with silken fingers.

What is it then, baby? If you want me too, what is your "but," because there is one, I can feel it in your mind.

Her tongue touched her bottom lip. Licked. Then her top one. Moistening both. *I love that you're hungry for me, Trap, but I'm just as hungry for you. I dreamt of taking your cock in my mouth again. I love the feel of you. Velvet yet so hot and hard.*

At her admission, his cock jerked hard. A fireball rushed through his body and seemed to lodge in his pulsating shaft. He lifted his head to look into her eyes, but his gaze fell on her mouth. That mouth had taken him to paradise. She had full lips. Pouty. A perfect bow. Sinful and tempting. He had loved watching her take his cock, her mouth stretched around him, working him. He bent to take her mouth with his.

I'll give you any fucking thing you want, baby. You name it, it's yours.

She opened for him instantly, her response hot. Fire burned through him. His veins ignited. His heart hammered right through his cock. Beating hard. Jerking and pulsing with hunger. He was used to that, but not like this. Not with this terrible brutal unrelenting need pounding through his body and centering in his groin. Heavy and aching beyond anything he'd ever known.

Then I want to go first. I have a feeling once you get started, I won't be getting my turn for a very long time.

She was not wrong about that. He kissed her over and over, drowning in her. Coaxing her response at first. She followed his lead easily, learning fast. Sex had always been great, but he'd never felt like this before. So on edge. So hungry. Desperate for her taste. He had planned to devour her, and he was doing just that.

Her mouth moved under his. Sweet. So sweet. A promise of paradise. Her hands slid up his chest and one curled around his neck. The other hand crept into his hair, fingers tunneling into the unruly mass. Her response added a new element, so that he deepened the kiss, his heart fluttering strangely. His arms pulled her close, locking her to him, but with a tenderness he hadn't known he was capable of.

Baby, you want to go first, I'm going to give you that, but when I say you're done, you stop. I'm going to be inside you when I get off. He was going to explode. The rockets were going off already. Everywhere in his body, hot blood surged. Cells were alive and firing. Fingers of lust, mixed with something far sweeter and heavier, danced up his legs and down his chest, centering in his groin, where hunger and need mixed into one throbbing, hard spike.

Trap was acutely aware of everything about her. Her taste. Her scent. The fullness of her lips. Soft yet firm. Her hot mouth. Her body moving against his, all those lush curves, yet so small and delicate. Her body was pure silk and felt like heaven against his. His hands were huge on her, stroking down her breasts to her belly, fingers unerringly finding the hourglass and then dipping lower to press into her tight welcoming entrance that was even hotter than her mouth.

Cayenne moved her body subtly, breaking the kiss, sliding her hand over the heavy muscles of his chest and then down to his defined belly. She loved the way his body was so hard, all that steel under his skin. Every muscle defined and rippling at her touch. Trap radiated hunger—for her. She had never felt more wanted or more powerful than she did at that moment.

She wasn't an insect to be pinned to an exam table, she was a desirable woman. No. More. She was Trap's woman. She loved being his woman. It was thrilling, exhilarating and scary all rolled into one, but she believed him when he said he would have her back and take care of her. She didn't need taking care of, but she loved that he wanted to. She loved that he knew she would want to take just as good care of him. She wanted to take care of him right then, because she was in his mind and once he got started, he wasn't going to give her this moment, and she needed it.

She had enjoyed the night before and giving him this would take a little time, allowing her nerves to steady. She wanted this, to belong fully to him, but that didn't mean she wasn't nervous. He was very well proportioned and that meant that he was big. He didn't look as if he could possibly fit inside her. That terrified her, because if she couldn't handle him, she would lose him.

For the last four months, ever since she'd first laid eyes on him, there in her cell when all hope had been lost, she had wanted him. Her voice was a weapon, yet it didn't work on him. For some reason, she loved that it didn't—that he could resist her commands and could turn the tables on her. She knew she could paralyze him with a bite, or wrap him in her silk if necessary, so she was safe enough, but still, she liked the knowledge that he was her equal in every way.

She kissed his chin and then his throat. He lay back, allowing her to take the lead. She loved that too. The fancy veils hanging around the bed added to her feeling of safety, creating a warm, sensuous cocoon for the two of them. She loved her webs, the masterpieces she created. She'd been exhausted, but the wide-open space had made her feel vulnerable. Given the chance, knowing she would wake up to Trap, she had put effort into making the intricate webs especially beautiful—and she'd succeeded.

She kissed her way down his chest. She hadn't been able to touch that part of him the night before due to the silken ropes she'd tied him down with. Now, she took her time, memorizing every inch of him with her mouth, tongue and fingertips. She traced each muscle with her tongue, lapping at his skin. He tasted masculine. Perfect. He felt masculine. That was even more perfect.

Her tongue teased at his hard, flat nipples. She suckled gently and then, when his breath hitched, a little harder. She flicked with her finger and brushed with her thumb, watching his face to see his reaction.

Baby, I'm burning up here. You want this, you need to get to it.

She smiled against his belly as she licked down the path of his ribs to that particularly hard area. She loved the way his muscles rippled under her touch. She threw one leg over his thighs, straddling him. Holding him in place while she took her time exploring.

So impatient.

He made a single sound. A growl. It seemed to rumble up from his chest and sounded like a large menacing cat warning it was about to pounce on prey and tear it apart. She took the warning for what it was. Her man was definitely getting impatient and he wasn't going to wait much longer. She loved that. Loved that he wanted her so much. Still, she was fairly certain, she could slow him down by giving him something else to think about.

She used her hands, now warm from his skin, to slide up his inner thighs, to cup the heavy velvet sac, rolling gently, all the while watching his face. She *loved* watching his eyes darken and the way the lines in his face deepened with desire—with need and hunger. She loved knowing she could do that to him even though she hadn't a clue what she was doing.

She had studied every book online she could find once the Internet was up and running again in Trap's home. He'd left one computer unprotected, for her to use, so she'd put it to good use, trying to learn as much about the outside world and, after seeing him at night, as much about sex as she could.

She put that knowledge to use, all the while watching his eyes, those blue flames burning hot behind the ice. Her fingers stroked and caressed. She bent her head, allowing her hair to slide over his bare thighs as she kissed the velvet softness and then used her tongue and mouth on him. His breath left his lungs in a gasping rush. His hips moved restlessly and one hand crept down to fist in her hair. All that told her she was doing something right.

She licked up his shaft, slid her tongue just beneath the crown while her thumb brushed over the soft, flared head, smearing those precious pearly drops. His breath hissed out of him.

Cayenne. The warning came through in a gruff, unmistakable command.

She smiled up at him, her gaze on his as she took him into her mouth. He was hot. Delicious. Thick and very, very hard. She loved the texture of him. The taste of him. She used her mouth, suckling hard and then butterflying her tongue before taking him deeper and then withdrawing. She worked at drawing liquid, at taking more of him into her mouth. It wasn't easy. He was thick, but she was determined. She enjoyed what she was doing and more, she *loved* what it was doing to him.

Don't look away.

She loved the sound of his voice. Low. Commanding. Edged with hunger. So erotic she was burning between her legs. She kept her eyes on his as she worked his cock with her mouth and tongue. His hips moved. Bucked. Drove him deeper. She knew her eyes went wide with shock, but she took him deeper and felt the answering rush of liquid heat between her legs.

Use your hands on my balls and my inner thighs.

Immediately she complied with her left hand, sliding it between his legs, massaging and kneading, but removing her right hand from the base of his cock was a little more difficult. That gave him the power. His hips stilled. His eyes went dark blue. Electric. She wanted to give him that. She did. Very slowly she pried each finger loose, one by one, forcing her hand to slide down to caress his very tight sac.

That's my girl. Beautiful, Cayenne. Feel what you're doing to me. Come into my mind. Feel this, how good it is.

His hips moved again, thrusting just a little deeper and then retreating before she could panic. Her lips stretched wide around him. She flattened her tongue to use it when she could and sucked hard when she was able. It was hot. Erotic. A little scary, but his gaze never wavered from hers and kept her from panicking.

She pushed further into his mind and instantly felt the heat rush through her body like a fireball. Her mouth massaged his cock, the roof, her tongue, and each time he pushed deeper toward her throat, she felt the almost convulsive ecstasy shooting through his body. That empowered her even more.

I love giving this to you, she admitted.

His cock swelled, stretching her mouth more, went deeper until she was nearly swallowing him. He felt so hard and hot. So erotic. She suckled and let him thrust, retreat, his hips still gentle, the movements controlled, but she could tell that control was slipping. She wanted that. She wanted to take him beyond his control.

You're done. My turn.

She wasn't done. She hadn't brought him to the point of no return. Her lips tightened around him, instinctively wanting to hold him to her. His hands went under her arms and he yanked her up and off of him, rolling to pin her body beneath his. The movement was so fast and so efficient, she had lost him before she knew what was happening.

She stared up at his face, the lines carved deep, his eyes nothing but blue flames. Maybe she was wrong. Maybe she had driven him past that point of no return. His hands moved over her body possessively, and everywhere he touched, she felt he'd branded her. Deep. Through her skin straight to her bones.

His mouth took hers, hard and long and delicious, taking her mind, melting it until she was squirming under him. Turning her into pure need. His mouth left hers and traveled to her right breast. He was rougher than he'd ever been with her, using the edge of his teeth. Nipping, even biting, his tongue caressing and soothing. His fingers rolled and tugged hard, sending streaks of fire straight to her clit.

Her sheath spasmed. The tension built and built. The burn grew hotter until she was pleading with him to do something. He kept at her body, his hands so big that when he stroked his palm down from beneath her breasts to her mound, he took in nearly her entire front with each sweep. She felt him everywhere.

His mouth went under her breasts, suckling. She hadn't thought the underside of her breasts could be so erotic, but when he added his teeth, a spear of lightning slammed through her body straight between her legs. She cried out and held him to her, or tried to. His head was already moving lower. He shifted his body down the bed, to pull her thighs apart and push her legs over his shoulders, leaving her open and exposed to him.

The position felt vulnerable, especially when his hands cupped her bottom and he brought her up off the bed straight to his mouth. He had said he was ravenous for her, and he wasn't lying. He fed. There was no other word for it. His mouth took control of her, and with the first thrust of his tongue, she was lost, sent rocketing into another realm.

There was no getting away from his mouth and the erotic noises he made while feeding on her. He liked her taste. He craved it. He clearly believed she belonged to him and so did her creamy honey. He devoured her. One orgasm crashed into another. She tried to yank his head up using a fist in his hair. She couldn't catch her breath, her body nearly convulsing with pleasure. He used his mouth like a weapon, his tongue, his teeth, suckling and stabbing deep. And then he added a finger.

The rush was full body, overtaking her like a freight train, the strength of the wave enormous so that she couldn't catch her breath, and panic began to take hold. Nothing could feel this good. She couldn't take it. She couldn't stop him. Another orgasm crashed through her.

I can't take any more.

Yes, you can. You will. You need to be ready to take me.

He was relentless. She did the only thing she could think of in her panicked state. She tried to wrap him in silk. She'd trapped him the night before, and she was certain she could just pull him off her enough to give her breathing room. His tongue licked up her clit, stabbed inside. His finger followed and then a second one.

She spun silk around his wrist and tugged. To her shock, his arm went right through the woven strands.

Baby. Gruff amusement. *I can go through walls. Do you think a little silk is going to stop me?*

Her breath caught in her lungs. He could have gotten loose the night before when she'd tied him up. Any time he could have gotten loose, but he hadn't. He'd allowed her to explore and feel safe. He'd given her that gift. That was enormous, so enormous, she forced air through her body and deliberately tried to relax. Giving back. Letting him have her. Letting him lead her.

His fingers stretched her and it burned, but it was a good burn. Fierce and hot. His tongue stole the ache and pushed her higher. This time, when she wanted the wave to crash over her, it didn't come. His mouth was gone. His finger was gone. He slid his body up and over hers, one knee keeping her thighs apart.

I'm big, baby. Let me do the work. I don't want this to hurt you.

He rubbed his face along her belly, the shadow on his jaw scraping erotically before he knelt up on the bed between her thighs, forcing them apart with the wide column of his legs. Heart pounding, she looked up at his face. He was beautiful. Wholly masculine. Her entire body pulsed and throbbed for him. When he pressed the flared head of his cock into her entrance she had to fight to keep from trying to impale herself.

It was like a hot brand invading. He pushed in just a short inch, and she gasped as he stretched her. He withdrew, waited a heartbeat, his eyes on hers, and then he pushed forward again. Slowly. Gently.

Trap. She wailed his name. Pleading in her voice. She needed him inside her and he wasn't cooperating fast enough. She *needed* him, but no matter how she squirmed, she couldn't get what she wanted.

My cock is thick, baby, and it's going to stretch you. We're doing this slow.

There it was again, that absolute, implacable voice that sent more liquid heat bathing just the broad head of his cock as he once again pushed inside. An inch. A slow, burning, send-fire-streaking-through-her-body inch. She caught her breath as he added a second inch, using a little more force to take his cock just a bit deeper.

Her body resisted the invasion, fighting him, even as her head thrashed on the pillow and she tried to shove her hips down hard to take him inside. She *needed.* She was empty without him, and that tension inside *had* to be released or she might not survive.

Trap tried to keep breathing, but she was so fucking tight

he wasn't actually certain he was going to get inside her. She was hot and slick and she wanted him—that was to his advantage, but she was so tight, squeezing him hard, clamping down, her sheath resistant, the inner muscles refusing to give way.

He rocked his hips back and forth, staying shallow before he retreated again. She cried out, a mewling, keening cry filled with pleas. Her breath came in ragged gasps, and her eyes had gone dazed and shocked. She was beautiful lying there, her fists clenched in the sheets, and her hair wild.

"Please, Trap. I can't take this. I need you inside me right now. *Please*."

"All right, baby," he said softly. "Breathe for me. Relax. Try to stay as relaxed as possible."

Little beads of sweat broke out on his body. He wasn't certain he was going to survive. She was so tight that pushing into her not only was difficult, it bordered on uncomfortable. Still, his cock was a relentless steel spike that wanted only one thing. He surged deeper, driving through tight folds, stretching her sheath, forcing the invasion to gain a couple more inches.

Her breath hissed out. He clamped his hands tight on her bottom to prevent movement. It was like being inside a molten lava tunnel, his cock surrounded by magma. Her body gripped his hard.

Scorching hot, Cayenne. A fucking vise. You're so fucking tight.

Is that a good thing?

The best. I swear, no one sucks cock the way you do. No one kisses like you, and your body is fucking paradise, baby.

He rocked his hips, savoring the feel of her tight body surrounding his. He withdrew partially and before she could protest, he drove deeper, and this time, he felt the crown of his cock pushing against her thin barrier. He'd managed to get a little more than half his cock inside her.

He looked down to see himself, her body stretched tight

around his. He'd thought seeing her mouth around him was erotic, but he fucking loved seeing his cock half swallowed by her. That beautiful red hourglass glistened with moisture.

You have to hurry, Trap, Cayenne whispered into his mind. *I'm burning alive. I can't stand it. Just do it.*

Tell me what you're feeling. He had to give her body time to adjust.

Stretched. Burning. Hurts, but feels so good at the same time. Please do something. I need you to move.

He moved one hand, sliding it up her body to her breast. His finger and thumb took possession of her nipple and he tugged hard, pinching so that the bite of pain flared in her eyes. At the same time he drove hard through the barrier and buried himself, those last few inches, to the hilt.

She screamed. Her legs slid around his hips, pulling him tighter, holding him to her. He stayed still waiting again for her eyes to clear. Waiting for her body to adjust to his size and girth.

That hurt.

I know. It won't anymore. Just relax and let your body adjust. Breathe for me.

Already he could feel her body melting around his. Scalding him. Gripping him with all that silk. He found he was the one who had to breathe to stay in control.

You ready for this, baby?

Her gaze locked with his. *I've been ready.*

He took her at her word, caught her hips in his hands and began to thrust hard. Deep. Powering through those tight folds. Letting the friction and fire take him. Each drive forward jolted her body, but he pinned her hips in place, so she had no choice but to take each stroke as he gave it to her.

Her breath hissed out of her lungs. Her mouth formed a shocked *O*. Her body flushed a beautiful rose. He increased the strength of his strokes, surging deep, letting himself lose a little more control. Giving himself up to the fire consuming him. He buried himself in her over and over. He'd been right all along. Her skin was silk, but deep inside, she was even silkier, as if that molten channel was alive and breathing around him, gripping him with silken strands, weaving tight until the friction was so abrasive the ecstasy bordered on pain. He fucking loved it and he never wanted to leave.

She was close. So close. He used his thumb on her clit to take her over the edge. She went over hard and fast, her sheath clamping down, convulsing around his cock, squeezing and massaging like a million fingers inside a tight silken fist. Mind-blowing. He kept moving right through her orgasm, rougher now, much rougher. Building her next one, pushing her up even higher.

Her gaze clung to his as the tension in her coiled tighter. As the need and hunger grew hotter and even wilder. She began to thrash again, fear creeping into her wide gaze. The green turned to brilliant vibrant facets like twin glittering emeralds.

It's too much.

It's not enough. Let yourself go.

I can't. I can't. Not again.

Yes, you can, baby. With me. Keep looking at me. I want to see it take you when I give it to you. So fucking beautiful, Cayenne. Nothing like this. Nothing like you.

He planted one hand on the mattress beside her head and the other framed her face, holding her head still so he could look into her wild, green eyes as he slammed home, over and over, each stroke harder than the last. Ecstasy. He could see it on her face. Knew it was carved into every line of his.

Her fingers went to his wrist. Fingernails bit deep. She lifted her hips to meet his. He could see the last vestiges of control slipping, and it was a beautiful sight. Her eyes went wide again. He felt the powerful quake rush over her, this time contracting every muscle in her belly and along her thighs as it hit like a tsunami. Her inner muscles clamped down like a vise, gripping him with all that scorching-hot silk. Milking.

Her eyes didn't leave his face, gaze clinging to his, her mouth forming his name even as her body tore his own orgasm from him. It started somewhere in his toes, or maybe it was the top of his head because that threatened to come off as well. As it went rocketing through him, he exploded. Jet after jet of hot seed poured into her. He felt that. The heat of it. The beauty of it. Her silky channel clamping down even harder. Shuddering. Rippling. Surrounding him with pure paradise.

He buried his face in her neck, collapsing over her. Unprotected. In his life, that had never happened. Not once. Until now, and he knew it was deliberate. That also branded him a bastard, but he didn't care. She was his. He was hers. This was their start, and he wanted a family. He wanted to tie her to him every way he could think to tie her. And he wanted her protected, more than anything else. A child would protect her.

She was writhing under him, her body still alive, the powerful waves ripping through her. She cried out again, her hands buried deep in his hair, turned her face toward him, and he felt the bite. A flash of pain that only added to the beauty of the sheer wild, almost primitive mating. And it was mating. He'd claimed her with every stroke, branded her his with his mouth and hands and body.

Beneath him she stiffened, her hands fisting in his hair, her breath coming in a gasping rush.

"Trap." She wailed his name. "I didn't mean to do that. I'm sorry. I have to get out from under you. I have to help you."

He didn't move, pinning her beneath him as she squirmed wildly. He managed to lift his head to look down at her. She looked terrified. Completely and utterly terrified. Distressed. Ashamed. For a moment it didn't compute. Her body was still rippling around his. Her feet went to the mattress and she tried to buck him off.

"Stop, baby," he whispered, staring into the green of her eyes. "You're all right. I'm all right. The world is the best it's ever been right now."

"I bit you. I didn't mean to, Trap. I swear it was an accident. When I get overwhelmed it's a compulsion . . ."

"Cayenne, calm down." He took her mouth because she looked close to tears, and he needed his mouth on hers.

He kissed her gently. Reverently. Tenderly. He kept kissing her until her body melted into his again and all that soft silk was under him, surrounding him with heat and fire and so much beauty he felt his heart convulse in his chest. She kissed him back. Giving him more in her kisses than she'd ever done before. Surrendering to him. He knew what she was doing, what she was telling him. What she was gifting him.

She'd bitten him. Injected venom. There were tears on her face, and he licked them away, following the tracks from her cheeks to the tips of her lush eyelashes. She hadn't meant to do it, and she expected the venom to paralyze him. He alternated kissing her with removing the tears from her face, all the while gliding gently in her, letting those aftershocks send more pleasure spilling through both of them.

It took her a few minutes before she realized he wasn't reacting to the venom. His body hadn't gone into a paralysis. He was still moving in her. Holding her. Kissing her. She pulled back into the mattress, her green eyes searching his face.

"Trap. I *bit* you. I injected venom. You could have a worse reaction. The venom is accumulative. I know because they tested it over and over on individuals, and if they were injected or bitten more than a couple of times they died. You could be in serious trouble." She studied his face. "*Why* aren't you in serious trouble?"

CHAPTER 14

Trap rolled, taking Cayenne with him, keeping his body locked tightly with hers. Her smaller body sprawled over his, and he reached down and jerked up a sheet, covering her. His hips kept up the slow, sexy glide. He was sated, happy, but still semihard. He knew it wouldn't take much to get him fully hard again, and the tight channel with the ripples of silken fingers fisting and caressing was doing just that.

"You should be paralyzed," Cayenne reiterated, green eyes wide with shock. Her hands smoothed over his skin. Clearly she was agitated and still upset no matter that he clearly wasn't reacting to the venom.

"I'm not," he said, and wrapped his palm around the nape of her neck to bring her head down to his so he could take her mouth again. *I love your mouth, Cayenne,* he told her, even as he showed her. *So fucking beautiful, you take my breath away, baby.*

She kissed him back. Poured herself into him. Into the kiss. One turned into half a dozen. She lifted her head the inch or so his hand allowed, staring down at him in wonder.

He liked that the back of her head fit nicely in his palm and her thick, wild mane of black hair tumbled around her face and body, pooling on his chest and the mattress under him. It was sexy. More than sexy. Every movement made him feel as if he was totally covered in silk.

"How, Trap? How come you aren't paralyzed?" She looked close to tears again. "I'm so sorry. I couldn't stop myself. It's a compulsion when I'm overwhelmed. I was so afraid it would happen. I tried to tell myself it wouldn't but . . ." She trailed off, looking more confused than ever.

"Baby. Really? Did you think a man like me wouldn't figure out how to be immune to bites? *Your* bite? I knew I was taking you to bed. I plan on getting you very excited in a lot of different ways. Self-preservation alone told me I'd better figure out how to cope with your bites."

Her wide-eyed shock slowly turned to comprehension and then she narrowed her eyes. "That's what made you late moving here, wasn't it? Instead of working in your own lab here, you worked it out in Wyatt's lab so I wouldn't catch on to what you were doing."

His hands spanned her waist, keeping her seated fully over him as she sat up. The movement took him deep, and instantly his cock swelled, going hard like a steel spike, pushing against her soft tissues, forcing her inner muscles to accept him all over again. He refused to allow her to leave him, so she sat there, her long hair a dark cloud shimmering around her body, her green eyes going emerald and her soft mouth frowning at him.

"Even when you're pissed as hell, you're so damned sexy I could eat you alive," he said. He did a slow thrust upward and watched her breasts sway with the jolt.

"I can't believe you."

"Your man believes in being prepared, and aren't you glad I was?"

She didn't reply, but threw her head back, grinding down on him. He lifted her nearly off him and then, controlling the pace, brought her back slowly over him, sheathing his cock in hot silk.

"Harder," she breathed, trying to twist her body to get what she wanted.

"Not yet, baby. I don't want you to get too sore. Just ride me slow." His hands urged her to accept the slow, easy, almost languid rhythm he set.

"Trap," she protested, but she did as he asked, rising slowly, her tight muscles dragging over him, creating a delicious friction for both of them. Creating a slow, scorching-hot burn.

"Slow can be good, Cayenne," he explained. "We're going to take this slow and easy until neither of us can take it anymore."

She moved on him, following his lead, her body so tight he could barely stand the pleasure as she wrapped him in heat and silk. Her hair swung around her with each movement, sliding over his skin. His gaze stayed on her breasts for several long spectacular moments and then drifted lower, to watch himself disappear inside her and then reappear as she lifted her body.

"Look, baby," he said softly. "Look at us. Fucking beautiful. Sexy as hell. That's my woman. I love the way you take me inside you."

She looked down at where they joined together, watched the long, thick length of him appear and then disappear as she slowly rode him. His hands found her breasts and began a slow massage. She bit her lip.

"Touch my nipples, Trap. They feel like they're on fire."

He did so immediately, his fingers tugging hard. He raised his head as he urged her body down over him so he could take one hard nipple into the heat of his mouth, suckling strongly, using his tongue and the edge of his teeth. She gasped, and he felt liquid fire bathe his cock.

"I need harder, Trap," she whispered. "Please, honey, this is making me crazy."

"You don't like it?"

"I do. I really do, but it isn't enough. Even my blood feels like it's on fire. I can barely stand the tension. I'm right there. So close, but I can't go over. I need to go faster and harder. Please, Trap."

He loved the soft plea in her voice. The need in her. The way she had no problems demanding and asking for what she wanted. He loved that she pleaded with him and wasn't in the least embarrassed to do so.

He gave her harder. Faster. Rougher. He used his mouth and his hands and cock to drive her up higher. He watched her face the entire time. Her every expression. The way her breasts bounced and swayed with each hard jolt. The way her eyes went hazy and her breath turned ragged. The flush turning her skin a rose color and the way her mouth opened and that shocked pleasure came over her face right before the orgasm took her, roaring through her so that her body clamped down hard on his.

Still, he drove into her right through that exquisite contracting, needing to watch her while he gave that to her before he let go himself, giving himself up to the same fire. He pulled her down over him, wrapping his arms around her, finding her mouth unerringly to take her gasping breath right down his throat. He loved that too.

Her heart beat hard against his chest. He could tell she was exhausted. He was too. It felt good. Not just good, great. He allowed himself a few minutes to just hold her while their breathing settled. The lacy veils of silken webs hung like artwork around their bed, creating such an intimacy that he felt his need of her crawling down his throat to wrap around his heart.

"Trap?" Her voice was a soft whisper running over his skin like fingers.

"Right here, baby," he whispered against her neck. He slipped his fist into her hair, sifting through the long, thick mass.

"I'm so glad you found a way to be immune to my bite. I think that might happen again sometime."

He could tell by her voice she was not only afraid that she might bite him again when their sex got out of control, but she knew she would because the urge was not as controllable as she would like. This time there was trepidation in her tone.

He gently tugged on her hair. "Good thing I find your bite sexy as hell. Everything about you is sexy, Cayenne. *Especially* your bite. I love that I'm the only man in the world who is safe around you."

There was a small silence. He felt her lips curl against his chest. Her tongue licked at his skin. "You're not *entirely* safe."

He laughed softly. Happy. He could sleep just like that— her sprawled over him, his cock still in her. Not that it would be fair to her. She needed care. He kissed her neck and forced himself to do the right thing. She had gotten to him as no one in his life ever had. "I've got to get up for a minute. Stay here and let me get a warm washcloth, baby," he said. "I'll clean you up and we can go back to sleep."

She made a little sound of protest, but loosened her arms.

Very gently, Trap allowed his body to slide away from Cayenne's as he put her on her back. She watched him as he got out of bed, her gaze drifting over his body. There was evidence of her innocence on his cock and thighs. He liked the way she looked at him, that dark green creeping into the vibrancy of the emerald.

"You told me that once I was in your bed, when I was yours, you were going to share some things with me, Trap."

He cleaned himself thoroughly, taking his time, wincing at her words and trying to think what he could say to her to keep her with him. He had promised that to her and he was a man of his word. She gave him honesty, and he couldn't give her less. He ran hot water onto a cloth and carried it back to the bed.

He sat beside her and gently drew her knees up. He opened her legs, using his hands on her thighs. He used the washcloth gently and very intimately to clean her. "I did say that, didn't I?" Happiness slid away to be replaced by knots in his guts. Hard, tight ones that told him the ice in his veins wasn't going to protect him. If he told her the truth about what was waiting for her, and that he knowingly dragged her into danger with him, what would she think of him? She already had enough danger surrounding her with Whitney sending his soldiers after her.

"Trap?"

"Give me a minute, baby." He needed more than a minute. She'd given him her body. Surrendered completely to him, just as he'd asked of her. He actually *liked* being in her company. Before, with any other woman, ice had come back, and sometimes, even when his body wasn't sated, he had to leave. Get away from the woman, because the moment she opened her mouth she made his head want to explode. He'd never had this before—this desire that had grown into a need and now was pure determination. He wasn't going to lose her.

He took his time getting rid of the washcloth before padding barefoot back to her. Sliding into bed, he drew up the covers, turning to her to slip his arms around her and pull her small body close to his. "You certain you want to hear this now, baby? You need more sleep. I'm not going to be through with you for a very long time. I plan on feeding you, fucking you and sleeping with you, for the next few weeks until neither of us can move."

"Sounds like a plan," she agreed softly, "but you promised me. I need to hear what you have to say."

He sighed and dropped his chin on the top of her head.

"Why don't you want to tell me?"

"You know why, Cayenne. You may not have been with any other man, but you're intelligent and you can also see the difference between a man like Wyatt and me. He's a good man and he's going to be a fantastic husband to Pepper.

I'm going to drive you insane with my personality. I'm going to hurt you when I'm not thinking before I snap at you. I don't like a lot of people around me, which means you aren't going to be attending a lot of parties and have tons of friends around you all the time because I'm going to want you with me, not out gallivanting around with your friends. I'm bossy and demanding and I'll expect sex whenever the fuck I want it. Adding more to my long list of sins isn't conducive to making you want to stay."

She slid her hand down his forearm to his hand—the one splayed possessively over her stomach. His belly knotted more. He hadn't even told her he was already trying to plant his child in her. She was new to all this and she wouldn't be thinking about getting pregnant, but he was determined they would have children right away. He was going to have a family with her. His own family. He planned to give her everything she wanted, make her his princess, surrounded by every protection he could give her. He didn't know how to give her sweet words, but he knew he could show her— eventually. He needed time though. Time to hook her and keep her hooked.

"So breaking this down, Trap, I will admit to being intelligent and to having studied the members of your Ghost-Walker team for the last four months. I visited Wyatt's home nearly every day, watching all of you."

He didn't like that. Her watching the other men. Maybe wanting one of them. He pushed his hips tight against her bottom. That beautiful, curved ass that swayed when she walked. An invitation, just like her soft, sexy voice and her lush mouth. The ass that was *his,* not belonging to one of the other men.

"Wyatt wouldn't suit me. Neither would any of the others. I'm a little obsessed with you, in case you haven't noticed. It was *your* bedroom I went to when I couldn't stand it and had to be close to you. I *had* to be close to you. You're the only person in the world who showed me kindness. More, you saw me. As a human being, not an insect or a threat."

"Cayenne." He murmured the protest against the top of her head. He didn't want her to ever have that image in her mind.

"At the risk of making you even more arrogant than you already are, you're the most handsome man I've ever laid eyes on. I love everything about you. Your height, how strong you are. Your eyes. The set of your jaw. I can describe every inch of your body, Trap. Every single inch. I love how you taste and how you make me feel. I love that you have a mind, and with that, comes a sexy, hot man. I want that for me. I don't want any of the others. They wouldn't suit *my* personality."

She was silent a moment and he felt her lips whisper across the back of his hand. His cock jerked hard and he pushed deeper into the cleft of her ass. She was warm silk and her body just melted deeper into his.

"I like your personality, Trap, and it's one I understand. I'm not easy, and I doubt that I ever will be. Yes, it hurt when you were so cold when we were in town, but you explained that and I understood. Now I know what to expect and why you need to be that way. I don't need you to be anything but who you are. If you're rude to me and I don't like it, I'm going to say so. We'll probably exchange hot words, and then I'll probably fling myself at you because I like to see all that ice melt and I know I can melt it."

He closed his eyes tight. He'd been alone so fucking long. Never had he ever considered that he might fall so hard so fast or even that he *could* fall. But there she was, the woman who could match the wild in him. She really would understand his driving needs in the laboratory, and he was fairly certain she'd be there with him, working right alongside of him.

"I don't like a lot of people around me either, Trap. Even if I make friends, and right now you have far more than I do as I don't have *any*, I don't foresee myself overcoming years of being alone in a cell and wanting to be with tons of people. Being with you is the longest I've ever been with another human being. I can't relax without my silks surrounding me. It's how I kept my privacy in the cells with all the cameras on me. I need them. I'm not certain too many other people are going to understand that. So you can cross that worry off your list. It's you I want to be with."

He heard the ring of honesty in her voice. She wasn't ever going to be the type of woman who liked to go to parties and get her photograph taken with him in order to have her fifteen minutes of fame in magazines. If anything, that would be another detriment. But she'd do it for him. He got that now. She was in as deep as he was in spite of his sins.

"I like your bossiness and your demanding because I can be the same way. As far as you making demands on my body—seriously, Trap? Can you not feel what you do to me? I look at you and melt. I want to have sex with you. I *love* having sex with you. I may not know what I'm doing exactly, but I learn fast and I know I can give you whatever you need. I trust that you'll do the same for me. Trap." She turned her head to look at him over her bare shoulder. "I want you with every breath I take."

There it was. Cayenne handing him everything. She didn't have to, and most women wouldn't. She didn't play games, she wouldn't know how. She was strictly honest and meant every single word she said. He let his breath out slowly, his fingers, as they stroked her stomach, reverent.

"My father was a mean son of a bitch, Cayenne. I didn't have one of those happy homes like you see in the movies or read about in books. He liked to beat up my mother and his children. He didn't work much, so he had a lot of time to think up ways to fuck with all of us. My mom worked and she didn't often see what he did to us, but eventually she decided to take us and run."

Her hand moved over his, stroking caresses, but she

remained silent. Waiting. Knowing it wasn't good, but wanting him to understand she was with him no matter how bad it was. He was in her mind and he felt that solidarity. It was strange to share space in one's mind because the loneliness simply disappeared. Every last vestige of it. Cayenne filled those deep cracks and wide gaps. Her strength. Her warmth. Her caring.

Trap had never really believed in love—not since he was a boy. He hadn't dared believe in it. He'd felt that emotion for his sister and his mother. Both had been ripped from him. He'd felt it for his aunt, and she'd been ripped from him as well. That had been soul-destroying. Utterly soul-destroying. He had forced away all emotion, turning himself into a glacier to survive.

Wyatt had found a small crack in the ice and wormed his way in. Then one by one the other team members had followed Wyatt until he accepted them into his life, but he still held himself aloof. Apart. There was no staying apart from Cayenne. None at all. He didn't want that. He wanted what he had right in that moment. That connection. That closeness.

"I was different. He fixated on that. My sister Dru was different as well, and she understood me when no one else did. My mother loved me, but I was strange and she didn't really have time for that strangeness. She worked all the time and coped with him, trying to keep him off of us. He grew to despise me. No matter how much Dru and my mother tried to keep him away from me, he beat the hell out of me and made my life as miserable as possible."

Cayenne's fingers tightened over his hand and she pushed back into him until she was practically sharing his skin. He found he couldn't get close enough to her. Sharing her skin was fast becoming a necessity. He trudged on, wanting her to understand why he was the way he was and what that would mean to her. She *had* to choose him. He couldn't see himself letting her go.

"In a way, I almost didn't mind. When he focused on me,

he wasn't going after my younger brother, Brad, or my baby sister, Linnie. He left my mom and Dru alone. One day, though, he broke my arm and a couple of ribs. We couldn't hide that from Mom and she took me to the hospital. He was arrested and taken to jail. Dru told Mom everything, and Mom decided it was enough and we left."

He slid his hand down her soft stomach until his finger could caress the soft triangle at the junction of her legs. He needed the soft feel of the hourglass. Her hand went with his and there was something sexy and also loving in that. He found stroking the hourglass, tracing the shape of it in all that soft silk soothed him.

"He found us. Mom took us across the country, and he still found us. He wasn't alone. He had two brothers. Like my father, they were vicious and cruel. They liked hurting others. They stayed outside pouring gasoline all over the walls and then coming into the house and doing the same in all the rooms. They'd planned it with him. My dad, my uncles, *planned* to murder his children and his wife."

He felt her breath hitch. Her stomach contracted and he pressed his fingers deeper into the hourglass.

"My father shot Linnie and Brad and my mother. Then Dru. She tried to protect me. There was so much blood, and I couldn't make it stop flowing out of her. Her eyes were open and she looked so horrified. Terrified. Lifeless. He should have shot me right there, with my body under hers, but my seeing him kill her wasn't enough for him. Knowing I was going to die wasn't enough for him. He wanted to beat the shit out of me one more time. I was nine fucking years old, he'd just killed my mother, my brother and my two sisters, and that wasn't enough for him. He wanted to beat the shit out of me one last time before he killed me."

"Trap." She whispered his name and pressed his fingers tight against her.

His heart tripped. Stuttered. She was so beautiful to him. Everything about her. She felt compassion for that little boy.

She wanted to wrap him in her silk and protect him from what was to come. He knew, because he was in her mind. Her hand was on his and he actually felt the silken slide against the back of his. He slipped right past need and hunger to something else altogether. Something he didn't believe he'd ever feel for anyone, let alone a woman. He'd protected his heart for years. With Cayenne, he just couldn't find the ice to keep her out.

"I went after him. I was nine years old and I went after him. I slipped on Dru's blood, Cayenne. It was everywhere. *Everywhere.* All over me. All over the floor and walls. I rammed my head into his crotch and I got the gun and shot him. He had a knife and he stabbed me with it a couple of times, but I didn't even feel the blade go in. Not then."

"Your belly and thigh."

She'd seen the scars. She knew them intimately. She'd even traced them with her tongue. He rubbed his face in her hair. "He kept slipping in Dru's blood. Even after she died she saved me. He wasn't dead, but he was gone. I made certain when I shot him that he wasn't going to live." He told her the stark truth. "Even then, barely nine, I knew anatomy. I knew where to place bullets to do the most damage and cause the most suffering. You need to know that about me, Cayenne. The worst. Because I'd fucking do it again if I had the chance."

"So would I," she admitted quietly.

Trap searched her green eyes until he saw the truth there and he believed her. He pressed his face against her hair, burrowed into it so the silk concealed his expression. She faced away from him, but he was confessing and he didn't take chances. "His brothers threw gas on him and all around the room. They lit it on fire and got out. I crawled through the flames and lived."

"The scars on your feet and ankles."

She'd kissed them too. Her hands had been gentle, soothing. Amazing. She'd nearly torn out his heart when she'd done that.

"I went to live with my aunt. She wasn't very old, but she took me in. It was just the two of us. I began making money because I invented shit and got the patents and then sold them. We lived well for a while. Apart from everyone else, but well. We changed our name and hid in a city. They—my uncles—found us. Kidnapped her. Tortured and raped her. Threw her on my doorstep after I paid the ransom. She was dead."

Cayenne's body jerked. Hard. She made a sound low in her throat.

"I hired the best detectives to look for them, but they're in the wind. I did everything I could to hone myself into something that could take them down, but I've never been able to find them. They said, if I found a woman, they'd come after her and they'd take her away from me and do the same to her—that I couldn't protect her."

"That's why you hid my face from the camera."

"Yes." He was honest. "Eventually, someone is going to get a shot of you, but I want to minimize that risk. I'll surround you with bodyguards, baby, but they'll eventually come at us. I waited to claim you, tried to talk myself out of it to protect you, but I'm too fucking weak to give you up."

"Trap." Her voice was gentle. "I *want* them to come after me. I'm not defenseless and there's no way they could hurt me without getting close. They get close and they're dead. We both know that. I have no problem making certain they can't do that to another woman. I'm the kind of woman who would have put a bullet in your father, one that made him suffer for as long as possible. That's who I am."

Again, her voice rang with honesty. She meant every word. There was no fear. None whatsoever. Just determination.

"Cayenne." He whispered her name, closing his eyes against the burn there. "You know what I'm telling you, right? What to expect when you're with me."

"Did you think I'd run, Trap?" she asked gently. "I might not know the first thing about relationships or cooking or having friends, but I know how to defend myself and I have no problems seeing beyond smiling faces. I could always tell the worst of my tormentors before they ever opened their mouths. I feel it like an oil surrounding them. The more vicious and cruel they are, the thicker the oil. Your uncles could walk up to me with halos on their heads and I'd know what they were."

"I don't like putting you in this position, Cayenne, but I can't give you up." He made the admission softly. "I want to put a ring on your finger and make it official. The moment I do that, the moment the world knows you're mine, wherever they are, they'll come out of the woodwork and make their try."

"Good. We'll be ready for them. And don't forget, Trap, while you're taking on all this guilt because of two men who have no idea who you are anymore or what you're capable of, I've got a death sentence on my head. Whitney will keep sending teams after me, which means, you'll be in harm's way because of me."

"I think I can get that particular order rescinded," Trap said. His finger stroked the hourglass again. She wasn't going to like the *how* of it, but he didn't feel the least remorseful. He *wanted* those ties to him. She had her silken threads, he had human ones.

She turned her head and looked at him over her shoulder. "What does that mean, Trap? *Exactly* what does that mean?"

He *fucking* loved that she was intelligent enough to be suspicious. She knew whatever plan he had, she wasn't necessarily going to be down for, although he'd kept his tone strictly neutral.

"Whitney likes to pair his soldiers. He gives the pair the skills to be an effective unit in a combat situation."

He spread his fingers wide again, covering her tummy, feeling the underside of her breasts with his fingertips. He stroked caresses along the twin curves. "I've never felt softer skin in my life, baby. I fucking love the way you feel."

"Trap, don't change the subject. I'm not going to be distracted."

"Is that a challenge?" A teasing note crept into his voice.

He had learned fun from Wyatt. He'd been sober, incapable of laughter, when he'd first met Wyatt. Then the members of his team, no matter how aloof he held himself, gave him a bad time. He'd learned to handle that as well. Maybe all that had prepared him for a life with Cayenne. All he knew for certain was that he enjoyed teasing her. He let the pads of his fingers swirl up and over her breast to brush the tips, those beautiful rosy tips that were so very sensitive.

She shivered and her hand came over the top of his, clamping him to her, right over her breast so the hard little peak pushed into the center of his palm. "Behave yourself and tell me what your plan is to get my termination order rescinded."

He liked her bossy. He liked her submissive. He liked every single thing about her. Especially that she could be lethal.

"I'm going to get you pregnant."

She went very still at his confession.

He moved his hand back down to cover her soft little tummy, ignoring her body language, talking his way right through it. "He's going to grow right here. Our child. He'll be smart, and we'll both give him all the love and happiness in the world. He'll have everything neither of us ever had."

"Trap."

Her voice was as still as her body. He actually felt her withdrawing from him, pulling her body into the fetal position, moving a slight inch from him, but he felt the loss. She couldn't separate herself any farther because he held her to him.

"Don't," he cautioned. "I mean it, Cayenne. Don't pull away from me. You know that's the only solution."

"We can't have a child so Whitney will leave me alone."

"Baby, think about this logically. He'll keep coming at

us. We might fight off fifty teams, but eventually, they'll penetrate our defenses and possibly get you. Or me. Or one of the members of my team. More than anything else, Whitney is looking for the next generation. He wants to see if the enhancements he gave us will be stronger in our children."

"My child won't ever be an experiment." There was outrage in her voice. Temper. Her body had gone stiff. He knew she would have scooted off the bed if she could have. "Not to save my life, or yours or anybody else's."

"*Our* child will never be used as an experiment, Cayenne. I can give you my word on that."

"I won't have a baby to save my life. That's no reason to bring a child into the world."

"Baby." He whispered the endearment softly. A reprimand. Very gently he forced her to turn over. "Look at me."

"I am looking at you."

"You're looking at my chin. I mean look into my eyes. Listen to me. You know me better than that."

He waited until she reluctantly lifted her gaze to his. There was fear there. Stark fear, pushing toward terror. His heart contracted. She was unafraid to face hit squads sent after her, or his two murderous uncles, but the thought of having a child filled her with anxiety.

He kept his voice soft. "You *know* me. You know what I am inside. I gave you the truth about myself and my childhood. Our child would be conceived in love. *Love*, Cayenne. I want a family. Children. I know that scares you, but we're both smart. We can figure it out. We've both got good instincts. We have Wyatt and the boys and Nonny and Pepper to help us out if we decide we hit a stumbling block and don't know how to handle something."

Her gaze drifted over his face. She held her breath and didn't seem to notice. He did. He noticed everything about her. Every. Single. Thing.

"Breathe, baby."

She pressed her hand to her stomach and shook her head.

"You should have talked to me about this. I'm just trying to get used to the idea of you and me."

"I know," he said quietly.

"This is a *huge* thing, Trap. You can't make decisions like this for both of us."

"I know," he agreed.

She narrowed her eyes. "Stop saying that. It doesn't mean anything. I *do* know you, and that is your arrogant, bossy, macho bullshit."

"It's not arrogance, Cayenne. Or macho. Or bullshit. I calculate everything. I can't help that about myself. My brain works on a problem and I find solutions. We need a solution to keep hit squads from coming at us every minute of the day for the rest of our lives. I need to keep you safe. I *need* that. You don't have to agree with me on this. You don't. It's my need, not yours. You're willing to take the risk, I'm not."

"Do you hear yourself?" She was outraged. She sat up, drawing her knees to her and holding on to her legs as tight as possible.

He sat up much more slowly, sliding back until he hit the headboard. He was relaxed. Watchful. Alert. But relaxed. He wasn't wrong. He'd gone through every single possible solution, and there was no other. Whether or not she stayed with him, Whitney would keep sending his supersoldiers after her. Eventually there would be a mistake on her part—on their part—and she'd be dead. That was unacceptable to him.

He wanted a child with her. He wanted more than one. He wanted several. They had a big home. A huge one. They had an entire team to help protect children. It was the *only* solution, and it was logical whether she wanted to admit it or not.

He reached for her and pulled her gently between his legs. She didn't unfold, or soften, but remained stiff, curled into herself. She seemed smaller than ever, a gift she had that helped her to disappear. She wasn't going to get that chance.

"I know having children scares you . . ."

"Trap, *you* scare me. *This* scares me. *Us.* A relationship. A commitment. You at least know what a family is supposed to be. You've lived in the world. You may have had a bastard for a father, but you had a mother and sisters and a brother. You had an aunt and Wyatt and Nonny. I had a tiny cell, my silks for privacy. I had techs darting me through bars so I couldn't hurt them."

She lifted her hands to show him her palms. "I had pins pushed through my hands, shoulders and ankles to hold me in place. I have scars on my ribs and feet as well as my palms. They studied me, took my blood, milked my venom. Tried to extract the silks. I've been shot, knifed and pitted against numerous supersoldiers all in the name of science. I don't know how to be what you want me to be, but I was willing to try . . ."

"Don't say *was*, Cayenne. We've hit a fucking bump, not the end. I know how you lived. Do you think I don't know? I *am* a scientist. I know exactly what those fuckwads did to you, baby. I'm going to erase it all. I am." He reached around her and caught her wrists, pulling her hands back to him, palms up so he could brush kisses into them. "We have time to get you pregnant and that gives us time to prepare for an actual baby. Time to get to be us. To learn the things we don't know."

She shook her head. "You're asking too much."

"No, I'm not," he said. "I'll never ask too much of you. You've been guarding Wyatt's girls. You came back and entered a fight with supersoldiers in order to keep them from being taken. You want children, Cayenne, same as me. You want a family. With me."

"*Someday.* This is going too fast. Way too fast."

"Four fucking months, baby, is not too fast. Not when I've had shit for years and you've had it all your life. Those days are over. We're going to look ahead, build us a family, and we're going to have the fucking ever after."

He pulled her onto his lap, his arms surrounding her. "I hear that you're scared. But I don't hear you saying you don't want my child growing in you. It doesn't matter when we have a child. Now or ten years from now, you're going to want that baby the moment you find out you're pregnant. You know you will."

She leaned back against his chest, turning a little more to rest her head against him, the first sign that he might be getting somewhere. He kept persisting.

"Cayenne, I *want* my child in you. Not just because it will keep Whitney from coming after you, but because once I realized that was the solution to our problem, the idea took hold and I found I wanted a child with you more than anything. I don't care if it's a girl or boy, only that it's ours and healthy."

She was silent for a long time. He waited. He was patient. He had methodically thought of and discarded a hundred ideas when the solution had presented itself to him. He'd been shocked. If he was truthful, even a little afraid. He'd never held a baby, but the thought of his child growing in Cayenne made him soft inside. He came to like the idea. Then want it.

"You don't have a child because of Whitney," she said, clinging to her stubborn. Her tone wasn't quite as combative. Her body had gone soft again, sinking into his skin, melting so the silk of her slid along his chest and belly. He instantly felt the answering need in his cock. He allowed it to happen. To build in him. She felt the growing erection against her bare bottom but she didn't shift away from him.

"No, we don't," Trap said quietly. "We have a child because it completes us. Because we love each other that much. If, when that happens, it makes Whitney back off, all to the good, but our child will be loved and wanted because he or she is ours."

She was quiet. He let his hands roam. Cupping her breasts. Thumbs sliding over her hard little nipples. He felt the answering heat rushing through her body. Silken skin melted more into him.

"I want you all over again, Cayenne."

She tilted her head to look at him. "I want you too, Trap, but you scare me so much sometimes. I don't want to get lost because I feel such emotion for you, and I want to please you. I want to give you everything you've never had."

He caught the cloud of dark hair in his hand and tilted her head back even more. "There is nothing I wouldn't do for you, Cayenne. Nothing I wouldn't give you if you asked me for it. I want to give you everything you've never had— especially a family. I need you alive for that. I need you lying beside me every fucking night. I need to wake up to you in order to give you the world. I know that sounds selfish and, baby, I *feel* selfish when it comes to you. You've trusted me with you this far. Come all the way with me. *All* the way."

She took a breath, and her vibrant green gaze moved over his face, taking him in. "Then okay. We'll do this. Together. But don't make any more decisions no matter how logical they are if they involve me, without consulting me first."

"Babe." His voice said it all. He was that kind of man. He knew it. She knew it.

Her breath hissed out of her. "Fine, but expect my temper when you do, Trap. It isn't going to be pretty."

"I know." And he did.

She pushed out of his lap and turned her head to lick up his chest, tracing heavy muscle. "This time, you'd better give me what I want and not go all commando on me and tell me I'm done. I'll be done when I want to be done. Got that?"

He got it. He was more than happy to give himself up to her very talented mouth. She'd given in to him and she could have any damn thing she wanted—especially his cock.

CHAPTER 15

———⟳———

Cayenne's heart beat a million miles an hour as she stepped onto the pier that was close to Wyatt's home. The last two weeks had been amazing. Trap spent most of the time in the laboratory. Wyatt came to work with him often, nearly every day. At first Cayenne had made herself scarce when he came over, but then she decided she needed to get used to being around someone besides Trap and she joined the two men in the laboratory.

Trap hadn't pushed her at all to do anything, but she could tell he was pleased that she'd made the effort. She found herself liking Wyatt. He had an easy charm, enabling her to relax in his presence. Still, she liked it best when she was alone with Trap.

Trap really liked sex. All the time. She did as well, so it was nice to know she wasn't alone in her needs. He was inventive and bossy but so was she. They worked together, and she had to admit, she was comfortable in their strange relationship. She spent most of her time trying to learn things that would make their huge house really a home. She wanted to do that for Trap. Watching various programs on the Internet helped, but even with numerous cooking shows to aid her, she had a miserable time learning to cook.

Baby, you have to stop looking like you're going to your doom.

There was humor in Trap's voice. Affection. Warmth. She wrapped herself in the way he felt for her, using it as armor as they approached the house. Trap took her hand and pulled her close, into his body, her front to his side, and then his arm swept around her, clamping her to him. She had no choice but to curl her fingers into his tight tee—the one that stretched valiantly across a wealth of muscle.

Do I look like that?

Yes, and it's adorable. So much so that if you keep it up, I'm going to carry you into the swamp and do you right there, just a few feet from the house.

Her nipples went hard and she glanced speculatively at the swamp creeping close to the Fontenot compound. She felt the rush of liquid heat between her legs the way she did whenever Trap used that voice. She *loved* his voice.

He halted abruptly. *You're thinking about it, aren't you? You'd let me.*

She was surprised. She'd never turned him down. Not once. He'd never turned her down. Ever. *Of course I would. Did you think I wouldn't?* In any case, sex with Trap was a far better option than being around people she didn't know. In fact, maybe it was the perfect time for seduction.

I love having you inside me. I love my mouth on you, the taste of you, the feel of you. Why wouldn't I go into the swamp with you? You could pick me up, I'll wrap my legs around your waist and you'll be inside me. What's not to love about that?

His arm tightened and he dipped his face low, toward hers. *Are you ready for me? Wet? Dripping my honey for me?*

She nodded, watching his expression closely. Trap didn't

give much away unless it came to sex. Then pure sensuality was carved into every line of his very masculine features. His glacier eyes flamed blue and became hooded and sexy. Like now. Her heart beat harder, her mouth went dry and deep inside she felt a spasm.

Absolutely. I'm always ready for you, Trap. You look at me and I'm ready. You touch me and I practically have an orgasm. Kissing me can give me a mini-orgasm. She touched her tongue to her bottom lip, tracing over it. Moistening it. Deliberately, her gaze dropped to the bulge in his jeans. *I didn't get to wake you up this morning the way I wanted to. You woke me and had your fun.*

He'd taken his time with her, his mouth between her legs, holding her down, making her take whatever he wanted to give her—and he wanted to give her a lot. She squirmed remembering how good it had been. How exciting and a little scary, because when he decided to be entirely in control, she was helpless against his strength. She loved every minute of it and he always made it worth it, but still, there was that little thrill of fear that only added to the pleasure he gave her.

Trap cupped her face in his hand. *Women don't like to get messed up when they're going out, Cayenne. Most would be embarrassed if their man wanted to take them out in the swamp and fuck them silly and then take them into a friend's house.*

She frowned at him and then switched from the more intimate telepathy to regular speech. "I don't understand, Trap. Why wouldn't they want their man to give them that?" Her hand strayed from his chest, lower, smoothing over his abs, to hook in the front of his belt, her fingers barely skimming the top of his growing bulge.

"They wouldn't want his friends to know what they were doing. And especially in a place like the swamp."

Her frown deepened as she struggled to comprehend what he was telling her. "That doesn't make any sense to me, Trap.

It isn't even logical. I always want you no matter where we are. What difference does it make, the location, and wouldn't your friends already know what we do? Is it supposed to be a secret? I assume Wyatt and Pepper have sex all the time. Why would we try to hide that from anyone?"

His hand came up under her chin. "Baby, you're making me as hard as a rock."

"That's a good thing, isn't it?" This time her hand slipped more, gliding over the thick length of him right over the stretched denim. "I like you hard as a rock. That means good things for me."

He groaned. "Seriously, Cayenne. You keep that up and I'm going to be taking you into the swamp."

"I just realized that with the differences in our heights, if you're on just a little bit higher ground than me, I could have you in my mouth without even having to get on my knees in all that dirt. Not that I would mind, but if my jeans get all muddy, I have to do laundry, and I've kind of had several disasters. There are a lot of how-to videos online, but they aren't very interesting. I keep going to the cooking channels."

He reached down, picked her up and started toward the swamp, using long strides to take them there. "That's it, woman. You can't talk about putting your mouth on me and expect me to go into a friend's home and not have the hard-on from hell."

She laughed and slipped her arms around his neck, leaning into him so she could touch her tongue just behind his ear. She kissed her way down his neck to his throat and the underside of his jaw.

"Hurry, honey," Cayenne said softly. "I can't wait for you. I've got the taste of you in my mouth now, and my panties are going to be soaked if you don't get them off of me." Seduction really wasn't all that difficult.

"Fuck. Woman, you make me lose control every fucking time." He increased his speed, nearly sprinting into the denser vegetation.

Several feet in, when the brush closed around them, he allowed her feet back on the ground. She was already pulling his belt loose and unzipping his jeans. His hands were on hers, but she got there first. No preamble. No warm-up. No hands. Her mouth slid over his cock like a tight glove, tongue working him, stroking and caressing as she suckled hard, taking him deep and then nearly releasing him to take him back into that hot, moist cavern.

Trap groaned and caught her hair, bunching it in his fist so he could watch her. She always looked as if she was loving him, her mouth stretched tight around his thick girth, her face soft and warm, her eyes a mixture of lust and something else that always took his breath. Rapture. She made him feel as if she couldn't get enough of him.

I can't get enough of you, she admitted softly. *I love how you feel in my mouth. Or when you're inside me. Sometimes, Trap, long after, I wake up and still feel you inside me. I love that feeling. I love this feeling. I love to give this to you.*

Her hands were there now, cupping his balls, rolling, lavishing attention on him while her eager mouth worked him. Streaks of fire rushed up his legs to center in his groin. The fire spread through his body until every nerve ending shrieked at him. His blood went hot, scorching him, as if lightning had jumped from the sky and entered him. Every sensation in his body raced to converge in his cock. In her mouth.

He tore at her jeans, shoved them down her hips. *Shoes, baby, kick them off. And then your jeans. Right fucking now. I don't want to come in your mouth.*

I want you to. You didn't this morning.

I want to be inside you. I'm not leaving you needy when we're going to be around other men. Fucking do what I tell you, Cayenne. Kick them off. Right. Fucking. Now.

She did it, because she nearly always gave him what he wanted. But she glared at him even as she tightened her mouth around his cock. *I'm going to have my way with you tonight, Trap,* she warned. *You're going to be the one tied up.*

The moment she kicked her jeans off of her, he yanked her up, hands on her bottom. He didn't wait because he couldn't. That's what she did to him. He positioned her over his aching, throbbing cock and then slammed her down hard.

Cayenne cried out, leaned into him and bit his chest without injecting venom. The flash of pain added to the wild, out-of-control, nearly savage thrusts as he hammered into her. She was always tight, squeezing down on him like a vise, her silken muscles massaging and gripping until he wanted to shout with pure pleasure.

You give me everything, he whispered softly into her mind. *You are everything. I can't imagine my life without you anymore. Never think I don't want you. Never think we aren't meant for each other.*

She lifted her head and looked into his eyes even as she ground down, meeting each upward thrust with a strong downward surge. She rode him just as hard as he rode her. She was just as out of control. But her face was soft, loving. He'd never seen that particular expression on her face or in her eyes as her gaze drifted possessively over his face.

I don't know what love is, Trap, but whatever I'm feeling is strong and lasting. I would do anything for you. Give you anything you wanted. That's how strong it is. Even when I'm afraid, I know I'll trust you to see me through it, because I have to give that to you. I can't do anything else.

She made the confession in his mind, her tight sheath swallowing his thick cock again and again. Hungry. Needy. Urgent. Almost brutal. He saw it on her body, the color coming over her, her eyes going wide, her mouth forming his name, her body clamping down on his.

He loved watching her when he made her come. It was the most beautiful sight in the world to him. That look of shocked surprise on her face, as if it was her first time—every time.

He loved the way her body shuddered with delight, the strong spasms surrounding him as the fire rushed through her, reaching all the way up her belly to her breasts.

Only then did he allow the sensations to take him. Only after he witnessed that exquisite beauty. That perfect moment he gave to his woman. He slammed into her four more times, each stroke harder than the last. His balls drew tight, so tight he groaned as he shot his seed deep into her. He swore her channel grew hotter and tighter, greedy for more of him, sucking him dry.

Trap buried his face in her neck, his heart pounding. Full. So fucking full. His woman had done that for him—given him everything—and she did each time he asked it of her. *I don't know what love is either, not the love of a man for his woman, Cayenne, but if it exists, it does in me for you. You understand me, baby? Do you hear what I'm saying to you? Because I've never said it to another woman and I never will. Whatever I have in me to give, it's yours.*

He hoped it was enough. There was a moment of silence. Of stillness. She pushed back to put a little space between them and waited for him to give her his gaze. He shouldn't have worried. He should have known. It was there on her face.

"Yeah, baby," he murmured. "You got it. You understand what I'm saying to you. No matter what I fucking act like, even if it's me being a bastard, you have this from me. You always will."

She leaned in and took his mouth. He loved that about her. She took him in the same way he took her. Claiming him. Using her mouth, her hands, her body, to let him know he belonged to her. Her kiss was sweet. Tender. Loving. Her tongue pushing into his mouth, searching, dancing. He let her have that because she turned him inside out when she did it.

Eventually he took over, like he often did, because he needed more. He needed her to know what she meant to him, and he kissed her like he meant it, because he fucking did. When he lifted his head her mouth trailed kisses to his jaw, his chin and then underneath to his throat.

"I just need you to know, Trap," she said, trailing more kisses along his collarbone, nuzzling his shirt aside so she could get to skin. "If you're a bastard to me, I will retaliate. I don't much like getting walked on."

His cock jerked hard inside her. He loved that about her too. She might look small and delicate, but she was pure steel. She stood up to him and gave as good as she got. What he appreciated most about that was that Cayenne chose her moments. She waited for him to get over being a bastard before she called him on it. When she did that, when she gave him those times, it only made him want to try all the harder to be a better man for her.

"Looking forward to that, baby," he assured her. His hands spanned her waist and he reluctantly lifted her off of him. "I should have carried something to clean you up."

"I did," she said, smirking at him. "You don't go very long before you want sex, Trap, so I thought keeping a few of those little towelette thingies would be a good idea." She picked up her jeans and pulled out a small square. Ripping the packet open with her teeth, she drew out the wet cloth. "Since I like feasting on your cock, I brought a toothbrush too." She flashed a little grin.

Trap took it from her and carefully wiped her thighs and in between her legs. She leaned into him and lapped at his cock.

"Baby, you'll just get me hard again."

"I know. I like you that way." She laughed softly and took out another packet to clean him with. "Seriously, Trap, I don't get why any woman wouldn't want this."

"I do you on a table and you're happy. The floor. The wall. Outside. On the roof. You just give that to me, Cayenne."

"No, silly. *You* give that to *me*. You also try to fix all my screwups. The laundry, our breakfast and dinners. You give me anything I want. I'm spoiled."

"I tie you up and take you the way I want to."

"I tie you and do what I want."

She pulled on her jeans, and he reached down to help her zip and button them. He didn't say anything else because he couldn't. She was there with him. Right there in the swamp, surrounded by brush and flowers and moss, and she didn't give a damn that she was wearing socks in the dirt and he'd just fucked her raw. She might not say "I love you" to him, but she showed him with everything she did. She made him feel it.

He pulled up his own jeans as she put on her shoes. Her head was bent and he could see the red hourglass in her cloud of black, shiny hair. The red gleamed through the glossy black silk. He couldn't help himself. He followed the pattern in her hair, caressing the red strands that often disappeared into the thick mass. He rubbed them between his thumb and finger, his heart hammering in his chest.

"You ready, baby?"

"Yes." She stood up, her gaze meeting his. "Thank you, Trap. I was so nervous about this, but you make me feel steady."

She was thanking him for carrying her off into the damn swamp and fucking her. She was killing him. Ripping him up inside. Shattering his heart into a million pieces and taking every piece into her keeping. He caught the back of her head in his palm and took her mouth, pouring himself into her, pouring every emotion he felt into that sweet, sweet mouth. He hadn't even known he could feel so much or so deeply.

She didn't hesitate, but then she never did. She kissed him back, just as deep, just as hot, giving him everything she was. He lifted his head before he turned around, took her home and tore her clothes off her. He could spend the rest of his life in bed with her.

She laughed softly as he threaded his finger through her

belt loop and pulled her in close to him. "You couldn't, you know."

"Couldn't what?"

"Stay in bed with me the rest of your life. You'd be bored. I watch you, Trap, and if you don't go into that laboratory, you start to get restless."

That was true. There was no denying it. She was very observant. He loved that about her too, because never once had she objected. Even when he'd worked forty-eight hours straight. She'd brought him food and disappeared. Then she'd come in with bottles of water, and he'd fucked her on the floor. He hadn't said a word to her, just caught her around the waist, ripped off her clothes and slammed inside of her. She was ready for him. Always ready. She'd left without a word between them, gathering up her clothes and leaving him to his work.

She'd returned at each meal, and she brought him coffee often. After the second time he'd ripped her clothes, she came in naked. He couldn't remember how many times he'd fucked her, but it was often. Several times on the floor. Several times against the wall and twice on a table. He'd loved that because he had his mouth between her legs and got a long taste of her.

The memories poured steel into his cock and he found himself grinning. He'd always had a high sex drive, but being around her, thinking about her, touching her, hearing her voice, all of it, just added to his need of her.

"You don't have to do this, Cayenne," he said softly, as they emerged from the swamp. "We can make excuses and head home if you're not ready."

"I *want* to learn, Trap. Eventually I'll work with you in the laboratory, but I don't want you to hire a cook. You can bring in someone to clean a couple of times a week, but I want to take care of you myself. And when we have children, I want to take care of them. I used to stay in Nonny's room because it felt like a home there. She has something intangible, but it's there, and I want to learn how to have that for our family. She's offered to give me cooking lessons. I'm not going to turn that down."

There was determination in her voice. He ran his hand down the length of her glossy hair. "Thanks, baby. I haven't had anyone caring for me since I lost my aunt."

"I'm going to be good at it, you'll see."

She was starting with nothing. No patterns, no skills, no prior experience or knowledge to draw on, but he could see she was absolutely determined. He could also see that soft warmth in her eyes when she looked at him.

"I know you will, Cayenne," he said as he walked with her up the stairs.

Nonny flung open the door, her faded eyes moving over the two of them. She smiled at Trap. "Missed you around here, boy. 'Bout time you brought your woman to meet me."

Trap drew Cayenne in front of him, one arm around her, locked right under her breasts. "Nonny, this is my Cayenne. Baby, this is Wyatt's grandmother. All of us call her Nonny."

Cayenne smiled at the woman. Nonny was ageless. Timeless. Her hair was gray and she wore it in a braid wrapped around the back of her head in a bun. She had a few wrinkles, but not many. Her smile was quick and real as she stepped back to allow them entrance.

"Wyatt, Ezekiel and Mordichai are goin' to take the girls out for a boat ride through the swamp. Wyatt's been talkin' to them about survival. He wants them to know all the dangers and also to give them a sense of direction just in case. Ginger likes to wander off, and we have to watch that one like a hawk because the other girls follow her lead."

"They're a handful," Trap agreed, as if he had great knowledge of little girls. "We're trying to have a baby, Nonny, so ours will grow up with Wyatt's."

Nonny spun around and fixed him with a glare. Both hands went to her hips, fists closed tight. "Trap Dawkins. You don' get a woman pregnant without marryin' her first.

You do that, and you'll understand the meanin' of a shotgun weddin'." She turned her complete attention on Cayenne. "Girl, you and me are goin' to have a talk."

Cayenne couldn't possibly take offense. She found herself smiling and nodding. Trap's hands closed over her shoulders.

"We're dealing with the paperwork, Nonny. Jaimie and Flame are making certain that Cayenne has a complete history and everything is in order. Once they give us the go-ahead, we'll get married. I give you my word."

Nonny studied his face for a long moment and then she grunted and nodded, as if in approval. Cayenne let out her breath. *She's magnificent.*

Yeah, she is.

Wyatt's so lucky.

We all are. She treats us all like her family, and she means it.

Cayenne studied the older woman as she followed her into what was the sitting room. That, she was certain, was Nonny's secret—she genuinely cared about the people around her. She welcomed them, took them at face value, and treated them as if they belonged to her. Cayenne wanted that for her own family.

Trap squeezed her hand as she sank into the chair Nonny gestured toward. "You'll be okay, baby? I'm going to go with Wyatt if you're comfortable with that. I need to be around his girls. I never thought I'd say this, but I miss them."

"I'll take good care of her," Nonny promised.

Trap leaned down and brushed a kiss on top of Cayenne's head. "Thanks, Nonny." He straightened, running his knuckles gently along Cayenne's face. "You two have fun."

"We will," Cayenne said, suddenly reluctant to let him out of her sight. She wasn't good at small talk. At talk at all. She was used to being with Trap, and maybe Wyatt in small doses, but she was going to be alone in a house with two women she didn't really know at all.

She pressed a hand to her churning stomach. She honestly hadn't considered what she'd feel like without Trap close by. Still, she kept her mouth shut, refusing to be such a coward that she would call him back when it had been her suggestion that he find an excuse to leave her alone with them. She watched him leave. Looked out the window to see him join Wyatt and the other two men in the front. Trap reached down, picked up a little toddler and settled her on his hip. The sight turned her heart over.

She turned her gaze back to Nonny and found the woman watching her closely.

"You're in love with him," Nonny said approvingly.

Cayenne once more looked out the window, staring at the man she couldn't imagine herself without. He was gorgeous. Tall and strong. His hair was always a mess, but she especially liked it that way. Every movement he made set his muscles rippling deliciously beneath his tight tee. The toddler on his hip looked tiny next to his large frame.

"I don't know what that is," Cayenne admitted softly, "but he's everything to me. I want to learn how to take care of him. To make him a home. I don't think he's had that, and I want to do that for him." She turned back toward the older woman, leaning forward, meeting her eyes. "I want that a *lot*. I'm hoping you can help me."

"Keepin' your man happy isn't difficult, Cayenne. Neither is makin' a home for him, not if it's important to you."

"I didn't have parents," she blurted out. "I have to learn everything out of a book or on the Internet. Cooking is especially difficult. I can get all the measurements right, but I make the worst messes. Half the time, Trap has to come in and help me get everything cleaned up. I don't want that. He works hard and the work he does is important. Eventually, I'm going to help him in the laboratory, but to do that, I have to be organized so everything else gets done. I don't mind him helping me with the laundry—which by the way

I screw up almost every time I do it. But I want to do the cooking. I don't know why, but it's important to me."

Nonny studied her face. "It was difficult for you to ask Wyatt if he'd ask me, wasn't it? But you did. That took courage. A little thing like cookin' isn't goin' to be hard for you after that."

Cayenne hadn't realized how tense she was. She forced air through her lungs and sank back. "I've never even talked to other women, not like this. Not Pepper, no one. I've never gone into a grocery store or paid for groceries. I don't know how to do those things. Trap's friends have been getting our groceries for us. He wants everything in place before we go out in public together. I think he actually wants us to be married."

Nonny didn't take her gaze from Cayenne's. "I don' know a lot about Wyatt's business. I do know that somethin' bad happened to Pepper and the girls. I know that same somethin' must have happened to you. You have no cause to be worried about makin' friends with me. You already did, just by puttin' the soft in Trap's face and meltin' the ice in his eyes. The way he picked up that youngin' was beautiful. He never did that before. Not once. Not slow and easy and natural. You gave him that."

Cayenne felt her eyes burn. She liked hearing what Nonny was saying to her. Movement in the doorway nearly had her spinning around in her chair, but the scent came to her and she knew it was Pepper, Wyatt's wife. She could actually smell Wyatt on her, their combined scents. She forced herself to turn slowly with a small smile on her face, even though she was back to being tense again.

Two people. Two women. Cayenne pushed down panic and smiled through the introductions. "I guess I have you to thank for telling Trap that I was imprisoned and awaiting termination," she said.

Nonny made a small sound in the back of her throat. "What did you say, child?"

Cayenne nearly bit her tongue. Clearly Nonny didn't have

all the details about her. She glanced nervously at Pepper, looking for direction.

"Nonny, just like the girls, Whitney and Braden put out a termination order on Cayenne."

"It's still in effect," Cayenne said. "So in coming here, I may have put you both in danger. If you . . ."

"Don' even say it," Nonny warned. "We're all in this together. I think it's time those boys earned their dinner anyway. They're hanging around here, pretendin' to work, eatin' every chance they get. A little guard duty will keep them sharp."

Pepper laughed softly. "Nonny's very good at handling all the men. I tend to hide sometimes, but she knows exactly what to do with them."

"I had me four boys to raise," Nonny pointed out. "Now I got me three little girls, Pepper and Flame, Gator's wife." The faded eyes went to Cayenne's face. "And you. 'Bout time I had me daughters what with all these boys I've got now. Gives a body a reason to keep goin'."

"What are the girls' names? Triplets, right?" Cayenne asked, her stomach settling a little more.

Nonny conveyed such warmth it was impossible not to feel welcome in her home. Pepper was more reserved; like Cayenne, she didn't have much experience with people. She'd had four months of being with Wyatt, Nonny, and the members of the GhostWalker team so she had a jump on Cayenne gaining experience. Clearly being around Nonny gave her advantages. She was already taking on Nonny's natural friendliness and warmth. Cayenne envied her just a little.

"Ginger, Cannelle and Thym," Pepper answered. "You know how Braden wanted us all to be spices. He was such a jerk."

"Whitney determined that those of us in France would be spices. He had two other labs that I heard rumors about in other countries, and if he has women or children there, you can bet they have a different category name. As I understand it from what Trap told me, those in the United States have flowers or seasons," Cayenne said.

"Flame's real name is Iris," Nonny said, "but no one calls her that. Whitney gave her the cancer—repeatedly. I know Trap and Wyatt are workin' as hard as they can to come up with a cure, at least for the type of cancer Whitney gave Flame. He wanted it to keep comin' back so she would have to go to him for treatment. Lily Miller is helpin'. She's Whitney's daughter, and she put Flame's cancer in remission, but we're all afraid it might come back again."

Cayenne was surprised that Nonny knew so much about Whitney's experiments. Although once she gave it thought, it stood to reason. Nonny had lived a long life and she was smart and observant. She had two grandsons who had joined the GhostWalker program and were married to other Ghost-Walkers. She hosted an entire team in her home. She had to see their differences and hear them talking.

"Whitney didn't want to see any of us as human," Pepper said. "He can distance himself from us so it's easy to look at us as experiments and he can terminate us, or do anything else he wants without feeling guilty."

Cayenne shivered, a cold chill creeping down her spine. Her hands ached. She rubbed them on her thighs, suddenly wishing Trap were there.

She felt Nonny's sharp gaze and forced her hands into her lap, threading her fingers together to keep from trembling. She didn't *ever* feel like this unless she was alone at night and couldn't shut out the memories of being pinned to a table like an insect with several men in lab coats poking and stabbing with needles and knives. Bile rose, and she felt like she might choke.

Baby. What is it?

He was there. Trap. Pouring into her mind. Filling her with warmth. With him. With his strength, but it was much more than that. So much more. She wasn't alone with her memories. He had them. He took them from her and made her whole.

Made her human. She felt him holding her, his fingers sifting through her hair, looking for the hourglass, stroking it and caressing it. Accepting who she was. He knew the worst of her, and it didn't matter.

I'm all right. Memories are too close.

Do you need me? I can come to you, take you home. Hold you, Cayenne. You say the word and I'm on my way.

She loved that. *Loved* that he would drop everything to get back to her. Her heart melted. Her stomach did a little flip. He'd already pushed the memories away, and she wanted to learn to cook. For him.

Baby. His voice, so soft, caressed her mind. She felt his love, that deep emotion neither really knew what to do with, filling her. *I don't need you to learn to cook.*

He didn't need it, but she did. It felt necessary to her. Cooking wouldn't define her, but it would make her feel more human. She needed to feel she could take care of Trap by means other than sex.

I need this, Trap. I want this. I'm interested in it and I think I can get good at it. I'm fine now, just maybe needed to touch base with you. She hesitated a moment. Took a breath and gave it all to him. *To know you're there for me.*

Always, Cayenne. Never doubt it.

She would never take that for granted, no matter how long they were together. She knew she wouldn't. She sent him warmth and broke the contact, aware of Nonny's steady gaze. The older woman leaned over and put her hand over Cayenne's. Her hands were warm, just like the woman.

"You're safe in this house, Cayenne," she said gently.

Cayenne blinked rapidly to keep the burning out of her eyes. She wasn't afraid, but she couldn't explain that to this woman. She welcomed a fight, she was in her element going up against Whitney's termination squads, but sitting in a house with two other women who were being sweet and kind and *friendly*, that was much more difficult.

"Thank you," she murmured, because she had to say something.

"Let's get started." Nonny patted her hands and then stood up to lead the way to the kitchen. "I've got everything we need set out for the cookin' lesson. The more tools you have, the easier it is."

"Trap has all kinds of tools in his kitchen," Cayenne admitted. "I just don't know what they're for. And I always make such a mess. After a while I get overwhelmed. I don't understand how it looks so easy on the Internet but when I try, I mess everything up. It's absolutely maddening."

Pepper burst out laughing. "I think, when I first tried to learn, Nonny wanted to throw me out along with the burned dishes. I turned everything into charcoal. I couldn't seem to remember when I had something in the oven or on the stove. I just would get distracted, and the next thing I knew, the fire alarms were going off and the house was filling with smoke."

Cayenne found herself laughing. *Laughing.* With two women. No Trap to hold her up, she was actually having fun. She wasn't the only one who couldn't cook, and Pepper wasn't ashamed. Even Nonny laughed with them.

"Malichai loves his food," Nonny said. "You should have seen his face. I wanted one of those nanny cams set up so we could get his picture every time he found out Pepper was doing the cookin' instead of me."

Cayenne knew what a nanny camera was because she'd read about it on the Internet, but she couldn't see Nonny trolling for information on the Internet. It was kind of funny to hear her say it. She glanced at Pepper, saw the look on her face and knew she wasn't alone in what she was thinking. Pepper burst out laughing and Cayenne found herself following suit.

Cayenne wouldn't trade this experience, being with the two women. It was her time having fun and gaining a connection. She loved it.

CHAPTER 16

Nonny raised her eyebrow, clearly reading both their expressions. "You keep laughin', you two. I got my ways to know these things. I thought that Wilson Plastics Company was a front for terrorists to make those dirty bombs. Brought Wyatt home. I wasn't very far off either."

"No, you weren't," Pepper agreed.

"Somethin' else is goin' on in the swamp. Years ago the government came in and moved five towns. Between them, the towns of Logstown, Gainsville, Santa Rosa, Westonia and Napoleon had over seven hundred residents, all that had to be moved. A lot of the people didn't want to go. They'd been born in those houses and grew up there, lived there all their lives. Still, they were all of them cleared out. Said they were testin' rocket engines for NASA. Even now, when they do fire them up, the houses outside the swamp shake and even the water rocks."

"I haven't been there," Pepper said, "but I thought they gave tours to the public."

Nonny nodded as she handed each of them a knife and

a chopping board. "They do. But that's all controlled, and you see what they want you to see. Used to be, we could take our boats into the canals and bayous where those towns used to be. A few years back, the military moved in. You try to take a boat in there or you go hikin' lookin' for plants to heal people, they come at you with grim faces and heavy artillery. They weren't doin' that to test those rockets. So somethin' else is goin' on."

"Have you mentioned this to Wyatt?" Pepper asked.

"Givin' it time. Lots of rumors. I want to sort them out and see before I go tellin' tales to my grandson. He's the kind of man who does somethin' about anythin' not right."

"That he is," Pepper agreed.

"We're goin' to make us some paella. The boys like this dish, so we've got to triple up on everythin'. Each of us will do enough for one batch, that way we're all makin' the right size servin' that you can use on your own for your men."

"What is paella?" Cayenne asked.

"It's chicken with rice, almonds, olives and mushrooms and Andouille sausage. I like to add me some crawfish sometimes, but not today," Nonny said. "A good staple and easy to fix if you have company. I need both of you to peel six of those small onions and I'll do the same." She caught up a small bag of onions, counted them out and gave each of them six. "After you peel the onions, you need to mince two cloves of garlic and then chop up a three-fourths cup of olives."

Pepper smiled. "No problem. I got this."

Cayenne moistened her lips and watched carefully as Nonny efficiently peeled an onion. There didn't seem to be any trick to it, but she was very fast. Cayenne mimicked her movements. There was no need for the knife, and she didn't cut away most of the onion trying to peel it as Cayenne had done at home.

When Nonny set the peeled onion aside, Cayenne studied her method for mincing the garlic cloves and then copied her.

"You just clean as you go. I keep a bucket handy to use for compost later and a garbage can for anything else." She gathered up the peels and dumped them. Both women followed suit.

"Now we got to cut up the chicken. Each of us needs three pounds. I take the skin off." Nonny demonstrated.

Cayenne took a deep breath. Skinning and cutting up a chicken was much more difficult than mincing a clove, but Pepper was already in action, and she was determined. In any case, she was really, really good with a knife. When she managed to cut up the three pounds of chicken fast she was rather proud of herself. Nonny indicated the compost bucket and they all dumped the remains.

"Cut a half pound of the sausage into rounds."

The girls found that easy enough and obeyed.

"If you were going to add in crawfish or shrimp, you'd do it with the chicken and sausage," Nonny said. "For today, in the Dutch oven, we're goin' to heat two tablespoons of olive oil, add the chicken and sausage, and we're makin' our own seasoning. See the little bowls there? The spices are in the middle. I use two tablespoons each of onion powder, garlic powder, dried oregano, dried basil, which I grow and dry myself."

The two women carefully measured out the spices into their respective bowls.

"Everyone makes seasoning different. I add quite a few, but you don' like that, or your man doesn', you just change it up. In this one, we'll add one tablespoon of dried thyme, one tablespoon each of both black and white pepper and cayenne."

Cayenne flashed a small grin. "Your recipe seems right for the two of us."

Pepper laughed. "So true."

"Add five tablespoons of paprika and three of salt," Nonny continued. "You want to mix it up really good. We just add seasoning to the chicken and sausage. No, no,

Cayenne, not the entire bowl," Nonny cautioned. "Just a little bit. The rest we store for the future in an airtight container. It will last a couple of months. We put the chicken and sausage in the oven and bake at 350 uncovered for fifteen minutes. It's best to set a timer. When I was younger and had the boys, they were a mighty distraction. Now I'm old and forgetful, so I always use the timer."

"That looks like *tons* of food," Cayenne said, trying to keep the horror out of her voice. "Do they really eat all that?"

Nonny nodded. "They're men, and they work all day tryin' to turn this place into a fortress and they need to keep their strength up. Each of them has bought land nearly all the way to Trap's compound. They're goin' to build homes or add to the ones they bought, so all through the swamp here, Wyatt's team will have a safe home base. They can have their families here."

Trap hadn't mentioned to Cayenne that his team members were all planning to settle in the area. She liked the idea that Pepper and the triplets would be so protected. Pressing a hand to her stomach, she found she was a little relieved that if Trap and she did have a baby, the child would be just as protected.

"So you have to cook for them?" Cayenne asked.

Nonny frowned. "I *want* to cook for them. I enjoy it, and I enjoy watchin' them eat whatever I make. I try to have beans or gumbo on the stove for when they come in at odd hours. I like havin' those boys around. Makes me feel my girls are protected. I got me a good shotgun, but some of these soldiers Whitney sends are a might trained."

"I like that," Cayenne said softly. "That you *want* to cook for them, that it gives you pleasure. I tried to explain how I felt to Trap, but I never know if what I'm feeling is normal. I just have this driving need to make him a home."

"There's nothin' wrong with that, girl," Nonny assured. "You love your man, and you want to do right by him. He do right by you?" Suddenly Nonny's gaze was piercing, as if she could see right through Cayenne to her very soul.

Cayenne held the older woman's gaze and slowly nodded her head. "He's so good to me, sometimes I don't know what to do with it. He's kind and funny and so sweet it makes me feel funny inside."

Pepper and Nonny exchanged a long look, both with raised eyebrows and disbelieving expressions.

"You're talking about Trap," Pepper said. "*Our* Trap?"

Cayenne didn't like her tone or her words. "Actually he's *my* Trap, and yes, he's always sweet. Well . . . Not in public. Then he's cold as ice, but he's got his reasons and I understand them, so it doesn't bother me." *Much,* she added silently.

"Trap is sweet to you?" Nonny asked.

Cayenne tried not to feel defensive. "He was the first human being to show me any kindness at all. When I was terrified one night, he was so good to me, letting me learn things on my own . . ." she broke off, blushing. "I don't know how he had so much control, and he's a man who needs and prefers control, but he was wonderful to me. And he built me an apartment. When I couldn't stand wide-open spaces, he didn't mind my . . . um . . . artwork hanging on the bed like drapes. He *sees* me. He makes me laugh."

"He sounds wonderful," Nonny said immediately. "He's the type of man who finds his woman and gives her the best part of himself. Some men are like that. He doesn't need or want approval from anyone else, but for you, he gives whatever he's got inside. He saves that for you. Exclusively."

Cayenne heard the approval in Nonny's voice. Trap was exactly like that. He gave himself to her, every single time. He actually took the time to explain himself when she instinctively knew he didn't ever do that with others. He gave her that look, his eyes going warm and soft, his expression the same, almost tender. He melted her insides every time.

The timer went off, and Nonny went straight into teaching mode. "Now we add the onions and cook for another forty-five minutes. Again, I set the timer. I try to stay around the kitchen or close to it even with the timer going. In this case, while the chicken is cooking, we can start the salad. We're serving a crabmeat salad tonight with the chicken. That should make the boys happy, and each of us can do exactly what we did with the chicken recipe. We'll triple it, each of us doing enough for six."

The door opened, and Malichai came in. He stopped abruptly when he saw the three women. "Whoa, there, Nonny. You can't have Pepper in the kitchen. I'm a starving man, and she has some kind of bad kitchen mojo going on. She's been cursed. Every time she's in here, the fire alarms go off and my food is ruined."

Pepper wadded up a napkin and threw it at him. "Go away. You're a bottomless pit, and for your information, the chicken is being cooked to perfection."

Malichai came closer to peer over their shoulders at the white lump crabmeat. "Woman. That is not chicken. Nonny, she can't be in here. I heard Trap brought his woman to learn from the best. Pepper is going to put that whammy on Cayenne and my brother will starve."

Pepper threw another balled-up napkin, this one hitting him square in the face. "Go away or I will burn the dinner and you'll have to go fishing and eat it raw."

"I've tried raw fish. A couple of times, when I was desperate for nourishment."

"Malichai," Nonny warned. "I've got the broom. You're disturbin' my cookin' lesson. These girls are doin' just fine so don' be distractin' them."

"I just need a bowl of that fine gumbo you've got on the stove," he wheedled, giving her his sweetest, most innocent look.

Cayenne thought he looked like a wolf, not a sheep, but clearly Nonny thought he was an adorable boy. She went straight to the stove and dished him up a very large bowl of soup, added her homemade bread and waved him out.

Malichai winked at Cayenne, glared at Pepper, and smiled angelically at Nonny, who shook her head, her eyes laughing, her mouth curved in a smile. He bent and brushed a kiss on Nonny's cheek. "You're the best," he murmured, clearly meaning it. He glanced at Pepper and Cayenne. "Sorry girls, no kiss for either of you. Wyatt would skin me alive if I touched you, Pepper, so you're just going to have to pine away for me. Trap would boil me in oil, Cayenne, so as sad as this is going to make you, you'll just have to learn to live without my kisses."

"We'll manage," Pepper called after him, as he went out the door.

Nonny shook her head. "That boy needs a woman."

"She'd never keep him fed," Pepper protested. "Although she'd be in stitches every day. On with the lesson, Nonny."

"Put your one pound of crabmeat into your salad bowls. Each of you has a head of iceberg lettuce. Break it into small chunks and add that with the crab. Immediately take anything you can't use and put it in the compost bucket so your work area stays clean. The small bowl is to mix up everything else we need. Chop the capers very fine. We only need a tablespoon full in each of the bowls. Add one teaspoon of lemon juice. I fresh squeeze mine. Always use the freshest ingredients. Add in a half cup of mayonnaise and some of the seasoning we just made up. We're going to put this in the fridge, and before we serve it, we'll pour our sauce over the crabmeat and lettuce, and garnish it with a little paprika and parsley chopped fine. See how easy that is? Now our salad is ready for dinner. The kitchen is still clean, Cayenne."

Cayenne looked around her. Everything was clean, and Nonny made it so easy.

Cayenne realized she was smiling. Malichai was funny, and Pepper, in spite of the teasing, or because of it, really liked him. She wasn't upset with his poking fun at her, and her laughter had been genuine. Nonny clearly had claimed Malichai as her own, and he obviously had great affection for her. And Pepper as well. Relationships were complicated, but they were very nice to have. She was more than enjoying herself. Because she was, she reached out to Trap.

Trap, I'm having so much fun. Nonny and Pepper are wonderful, and Malichai is so cute. Really funny and cute.

There was a moment of silence. *Baby, he's not that cute.*

She found herself smiling at his reaction. He sounded a little grumpy. *He said no kisses for me because you'd boil him in oil. None for Pepper because Wyatt would skin him alive. He didn't seem all that afraid.*

I'd skin him before I boiled him, so he'd better be afraid. The grumpiness had disappeared to be replaced by a faint sense of humor. *Glad you're having fun, baby.*

The women passed the time writing down recipes for Cayenne. Nonny took care to explain how to do things Cayenne didn't understand. When the timer went off again, they added to the chicken and sausage mixture again. Each one added their minced garlic and two and a half cups of uncooked rice, mixing it well. Then each added one cup of dry white wine and three cups of chicken stock.

"We cover this and cook it another forty-five minutes," Nonny explained as she set the timer again. "When it's done, we'll season it with our spice mixture, sprinkle in a little oregano, three and half ounces of blanched almonds and three-fourths of a cup of chopped olives. We can add the last two cups of chicken stock to the mixture and then keep it hot in the oven. When we serve it, we'll sauté mushrooms in butter for about five minutes. You want to do that at the last minute. We'll sprinkle those on top and we've got an entire meal. I always serve my homemade bread. The next lesson, we'll bake bread."

Nonny went to the refrigerator and pulled out a large

pitcher. "I made us some homemade strawberry lemonade. Thought we could pour it over ice and sit out on the porch. I need me my pipe while our dinner is cookin'."

"That sounds wonderful, Nonny," Cayenne said. "Um. I mean the lemonade, not the pipe. Do you really smoke a pipe?"

Nonny nodded and gestured toward the cabinet. Pepper got out three tall glasses and put them in front of Wyatt's grandmother.

"Been smokin' a pipe since I was about ten years old. Back then, it wasn't considered bad for you. Wyatt tells me to stop, but I'm already eighty. Not goin' to give up somethin' I love at this stage of my life."

They settled on the porch, Nonny in her rocking chair, looking out over the water. Pepper and Cayenne took the chairs facing the swamp. A cool breeze ruffled their hair and felt good against their skin after the heat of the kitchen. Cayenne pressed the icy glass to her forehead before she took a sip. The moment she sampled the drink, her gaze jumped to Nonny's face.

"This is amazing. I definitely want to learn how to make this as well. How do you make everything taste so good?"

"She pours love into it," Pepper said, before Nonny could answer. "I've watched her, and no matter what she says, that's the truth. That's her secret. She puts a recipe together just like everyone else, but she pours love into it and makes it a miracle."

Nonny smiled at Pepper as she lit her pipe, rocking, the chair creaking slightly, soothingly. A kind of comforting, homey sound. Her face was soft and warm, and when her gaze rested on Pepper, there was love there for anyone to see. She looked the embodiment of love.

"Child," she said, her voice low as she smiled at Pepper. Loving.

Cayenne's breath caught in her throat. Nonny was everything she was looking for. Her example. The truth about families and how to go about making them. Pepper had already learned from her. Cayenne had subconsciously known it. She'd been drawn back to Nonny's bedroom time and again.

"Before." Cayenne waved her hands toward the swamp. "When I was alone and afraid and had nowhere to go, I looked for Trap. It was always Trap I needed."

Both women were looking at her now. She had their full attention. She didn't know how either of them would react when she gave them the truth so she stood up and walked to the thick column that ran to the porch roof. Circling it with one arm she raised her chin and looked Nonny straight in the eye.

"I came here. A *lot*. Nearly every night after the first two weeks. I had no food, no clothes, I was living in the basement of the old plastics building. I didn't know how to exist in the world. I'd lived in a very small cell my entire life."

Something stirred in Nonny's eyes. Something deep. Cayenne felt that look penetrate straight through her heart to her soul. Nonny was giving her something huge. Claiming her without words. Just as she'd claimed Pepper and her three little granddaughters. Just as she'd claimed Malichai, Trap and the rest of the team members. Hers. They were her family, and she'd be loyal to them and love them until the day she died. She said that with one look. Without a single word, and still, Cayenne, who knew nothing of love and family, understood.

Cayenne blinked back tears, her fingers digging into the wood. "I slipped past the guards and stayed downwind of the dogs. I'm ashamed to admit that I came into your house while you were sleeping, Nonny. I would go to Trap's room and just sit in it." More like cling to the ceiling or the wall, but she wasn't going to admit that. "When I wasn't with him, I went to your room. I didn't know why at the time, but being there, with you, brought me comfort. I felt hope when I was there. I shouldn't have done it, not with you sleeping, I knew it was wrong, but I couldn't stop myself."

She blurted her confession fast. She hadn't felt it was

wrong to be in Trap's room, but she *knew* she shouldn't have sat for hours in Nonny's room.

"Child." Nonny took the pipe from her mouth and held out a hand to Cayenne. "Come here to me."

It was the last thing Cayenne expected, but given what she knew about Wyatt's grandmother, she should have. She pried her fingers from the safety of the column one by one, her heart pounding so loud, it sounded like thunder in her ears. She took three steps toward that outstretched hand.

Something hit the column just where her head had been, smashing into the wood, sending splinters everywhere. The sound came a beat later, the rolling thunder of a long-distance rifle shot.

Cayenne flung herself in front of Nonny. "Pepper, Nonny, get down."

Pepper was already crawling toward cover. Nonny couldn't move that fast. She jerked out of her rocking chair and turned toward the door. Cayenne leapt into the air, an instinctive, strange move that after, she would never know why. The bullet took her square in the chest, driving her backward into Nonny's body. Had she not taken the bullet, it would have struck Nonny between the eyes.

Nonny wrapped her arms around Cayenne as they both went down. Pepper scrambled on all fours to try to get to them to help Wyatt's grandmother pull Cayenne's limp body into the house. Behind them, the door was flung open and Malichai was there, crouched low. He caught Nonny under her armpits and yanked her inside. She had her arms around Cayenne and dragged her in as she was being pulled in.

The second bullet went into Cayenne's limp body, hitting her lower, on her left thigh, tearing through her jeans. Blood spread across her chest and over her leg. Pepper dove into the house and Malichai slammed the door.

"Draden's on the roof. He took the night shift. He was asleep in the house while I was on guard. He's already on the roof and in position now. He'll take out the sniper. We've got a team coming at us. At least five," Malichai told the women, even as he ripped open Cayenne's shirt with one hand, his fingers at the pulse on her neck with the other.

"She's alive," he said. *"Fuck!"* He shouted the expletive. "I should have seen this coming. Gino's here as well, he's already in the swamp. Everyone else is working on Joe's place down the road. I sent for them, but we're going to take a lot of heat before they get here."

Nonny gave him a cool look. "It isn't necessary to use such language, Malichai. Pepper, in the front bathroom under the sink is a large first-aid kit. I'll need that. My shotgun's just inside the parlor door. Bring that as well. You know where Wyatt keeps his weapons."

Pepper nodded and raced to the other room, staying low, away from the windows. Another bullet crashed into the door, low, but the armor plating Wyatt had installed stopped it from coming into the house. An answering roll of thunder told them Draden had spotted the sniper and had taken his shot.

Malichai pressed his hand over the bullet wound in Cayenne's chest. It was right over her heart. *Directly* over her heart. Already the area around the hole was swelling and turning color fast. Blood ran like a small river, but when he placed his hand over the wound, he actually felt the bullet. It should have penetrated *through* Cayenne. She was small. The bullet could go long distances and punch through walls. Malichai was certain it was an AI sniper rifle.

"I can feel the bullet, Nonny. She's not wearing armor. It should have gone right through her. Put your hand right here and apply pressure while I check the one in her leg," he instructed.

He used his knife to rip her jeans open. There was a lot of blood, and he did the same thing he'd done with the chest wound—pressed his hand over it in order to apply pressure. Again, he swore he felt the bullet. It had only penetrated about the length of the bullet itself.

"Both bullets are still inside her. There's no through and

through. We'll have to get them out. I'm going to carry her into the bedroom Trap was using. I'll need to hook up an IV to get fluids in her. The way she's bleeding, she might need a transfusion."

Pepper was back with the first aid kit and Nonny's shotgun.

Draden took out the sniper, Malichai, Gino reported. *I've located four others. They're moving on the house now. I'm going to try to spot them for Draden. Cayenne told us to take them in the throat. If I can maneuver them out into the open for Draden to get a shot, we can take out a couple before they reach the house. Is Trap's woman alive?*

She's alive, but I don't know how. He scored a direct hit right to her heart and another on her thigh that should have gone through, taking out her bone and severing the artery. She's breathing though. I need time. Can you keep them off of us?

We'll keep them off of you, Gino assured. *Keep her alive. I've never seen Trap like he is with her. Almost mellow. We're not losing any of our own to Whitney or his robot soldiers.*

Malichai set up the IV right there on the floor of Wyatt's home. He'd done the same thing in far worse conditions. On battlefields with mortar fire striking close. On a spinning, bumping helicopter taking fire. Still, when his hands were *always* steady, he felt a slight tremor. This woman was one of theirs. They couldn't lose her. He'd never be able to look Trap in the eye again. He'd never be able to live with himself.

He lifted Cayenne into his arms and carried her to the back of the house where he placed her on the bed Trap had used when he stayed there. He hung the bag of fluids on a hook on the wall and opened a tray of surgical instruments always kept in a sterile pack.

"Pepper, Draden and Gino are going to try to keep them off of us while I do this. I'll need Nonny's help. You'll have to be our last line of defense. If they get close, let me know."

Pepper nodded. The entire team knew she had a major problem with violence, but when it counted, she would come through. Violence made her horribly ill, and haunted her for weeks, even months after, but she would do whatever it took to protect them. Malichai knew he could count on her and he didn't give it another thought as he rushed to wash his hands and don sterile gloves.

It had cost Trap to allow Cayenne the decision to be alone with Nonny and Pepper, but she needed to know she could make her own friends, have her own relationship with the others without him. He wanted that for her, and the only way he could give it to her was by making himself scarce. That put him on the boat with Wyatt and the three little girls. It would also give him a chance to study the toddlers. He wanted his own children and he was determined to be a good father. Wyatt was a good man. A good friend. He was also the best father Trap had ever spent time around.

Wyatt took the time showing the girls the various plants and wildlife. He spotted alligators for them and talked about the differences in canals, bayous and marshes. They were toddlers, but they listened attentively. Trap spent a lot of time watching their smiles, evaluating them and their well-being. All three girls were venomous. They had capped their teeth and all got terrible rashes. The caps had to be removed. Trap had studied the venom sacs in the hopes of removing them, but that wasn't going to happen anytime soon. The way they were situated, it was a difficult and dangerous operation.

Wyatt and Trap had turned their attention to finding a specific antidote and eventually a vaccine those caring for the girls could take to prevent accidental bites from harming them. That earlier research had enabled Trap to find a way to break down the venom Cayenne injected into his body much faster.

"We're going to stop the boat here and let the girls run a bit," Wyatt said. "They need the exercise. They're fast and they need to run off energy. I've cautioned them to listen and stay together. I'll be running behind them."

Trap nodded. "I'll stay with the boat." He found being apart from Cayenne difficult. They'd shared each other's body as well as mind. He'd always been alone. When he was in his laboratory or had turned his attention to a problem, he lost himself in it. He could concentrate wholly on it and nothing else penetrated. Not the need for food or drink or sleep. He could go for days and nights working without a break. During those times, he never thought about anything but his work.

Now he thought about Cayenne. Always. She was there in his mind. When he was away from her, he felt uneasy. He knew, logically, it was because he hadn't been able to prevent the loss of his family, but more, it was because they shared the same mind. It was impossible to feel alone when she was with him, filling every dark place, removing all dark thoughts. He'd been alone so long, now he had her.

She thought her need for him was greater than his for her, but that wasn't the case. He was man enough to admit that. Once he'd found her, once he knew they were compatible in every way, she'd wrapped herself around his heart, around his very guts. More, she was entrenched in his mind.

He didn't let her go, not all the way. He kept that thread between them, like one of her thin silky feelers. Monitoring her. It was wrong on so many levels, spying on her innermost thoughts. He had never been a jealous man, or a possessive one, until Cayenne. Women came and went. He didn't want them close. His need for Cayenne consumed him. She made him whole. She made him a better man. She did it all by giving herself to him without reservation. Anything he asked. Anything. Most importantly, she gave him complete trust in and out of the bedroom.

For a woman to hand a man that kind of gift—he couldn't imagine anything greater. She let him do anything he wanted, and in return, he worshipped her. She didn't know that, because he wasn't like she was. She didn't play games. She gave him complete and total honesty at all times. If he asked a question, there was no hedging. She gave him the answer. She didn't hold back from him. He hadn't learned that yet. He still protected himself, and the more vulnerable he was, the more he tried to keep that protection in place.

Trap knew there was no going back to a life without her. She had become his world, inside or out of the laboratory. He didn't want to go back. He just didn't like separation and vowed, from now on, he was going to stick close to her. She didn't seem to need space from him, so he was going to take advantage of that.

He knew absolutely he was the needy one. He was also a first-class bastard. He was selfish. He always had been. He did what he wanted when he wanted. He had become used to being rude and expecting those around him to put up with it. At first, he'd wanted to drive people away and keep them at a distance. Now, that behavior was ingrained in him.

He could have anything he wanted. He had that much money. He wanted a machine costing a couple hundred thousand, or a million, he bought it if it was important to him. His assistant provided anything he asked for and would answer his call even in the middle of the night. He was used to deference when he addressed others. He was used to getting his way in all things.

He not only wanted Cayenne—he needed her. That meant he would use everything at his disposal to keep her tied to him. Everything he'd told her about having a child and saving her life was true. He had finally found her files on the computer. He'd read them carefully. He knew when her period was. He had already calculated when she could get pregnant. He'd waited to say something to her until he was certain he'd managed to plant his child in her. He had known all along it was wrong. He also had known she would forgive him.

He pressed his hand to his heart. The physical reactions to her were getting stronger. Separation anxiety was growing with every moment they were apart. He forced himself not to call Wyatt back. Ezekiel had trailed after Wyatt to protect the family on their outing. Trap was grateful he was alone. He knew Zeke or Wyatt would have known he was in distress and they were astute enough to guess that being away from Cayenne was the reason.

He felt her then. In his mind. The sudden alarm. Near panic when Cayenne didn't panic. Trap leapt to his feet, his shout sending birds lifting into the air. *Cayenne.* He reached for her. There was a moment of clarity. He knew she threw herself in front of Nonny, and as Wyatt's grandmother rose from her chair, Cayenne leapt up to cover her head as best she could with her own body.

The bullet drove her back into the older woman. Both went down. The second bullet struck, a one-two punch. Cayenne was already fading, barely feeling the second bullet. She had shut everything down deliberately, realizing the bullets penetrated deep enough to do damage. She was bleeding and she didn't know how bad either of the wounds was.

He was in the boat, ready to start it when first Wyatt arrived, two of the toddlers on his hip. Ezekiel followed with Ginger, racing through the swamp to gain the boat before Trap had taken off.

Cayenne. Trap reached for her. Allowed Wyatt to take over. He sank down on the seat and gripped the edge of the boat, uncaring that his enhanced strength might leave evidence behind. He waited. Reached for her. There had been a flash of intense pain. He'd *felt* her heart jar. Hard. As if shock waves had shaken it. For one moment, her heart's rhythm had changed.

He'd had her close. Warm. Inside him. One second could change his life. He knew that. It had happened twice before. One second had changed everything. Taken his family. Taken his aunt.

Not you, Cayenne. Don't you fucking die on me. You aren't leaving me. Do you understand? Whatever happened, you keep breathing. For God's sake, baby, don't you fucking die.

"Trap." Wyatt's voice was ultra-quiet. "The girls can't breathe. You have to get it under control."

The voice registered, but he really didn't hear the words. He was someplace else. Inside himself. Someplace no one could reach him. Get to him. Make him feel anything but sheer ice.

Trap's gaze jumped to Wyatt's. He embraced the cold. Hid himself there. Became a fucking glacier. His hands were steady. He knew his eyes were devoid of all feeling because he wasn't feeling. He couldn't feel. Not without her. Not ever again. He'd given himself this one last chance. One. To live. To not be the cold lethal monster he'd shaped himself into in order to exact revenge.

"Trap." Ezekiel's voice penetrated the ice in his veins. "The girls have to breathe. So do we. You don't get it under control, none of us is going to make it back to her."

Trap looked around him, blinking to bring it all in focus. The air density surrounding and in the boat went back to normal. He couldn't reach Cayenne. She wasn't there anymore. He took a deep breath and let it out.

"When have I ever lost control, Zeke?" His voice was as devoid of feeling as the rest of him. There was nothing left but ice—and the need to kill.

"Malichai reached out. He's taking out the bullets. She's alive, but they've got trouble, at least two, maybe three more coming at them. Gino's in the swamp and Draden's on the roof," Wyatt reported.

"Wyatt, you can't take the girls to the house. Let me off in the swamp, the trail we made leading through will bring me in behind them." Trap stared straight ahead. It was up to Malichai, not him, to save Cayenne. But he could kill everyone who had tried to take her from him. He'd spent a lifetime learning how. And if she survived . . . this bullshit was *never. Ever. Fucking. Happening. Again.*

CHAPTER 17

The moment Trap's foot touched dry land, he was running, merging with the brush and trees, heading into the dense vegetation toward the narrow trail the GhostWalkers had created to allow them access through the swamp between their homes. He expanded his senses to encompass the area between him and the house. Gino was already reaching toward him with his mind and they nearly collided there in that psychic place.

I'm coming toward you. Draden's on the roof. Pepper is armed inside while Malichai and Nonny work on your woman. Draden took out their sniper. We've got at least three more approaching the house.

Four, Trap corrected. *I'm coming in behind them. I'll take out as many as I can, you stay close to the house to keep any of them from getting to the others.*

A third voice entered the conversation. *I'm a couple of miles from the house, in the bayou,* Wyatt said. *Getting the girls undercover. I hear helicopters. Two of them. Draden, if you're exposed, you need to use the blinds.*

One of the first changes made to both Wyatt's home and Trap's was the installation of cover for the men using sniper rifles on the rooftops. They could slip into one of the camouflaged tubes that looked part of the roof and never be seen, even from the sky.

Helicopters mean business, Trap said. *They're coming at us with more than a five-man team. Pay attention to the swamp side. They won't make their entry via water because they'll be too exposed. They'll have gunners on the helicopter. Draden, can you take them out?*

If they expose themselves, Draden replied.

Trap never slowed down, using a ground-eating pace to cover the distance and fall in behind the team moving in for the kill. He couldn't think about another team approaching the house from a different direction. He had to trust Gino, Draden and Pepper for the moment.

He heard the sound of a footfall and the whisper of clothes brushing through leaves. He kept moving fast—very fast—maintaining silence. He spotted the rear guard. He was running at a much slower pace than Trap, his automatic cradled in his arms as he scanned the surrounding swamp. It was more cursory than anything else. He had no idea death was a pace behind him.

Trap transferred his knife to his left hand as he came up on the man. His hand snaked out and he sliced the vulnerable throat as he blew past. The cut was deep and long. He'd used a tremendous amount of strength as he swung his arm back to meet the man so the soldier literally ran into the slice of the blade. The cut nearly severed his head. Trap didn't lose his pace, but kept running, not even looking back to see or hear the body fall.

One down, he reported.

Now he could hear the thump of the helicopter blades as the two machines closed in over the swamp, rushing to aid their team.

Helicopters over my head right now. Two gunners in

position in each. I believe the team leader is directing the action from the second helicopter. For one heart-stopping moment, Trap allowed the full meaning of those two helicopters to penetrate.

His breath caught in his lungs and his stomach rebelled before he managed to shut that shit down. He couldn't think that Whitney was sending everything he had against Cayenne. He wanted her dead. Gone. Whitney knew she was nearly indestructible and he couldn't afford for her to be in play. That meant Whitney was brewing up some plot against the GhostWalkers or one of their members and he didn't want interference.

Cayenne was small and could get in and out of places most of the GhostWalkers couldn't, but still, how could one person be such a threat to Whitney? She hadn't made a move to go after him. Why was it that Peter Whitney wanted her dead, so much so that he would send more than a five-man team after her? Why risk his soldiers? He didn't have that many, and they didn't last long. They weren't psychologically prepared for their enhancements and most broke fast. He was also risking an entire team of GhostWalkers as well as Wyatt's little girls. This attack made no sense.

Trap shut down his emotions hard, but his brain kept processing even as he ran, the helicopters directly overhead. He caught flashes of them through the trees, large silver birds, doors wide open, gunners manning their large caliber gun.

Fuck. They've got a .50 cal FN M3M/GAU-21 machine gun.

Badass, Draden said. *Eleven hundred rounds per minute. Serious fire power. They've come to kill.*

It doesn't make sense. They have no way of knowing that Wyatt's three little girls aren't home. Whitney wants them alive, doesn't he? Trap asked.

He could no longer hear three bodies moving fast through the swamp. Two, a good distance ahead, but not all three. He slowed instantly and then came to a halt. There was a strange buzzing in his head that told him at least some of Whitney's soldiers had telepathy and were in communication.

I've got the girls undercover in the swamp, Wyatt said. *Pepper, I need to know you're all right.*

I'm good, in position to protect Malichai, Cayenne and Nonny. Take care of the girls, Wyatt. Don't worry about me, Pepper said.

Status on Cayenne, Trap snapped because he *had* to know in spite of all resolve not to allow himself to think.

Malichai has already started on Cayenne. They're extracting the bullets now. She's alive, Trap, but her heart and lungs took a beating.

First helicopter in sight, Draden reported. *The second is hanging back. I don't have a clear shot. Trap, you might have to take that one if they stay out of my range.*

Roger that.

Trap studied the swamp ahead, pushing all thoughts of his woman as far from him as possible. The foliage was thick in some places, lending cover to anyone lying in wait for him. A small clearing of only about seven feet by eight feet where two trees had dropped was just ahead. On both sides, the swamp was edged with cypress trees and veils of moss hanging, again providing cover. He studied the entire layout, cataloguing everything in seconds. The temptation was to skirt the clearing and move to the outer rim of the swamp.

The sound of Draden's rifle cut through the air. The quick one-two Draden was famous for. He'd placed both shots precisely in the pilot's head. The lead helicopter lurched. Spun. One of the gunners went flying. The other fell back into the spinning craft. The helicopter continued to spin as it fell from the sky. The wheels touched earth. Bounced a few feet into the air spinning like a top. The craft listed to the side, the left back wheels touched first, almost gently, and then crumbled as the helicopter spun on the ground.

It looked as if for a moment time slowed. The helicopter

continued to tip to the side. The tail crashed into the ground, as the entire craft swept around in a circle on its side, throwing up dirt, debris and pieces of the wheels and tail. The rotor collapsed into the dirt, crumbling, forcing more debris, plants and dirt into the air, so that the sight was nearly obscured from vision. The craft, on its side, continued to spin as more debris flew into the air. It seemed alive, thrashing wildly for a moment, and then it came to a rest on its side, completely broken.

The second helicopter pulled back deeper into the cover of the swamp, hovering behind the taller trees where their leader barked out orders to his ground crew. Trap felt those orders like a tedious buzzing in his ear. He kept his gaze fixed on the tiny bit of clearing covered with vegetation, rather than the temptation of the moss-covered trees. The man they'd left behind to deal with him was in that clearing.

I know you're there, he whispered into the midst of the buzzing.

There was an abrupt silence, as if the leader heard him. Not just the leader, but the entire team. He was a strong telepath and he *wanted* them to hear him. He willed them to hear him.

You should have left her alone. He stayed still. Motionless. He was inside the grove of trees, surrounded by brush, so even if the helicopter swung back to aid the rear guard, they wouldn't spot him. They could sweep the area with their powerful gun, but they'd kill their own man as well.

You'll never find me, the rear guard hissed. *Keep looking, you big son of a bitch. They'll be on that insect before you ever find me. It's already too late.*

There was a heartbeat of silence and then a furious hiss of command. The leader wasn't in the least bit happy that his rear guard had engaged with the enemy.

Trap stared at the small clearing of leaves, calmly calculating the cubic feet and how best to direct his blast. He knew Gino was in front of the other two men and any others converging on the house. Gino was a ghost. Phantom wind, they called him. No one saw Gino, even when he made his kill. One moment no one was there, the next the body was already dropping to the ground and he was gone. Trap trusted him to do his job.

He sent a gust of air, lifting the vegetation to reveal the rear guard lying prone. Trap changed the actual chemicals in the air, a gift he had in abundance now, one that he'd practiced and honed, one he used when he went into enemy camps and left behind the dead. Gasses changed. The strange shimmer, a veil more opaque than translucent, surrounded the guard.

The man coughed. Tried to push himself up. Coughed again. Spat blood. Collapsed. Keeping to the edge of the heavier brush, Trap skirted around the clearing, holding to cover, keeping an eye on the dying man. Once around the rear guard, he picked up his speed, running full out to catch up with the last two team members.

Two coming in from the south side, Draden reported. *Gino, they'll be on top of you in another couple of minutes. I don't have a clear shot at either of them.*

Take the two about to break out of the swamp, running full out, Trap ordered. *They know I'm coming up behind them because I made a little noise to let them know. I'm hoping the helicopter will try to cover them.*

He could hear the buzz as the team leader gave orders from his vantage point in the sky. The helicopter began to move cautiously, trying to find a way to shift into position to cover the two men trying to gain access to the house. Trap ducked into the cypress grove and circled back around until he was directly beneath the helicopter. He inched forward, staying as low as possible, making certain no leaf stirred to give him away.

Looking directly up at the silver bird, the two gunners at the ready and the team leader using binoculars to watch the open ground between the swamp and Wyatt's home, he looked upward toward the sky. The air around the helicopter was made up of a mixture of gasses, mainly oxygen, nitrogen with smaller amounts of argon, water vapor and carbon dioxide along with a very small amount of other gasses.

By changing the gasses in the air beneath and around the helicopter, Trap changed the actual density of the air. He did it fast, not giving the pilot time to figure out what was happening. Even with his instruments to guide him, the pilot would know that nothing changed air density that quickly and he wouldn't believe what he was seeing. The rotor RPM decayed rapidly until the blades simply ceased rotating. The bird dropped like a stone, forcing Trap to dive to relative safety.

The helicopter crashed hard, breaking apart, scattering bodies, equipment and debris over a wide area. Trap hurried forward, knife in hand. The pilot and team leader were both dead, killed on impact. One of the gunners was still alive, spitting blood and trying to get to a weapon. Trap cut his throat. He found the second gunner a distance away, body in two pieces.

Helicopter down, crew dead.

I've got three coming at me from the south, Gino reported. *I'll take them.*

Two are moving in from the east, the canal side, Draden reported. *No way for me to get them.* The sound of his rifle was loud. Two shots. Close together as Draden nearly always did. It was his personal trademark. *Both runners close to the house down. Took them in the throat.*

I'm moving toward the river, Trap reported. He waited a beat but the wall in his mind was beginning to crumble. He had to reach out whether or not that way lay disaster. *Malichai, give me a report.*

She's alive. Her skin has some kind of built-in armor. I swear it feels like silk, but the bullets couldn't penetrate very far. The skin worked like a vest. It's crazy, Trap. Her organs took a jolt, her heart nearly stopped, but it's back to beating steady again. Her thigh needs attention, but I don't think she's going to need more than a few stitches.

Trap found he could breathe again. She was fucking glued to his side from here on out, and he didn't give a damn whether she liked it or not. Guarding her. Keeping her safe. That was *necessary*. He set out running again, choosing a course that would take him close to the canal and the cypress trees weeping moss there.

Something else strange, Trap. Her bones are different. They don't feel the same. Nothing's broken, but her femur should have been. The impact of that bullet should have taken it right through her body, but it stopped in her skin. Still, it should have broken the bone. And man, I have to tell you, no one has skin this soft.

Trap didn't like that one bit. *You don't need to notice that. Just keep her alive so I can strangle her.* He was going to do something to ease the raw, gaping hole in his gut. She'd done that. Gutted him with this shit. He'd had enough. She was going to do what the fuck he said when he said it, and if that made him a bastard, too fucking bad.

You're broadcasting loud, Wyatt said, amusement tingeing his voice.

There's nothing fucking funny about her getting shot. Twice. Trap spat the declaration at Wyatt.

No one thinks her getting shot is funny, bro, Wyatt pointed out. *Only your reaction. Never saw you lose it before.*

Trap heard them now, two of them. They were moving slow, single file. He ran silently until he was parallel with them, ignoring Wyatt. Whitney's supersoldiers seemed tireless, not even breathing hard. This close he could share their telepathic link.

We've got to get the son of a bitch on the roof, Jerrod, one said. *He took out the last of our first team.*

They weren't all that anyway, Jerrod said. *I'd like to know why these boys are protecting that hideous creature. Do you suppose they don't know what she is? A fucking spider?*

You're just pissed because your brother tried to fuck her right in front of you all and she killed him.

Whitney should have let me kill her.

Whitney thinks he's god almighty. His little experiments are getting more bizarre, and he's losing his backing. If we don't shut down this shit fast, he'll have an army of insects coming after us.

Trap drew in his breath sharply. These soldiers hadn't been sent by Whitney. The soldiers that had come, a few months back, for Wyatt's daughters hadn't been sent by Whitney either. They thought Braden had sent them. Another faction was in play. But who? If not Whitney, who?

He couldn't ask his fellow GhostWalkers, because if he could hear these two men, they could hear him. He sprinted past their position, inwardly cursing that he couldn't wait to hear more. They were gaining on the house. He couldn't allow them that close to Cayenne, Pepper or Nonny.

He got ahead of them and crouched low, once more sending poisonous gasses into the air so that they ran straight into them. The air shimmered with a particular glow that was a dead giveaway, but no one ever seemed to understand what it was until it was too late. He'd moved into enemy camps, that shimmer drifting ahead of him. Even when the enemy coughed and went to their knees, it still didn't register that they shouldn't breathe in the air around them.

In the swamp it was much easier to conceal. The shimmer looked a bit like drifting tendrils of fog coming together to form a veil. He heard the two men's footsteps stumble. They coughed. Cleared their throats. Spat. One tried to take a drink. One tried to speak. He didn't wait for them to succumb to the change in air. Gino was somewhere and needed backup. He stepped right in front of both of them, sweet air caught in his lungs. His knife slashed deep across each throat in one continuous motion and he was gone before the bodies dropped.

Two more down.

I've got one down here, Gino reported. *The other two have holed up.*

Whitney didn't send them. They're supersoldiers, but they belong to someone else, Trap reported. *Mine are all down. If we can get one alive, we might be able to interrogate him.*

I'll do my best, Gino said. *One's asking for deliverance right now. Give me a moment to oblige him and I'll ask politely of the last one.*

Trap crossed the swamp, using the trail they'd built and then swerving toward the location Gino had given him. He spotted a soldier easing his way on his belly, using toes and elbows to drag himself forward through the thick vegetation, eyes trained on the house. Trap didn't dare change the air because he didn't know exactly where Gino was.

The soldier eased himself over the thin trunk of a sapling that had gone down a few years earlier. It was broken in places and rotting. Only a few inches in diameter, it was still quite long. The soldier's stomach seemed to hang up on it for a moment. There was a gurgling sound. Blood splashed on the leaves around the sapling. Trap tried to spot Gino. He had to be somewhere on the ground. The soldier had been facedown, only a few inches off the ground, and yet Gino had cut his throat. The soldier had to have been staring right into his killer's eyes when he died, but Trap couldn't see his fellow GhostWalker.

Nice job, Gino.

I can handle this, Gino replied grimly. *Draden can cover me, you get to your woman. Should have been on top of this, Trap. I'm sorry I let that sniper anywhere near her.*

Not your fault. I should have been with her. She wanted to do this alone. Said it was important to her. When a woman tells you it's important and your gut tells you no fucking way, go with your gut, Gino.

Copy that.

Trap made his way to the house, leaving the last soldier to

Gino. Gino wanted to interrogate him. They didn't have a whole lot to offer in return for information. Trap doubted that the soldier would believe them if they offered to spare his life. Still, Gino could make him very uncomfortable and plant a tracking device in his body while he questioned the man.

He stayed under cover as long as he could, not wanting to risk getting shot by the last remaining soldier. Crouching just at the tree and brush line, he waited. It took less than five minutes.

I've got him. You have to go.

Trap didn't hesitate. He had to see Cayenne for himself. See that she was alive. If she was, he didn't know exactly what he was going to do with her. The rage buried so deep, rage he'd held for nearly all his life, was there. He could feel it. Powerful. Dark. Lethal. He'd spent years building a glacier to keep it covered. In that moment, when the first bullet had taken her, driven into her body, jolting her heart—that bullet had lodged into the very heart of his glacier. Great spiderweb cracks had radiated out from it, and now that rage was rising to the surface and he was helpless to stop it.

He knew Malichai would have had Pepper or Nonny inform headquarters that they were under fire. That contact would send a team to clean up the mess. They wouldn't want the bodies strewn around the forest so a medical examiner could speculate on the deaths. They'd already be on their way. That didn't matter to him.

At first he used ground-eating strides to cross the yard to the house, then abruptly he found himself running, using his enhanced speed. He jumped, clearing the long row of steps leading to the house. Like most houses in the swamp and bayou, the Fontenot home was built the traditional way, raised off the ground in case of a flood. His jump landed him on the wraparound porch Nonny loved so much.

He yanked open the door and at the last minute called out his name so Pepper or Nonny or both wouldn't shoot him. He didn't break stride as he went into the house. Pepper moved away from the door, her face lighting up when she saw him and then darkening to a frown when she *really* saw him. She bit her lower lip and stepped aside.

"Trap, Cayenne's fine. She just has bruises and a few stitches."

Pepper tried to soothe him, but he barely registered her voice. He couldn't assimilate her reassurance. There was no way to calm the deadly beast rising like the molten lava in a volcano. He tried to breathe it away because now it was in his belly, hot and ugly, swirling like the fireball it was, spreading through those various cracks so there was no dam that could possibly stop them.

He moved unerringly through the house, his footsteps utterly silent. In his ears, his heart thundered. Roared. The jackhammers were back, driving deep into his skull with every step he took. The scent of blood was heavy, mingling with Cayenne's fragrance. That sent the rage swirling a notch higher. The blood scent nearly obliterated Cayenne's beautiful exotic natural perfume just as the bullets had almost taken her from him.

Nonny stood in the door of his old bedroom, but after taking one look at his face, she reached inside the room, caught Malichai's arm and tugged. Malichai filled the doorway, opened his mouth and closed it, reading Trap's darkened face and the lines carved deep. Both stepped outside the room and aside, allowing him to brush past them. They wisely closed the door, leaving him alone with her.

Cayenne was in his bed—the bed he'd lain in for four long months. He'd dreamt of her being in that bed. Fantasized about her being there. Jacked off thinking about her and what he'd do to her—all in that bed. Now she was sitting up in the damn, *fucking* bed, smiling up at him as if nothing had happened. As if she didn't have a care in the world. All around her was the aftermath of her surgery. The empty bags of fluid and blood. Her bloody clothes shredded and on the floor. More blood—all hers—saturating the cloths they'd used to try to stem it.

"What the *fuck* do you think you were doing?" The words hissed out of his mouth. Low. Lethal. It felt like an explosion in his chest. His chest hurt more than any injury in his life had ever hurt him, and he'd had plenty.

Cayenne frowned at him. She studied his face for a long time. He remained still, just inside the door, every muscle locked in place.

"Are you angry with me, Trap?"

She sounded shocked. Innocent. As if she didn't know she was his entire world and she'd nearly allowed a bullet to take her from him. He wanted to shake her until her teeth rattled.

"What the fuck do you think, Cayenne?" He bit the words out, enunciating each. His breath came fast, as if he was running through the swamp again, running to keep those soldiers off of her.

Trap leapt across the room and yanked up the thin tee she was wearing. One of his old ones he'd carelessly left behind when he'd packed to move to his new home. Packed to move wherever the hell Cayenne was, because even then, he knew she was home.

"*Hell* yes, I'm angry. Have you *looked* at your body? That bruise covers your entire chest. *Both* breasts." He yanked the covers down to expose her legs. "Your thigh. You could have been killed."

She touched her tongue to her top lip. Then outlined her bottom lip. He wanted to lean down and bite that full lower lip and if she kept it up, that was exactly what she was going to get. Hard. He was going to bite that lip hard and leave his mark on her.

"Trap." Cayenne said his name gently. "I'm perfectly fine. If I hadn't covered Nonny like I did, they would have killed her. They weren't only coming after me. I feel things and their energy hit me before the bullet was fired. I had a much better chance of survival than Nonny."

He crouched beside the bed, his face inches from her. "You fucking don't get to take that chance. Your life isn't yours anymore. You need to get this right now, Cayenne. I'm not fucking around with you. You belong to somebody. That somebody is *me*. You gave yourself to me. You let me believe I could fucking live again, not just exist. Not walk around like a fucking zombie. I could live. *You* did that. That gives you responsibility to keep yourself alive. Not throw your ass in front of bullets because you think you're fucking invincible. You're not."

"Trap." She whispered his name, reached out to touch his face.

He couldn't bear her touch. Not right then. He would shatter into a million pieces if she touched him. He batted her hand away.

"Don't try to sweet talk your way out of this. If you didn't have bruises all over you, I'd bend you over the bed and use a fucking strap on you. You wouldn't sit comfortably for a couple of weeks and maybe you'd think about what a fuckup this was every time you tried."

She touched her tongue to her upper lip and then moistened her full lower lip with her tongue. He was up abruptly, pacing away from her, fury riding him so hard he shook with it. She just sat there, looking innocent. Not comprehending the enormity of what she'd done. Not understanding what she was to him. *Not feeling the same way.*

"I have to get out of here. I'll be back to get you in a little while."

"I'm going with you." Cayenne flung the covers all the way from her body and swung her legs off the bed to the floor.

"You're not." He glanced over his shoulder and nearly froze. Every muscle locked in place. Her face was set in stubborn lines. That beautiful face, heart-shaped, her silken skin inviting touch. Eyes large, a vibrant green framed with impossibly long, thick, black lashes. Straight nose and that exotic, perfect mouth. Her chin was up in a line that challenged any man.

"I am."

The roaring in his head increased. "You don't have one fucking ounce of self-preservation in you, do you?"

She narrowed her eyes at him. Lifted one hand to the mass of dark hair falling around her face, down her back and pooling on the sheets. Her hand actually shook, and the vulnerability there on her face and in that action caused his heart to seize in his chest.

"I had to sit here knowing you were out there, Trap, with soldiers I brought here. Soldiers bent on killing everyone. Soldiers you were facing in the swamp while I was lounging around in a bed. So, yes, I'm going with you, and I'm going to make certain I have you in my sights for as long as it takes to get rid of this terror inside of me."

She stood up. Trembled. He was there instantly, settling his hands around her upper arms. His fingers closed around her silken skin. He felt the movement of muscle beneath his vise-like grip, but she didn't pull away from him. She was cold, as she often was and actually leaned into his body for warmth and shelter.

His heart contracted. Hard. Tight. He tightened his grip on her, not knowing what he was going to do. Not trusting himself. For the first time, he was afraid for her. Really afraid. She'd made him open himself to her. She became part of his life. Not just part. She became his life. She acted instinctively and she'd almost been killed. That was a part of her character.

She'd lived in a little cell thinking of herself as not human. As an experiment to be studied. She'd been pitted against teams of trained soldiers determined to kill her, and she'd come out the victor. She was fearless in battle.

"Damn it, Cayenne, you aren't disposable. Your life is

worth something. Everything. You can't keep thinking the way you do."

She tilted her chin at him, her green eyes searching his face. Brooding. Moody. Those lashes fanned the high cheekbones concealing the brilliant green of her eyes and raised again to reveal multifacets. Gems of emerald. His breath caught in his throat. This woman was his. She was his everything, and she went into battle prepared to die. Fearless because she didn't believe she had anything to lose.

"You have *me* to lose, Cayenne," he corrected. "You die, and what the fuck do you think is going to happen to me? You can't give a man who had nothing everything, and then take it away from him. You don't get to do that. I lived in a void. It was a kind of hell, and maybe I thought I belonged there because I didn't die with my family. I believed for so long I didn't deserve a damn thing because if I hadn't lived, they wouldn't have touched my aunt. I had nothing. *Nothing.* Do you fucking understand that? I had nothing until you gave me you."

She took a breath. He could see her pulse pounding in her throat. He wanted to bend down and lick it. Taste her skin. Taste her passion. But he couldn't because she'd been shot. Twice.

"The thing is, Trap," she said softly, "I *do* understand. You're not in this alone. I had nothing. I lived in a void, a kind of hell. Maybe I thought I belonged there because I was convinced by everyone around me that I wasn't human. I believed I didn't deserve anything at all. Until you saw me. The human. Until you chose me. I had nothing to live for. I had nothing at all, until you gave me you. So please don't tell me I don't understand. You were out there, in danger. You pushed aside all feeling and you did your job. When you did it, you weren't thinking about whether or not you could be killed and what would happen to me if you did. You simply did what you were trained to do. You aren't less than me. I don't love you less."

His heart clenched so hard he thought it might shatter. *Love*. There it was. She said it. Brought it right out into the open. He had skirted carefully around that particular word and the terrible emotion it conjured up. A single word couldn't describe the way he felt about her. There was no getting around it. The powerful, overwhelming emotion he felt for her had to be love and more. More than love. Worship maybe. Whatever, she couldn't leave him.

He didn't know if he was steadying her or himself when he pulled her closer to him, when he fit her small body against his side. It wasn't the revelation of how she felt that got to him. It was her voice. That soft, shaky admission. Close to tears. The revelation of love. Of fear. No, not just fear. A soul-shattering terror. It was there in her voice. In her mind.

Cayenne always gave him everything without reservation. She wasn't ashamed of her feelings or what that exposed to him. She didn't care that by knowing how she felt, he might have power over her. She just gave him everything. Straight up.

His hand moved over her face, brushing aside her hair. "Baby." He said it softly. "I can't breathe right now."

"Then kiss me and I'll breathe for you," she whispered back. In that voice. The one that could turn a roomful of decent men into a pack of salivating hounds. The one that sent fingers of desire dancing up his thighs and down his spine to spread through his bloodstream straight to his cock.

He didn't deny either of them. He *needed* to kiss her. More than he needed to draw air into his lungs, he had to kiss her. He bent his head and took her mouth. She opened to him instantly. He didn't take her along for the ride on the kiss, she participated fully. Her lips were soft, his were hard. She was cool. He was hot. His mouth melted her as he took possession, his tongue stroking along hers. She had paid close attention every time he kissed her or touched her and she learned fast.

They exchanged breath. Air. Passion. He felt it, the rage

retreating under the force of her love. Of her giving. She gutted him with her kiss. With her love.

You give me everything. All of you. I can taste you in my mouth. In my lungs. You're wrapped around my heart. Stamped into my bones. He gave her that because she deserved to know. She had to know. *Baby, you can't risk yourself. I wouldn't survive the loss. Not intact. You have to give me this.*

Trap. She kissed him again, melting into him. *I would give you anything. I want to give you what you're asking, but you aren't being logical.*

Fuck logic. He lifted his head, his hand spanning her throat, his thumb on her jaw, holding her head still. "Fuck logic," he said aloud for emphasis.

That little tongue of hers came out again, moistening her lips. Lips swollen from his kisses. "I have to be me. I'm a warrior, just like you. I have to be me. You have to love that part of me, Trap, just like I love all of you. Was I terrified for you? Yes. Did I know you had to do it? Yes. Did I believe in you? Yes."

"It isn't about believing in you." He raked his free hand through his hair, wanting to fist it and tug in sheer frustration. "I can't do this with you in danger."

"Yes, you can. You have to. Because we're always going to be in danger," she said. "When we have children, they'll be in danger. You have to trust us. Trust me that I know what I'm doing just like you know."

"They have armor-piercing bullets. You think they aren't going to use them?"

"They did. That's why the bullet penetrated almost completely through the silk, but Trap, I knew it would. I've been shot before. Did you think they hadn't used them on me when I was in that maze with them? They tried everything. I couldn't let Nonny die. I won't be able to do anything but stand in front of our children either. That's who I am."

"Fuck." The word exploded out of him.

"Trap."

That was her answer. That would always be her answer. He could dictate, and he knew he would, but she would go her own way when she believed she was right. The rest of the time she'd give him everything.

He repeated the expletive several more times. She kept her eyes on his. He shook his head. "We do this your way, baby, and you're fucking locked to my side. And by that I mean you go where I go, and you do what I say when we're out in public. You have any more cooking lessons I'm there, not *cute* fucking Malichai. You got that?"

Her green eyes moved over his face. Soft. Warm. Loving. Turning his heart over. Making it stutter hard in his chest. A slow smile curved her mouth. That beautiful mouth he was putting to work the moment they got home.

"I got it, Trap."

"You giving that to me?" he insisted. He wasn't going to give her wiggle room. She was going to be with him for a long time. He wasn't certain when the terror would recede enough to give her breathing room.

"I'm giving that to you."

"Tell me what *that* is."

"I'm glued to your side and you're with me even when I do more cooking lessons with Nonny. You owe cute Malichai your thanks. He took good care of me."

"Don't want to hear that, baby." But he could breathe now. Draw air into his lungs and let it out without that raw burn. Without the pain in his throat and the visceral tearing of his gut.

She leaned into him very heavily. "I want to go home, Trap. I want to be in our bed with our silks cocooning us. I want to feel your heartbeat. I want your cock in my mouth and then in my body. Deep. I want to feel you pounding into me hard and rough so I know you're alive and that you're mine. Can you give me that? I'm giving you what you need. Give me what I need."

His thumb moved along her jaw. He doubted if there was a man alive who could hear his woman ask for that and turn her down. "We have to be careful of your bruises, Cayenne."

"I need this more than I need to worry about a few bruises. Take me home, Trap."

CHAPTER 18

―――――――――⌇―――――――――

Trap took his time examining every inch of Cayenne's body. She lay sprawled out beneath him like a gift. A feast. A treasure beyond all price. Her hands stroked through his hair, fingers sifting, rubbing along his scalp as he kissed his way along her collarbone and down to the dark bruises marring the lush curve of her breasts.

"Baby, we're getting married right away. I don't want an argument about it either. Flame sent the papers. Gator's bringing her with him. They missed Wyatt's wedding because Gator was out of the country. Flame's been anxious to meet her three nieces, so our wedding will be the perfect opportunity."

She smiled, looking serene. Her hands communicating love right through the strands of his hair. "You were in touch with them, planning our wedding even before you talked to me?"

He nuzzled the valley between her breasts gently. She drew in her breath sharply. He licked along the dark bruises tenderly, wishing he could heal her with his mouth. With his love. "They were in touch with Wyatt, and he told me earlier. They gave him the information that your background was complete and any reporter looking into you would believe the history they created for you. Wyatt knows I mean business. I'm not waiting to make you mine. Tomorrow I leak the news to the magazines and papers. I want to send a photograph of the two of us together as well."

"You're daring your uncles to come out in the open."

Again, her voice was matter-of-fact. Giving him everything. This time he wasn't fooled. She *would* give him everything because she liked to please him. She wanted him happy. But the moment she felt she needed to do something he wouldn't like, Trap was well aware his woman was going to do it. She made that plain enough. He couldn't have everything his way.

He licked up the side of her breast. He couldn't suckle the way he wanted to. She was far too battered, so he contented himself with kissing every inch of the deep bruise that spanned both breasts and under them. It wasn't enough. He had to *feel* for himself that every inch of her was unharmed.

He took his time on her arms, using the pads of his fingers to run lightly over the undersides while his mouth inspected above. He found a series of small bruises up high on her biceps and knew Nonny had tried to catch her as she flew backward when the bullet struck. His gut clenched all over again. Knots tightened until they were hard and threatening to snap into pieces.

His teeth nipped her wrist in punishment. His tongue soothed. The small chastisement wasn't enough to rid him of the moment in his mind. He knew it was burned there. That single moment when he was certain she'd been taken from him. He kissed his way back up her arm to her shoulder.

Trap pressed his mouth against her vulnerable neck. "You don't get shot again. *Not.*" He bit that sweet spot between her shoulder and neck. Hard. She made a single sound of protest, but she didn't move. She didn't try to stop him. He licked at the mark and then suckled, leaving his brand on her. *"Ever."* He switched sides, his tongue gliding over her nipples, the gentlest of licks. Heart pounding. Blood roaring a protest in his ears. His lips moved against that same spot on her left shoulder. *"Again."* He whispered it softly and then bit down again. Soothed with his tongue. Suckled until his brand was there.

He kissed his way to her ribs. "Do you understand me, Cayenne? You don't get shot again. Next time I'm not going to be nice about it."

"Honey."

She breathed the endearment, and he thought he might shatter into pieces. She didn't do that. She rarely called him anything but Trap. She hadn't moved her hands from the sheets. She kept giving to him. Showing him how she felt.

"Say it, Cayenne."

"I won't get shot again."

He caught that soft silky skin between his teeth along her left side and nipped. "Say it and fucking mean it, baby. Don't try to placate me."

"I want to give you anything you need, Trap, but how can I promise that? I'll do my best to never get shot again. You have my word on that."

His hands moved to her waist, holding her for a moment. Just holding her. His hands were big and he could almost span her waist. He took a breath and let the knots in his gut ease. Just a little.

"You stay close to me. When we're out of this house, you're right next to me."

"I *want* to be next to you. I need to know you're alive and well too, Trap," she assured softly, and then, being Cayenne gave him more. "I'm not planning on letting you out of *my* sight for a long while."

The knots disappeared and he could breathe easy again. The roaring in his head dissipated. He was extraordinarily gentle with her. He kissed each rib, tracing the indentations with his tongue. She squirmed. Her hips lifted, pushing into him suggestively.

"Not a chance, baby. You were nearly killed. I felt that jolt to your heart. I *felt* it. The flash of pain. For one moment I thought you were gone. It was the longest, most agonizing moment of my life. Even then I had to wait for a report on how bad it was. So I get this. I get to take my time and inspect every inch of you."

There was heat in his voice. Command. Demand. He didn't give a flying fuck either whether or not she wanted this different. He'd give her different another time. This was his time. His need. It wasn't about lust or hunger. It was a need so deep, so elemental and primal, he couldn't even explain it to her.

She stilled, but the hands in his hair clenched tighter. "After you get what you need, Trap, you have to give me the chance to do the same."

"Don't worry, baby," he assured, nuzzling her belly button. He licked along her soft belly and rimmed the little button before dipping his head lower to trace each hip bone. She shivered in response, but held herself still. "I want your mouth on me. I even need it, but not yet. I'll be careful of your thigh, but the rest of you is in working order, and I'm going to make certain I spend time claiming what's mine."

She was shot twice. Her heart had suffered a terrible jolt and she had massive bruises, but in spite of all that, it was clear her body had superior healing ability. He could see that, although she was sore, she wasn't really hurting that bad. Already her body had tried to heal itself. That ability shocked him.

"You like that word." There was a smile in her voice.

"What word?" He was fascinated with the silk of her skin. He loved the feel of her, the way she seemed to melt into him. The way she went from cool to hot under his touch. He loved making her breath hitch. The little purr in her voice when he touched a sensitive spot.

"*Mine.* You use that a lot."

"You are mine, aren't you?" To add emphasis to his claim, he shoved both hands beneath her beautiful, rounded ass and lifted, fingers sinking into firm muscle there.

She gasped as his warm breath slid over her damp entrance. "Yes."

"Your body is mine, right? All for me? That mouth is mine. So fucking beautiful. The way you kiss me, drowning in our kisses, giving me that. It's mine, right? No one but me kisses that mouth. Not. Fucking. Ever."

He dipped his head and swiped his tongue along the inside of her left thigh, careful of the bruise that had spread from the front to both sides. Just from the time he'd first seen it until this moment, it was already fading in color.

"It's yours," she agreed.

"I love the sight of that mouth wrapped around my cock. So beautiful, Cayenne. In my wildest imagination, I couldn't have conjured up the image of you sucking on my cock the way you do. Loving it. Lavishing attention on it. Enjoying it. That's mine, right? That mouth. All mine. All for me."

He licked up her right thigh, and then pressed his mouth right into the middle of that silky red hourglass he loved so much. He stroked with his tongue. Traced each distinct line pressed there in the middle of the midnight black curls.

"Yes." Her breath hitched in her throat. At his explicit words, droplets of liquid honey seeped along her entrance.

He felt the tension coiling in her. Her stomach muscles contracted. Her sweet bottom, even her thighs, but she didn't move. She kept her hips still for him. Giving him that. He lapped at the tiny drops.

"I love the way you taste. Sometimes I just want to eat you alive. Devour you. Spend hours right here, harvesting every drop you can give me and making more. This is mine too, isn't it baby? All for me."

"You know it is, Trap," she murmured, her fingers now curled into two tight fists in his hair.

"All the honey you can give me. That's mine. That sweet, scorching-hot silk that wraps so tight around me and strangles my cock, milking every fucking drop of my seed right out of me. That's mine, right?"

"All yours," she agreed. Now her voice had gone raw. Low. So sensual he felt it vibrating in his cock.

He didn't ask her again. He plunged his tongue deep. He needed this, the taste of her pouring down his throat. The affirmation that she was alive and that she was his. He held her hips still while he took his fill, while he drove her up over and over with his mouth and tongue and teeth. He couldn't use his hands because she could no longer control herself, her breath coming in sobbing pleas. Her head tossing on the pillow. She lost the purchase in his hair and transferred her grip to the sheets, fingers digging deep, bunching the material into the palms of her hands.

He didn't stop, even when she begged him. He lost count of the times he demanded her body go over, but in the end there was no counting where one climax started and the next ended, they simply rolled into one another.

When he was so hard and thick and aching that he thought his body would explode, he lifted his head and started the crawl back up her body, rubbing his face and her nectar on her belly. When he reached the pillows, he rolled off the bed to stand up. At the same time, he caught her under her arms and pulled her to the edge of the bed. "Scoot your bottom all the way to the edge of the bed, baby."

She didn't ask questions or protest. Her green eyes were on his face. Trusting. Watching. Learning. He loved that in her. She obeyed instantly, positioning herself there at the edge of the bed.

"You're going to give me this too? The way I want it?"

"I'd give you anything, Trap," she said. "My body is yours. I'm yours. We just established that. Tell me what you want."

His belly tightened. His cock jerked. She sat there in the

bed. His bed. Their bed. Waiting for his command. Looking up at him with her green eyes and that mouth of hers. Just waiting for him to tell her what he needed. His woman. Cayenne. His heart pounded. Hurt even. He had this now. Her. This incredible woman belonged to him.

The silks she'd fashioned hung from the ceiling in long beautiful lacy patterns, cocooning them inside the small area, creating an intimacy like no other. It was their space. The bed was up higher on a platform, allowing him to stand close, his cock right next to her mouth. He'd had this built calculating the exact measurements needed and had his bedroom constructed accordingly.

The headboard was wide with numerous sturdy intricate dowels that were built for a specific purpose. He liked to play, and his bedroom was where he liked to do it. The bed had also been made to his specifications. He loved the idea of playing, having her at his mercy, but not now. Now was for worship. Now was for affirmation. He was loving her the best way he knew how. He was claiming her. Letting her know she was his and he'd spend the rest of his life finding ways to make her happy.

His hand came up to circle the wide thickness of his aching cock, a casual gesture he was barely aware of. He still didn't feel lust in the way he normally did. This was so much more, a ritual he needed. A giving he craved. Still as elemental. He saw that same primal need in her eyes. That same terrible necessity that was so brutal, so urgent, neither of them could resist it.

"Open your thighs wide, baby," he ordered softly.

Cayenne did so immediately, spreading her legs wide for him, her eyes on his.

"I want you looking at me. Just like that. I want to see your eyes, Cayenne. I need to see your expression."

Her small tongue slipped out. Moistened her lips. He groaned at the sight of her gleaming lips. So wet for him. His gaze dropped lower. Between her legs. She was wet there for him as well. He knew she would be. Cayenne lavished him with love. Gave and gave. He wanted more, and he was going to take it.

He pressed the burning head of his cock against her lips. She surprised him by kissing him. Not once, but several times. Her hands cupped his heavy sac, fingers caressing and stroking. The action lifted the lush curves of her breasts. Her nipples were tight little buds. It took willpower to resist their allure, but she was heavily bruised there and he didn't want anything else to hurt her—ever. Even with the bruises fading so swiftly, he wasn't about to take any chances of hurting her.

Her tongue slipped out of her mouth again and she licked over that broad, velvet head, making a little sound of happiness. His gut clenched hard. His cock jerked in anticipation. Her mouth engulfed him, tongue fluttering like butterfly wings along his shaft, the tip reaching that spot right under the crown. Pressing. Laving. She used broad strokes and then took him deep, released and did it again.

The sight of her loving him that way was almost too much. He was on fire. Fucking fire. Deep inside the ice melted, but the rage was gone, replaced by something altogether different. A molten volcano, buried deep beneath the glacier had begun to make its escape. The emotion erupting wasn't anger or rage. It was just as deep, just as overwhelming, but it was a surge so powerful it shook him. Love. The emotion gripped him. Stunned him with its force.

She spread lightning through his veins. Her mouth scalded him. Sent pure fire spreading like a wild conflagration through him to come together in his cock. He reached for her head, two fists in her hair, tugging. She didn't obey him. Her mouth tightened.

"I'm not coming in your mouth, Cayenne," he said. "Fucking let go now."

She smiled at him around a mouthful of cock. Her eyes smiled at him. Her mouth moved again, one long stroke that took him so deep his heart contracted. Her tongue teased up his shaft and then she let him go.

"On your hands and knees, facing away from me, right there on the edge of the bed." His voice was hoarse. Who wouldn't be? She loved touching him. Sucking him. Her hands caressed him, left him reluctantly. But she obeyed. She gave him that too. Because she was Cayenne. The woman created entirely for him.

He stood at the side of his bed, his eyes on her shapely ass. That was his too. All of her. Every damn inch. He couldn't resist rubbing her buttocks, those firm, silky muscles and down her thighs. She was beautiful, on her knees, waiting for him, totally exposed. Totally vulnerable. Trusting him.

If you hurt at all, you tell me. He waited.

I'll tell you, honey. I swear. I need you right now.

That was it. Right there. She trusted him implicitly to give her pleasure, to see to her pleasure no matter what he did to her. That gift was beyond any price. He stepped close, so close he could feel the heat waiting for him. That scorching tunnel of silk waiting to surround and strangle him.

The thought was too much. He caught her hips and slammed home. The sensation of her scalding muscles gripping him so tightly as he invaded, as he drove so deep he felt the bump as he touched her womb. She screamed.

"Trap. That's so good. Perfect. Like that. Do me just like that."

"I'll do you however I want." He stayed buried in her. Holding her to him. Feeling those muscles trying to strangle him, pouring into her mind to ensure she wasn't hurting anywhere. He wanted only pleasure for her.

She wiggled. "You have to move. I'm not going to survive if you don't move. I need this too, honey. Please move. Hard. Rough. I want to feel you. Let go this time. Completely."

"Baby." The thought of that—of losing himself in her—was such a temptation. Too much of one.

He pulled back and surged forward. Hard. Deep. Again

and again. Fire streaked up his body, sizzled along every nerve ending in tune to her ragged breathing and soft cries of pleasure. Her pleas became demands. He loved that when he took her hard and rough, she pushed back into him, eager for more. So eager, she made her own demands.

He pounded into her, and let the fire take him. Consume him. He lost himself in the sheer beauty of her body. In the love he had for her and the knowledge that she gave herself to him so completely. He could have her any way he needed her and she'd give him that.

She pushed back, meeting his every stroke. Hard. Her breath hissing out of her lungs. Her body gripping his hard. Taking him deep. The scorching silk surrounded him, that tight, fiery tunnel of sheer bliss. He felt the coiling tension in her, heard the change in her breathing, the moans that sounded like music to him, and he knew she was so close. The need to give that beautiful gift to her was in every loving stroke of his body.

Lust was there, but love was the most prevalent, overwhelming emotion, tied so tightly with his lust that he couldn't separate the two. The emotion made every streak of lightning, every fiery flame rushing like a fireball through his body so much stronger, sharper and raw.

Her body clamped down on his. Her breath hissed out in a long scream of his name, triggering his own release. There was no holding back the volcano. His cock erupted, slamming deep inside of her, his seed splashing into her scorching channel, filling her, pushing her climax higher. His cock jerked hard, over and over, as she milked him violently for every drop her body could wring out of his.

He couldn't move, his legs unsteady as he gripped her hips so she wouldn't collapse onto her bruised chest. Clearly her body had healed quickly from the injury, leaving behind the discoloring, but she wasn't nearly in as much pain as she should have been. He held her still until he could breathe again. Only then did he slowly pull out of her and guide her over onto her back. She sprawled out on the mattress, her breathing still ragged, her breasts heaving.

He followed her down and wrapped his arm tight around her waist. He pulled her into the protection of his body. He was completely sated, his cock limp and still feeling the burn of bliss. He pressed the length of him against her thigh.

"I have to clean up," she said softly.

"Don't. Go to sleep with me in you. I'm planting my babies in you. I want to go to sleep knowing that's happening." He murmured the order against the cloud of her dark hair.

"Trap. You're getting arrogant. And bossy." There was amusement in her voice, but she didn't stir. Her body stayed tight against his.

"You make me that way, baby." It was the strict truth. He knew he could have what he wanted, because she loved him and would give him anything.

She laughed softly, and the sound was like a miracle to him. "I'm in your mind right now and I'll give you anything *within reason*. I like to be there when you're inside me or when my mouth is wrapped around your cock. I like how I make you feel. It's sexy and makes me feel especially good knowing I'm the one that makes you feel like that."

"Baby," he corrected, because it was the truth. "You'll give me any fucking thing I ask you for. You think I don't know you by now? You think I don't know what's the most important thing in your world? I know, because *you're* the most important thing in mine. I'd give you the fucking world. You won't do less. You're far more giving than I am. So don't try to fool me. I ask, you're going to give it to me."

She sighed. "You're such a pain, Trap."

"I know, baby. Go to sleep. You have about two hours and then I'm going to be waking you up again. I've got plans for you."

"I'm injured," she pointed out. Her voice was mild. Not a protest. She didn't care that she was injured.

"There's no need to remind me. It's burned in my fucking

brain, Cayenne. You keep bringing it up and I'm going to injure your beautiful ass for you."

She laughed softly. "Trap, you're so full of it. Even if you did, I'd have your cock two seconds later. That wouldn't be much of a punishment."

His hand cupped her face and turned it toward him. He didn't want her to have any doubts about the man he was. "You're right about that, baby. You'd have my cock. My mouth. My hands. But I wouldn't give you release, and I wouldn't let you give it to yourself either. Not for a long, long time. I don't have to hurt you to punish you. I would *never,* under any circumstances hurt you. But you'd pay for making me relive that fucking moment over and over."

She shivered. Her eyes went dark green. Sexy. Her tongue came out and licked her lips. Top and bottom. She pressed her body closer. "I'm not certain I could take that, Trap."

"You'll take it. And then I'll make it so good for you that you'll scream my name over and over. Never doubt that I'll make it good for you." His arm tightened. His fingers slid over her face gently. Tenderly. "I love you, Cayenne. So much. Maybe too much."

She smiled and turned onto her side, facing away from him, pressing her bottom into his lap. "I love you that much too, Trap. Way more than is good for you."

He needed that. Her loving him like that. He was clinging too hard. Needing too much, but she gave him that. He knew, with time, he could ease back, but right now, with danger surrounding her, with his past so close, he couldn't let go. As always, he knew, she would give him exactly what he needed. He waited to sleep until he felt her body relax completely and her breathing even out. Then he followed her.

Cayenne's heart pounded hard. She wanted to bolt. It took every ounce of self-control she had not to lean over and bite Nonny, paralyze her and escape out the window. Other than

Trap, no one had ever fussed over her. She wasn't used to being the center of attention. The dress felt foreign on her body. It was beautiful, no doubt about that. Trap always provided her with the best of everything.

Her wardrobe had grown significantly. She didn't know why. They lived in the swamp, away from most people. Nonny and Pepper were her only friends, and they wore jeans most of the time like she did. Well, Pepper, when all three women had a little too much of Nonny's homemade strawberry wine, had confessed she wore long skirts so she didn't have to wear underwear and Wyatt could catch her anywhere in the house and have his way with her. It was an exciting game between them finding a hiding spot surrounded by their family. At home, Cayenne rarely wore clothes. If she did, it was a shirt, but she supposed once she had children, long skirts might just be the perfect attire.

"You look beautiful," Nonny said.

Cayenne smoothed her hand down the white silk dress that clung to her curves and dropped to the floor in panels of beads and lace. She couldn't fault the gown. It was exquisite. It fit perfectly. She wanted Trap to see her in it, but he wasn't the only one out there waiting for her. Pepper and Nonny were standing up for her. Draden and Wyatt were standing for Trap.

The triplets, dressed in long ruffled peach gowns, raced around the room, so excited they couldn't keep still. Everyone was waiting, and she couldn't move. She was frozen to the spot and near tears. She couldn't walk out there with everyone watching. It wasn't just Wyatt's team—men she was familiar with—and that would have been hard enough. Wyatt's brother Gator was there with his wife, Flame, and several members of Gator's team. All strangers. Flame was nice. Very nice and she seemed understanding. But to have all of them staring at her . . .

Her palms hurt. She closed her fingers, forming a fist, her palm covered. She could feel the needles going through her skin, penetrating deep. Pinning her down. An insect. She felt venom rising. Her mouth hurt from keeping her lips clamped tight.

"Cayenne?" Nonny's voice sounded far away.

Trap. She reached out telepathically. He wasn't supposed to see her before the ceremony. She knew that. Knew they would all disapprove, but she needed him. She was desperate for his strength.

Baby. What is it?

She clung to his mind, knew he was surrounded by his friends. All the men he knew. Still, he answered her immediately.

I can't . . . She trailed off. She could marry him. Just not like this. Not with everyone staring at her like she was an insect under a microscope. She wasn't a true arachnid because she didn't have eight legs. But still, she preferred that to the *insect* that all the men liked to call her. If they were referring to the spider in her, they should at least get that part right.

The door swung open and he filled the space, his wide shoulders and tall frame taking nearly every inch of it up. He was dressed in a black tuxedo and he looked gorgeous, the most handsome man she could possibly imagine. He took her breath away. Nonny scowled at him. Pepper tried to shoo him out. The little girls screeched a welcome and ran to throw arms around his legs. His hands automatically went to the girls' hair, but he didn't look at any of them. Only her. Only Cayenne, as if she was all he could see.

The terrible burning in her lungs eased, and for the first time in hours she felt she could draw air all the way in. He absently patted the girls on their heads and then, eyes still on her face, strode right in, closing the door behind him, muting the noise and blocking all view of her to their guests.

"Baby," he said softly, as if they were the only two people in the room. His voice was black velvet, intimate. Brushing over her skin like the pads of his fingers. Featherlight, but commanding. His voice steadied her instantly. "Talk to me."

She swallowed hard, feeling a coward. He needed this from her, and she always wanted to please him, to make him happy. She knew this was important to him, but she couldn't make her feet move. Trap had called a reporter he sometimes talked to, one he respected more than most. He'd given him the scoop that one of the world's most eligible bachelors was off the market and getting married in a few days. There was a picture of the two of them, smiling at each another, and a brief write-up on her, with a background she still was memorizing.

Trap had even given her dance lessons every night so they could dance after they were married. Trap seemed good at everything he did. He was graceful, fluid even, like a cat, and when he moved across the floor to the music, his rhythm was impeccable. In the privacy of their home, she loved it. She loved the feel of his body against hers, the masterful way he guided her steps, the shared laughter. She didn't feel awkward at all. She actually felt happy. His woman. But not here. Not in front of them all.

Trap gently moved Nonny out of his way. "Baby, you should have called to me the moment you started getting nervous. There was no need for you to get so frightened."

She moistened her lips. "This is important to you." Her voice was low. A confession when she hadn't even told him what a coward she was.

"*You're* important to me. Talk to me. What's wrong?" He wrapped his arm around her waist and pulled her into his side, under his shoulder, shielding her the way he did with his body.

"There's too many people," she admitted, her fingers finding the lapel of his elegant jacket. "I can't walk out there in front of them with all of them staring at me." A small shudder went through her body. "I know they're your friends and you want them here. I want them here for you as well, but I can't seem to move."

She was close to tears. Too close. It would ruin the makeup Pepper had so carefully applied for the photographs. Nonny explained the importance of pictures and showed her several of the family albums. Pictures of her four grandsons decorated the walls. There were beautiful photographs of Gator and Flame as well as Wyatt and Pepper in the parlor and along the wall above the stairs. Cayenne wanted to line her walls with pictures of Trap and her, or just Trap. She wanted her home to feel the way Nonny's house felt.

Trap bent his head to hers, his strong fingers under her chin, tilting her face toward his. "Baby, you don't have to go out there alone. This is our ceremony. We get to make up the rules."

"I've already ruined everything because you aren't supposed to see me ahead of time."

"Do you think I've ever, in my life, given a flying *fuck* about the rules? I haven't. That's the answer, babe, I've never cared about rules. You don't want to walk out there alone, without me, we walk out together. The girls can go ahead of us. No one's going to care. They're just happy you got me all wrapped around your little finger so they can give me hell whenever they feel like it."

She couldn't help it. He made her want to laugh. It was such a Trap response. "You can't swear in front of the girls. Nonny told me if you keep it up, she might have to wash out your mouth with soap. I like kissing you and you might not taste as good."

Trap grinned at her, completely unrepentant. He kept her pinned to her side. "Let's do this, Pepper. Nonny, you get them to start the music and we'll get married. The sooner we're married, the sooner I get to have you in my bed."

Cayenne frowned at him. "I was just in your bed."

"Yeah, baby, and once I had that taste of you, I needed more. It wasn't enough."

"Trap!" Nonny said sharply. "We have children in the room."

"With Wyatt around, Nonny, I think those girls are going to grow up knowing what their men are going to be expecting."

Nonny shook her head, raised an eyebrow at Pepper and pulled open the door to signal to Wyatt to put on the music. She went first, followed by Pepper and the triplets, who solemnly flung flower petals in all directions. Trap kept her clamped to his side, his large body protective, partially shielding her as they followed the little girls.

It was a very short walk. Rows of chairs had been set up in the room with a path between them so the wedding party could make their way to the minister. Cayenne found her heart beating so hard she feared Trap would hear it. He knew she was nervous because she was trembling uncontrollably. She didn't look at anyone, just stared straight ahead, concentrating on Trap. The feel of his hard body moving so close to hers. His breathing. The strength in his arm as it wound around her waist. His massive chest where her hand lay.

Baby, thank you for doing this. I know it's scary for you, but once it's done, you're legally my wife and I'm your husband. I've always been yours, but this makes it official to the rest of the world.

She felt his fingers flex on her waist. *I want to make you happy.* She did. More than anything else, she wanted Trap happy. She knew the demons he had. She had her own, but she never had a family to lose. Now that she saw Nonny, Wyatt and Pepper and their daughters, she understood what having a family meant. He'd had that and it had been ripped from him. She couldn't undo the past, but she wanted to do everything in her power to give him something just as beautiful. Maybe, if she was lucky, even more so.

It was a very short ceremony. She repeated the vows in a low voice. Trap sounded firm. He never once took his arm from around her until he had to in order to put the diamond band on her finger, pushing it next to her diamond engagement ring. Pepper had gasped when she saw the ring, but had just smiled when Cayenne asked her why.

Trap's expression, the look in his eyes, when the minister pronounced them man and wife, had tears burning close. She knew, in that moment, she'd done something huge to make him happy. His kiss was everything she'd come to expect. Hot. Hard. Commanding. Demanding and possessive. Catcalls and whistles erupted along with applause.

Trap didn't leave her side after the ceremony either. He did most of the talking to the GhostWalkers as everyone celebrated with copious amounts of food. The music started and Trap whirled her onto the dance floor, holding her close to his body, enfolding her into his arms as if she were the most precious thing in the world.

"You are," he whispered. "Have no doubt that I'll always take care of you, Cayenne."

"I plan on taking care of you," she told him, meaning it.

She vowed silently to love him better than anyone else could possibly do. She moved in his arms to the rhythm of the music, drifting on a tidal wave of love. Of need. So close to him, it was impossible not to feel hunger for him. Pepper and Nonny had bought her an outfit for bed, one she was more than delighted to show him *before* going to bed, but she didn't see why she would want to wear it *in* bed. Still, they told her he would love it, so she knew she'd wear it.

"Phone's for you, Trap," Wyatt said, tapping him on the shoulder.

"I'm a little busy." Trap didn't look up, his arms around Cayenne as they moved across the dance floor.

"I think you'll want to take this one," Wyatt said. "It's an assistant who is holdin' for Violet Smythe. The Violet Smythe in the running to be a candidate for the vice presidency. The same Violet Smythe who was married to Senator Ed Freeman who set up Jack and Ken Norton from Team Two in the Congo. The same woman who betrayed all the women in Whitney's compound when they were prisoners being forced to be with men they didn't want to be with. *That* Violet Smythe."

The room went instantly silent. Ryland Miller, head of Team One, Gator's team, stepped away from the wall where he'd been lounging. "She recently pulled the plug on her husband. He'd been in a vegetative state for some months. We believe she did so on Whitney's orders. It's rumored she might actually be paired with Whitney, but no one has confirmed that as of yet. Clearly she is in league with him."

"Why would she be calling Trap?" Draden asked.

Trap shrugged. "Doesn't matter. I don't have anything to say to the bitch."

"Trap," Nonny snapped. "Do not refer to a woman as a bitch, even if she is one."

"Sorry, ma'am," he muttered, not looking in the least sorry.

Later, Cayenne was fairly certain that she was going to hear all about Violet Smythe, and he wasn't going to be calling the woman Violet or Smythe.

"Take the call," Wyatt said. "We need to know what she's up to."

Trap sighed. "This is fucking annoying. It's my wedding day. I don't want to talk to, or have to listen to, a lying bitch, but if you think it's necessary, Wyatt, I'll do it. Did you set up to record the conversation?"

Wyatt nodded. "We're on it. Put her on speaker so we can hear."

Trap threaded his fingers through Cayenne's and tugged until she followed him across the room to the phone. The room was so silent, she was certain they could have all heard the proverbial pin drop. He clamped her to his side, one hand at her waist but fingers sifting through the thick strands of hair curling at the hollow of her spine.

"Dawkins here." He sounded abrupt. Rude. Annoyed.

"Please hold for Senator Smythe," the voice intoned.

Trap waited until the silver voice spoke in his ear. "Dr. Dawkins?"

"Next time, if there is one, you want to speak to me, don't have some joker tell me to hold for you. You want to talk, be on the fucking phone."

There was a small silence. "I understand, Dr. Dawkins." The voice was strictly neutral now. "I wanted to talk to you about something important as well as exciting. I'd like to do that in person and hope you'll accept my invitation to a ball. It's actually a fund-raiser to raise money for the presidential campaign. More importantly, I would like to have a meeting with all the top scientists we have here in the United States. I'm running with the presidential candidate on a platform that is very dear to me. I'd like the United States to be the country to find the cure for cancer. I don't doubt that it can be done if I can bring all our top people together to work for the same goal. Not for glory or money, but to actually help mankind. There isn't a family untouched by cancer. The formal invitation will be in the mail for you and your wife. I know you're getting married, Dr. Dawkins, and I would very much like to meet you and your wife. Are you at all interested?"

Curing cancer. Trap turned his head to look at the woman standing in Gator's arms. Whitney had used her body, even when she was a child, to experiment with curing cancer. He actually *gave* her cancer repeatedly. No one would ever pass up a chance to meet with the top researchers in their fields when they came together to find a cure for cancer.

"I don't work alone. Dr. Fontenot is my partner. I'm also in the military and I run missions." He wanted to make that clear.

"I understand. I know Wyatt Fontenot works with you, and of course, he and his wife are also invited."

"I'll be bringing a security team."

"We'll have plenty of security, Dr. Dawkins."

"I bring my own or I don't show."

"Of course. I look forward to seeing you."

Trap hung up the phone and turned to the others in the room. They'd all been able to hear the entire conversation.

"She's up to something," Flame said. "She may be bringing all the top researchers together, and maybe they'll even find a cure, but she can't be trusted. Not for a minute. She's up to something."

"I agree," Wyatt said. "The question is, what is it? What does she really want?"

Ryland shrugged. "The only way of knowing is for Trap and Wyatt to meet with her. Trap will be bringing a very large security team with him."

CHAPTER 19

———

Trap closed his fingers around Cayenne's slender wrist—the wrist adorned with a brilliant emerald bracelet. He found he suddenly preferred emeralds when he'd always been a diamond man. Cayenne subsided on the leather seat of the limousine and looked up at his face. He knew what she saw. He'd gone where he always did when he was in public, his face stone, no expression, no emotion.

He tightened his fingers until they shackled her, until they were a shackle around her small, delicate wrist. "You don't leave my side for any reason, Cayenne. Do you understand me?"

Wyatt, sitting across from them, glanced at Trap sharply, but turned his head and looked out the darkened window at the spectators lining the streets. He didn't say a word, and Trap knew he wouldn't. This was between Trap and Cayenne and Wyatt wouldn't interfere—unless he thought Trap would lose his mind—a distinct possibility.

"Trap." Cayenne's voice was soft. Gentle. Loving even.

"We have nearly two full GhostWalker teams here for security."

"I don't fucking care." He bit the words out, yanking her closer to him. She looked so damned serene, not at all as if they were going into a major ambush. "This isn't a party, baby, this is a fucking nightmare. A trap. They have something planned, and that something could be another attempt to kill you. When I tell you to stay at my side, I mean no more than an inch from me. I want to feel your hand on me at all times."

She continued to look up at him, her eyes as green and vibrant as the bracelet on her wrist and the necklace at her throat. She had no idea what they cost, and probably would be upset with him if she did know, but he liked seeing them on her. The earrings in particular, framing her face and surrounded by the cloud of dark hair, highlighted the green of her eyes. She took a breath.

"Honey, I'm not going to leave your side." Her hand came up, fingers brushing at the lines etched deep in his face.

Her touch always undid him. That look on her face. She didn't hide her emotions, not like he did. That look was pure love and it always rocked him. Sent shock waves through his system and turned him to jelly. He bent his head and took her mouth. Hard. Possessive. Angry. He didn't want her here. He didn't want her anywhere near Violet Smythe and her schemes.

Flame had done Cayenne's makeup. Not much, just enough to highlight her beauty. He took the lipstick right off. All that gloss that emphasized the beauty of her ruby red bow of a mouth. He loved her mouth, and that gloss sent heat coursing through his body and centering in his cock. She tasted exotic, just the way she looked, and he didn't give a damn if Wyatt was witnessing his raw vulnerability. Not. One. Fucking. Bit.

Cayenne didn't protest that he was ruining her makeup— she kissed him back. Giving herself to him. Reassuring him.

He lifted his head, one hand framing her face, his gaze drifting over her. Brooding. Pushing down the feeling of dread. They were walking into a trap. He knew that with certainty. He just didn't know whose trap it was or what they wanted.

His thumb slid over the perfection of her skin. Silky soft. "The uncles could be close. The series of articles Doug Levi did on us will bring them out. The taming of the beast was a good slant. I want you to keep your eyes open."

"I will, Trap." She gave him that too.

For some reason that just pissed him off more. "Don't fucking appease or patronize me, Cayenne," he snapped. "I *know* something's going down tonight. I know that one hundred percent. You can't fuck up tonight."

Wyatt stirred. *You're being a dick and damn fool.*

I don't give a flying fuck. She needs to get this.

Wyatt heaved an exaggerated sigh, but kept his mouth shut.

Something moved in Cayenne's eyes. Not anger. Something nameless. She sat still, her emerald eyes sparkling like the gems adorning her body. She wore a one-of-a-kind, designed specifically for her, Oscar de la Renta ball gown of shimmering silver. She wouldn't like how much that cost either, but she looked stunning in it. The gown clung to her curves, showing off her hourglass figure.

He'd gotten his way with her hair. The women had insisted she wear it up, that Cayenne would look more sophisticated. He wanted it down. He loved the silken water-fall and how, when she moved, the unexpected red hourglass appeared and disappeared. She wore it down for him, just like he knew she would. Because he asked her. It was always that simple. He asked, she gave it to him.

He tried to push down the ice-cold anger. The rage in him. Ice-cold was far worse than burning hot. She couldn't look at him with those eyes, her tempting mouth and love on her face, so damn calm when he knew she was walking into danger.

"Trap, I'm not afraid."

"You should be."

"I'm not. You'll be with me. The entire team will be with us. We can do this. No matter what they throw at us, we've got this. I love you. I'm not going to lose you to them. You aren't going to lose me. As for your uncles, I hope they're so stupid that they make their try for me."

His thumb slid over her silken skin again, traced her high cheekbone and then swept the line of her jaw. "I love you with every fucking cell in my body, Cayenne. You're all I've got."

He made the confession because she had to know. The money. The fame. None of it mattered. *She* mattered. He didn't even know how it happened. He just knew he wouldn't survive if she were taken from him. He'd lost too much. He couldn't go through that and survive intact. He didn't care if he was revealing everything to Wyatt or not. *She* had to know. She had to understand what would happen if he lost her. Maybe Wyatt needed to know as well.

Her hands framed his face. She leaned into him, her emerald eyes boring into his. Piercing him right to his soul. "Listen to me, honey. Hear what I'm saying. You look at me and you see a woman you love, someone vulnerable. Someone you want to protect and care for. You do that well. You love me better than any other man could. I know that. But you have to see who and what I am. Look at me and really *see* me. If you do that, you won't be afraid for me. Afraid for us."

His gaze roamed her face, his heart pounding hard in his chest. She was so beautiful. So small and delicate. Her gaze remained steady on his. The love was there. That soft silken skin. The cloud of hair he loved to sink his fingers into. Her body, the one that belonged to him. The one she gave him. The one that brought him unimaginable pleasure.

His heart constricted. It hurt to look at her. To see her beauty. To see that look of love on her face and know it was all for him. He *did* know her. All of her. That voice that could lure men, make them forget, make them do her bidding. He was mostly immune, but it was because his brain was always occupied with other things and could dull the impact. The silk she spun. So lovely. An art form really. Silk she could bind around a person in seconds. Her skin, that stunning expanse of skin that was really armor so strong it could stop a bullet.

There was her mouth. Alluring. Tempting. More than beautiful. Deadly. She could smile and kill in seconds. She didn't hesitate under fire. She had good instincts, and she moved like lightning. For him, that lethal, deadly side of her was part of her siren's call. Part of what he loved so much. One moment all silk and vulnerable. He loved when she lay under him, helpless, pleading, *begging* him for release, knowing at any moment she could lose complete control and sink her teeth into him. He lived for those moments when it happened. He had the bite marks to prove it.

She was lethal to anyone but him. He loved knowing that. He loved that with the rest of the world she was shy. A hidden danger. She clung to him. Relied on him. *Loved* him. She gave him everything, but anyone else could be in trouble. *Everyone* else could be in trouble.

A slow smile formed, first in his gut, unraveling the tight knots, worked its way up his chest so that the constriction in his heart eased, and then made its way to his mouth, softening the hard line there. "I see you, baby. I see everything about you, and I get you."

Her gaze moved over his face and the tension in her dissipated. She sent him a slow smile. "We've got this, Trap. I'm not saying it will be easy or that there won't be danger, but we've got this. You. Me. Together." She leaned into him. "Do you get what I'm saying now?"

She took his breath away. Her exquisite loveliness. Her delicate vulnerability. Her absolute confidence. The fact that beneath the beauty was a weapon so lethal, her creators were terrified of her. She was fucking perfect, and she was his.

"I get you, baby. Let's do this and go home so I can spend hours making love to you." He meant that. He liked fucking her. Rough. Hard. Tied down. On her knees. Any way. But he *loved* making love to her. Taking his time. Letting his body show her how he felt inside. How she could turn him inside out. How he worshipped the ground she walked on. How he worshipped *her*.

Like I needed to hear that.

Trap ignored the amusement in Wyatt's voice and took Cayenne's mouth one more time, watched her repair the gloss as if she'd been doing it her entire life and hadn't just learned a few short weeks earlier. He buzzed their driver and the man came around to open the door for them.

Wyatt stepped out first. Paused there. Scouting. He stepped aside for Trap. Trap emerged next, allowing his gaze to sweep the crowd of spectators and reporters just as Wyatt had done, his body blocking Cayenne's while he did so. He took his time, waiting until Draden and Gino moved into position to guard her. Guard them.

He stepped back and extended his hand to her. Cayenne took it as if she'd been born royalty. She'd been devouring every video clip of galas she could find, studying the women and how they acted. She observed how they dined formally or informally over and over. How they moved, talked, danced. Everything she could find that would help her. She learned fast, and now, as she took his hand and gracefully exited the limousine, he couldn't help but be proud of her.

She didn't look scared or shy. She looked serene. She even tilted her face up and smiled at him as dozens of flashes went off. Only he saw how her gaze clung to his, drawing on his strength. He loved that. His little lethal warrior needed him. Not for saving her life, or kicking a man's butt, but just to get her through being in a very public situation. Again, no one else would know, only him. It was something she shared with him alone, that reluctance to be in a crowd.

Every protective instinct he had came surging to the

forefront. He tugged her to his side, watching the way her body moved beneath the dress. The designer was brilliant. He knew women and how material best draped on their bodies, how it came alive, moving with them, heightening their beauty. Her dress was a miracle of silken fabric, shimmering with every step she took, emphasizing her curves and the grace of her body as she moved in close and took his arm.

Wyatt closed in on her other side. Gino stepped in front of them, leading the way toward the doors of the hotel where the fund-raiser was being held. Draden prowled behind them. Trap spotted Ryland at the double glass doors, just inside, looking handsome and casual in his tuxedo. Ryland brought five of his team members, including Gator, Wyatt's brother, to help with security. Nearly all of Trap's team was present. They'd left Diego and Rubin Campo, two members of their team, with the rest of Ryland's team to guard Pepper, the triplets and Nonny. None of them were taking chances.

Wyatt and Trap, with Cayenne in between them, stopped at the VIP security line, the one set up for the scientists, to present their engraved invitation to the guard. He immediately allowed them through, nodding his head in deference to them.

Ryland wandered through the large lobby parallel to them, his wife, Lily, on his arm. At the double doors to the ballroom, Trap spotted Gator and Flame talking together. Although he appeared completely involved in the conversation, Gator's gaze continually swept the entire area, noting everything and everyone in it. As Trap, Wyatt and Cayenne went through the elaborately carved doors into the ballroom, Gator and Flame fell in behind them.

The moment Trap entered, he felt the tension, stretched like a thin wire in the room. One glance told him there were several supersoldiers inside, most covering the various exits. *How many?* He didn't care if they knew he spoke telepathically. They wouldn't hear what he was saying unless he wanted them to.

Malichai answered. *My count is seven inside the ball-room.* He was positioned up above, on the long sweeping balcony overlooking the room.

Nine, Ezekiel answered. *I've got two more on the roof with rifles.* He was outside the building, across the street. His job was to keep them alive while they moved in and out of the building.

I've got one just inside the kitchen, Mordichai reported. *He's trying to blend in with the catering staff. He's smaller than most of the soldiers but still stands out like a sore thumb. I also saw two setting up with the band earlier. They're roaming the halls.*

Trap put his hand over Cayenne's as they moved through the crowd, Wyatt sticking to her other side, Gino clearing a path for them.

So we know they've got twelve supersoldiers to supplement their regular security staff. That's interesting. Is Whitney here? Are you running facial recognition, Ryland? Joe Spagnola, Team Four leader, asked from his position on the balcony.

Jeff is in the security room. He's doing that now, Ryland answered.

Senator Smythe at six o'clock, Wyatt reported.

You heading that way? Joe asked.

She wants to talk to me, Trap said, *she can come to me. I'm not her fucking servant.*

You're such a hard-ass, Joe murmured, amusement edging his tone.

Cayenne's fingers curled on his arm. "She's using her voice." She nodded to where Violet was holding court, looking spectacular in her low-cut gown, her laughter tinkling like sweet-sounding bells. "Do you hear those notes? She's embedding a compulsion. You'll have to be careful, Trap."

"Don't worry, baby, the only woman capable of ensnaring me is you. I've got something going on in my brain that prevents voice compulsion from working."

"*My* voice. I don't try that hard with you," Cayenne corrected. When he raised an eyebrow at her, she shook her head. "I don't. Not even that first meeting. I was terrified and I wanted out of the cell, but you opened that cell of your own volition. No one had ever done anything for me before, not without wanting something huge in return. You didn't ask for anything."

"I've got you to protect me, baby. We'll head away from her and see just how anxious she is to talk to me."

Wyatt nodded his approval, and they moved away from Violet, who was surrounded by a group of about eight men. They headed toward the long tables of hors d'oeuvres. "Might as well eat while we got the chance," he added.

Cayenne laughed. The moment she did, heads turned toward the sound. Trap noted that included the men circling Violet. Violet's eyes darkened, but she kept her smile, ever the consummate professional.

Cayenne didn't seem to notice the attention. Trap didn't like the way the men were looking at her, already captivated by her.

It's her voice, Wyatt said thoughtfully. *It's overriding the senator's voice and Smythe is aware of it. She doesn't like being upstaged.*

She needs money for the campaign. Money and allies. I see why she's so popular now. She doesn't have to work that hard, just send out the right notes and supporters flock to her. What the hell does she need us for? Trap said, drawing Cayenne closer.

She put one hand on her belly. He felt the heat instantly. When he looked down at her, she had a question in her eyes.

"Nothing, baby," he assured. "You're just getting a lot of attention. I'm going to have the boys move in a little for protection."

"I don't need protection," she said, narrowing her eyes at him. "I thought we had this discussion and you understood."

He grinned at her. "Not for *your* protection, babe. These men keep leering at you and then heading for the bathroom to jack off, I'm going to have to kill a few of them just to keep from having nightmares."

She rolled her eyes at him. "The senator has her sights set on you, Trap. Stop distracting me. I'm the only one capable of protecting you from her. Look at her fingernails. Bloodred. Sharp. She could kill with those daggers."

Cayenne was serious. Trap flicked a glance toward Violet. She was making her way across the room toward them.

"Let's dance, Cayenne," Trap said, sweeping his arm around her and moving her away from the tables toward the dance floor, his back to Violet.

What the hell are you doing, Trap? Joe demanded. *Isn't the point to talk to the woman and figure out what the hell she wants?*

I can't make it easy, Trap said. *I have a certain reputation. If I make it easy, she'll be suspicious. I can't go to her. She has to come to me.*

And what if she decides you aren't worth it? Joe asked, sarcasm dripping.

I am worth it, Trap said matter-of-factly. He knew he sounded arrogant, but the fact was, he was one of the most intelligent human beings in the world. There was no disputing that fact. If Violet meant what she said about bringing all the top minds together for one goal, he *was* the top mind. She needed him. *She's in league with Whitney. We know that. He has been working on cancer research for a while now. She knows I have. My guess is, she'll give us access to Whitney's research without the references to the experiments using children.*

Trap pulled Cayenne into his arms, held her body close to his. He loved the feel of her against him. Her arms slid up his chest to his neck. He leaned down. It was well worth the backache to hold her so close and move their bodies to the music. He could shut out the reason for being there. Shut out the scent of men's arousals as they danced close to be near Cayenne's swaying body. He let her scent drown out the testosterone in the air. That exotic, potent fragrance unique to her.

His team would watch his back. He had gone into battle with them countless times. They wouldn't let him down any more than he would them. For just those few minutes, he let himself drift on a tide of need, of hunger, of heat and sin. Holding her close. She moved like an angel or a temptress, her body, in that silken gown, sliding over his senses like the finest of wines.

The song ended, and Trap transferred his hold to Cayenne's hand to lead her off the dance floor. Violet wasn't taking any chances. She was right there on the edge, smiling directly at him. Making it clear she was waiting for him. He was known for his rudeness, but it was her invitation and he'd accepted it. He sauntered over to her, keeping Cayenne in close.

"Thank you for coming, Dr. Dawkins," Violet said. "Or do you prefer to go by Johansson?"

Her little warning didn't throw him. He felt Cayenne press her hand deeper into his side, but she kept her smile.

"I haven't used Johansson since my father murdered my family," Trap said easily. "I adopted the name Dawkins."

"Of course. So much paperwork to get through on everyone. Forgive me." Violet used her voice. It was subtle. Very subtle, but he felt the stream of compulsion on the edges of his mind. "And this is your wife? Cayenne, isn't it? An unusual name."

"As you know, like you, I'm one of Whitney's orphans," Cayenne said. "Perhaps, Violet, we can dispense with the games."

She used her own voice, and Trap had to admit the compulsion was stronger. He felt the energy crackling between the two women. Violet shook her head several times to rid herself of the suggestion Cayenne had planted.

"Perhaps we should go somewhere private," Trap

suggested. "You bring a couple of your security people if you need to feel safe."

"Why wouldn't I be safe?" Violet asked. "You're hardly going to assassinate a U.S. senator and running mate for the presidency."

"You haven't actually gotten that yet," Trap pointed out. "Isn't all of this to raise money?" He leaned close, his gaze sweeping with contempt down her body and then back up to stare straight into her eyes. "Isn't Whitney backing you?" His voice implied all sorts of things, mostly that she was sleeping with a monster for his money.

Her lashes swept down and then back up. "Follow me. You and Dr. Fontenot."

"Cayenne comes with me."

It was her turn to give him a contemptuous look. "You have to have a security blanket?"

"I have to make certain you aren't making another attempt to kill her." It was a shot in the dark, but he took it.

Violet stepped back, one hand moving defensively to her throat. "Why in the world would I do that?"

What are you doing, Trap? Joe demanded. *Whitney ordered the hit, not Violet.*

Violet? Trap echoed. *Not Violet?* None of them called her that. Not when discussing her. Not ever, unless they were addressing her and thought it would irritate her not to be called Senator Smythe.

"You tell me," Trap said aloud. "Did you send the team of souped-up soldiers after my wife? Did you want her dead?"

Violet stared at him for a long heartbeat. "Of course not." Abruptly she turned her back on him. "Follow me."

She's lying. Cayenne pressed her hand deeper into his side. There was a hiss of anger floating through her musical tone. *She did send them.*

Gino swung in directly behind Violet. A phantom so close he could breathe on her neck or snap it any moment.

She didn't feel him there, his pace matching hers exactly, his footfalls in perfect sync. Trap, Cayenne and Wyatt followed him, and Draden stepped behind them, covering their backs.

You can't know that, Joe snapped. *Stick to the plan. Find out what she wants and stop accusing her of things we can't prove.*

Cayenne knows a lie when she hears it. I do too, Trap bit out. *That woman sent those soldiers knowing those three babies could have been at home. The soldiers were trying to kill all of them, Joe. She did that.*

There was a small silence and then Joe made his decision. *Pull back. We don't have a security team in that room. You have to stay where we can protect you.*

Violet yanked open a hidden door that looked as if it was part of the wall. She stepped inside without hesitation. Gino followed her in. Trap swept his arm around Cayenne's waist, halting her. For all he knew, Violet had a team of soldiers inside, waiting to cut them down.

Room's clear, Gino stated.

I don't like it, Joe said.

Gino says it's clear, you know it is, Wyatt said. *We need this information.*

Trap? Joe prodded.

I agree. Gino doesn't walk into traps. I say let's hear the lying bitch out.

Cayenne's hand gave him a slap of a reprimand—or a pat of approval—on the ribs, he wasn't certain which, but he barely waited for Joe's go-ahead before he stepped inside, taking Cayenne with him. Wyatt was right there with them, pressing close to Cayenne on the other side of her, shielding her body as they moved toward the chairs set in front of a fireplace. Draden closed the door behind them, and then stayed in front of it, his arms at his side, looking relaxed. He moved like lightning, and he never missed his target. Never that Trap knew of anyway.

No one sat, waiting for the senator to do so first. She didn't. She paced back and forth in front of the fireplace, her steps quick and fluid, all nervous energy. She finally turned toward them, realizing they weren't sitting.

Violet waved toward the chairs. "Please. Hear me out. I invited you here for a very important reason."

Wyatt gestured toward a chair. "You sit, ma'am."

Swift impatience crossed her face. She flung herself into the nearest armchair. "They aren't rigged to blow up the moment you sit in them," she snapped.

"I was raised by *ma grand-mere*. She taught me to be a gentleman. You don't sit, then I don't sit."

Violet's gaze swept him. "Of course. But Dr. *Dawkins* has no excuse."

"No," Trap agreed. "I'm not a gentleman, not unless I'm around a lady, which you're clearly not." He deliberately waited until Cayenne sank into a chair before he followed suit.

"Why are you being so difficult?" Violet demanded.

"Because you're trying to use compulsion on me, on all of us, and I don't like it. Stop trying to force us into doing your bidding. It isn't going to happen," Trap snapped. "This is a complete farce—you bringing up my past as if that's going to throw me. That's a game, bitch, and you know it. I call it like I see it. You're a senator because your husband was a senator and when *you* pulled the plug on him, you went on television every chance you got, playing the sad widow patriot and using your voice in order to make the world sympathize so you could be elected to take his place."

Every vestige of color leached from Violet's face. Again her hand went to her throat. She pulled out a chain and wrapped her fingers around the two rings, making a fist, covering them like hidden treasure. She leaned toward Trap. "You don't know the first thing about me, so don't presume that you do."

"I know you've been shoveling shit at us since you

opened your mouth." Trap's voice lashed like a whip, something he was very good at. He ignored the warning hand Cayenne put on his thigh. He wrapped his fingers around it and held it to him, pressing her palm deep.

She's really upset, Trap. When you mention her husband, she becomes very agitated.

"I didn't pull the plug because I wanted to," Violet said, her voice low, her eyes on the floor. For one moment, her face looked ravaged. When she raised her eyes, she looked so completely grief-stricken, Trap couldn't help but register the look. He'd seen it in his own eyes every time he looked in the mirror after his aunt had been murdered. Bleak. An endless agony one couldn't escape. Violet couldn't fake that kind of grief. No matter how good of an actress she was, she couldn't fake that.

"The only one who might have been able to save Ed was Whitney. He dangled that carrot in front of me so often, forcing me to help him with his schemes, but he never operated. There was a new protocol. It wasn't being used yet, but he knew how. He could have done it. A surgery and a drug. I brought my husband . . ." Her voice hitched on a sob. She choked it back and lifted her chin. "We flew into one of Whitney's safe military airports. He was supposed to help him. Instead he paired me with him. *Paired* me with *him*. With *Whitney*."

There was so much hatred and anger in her voice, Cayenne winced. Trap curled his fingers around hers protectively and kept her palm pinned to his thigh.

She's telling the truth, Cayenne confirmed. *Every word is the truth. So is her emotion. The anger. The grief.*

"I did despicable things for my husband, to keep him alive, before he was shot and again after. I did everything Whitney wanted, including betraying my friends, my sisters—the others from the orphanage. Still, he didn't keep his word. There was no saving Ed. I knew that." Violet pressed her hand to her mouth. "When he told me to go into the hangar and pull the plug, I did."

Her voice broke and she struggled for a moment with her emotions before she could continue. No one said anything. Waiting.

"It was the only way I could get free of Whitney. I knew he hadn't paired himself with me, that it was only one way, not both. I knew that. He wanted me to worship him, do whatever he said. And I did. I became a senator, and I put myself in the position to be chosen as a vice presidential candidate. He thinks he'll continue to use me as his puppet and believe, me, that's *exactly* what I want him to believe."

That is true, Cayenne confirmed. She leaned toward Violet. "Then why did *you* send the soldiers after me? And don't deny that you did that. You did. He doesn't want me dead anymore, does he? I'm paired with Trap. We're together, and more than anything else he wants a baby from our pairing. He wants Wyatt's children. You ordered the hit, not Whitney. Why did you do that? You need to tell us right now. You *want* to tell us."

Trap stared at Cayenne in awe. She'd never used that tone. The one that slipped inside one's brain and insisted on obedience. So low. So perfect. The voice of an angel. No one, not even the devil, could avoid her voice or resist the soft command. She'd been telling him the truth when she said she'd never used her talent on him—not her full talent.

Baby, I'm going to have to reassess whether or not I've actually had the upper hand. He let the awe and pride in her show in his voice.

I love you, Trap, but you've never had the upper hand.

He brought her hand to his mouth, turned it over and pressed his lips to her sensitive wrist making her shiver. He waited for her gaze to jump to his face. His tongue touched her pulse. It jumped and her eyes darkened. He smiled against her bare skin. *I have the upper hand.*

"I did send the soldiers, but not for the reason you think," Violet said. "I knew you would wipe them out. It isn't like he has an endless supply. He takes the rejects from the program, the ones who test high in psychic ability, but low in the psychological ones. He knows they'll burn out eventually, because when enhanced, they're too aggressive and become killers. He doesn't care about that because he says they would never make good soldiers to protect our country and he might as well give them a purpose. He binds them to him some way so they're completely loyal to him."

"You knew that. You knew he had a breeding program and some of these men were forcing the women to have sex with them. You *knew* and you turned your backs on them," Wyatt accused.

She nodded. "For Ed. I had no choice if I wanted to keep him alive."

"They were raped repeatedly," Wyatt said.

"I know." She lifted her head. "I *know*. Do you think I sleep at night knowing what I let happen in order to try to protect my husband? I don't. I hate what I became. What I've become. Still, if I could have him back . . ." She broke off.

Wyatt leapt out of his chair and paced across the floor, fury riding him. "You knew my children and my grandmother were in that house. My *wife*. The woman I love the way you loved your husband, and you still sent a full team of soldiers—a *full* team and two helicopters."

"*His* helicopters. *His* soldiers," Violet hissed. "How else can I bring him down? You're soldiers. Trained. An elite force. You did your jobs. And you wiped out an entire *full* team. But you left one. The man you interrogated went running back to Whitney and he would have blown everything. I had to kill him before he connected with Whitney and make it look like he'd died because of wounds he'd sustained. Fortunately, Whitney trusts me just about as much as he could ever trust anyone." She sounded scathing, as if they were guilty of not doing their jobs.

She's lying about that man going to Whitney. He went to her, Cayenne said.

Wyatt suddenly flung his body in front of Violet's, hands slamming down on the arms of her chair, leaning in close to her. "You *bitch.* Did you not hear me? Do you not understand? You sent those *trained* soldiers after my wife. My children. *Ma grand-mere.* Nonny would have been killed if Cayenne hadn't jumped in front of her. Their deaths are not acceptable for your revenge. They aren't expendable."

Violet didn't flinch. "It didn't occur to me that Whitney's soldiers had a chance to kill anyone, let alone your family. I presumed that you had protection in place for them."

"Cayenne was shot. Twice." Trap took up the attack when Wyatt, clearly disgusted, prowled across the room to keep from strangling the woman.

Violet's gaze swept up and down Cayenne. "She looks alive to me."

Trap's breath hissed out. The air shimmered. Turned opaque. The shimmer drifted in a circle around Violet's chair, wrapping her up in a soft, incandescent veil. She coughed. Once. Twice.

Trap stared at her, not breaking eye contact, watching as she began to choke. To change color. He didn't blink. Didn't move. Stared at her as any lethal predator might his prey.

CHAPTER 20

————⟲————

What the hell are you doing, Trap? Joe snapped. *What's going on in there?*

I'm killing this fucking bitch, Trap replied. *She allowed women to be raped repeatedly, held prisoner and experimented on for her own gain. She knew Whitney was giving Flame cancer and she didn't care. She sent a full team of trained soldiers to Wyatt's home where his children and wife were. She couldn't care less that Cayenne was shot. She's not worth it, Joe. She's the enemy, and we take out the enemy. Can you imagine what she'll do if she becomes the VP?*

I am ordering you to stand down. Right now. You stand down. Joe poured command into his voice. Trap wasn't a man to accept commands unless he totally respected the man heading his team. He'd always given Joe respect. He'd never once disobeyed his order. Joe, and the team, had covered for him more than once when he'd ignored a directive coming from above Joe.

I overheard those soldiers talking about Cayenne, calling her names, acting like she was filth, an abomination to be stamped out. Those soldiers were loyal to Violet, not Whitney, no matter what she says. So screw her, Joe.

Stand. The fuck. Down. That's an order.

Cayenne very gently brushed her hand over Trap's face, her fingers lingering along the seam of his lips. "Honey. Let it go."

Trap stood up so fast his chair rocked. He stepped away from the group, but before he did, he blew air into the center of the opaque mass. Turning his back on Violet he paced across the room to stand beside Draden.

Violet fell out of her chair onto the floor, her hands around her throat, her body spasming. None of the men moved to help her. It was Cayenne who went to her knees beside the senator.

"There's a pitcher of water and glasses over there on the sideboard," she said quietly. "Trap, I need a glass of water now."

"This is fucking bullshit and you know it, Cayenne. She's a lying bitch who will do anything to get her way. She'll lie and kill and watch women she was raised with be raped and tortured in order to get what she wants." He poured water into a glass and brought it to her. "She'll let children die, put them in danger, if it serves her purpose. I don't want you fucking touching her."

Violet sat up, coughing heavily, dragging clean air into her lungs, her body trembling. She took the glass of water Cayenne held out to her and drank deeply. Cayenne stood and leaned down to take her elbow. Violet drew back as if contact with Cayenne might contaminate her.

"I would prefer not to be touched," Violet said, her voice haughty in spite of her coughing. "I have an aversion to . . ." Her gaze swept up and down Cayenne's body. "Insects," she finished, clearly meaning to insult.

"*Fucking* bitch." Trap reached down, caught Cayenne's arm and yanked her up and to him. He enfolded her in his arms, sheltering her against his body, against his heart.

"Actually, Senator," Cayenne said, turning in Trap's arms

to face the woman. Trap locked both arms just under her breasts, holding her in place so she couldn't help Violet up. "A spider is not an insect. It's an arachnid. I'm neither. But then you know that. You were striking out because Trap scared you to death, although I know you're telling the truth when you state you have an aversion to me—to what I am. I suggest you tell us why we're here so we can leave before someone gets hurt."

Violet struggled to get to her feet. She had to use the chair to pull herself up. Her breasts were heaving, nearly coming out of the tight bodice of her gown as she continued to struggle for air. She collapsed back into her chair and gulped more water from the glass she'd refused to relinquish while she fought to get up.

When she had her breathing under control and she could speak again, she waved toward the chairs. "Thank you, Cayenne, I appreciate you coming to my assistance." Her voice was stiff and the senator didn't look at her when she forced herself to be polite.

Cayenne nodded, but Trap didn't allow her to move. He kept her at a distance, holding her, back to him, facing the senator.

Violet moistened her lips, took another drink of water, her hand shaking. She noticed the water moving in the glass, giving her away, and she put it down on the little table beside her chair.

"I thought you were paired with Whitney," Wyatt said. "If that's the case, why are you opposing him? Why aren't you showing him the same devotion you did your husband?"

Violet's gaze swept over him. "You know why." Her voice was low. Still shaky.

"Because pairing gives a powerful physical attraction, not an emotional one," Trap said. He felt Cayenne's gaze burning into him, but he didn't look at her. "Whitney can't control that. He doesn't understand the emotional because he doesn't feel."

"He feels other people's pain," she corrected, wiping her mouth, taking the last vestige of lipstick. "He knows that I know he is responsible for Ed's death. He likes the idea that I'll serve him all the while aware that he killed the man I love. He knows that it hurts me, but that's his enjoyment. The only time he's truly happy is when someone else is in pain. He prolongs it, so he can watch."

"So these experiments of his are more self-serving than patriotic?" Wyatt asked.

Violet frowned, hesitating. Finally she shook her head. "I wouldn't say that. He's a patriot. He honestly believes he can cut down on the deaths of American soldiers. He absolutely wants to create soldiers who are elite and have far better chances of survival. His ultimate goal is that those soldiers will create the next generation of soldiers. He believes in what he's doing."

She was obviously reluctant to admit that. "Saying that, he despises women and feels they are disposable. The same with female children. Any girl in an orphanage is at risk if she has the slightest psychic ability. He 'sees' the ability. I don't know how, but he knows. He also 'sees' what he calls a 'true' pairing. He thinks in terms of soldiers and what they can do together, but I think it is more like Dr. Fontenot suggests. The pairing is both emotional and physical as well as psychic. That's why it's so deep."

She pressed her closed fist to her mouth. It was shaking. "Ed wasn't psychic, but he loved me. He truly loved me. Whitney didn't understand that bond. He isn't capable of feeling it, so he can't really understand it."

"Your husband set up the Norton brothers, sending their team into the Congo, straight into an ambush. You knew about that, didn't you?" Trap asked.

"You don't understand. Whitney wanted a diamond. It was important to his research. In order to get what he wanted, he used my husband."

"In order to get what your husband wanted, the two of

you sent *our* soldiers into an ambush knowing the likelihood of their survival was very slim," Trap snapped.

Violet sighed. "You deliberately don't want to understand. Politics is a road of sheer treachery. You have to have allies. You have to tread carefully. It's all about making the right connections, and in doing that, you often have to compromise your code of ethics. That's the way the game is played. It's been that way forever. I didn't make up the rules. It could have been any senator Whitney approached with his offer."

"You know, *Senator*, even though I think some of what you're saying and how you're acting is genuine, there isn't any difference between you and Whitney," Trap snapped. "He tortures little girls and forces them into sexual slavery in order to get what he wants. He believes the end justifies the means. You know that's all going on and you let it, you betray those women and you send in soldiers with children around . . ."

"*Vipers*. Made in a petri dish. You know what he does. You know none of you, including the children, are truly human anymore."

"There it is," Trap said. "You didn't give a damn whether or not the girls lived through the attack. All you cared about was making sure what you wanted happened."

Wyatt leapt up and stood over Violet, his fingers curled into fists.

Stay calm, Wyatt. Trap's already a hothead. I don't need both of you to lose it in there. We have to find out what she wants. Joe's voice was devoid of all feeling.

Wyatt swore and turned on his heel, shoving the chair out of his way so he could stalk across the room.

"To take down *Whitney*," Violet emphasized. "If we manage to rid this world of him, the girls will no longer be in danger. He has seven laboratories he uses for experiments. Laboratories where he and his people create genetic mutants. Disgusting, nonhuman beings. Creatures that kill without mercy." There was sheer revulsion in her voice, in her mind.

She actually shuddered, not even seeing Trap's reaction. She was too busy trying to persuade them that she was right.

"Seven monsters just like Whitney oversee those labs for him. You took down Braden, but that leaves six more. I don't have those locations, but I know they exist because I've heard Whitney talking to the men and giving them orders. I know he flies to them whenever he feels like it. He gets help from so many people in power. If I get to be vice president, I can find those people and get rid of them."

Ask her who set our team up to be ambushed in Afghanistan, Joe commanded. He was still feeling the effects of his injuries.

"Who sent our team into an ambush in Afghanistan?" Trap demanded. "And tell the fucking truth because we'll know if you lie."

She raised her chin. "He did that. Not me. He wanted Wyatt home."

That's a mixture of truth and lies, Cayenne whispered into Trap's mind.

"But you knew he was doing it, didn't you?" Trap snapped.

Violet shrugged. "I couldn't stop him."

Cayenne hesitated for the first time. *I think it was Violet that did it and Whitney knew, but honestly, I don't know for certain, only that she was very aware and feels no remorse. At. All.*

"But you could have warned us all," Wyatt said. "Just tell us why you brought us here so we can go. Being in your company offends me."

"Is that so?" Violet's gaze narrowed on him. "You live with a snake and your best friend lives with a spider. Your children are venomous creatures, and yet you can't be in my presence because you say it offends you? Do you have any idea of the monsters he's created?"

"I'm looking at one," Trap said, "so yes, I do. Tell us your fucking plan or I'm walking right now."

Cayenne's fingers curled around his and then brushed the back of his hand. Slowly. Gently. There was something beautiful to him in her gesture. She wasn't in the least bit affected by Violet's vile prejudice. He could sense his teammate's reactions to Violet's bigotry. They all loved Pepper and the girls. They were beginning to have affection for Cayenne, and in any case, she was theirs. They looked after their own, and all of them were offended on her behalf. Cayenne remained the calmest of all of them, her gaze on Violet, her hand in Trap's.

"I want to bring together all the top scientists we have to work on cancer research. I have Whitney's research." She sounded triumphant. "Everything he's compiled over the years. I know you've been working on producing some kind of molecules to surround and strangle cancer cells. There are so many breakthroughs happening right now, so many people coming up with ideas, but Whitney's tried all sorts of experiments. He documented them all. Flame wasn't the only woman he gave cancer to. She was the only survivor, but his research provides a platform for all of you to start from. It will advance your work by years."

"Why haven't you assassinated him yet?" Trap asked.

She swallowed hard. "I can't do that. There's no way. It's impossible."

Because she's paired with him. She isn't strong enough, Joe said. *Get this over so we can all get the hell out of here.*

"You'll have all the funding you need, Dr. Dawkins, I can guarantee that. You'll have access to the work of the greatest minds we have in the United States. I know curing cancer is doable. I know absolutely you can do it. You and Dr. Fontenot. When the two of you published your paper on protein and sugar molecules and the possibilities of what they could do to fight cancer, so many other researchers jumped on that. You opened new doors. This platform will ensure that we will win the election. Once I'm in power and I can ferret out everyone who supports him, I can take him down."

She's lying, Cayenne said instantly.

Are you certain?

She wants to win the election and she intends to hunt for Whitney's supporters. There was truth there. She genuinely wants a cure for cancer. That's truth enough, although her reasons are self-serving. But taking down Whitney was a lie. I think she wants power over him, but she doesn't intend to destroy him. More, she is involved with others, people in power, I can feel their influence on her, ones who would destroy Whitney's GhostWalker program. Others who have her same prejudice.

Cayenne, Joe broke in. *Are you absolutely certain she's lying about destroying him? Absolutely, without a doubt, certain.*

Yes. There was no hesitation on Cayenne's part. *Her voice changes pitch when she's lying. I can hear the difference. Also, there are changes in her body, physical changes that are so minute, you can't see them, but I feel them.*

Trap, tell her that you'll think about it. The idea of seeing Whitney's research is certainly intriguing, Joe said. *And then get out of there. This is turning my stomach.*

"I can't pretend the idea of seeing Whitney's work isn't huge," Wyatt said, when Trap remained silent. "We've worked on various ideas for curing cancer, but his work might really advance ours by years, Trap. If she can bring other researchers together, and we have more funding, we really might be able to make this happen."

Trap pulled Cayenne up and turned his back on Violet as he strode toward the door. "We're in, but there better not be any more attacks on our families." He turned his head and pinned Violet with his ice-cold gaze. "You'd better fucking hear what I'm saying to you, bitch. I'll kill you. If I don't get you, one of the others will. In case you don't believe me, you remember what happened in this room, and right now, you have a fucking phantom behind you who could snap your worthless neck in seconds."

Gino emerged behind her, his arm dropping and then locking around her neck.

"Right now, this moment, you're one second from death." Trap paused to allow her predicament to fully sink in. She'd all but forgotten Gino was in the room. He'd been too still, too quiet, fading into the background. She had no idea when he'd come up behind her, because she hadn't heard him—or smelled him—or felt him and she had a built-in radar for trouble. "You will have every GhostWalker from every team coming at you, not Whitney, if there's an attack on any GhostWalker again. Do you understand what I'm saying to you? It won't matter that you're the vice president or the president. No one, nothing will protect you from us."

Gino let her go and moved away from her, not even looking at her when she turned her head toward him. She touched her neck with shaky fingers. "I can't control Whitney. You know I can't."

"True, but you can warn us. You can get word to us when he's up to something," Wyatt pointed out. He was already walking to the door, following Trap.

Trap yanked open the door. "Pull yourself together, Senator, you've got bullshit speeches to make. Go ahead and tell the others Wyatt and I are in. That ought to buy you a lot of funding."

He tightened his arm around Cayenne and swept through the door, taking her with him. Stalking across the room, he didn't look right or left. His face was a mask of indifference. He appeared totally aloof. Cameras were on him, people greeted him, and he kept moving, never changing expression, never answering anyone.

Trap said nothing at all as the limousine took them through the darkened streets to the airport. Cayenne didn't feel much like talking either. Being in close proximity to Violet left her shaken. She'd been surrounded, from the day she'd been born, with cruelty. Viciousness. There was an oily feel to the aura surrounding the person that made her sick to her stomach.

Violet wasn't vicious, but she was deceitful and selfish, capable of great cruelty. She was capable of only accepting what she wanted as her reality. She couldn't see anyone else's point of view. She believed in her own greatness and believed that it was perfectly okay for her to remove anything or anyone that got in her way. Her aversion to Cayenne was deep-seated, as was her revulsion of Wyatt's daughters and his wife.

They'd been in the city three days preparing for their meeting with the senator. Both she and Trap were used to spending long days alone. Although they'd stayed in the penthouse, the team was often with them. When they went out they were surrounded. Sometimes Cayenne felt as if she couldn't breathe, and she knew it had to be the same for Trap.

They'd given his uncles several opportunities to make their try, appearing often in public. Those times, the underlying tension had been terrible, but the uncles hadn't shown up. Trap's mood had gone from bad to just plain foul. She couldn't blame him. He'd geared himself up to face the men who had helped to destroy his entire family and in the end had taken his last happiness from him. They'd changed the entire course of his life, and still, they were somewhere, hidden by the very money he'd given them for his aunt's safe release.

At the airport, Ryland's team boarded their private plane for home. She liked them all, especially Flame and Gator, and actually hugged them before waving as the two teams split. She waited until they were in the air before she went into the large, well-appointed bathroom to change out of her evening dress. The silk slithered to the floor to pool at her feet, leaving her in nothing but her panties. Every time she'd moved in that silk, her body had come alive with need for Trap.

She stretched and reached back to braid the long thick hair, needing to get it out of her face. She pulled on her soft, vintage jeans, her favorite pair, the ones Trap had bought her that fit like a glove. It felt good to become her again. She loved the dress and even the one dance she'd had with Trap, but she much preferred the swamp and their enormous, ridiculous home.

She pulled a T-shirt over her head, going without a bra. She much preferred to be naked, but that wouldn't do until they got home. In the meantime, she was going for comfortable. She would put her shoes on later—much later—after the flight. Right now, she wanted to sleep. To get her mind as far as possible from Violet and the things she'd admitted.

Cayenne began to make her way back to her seat where Trap waited. The plane hit turbulence, shifting in the air. Bumping. Her heart jumped. She wasn't used to flying, and it was a little frightening to have the airplane, so high in the sky, jolting like it might go down any moment.

The next lurch sent her sprawling forward. Malichai caught her, grinning at her with his devilish smirk. "Falling into my arms *again*, woman? I know you find me pretty, but seriously, Cai, I'm not for sale." He winked at her, his white teeth flashing even as his hands steadied her.

"You're breaking my heart."

He didn't let her go and when the next bump came, it flung her forward so that she fell almost in his lap. He pulled her into his lap, holding her steady while the plane dipped and shuddered.

"You aren't afraid, are you?" He kept his voice low.

She was grateful for the consideration, even though everyone on the plane had acute hearing and probably, now, all of them were aware her heart pounded like crazy. She swallowed hard and glanced across the plane where Trap sat. His eyes were on her, all that ice making her shiver. Glacier-cold. But beneath the ice she saw that blue flame, the one that burned so cold it was hot. He looked—furious.

"I'm a little afraid. I don't like flying," she admitted. She pushed out of his lap and stood in the wide aisle, holding on to the back of his chair. "I just want this over."

She made her way to Trap, hanging on to each of the chairs as she went. When she neared him, his hand snaked out, settled around her wrist, and he all but yanked her into her seat.

Cai? Since when does he call you Cai?

She frowned at him and subtly moved her wrist in the hopes that he'd release her. He didn't. *He doesn't call me that. At least he never has before.*

She closed her eyes, determined to ignore his foul temper. She was tired. Exhausted. Sick to her stomach thanks to the turbulence and he wasn't helping. She didn't like the city any more than he did. More, she didn't like being in public *at all.* She was trying to be friendly to his team members because they were his friends. She stopped trying to take her hand back and forced herself to relax.

You aren't wearing a bra. You like rubbing your breasts all over him?

What are you talking about? Trap, it seemed, was spoiling for a fight. She was too exhausted to rise to the bait, so she pressed her lips together and kept her eyes closed.

"Hey, Cayenne." Malichai made his way up the aisle to drop into the seat opposite her, next to his brother Mordichai. "Can you tie just anyone up with that silk of yours?"

Her heart jumped. She opened her eyes and regarded his teasing grin. It was open. Friendly. Genuinely interested, but more, something she couldn't quite read at first—a kind of camaraderie—because she'd never had it directed at her before. The others moved closer as well, changing seats until the attention was directly on her. She *hated* that. She glanced up at Trap for some direction, but he gave her none, staring impassively straight ahead.

What did women do when they found themselves the complete center of attention? These men worked with Trap.

They were his friends. She wanted to fit in, to become part of their team. She knew it was important they accept her. Still, her silks were private. A part of her she didn't reveal ever to others if she could help it. She didn't see the silk as a weapon. It was her art. The beautiful part of her existence when she was alone in her cell. Her silk kept her safe.

More, it had been the silk her tormenters had tried to rip from her by force. The pain had been excruciating. Trap's teammates couldn't know that and she didn't want to enlighten them, so she said nothing.

"Leave her alone," Trap said unexpectedly, coming to her rescue.

The relief was tremendous, but when she looked up at his face, his sculpted masculine features were completely devoid of feeling.

"I'm with Malichai," Draden said. "I'd like to see what you can do. You managed to get the drop on Trap once. Have you done it again?"

"Maybe tied him up a time or two?" Malichai suggested, with a teasing leer.

She tried to control the blush moving up her body into her neck. She squirmed, forcing down the memory of her mouth and hands on Trap's body for the first time.

"Could you tie me up?" Malichai persisted. "I think I'd like that."

The men burst out laughing, and several had comments to make ribbing Malichai about needing a dominatrix in his life.

"Do it, Cayenne," Draden urged. "Wrap him up in silk."

She moistened her suddenly dry lips. She had no experience to draw on. They were all joking, teasing Malichai. Really, it was more about him than her, although they were all curious.

"I read spiders have seven different types of silk," Mordichai said. "Use the kind on my brother that will make it difficult for him to get free. Tie him to the chair."

The others burst out laughing at the idea and urged her to do it. Heart hammering, she lifted a hand toward Malichai. Trap's hand hit hers so hard she actually felt the sting and then his fingers were clamped tight around her wrist and he jerked her hand into his lap.

That's mine. It belongs to me, not them. Icicles dripped from his voice. *You fucking never give that to another man.*

What am I supposed to do? She genuinely didn't know.

You say no.

Sometimes the intensity of Trap's moods wore on Cayenne. She had spent long periods of time alone without the constant bombardment of energy swirling around her before she'd ever met him. Now she felt overwhelmed by every new experience. She felt vulnerable and off balance. She didn't know how to act and couldn't seem to find a way to breathe without taking in Trap's ice.

"I'm tired, Malichai. I'm going to ignore you and go to sleep. I'm ignoring *all* of you." Mostly she wanted to ignore Trap and his foul mood. She experimented with tugging at her hand to try to gain her freedom, but Trap just tightened his hold on her and sent her a quelling look with his hooded lids at half-mast.

The men dispersed, going back to their seats. Malichai was last. He winked at her and reached out to tug on the long braid before going back to his seat. The team continued to talk to one another, mostly joking, especially Malichai who joked with everyone. She liked him. Liked the way he distracted the others and got them laughing.

You don't have to like him so much.

She glanced up at Trap with a smile on her face, but it faded quickly. He wasn't looking at her, but staring straight ahead, that same glacier in his eyes. The pad of his thumb stroked along the back of her hand, but in his mind, there was a swirling of something unfamiliar, an emotion she couldn't put a name to.

It's called jealousy, Cayenne. When a man's woman

looks at another man and fucking likes that man right in front of him, he feels jealousy.

Jealousy? She echoed the word, not believing it.

Don't pretend you don't understand because you're inexperienced. The most inexperienced girl on the planet knows not to crawl around in other men's laps and rub her tits all over that man in front of their husband.

Her breath hissed out between her teeth. Holding on to her temper was becoming a problem. *I was not crawling around in anyone's lap. Or rubbing my breasts over him. You know I don't like to wear clothes.* She nearly groaned. She shouldn't have said that.

Really? Because from where I was sitting you were. You want someone to fuck you, baby, we can go to the restroom right now. You can strip, not wear a stitch. I'll be fucking happy.

That is so not happening. I don't want you to touch me. In fact, give me back my hand.

You don't think I can tell when a woman is aroused? From the moment you put on that fucking dress you were aroused. It was an accusation, nothing less.

It's silk, she said, unable to believe what she was hearing. *When I moved, it moved against my skin . . .*

Exactly. Your skin is silk. What do you think happens when you rub yourself all over a man?

He was impossible. Totally. And unfair. *You're in a foul mood.*

Watching you eating another man with your eyes and catching you thinking about him does that to me.

I was not eating him with my eyes, she denied. *I'm trying to be friendly to your friends.*

Is that what you call it? You were flirting. You actually were going to tie Malichai up. He yanked her hand against his thigh. Hard. Pressing her palm deep into his heat. *What the hell do you call that? Your body is mine. Your fucking silk is mine. Not his. Not any of theirs. Only mine. Only for*

*me. Damn it, Cayenne, get a clue. What did you think he'd
be thinking of if you tied him up? I do not want my friends
to go to bed at night jacking off thinking about your body
and what you might do to them after you tie them up in silk.
Or is that what you wanted?*

*Oh. My. God. You did not just say that to me. That is so
disgusting, Trap. Let go of me. I can't believe you'd say that
to me. I was trying to fit in with your team. I thought you
wanted me to fit in.*

*I want you to fit in, not give them the impression you're
willing to fuck them.*

Her breath caught in her throat. Anger ripped through
her. Venom rose and she had to fight to keep it from moving
all the way into the twin hollow teeth waiting to receive it.
She took several deep breaths. One of them had to remain
sane. Clearly, Trap wasn't.

*Why are you picking a fight? This doesn't even make
sense. I'm not in the least bit attracted to Malichai and you
know it.*

*You think he's cute. Hell. You seem to spend a great deal
of time thinking about him. I don't like it and you can fucking stop it.*

Cayenne stared up into his implacable face, those hard
features, the lines etched deep, the jaw set. His grip on her
hand never once relaxed and she had no hope of pulling away
from him. He didn't look at her, and she hated that as well.

Trap. She sighed, seeking a way to defuse the situation.
He always lost his mind when they were out in public. *You
have to know I think you're gorgeous. The most handsome
man I've ever seen. You know the physical reaction I have
to you. You know I love you. You have to know that. I tell
you and I show you. Every time I touch you, I show you. It
doesn't make sense that you're jealous. You know I'm only
attracted to you.*

*How do I know that when you're flirting? Letting another
man put his fucking hands on you?*

She bit back her first retort, took a calming breath and let it out. *He saved me from falling. Would you rather have seen me facedown on the floor?*

Better that than his lap.

She wanted to scream. Really scream in sheer frustration. She knew Trap could be difficult and rude. She knew he could shut down his emotions. This wasn't shutting down. This was feeling. The emotion he was feeling wasn't good. She couldn't believe he was jealous. It just didn't make sense to her. She tried hard to go back over everything that had transpired to check her own behavior.

She'd been nervous. She didn't like to fly. The plane was all over the place, and she would have fallen if Malichai hadn't steadied her. The next jolt he had pulled her into his lap, but . . . Had she clutched at his shoulders for support? She didn't remember.

Damn it. Stop fucking thinking about him. Trap leaned into her, yanking her hand up his thigh, nearly to his groin. So close she could feel the heat pulsating right through his jeans.

She'd been trying to figure out if she'd given him a reason, and he was just making things worse.

You make it easy to think about anyone but you. The moment the retort was out of her mouth, she knew she'd made a terrible mistake.

Trap dragged her hand over the large bulge in his slacks, forcing her palm to curl around all that heat. *Then I'll make it easy for you to think about me. You like this, don't you, Cayenne?* His hand moved hers up and down, stroking his thick cock through the material of his trousers. *You remember how I feel? How I taste? If you can't wait, I can indulge you right now.*

Stop it. She tried to tug her hand out from under his. *I don't want you.*

Really? I can see your nipples hard as twin rocks. You

think I put my mouth on you that you aren't going to give me whatever I want?

Furious, she tried to pull away, unsure if her anger was directed entirely at him. She couldn't help the little throb of reaction in her deepest core just touching him. And she could taste him in her mouth.

He tightened his fingers around hers so that she could actually feel his pulse through the material of his slacks. His heartbeat. The jerk of his cock. Her breathing turned ragged. Labored. He was far stronger than he was.

You could build us a cocoon, baby. Nice and thick. Suck my cock right here. I'd like that. Wouldn't you? Then the team could see your handiwork. The silk you want to show them so badly.

If she could have, she would have slapped his face. For one moment, she had actually felt the terrible call between them, that sensual, hot grip of need and hunger that pulsed between them. Now she felt pure fury.

You're being a world-class bastard.

Baby. I am a world-class bastard. That's the man you fucking tied yourself to. His fingers moved over her wedding rings. *You knew exactly what I was like going into it and you aren't going to back out now because you get raked over the coals—justifiably—for nearly giving your silk to another man.*

Her breath hissed out between her teeth. She wanted to bite him. Hard. Inject enough venom in him to force his mouth closed. The temptation was strong, but he had ensured her venom wouldn't work on him.

First of all, I never once intimated to you that I was going to back out on our marriage. I gave my word and my word is every bit as good as yours. More importantly, you ass, your accusations aren't justified. You know very well I was making an effort with your friends on your behalf.

Because I want you to crawl into their laps. His voice dripped sarcasm.

She was so done with trying to be reasonable. She wanted to scratch his eyes out. He wasn't even looking at her. *If we're going to have a fight, you can at least look at me.*

We're not going to have a fight. You're going to sit next to me all the way home. When we get to the house you're going to get in my bed. The others will go to their homes and we'll be alone. I'm done with this conversation until then.

Now he didn't want to fight with her. Great. Cayenne was done with it as well. She hated it when he went all arrogant and bossy on her like this. In bed, that was fine, she could be just as arrogant and bossy. That was fun. This was . . . *not*.

You're being a bastard, Trap. You're angry with Violet, not with me. Don't take it out on me.

Then stop making it easy by thinking of other men. Another man touches you, Cayenne, and I'll fucking kill him.

She remained silent. He sounded like he meant that. Right now, in his present mood, she wasn't certain what to expect. He was just a little scary like this. His hand still pressed hers directly over his heavy erection. How he could have an erection when they were fighting, she didn't know. Clearly she didn't understand men—especially him.

For the rest of the flight neither spoke. He didn't release her hand, not once. Even when she felt him relax a little and tried to tug her hand free, he just tightened his grip again and sent her a cold look. The blue flame was still flaring beneath the glacier. She figured that didn't bode well for when they were alone.

Their vehicle was parked at the airport along with various SUVs the other team members had. Trap kept her locked to him so she didn't get a chance to really say much in the way of thanks or good-bye to the others. Trap actually walked her to the passenger side, unlocked the door, nearly threw her up onto the seat and leaned in to lock her seat belt around her. She stared out the window, hating that when he grazed her breasts with his jaw, her nipples tightened.

She hated that reaction. Hated that all the way home, the

tension between them built—and that it was building into something violent and sexual. She tried to breathe, to force her mind to think why Trap acted the way he did, but the tension in the Rover was too intense to think straight.

"Take your shirt off."

His voice was hard. Commanding. It took her breath away.

"What?"

"You fucking heard me, baby. You didn't want clothes on, take them off."

CHAPTER 21

Cayenne drew in her breath. It was no longer dark out, but they were on the narrow track leading to their home. No one ever drove that road but them and the occasional team member visiting them. If she took off the tee—and the material was already dragging across sensitive nipples—she could be seen if they happened upon anyone. It wasn't that she was particularly modest, but she knew Trap was already at a breaking point. She didn't want to experience any more of his silly jealousy.

She knew Trap's foul mood, his dark jealousy and his holding so tight to her had nothing to do with any of the things he thought they did. He was experiencing something else disturbing, something big. Now that she was away from the close proximity of others and she could breathe again, she realized the feeling she got from him was different than the accusations he made. She needed a little time to work out what it was.

"Cayenne, you aren't going to like what happens if I have to tell you twice. Get your fucking shirt off."

She had no idea why she found it hot when he used that particular voice. She moistened her lips, unsnapped her seat belt and pulled the shirt over her head. Her breasts were full and they jolted and swayed with every pothole in the dirt track the tires hit. She felt very exposed. The seat was high and the windows, although tinted, made her feel on display. She brought her hands up to cover herself.

"Don't. I want to see you. Take off your jeans."

"Trap."

"Take them off, baby."

This time his voice gentled, and that was somehow more commanding to her than his edgy voice. She swallowed a protest and dropped her hands to the waistband of her jeans. She knew he was still angry. Still thinking he was riding on the fury of being jealous. She knew better. At the same time, she wanted this from him. This claiming. She wanted to give him whatever it was he needed to feel that she was his. For her, his need always became hers.

"And get rid of the panties. You aren't going to need those either."

She shimmied out of the jeans, pushing them down her hips and then her legs until she could kick them off. She sat stark naked on the seat, aware that Trap had slowed the vehicle. She wanted him to speed up, not slow down.

"Turn on the seat toward me, your back to the door."

She heard the snick of the lock as he ensured the door couldn't accidentally open. She did what he asked, her breath catching in her lungs.

"Bring both legs up onto the seat, bent, feet close to your bottom, but apart. Spread your legs. Wide. Open yourself to me."

Already her breathing had gone ragged. She could barely pull air into her lungs. He was making her outrageously hot without even touching her. She could feel her body dampening. Growing hot.

He took his gaze from the road and then dropped one hand to his slacks. He opened them easily and drew out the thick length of his heavy erection. One hand circled his shaft with a fist, and began a slide up and down.

"Touch yourself. Your breasts. Just like I taught you. Your nipples, baby. Don't be so gentle. Think about how good it feels when my mouth is on you. When my teeth are on you. You like that little bite of pain. It makes you feel alive, doesn't it?"

She did what he said, using her thumbs, then her fingers and thumbs. Her breath quickened more. Tiny droplets teased the curls on her mound.

"Answer me, Cayenne. You like when I use my teeth, don't you?"

"Yes." She pinched and tugged harder so that her breath exploded out of her lungs.

"Your nipples were so hard rubbing against the silk of your dress, weren't they?"

"Yes." She couldn't breathe. She continued to torture her own nipples, feeling the heat of his gaze as he switched between watching the road and watching her.

The vehicle was in a slow crawl now. The swamp enclosed them in its perfumed beauty even as the sun dazzled them through the windshield. The tires continued to find every pothole and uneven track so that her breasts bounced, pulling against her fingers as she tugged at her nipples.

"That T-shirt rubbed too, didn't it? You're that sensitive, aren't you? The material touching your bare nipples made you hot."

She couldn't deny it, and she could see where he was going with this. "Trap." She stopped what she was doing in an effort to get her brain back so she could defend herself.

"Fucking answer me." He snapped the words at her like the lash of a whip. "And don't you stop."

"Yes," she had to concede, her hands obeying even though her brain hadn't caught up yet.

"Now bring your hand down your body, but don't stop the rough nipple play. Slow with that hand. Feel your skin, all that silk. You like how that feels, don't you? Slow. Stay slow. Keep your eyes on me. See what you're doing to me. You make me so fucking hard I think I'm going to come apart sometimes. Look at my cock. Look what you do."

She swallowed hard, her hand sliding down her body to find her mound. One finger stroked over it while her other hand kept at her breast. Her gaze was on his hand wrapped around his thick shaft. The broad, flared head glistened and he rubbed at it with his thumb, spreading the moisture as his fist pumped. The sight was mesmerizing. Beautiful. Sexy.

"Push your finger inside. Deep. Fuck yourself with your finger, baby. Find that sweet little clit of yours and work it."

She did what he ordered. It felt good. *So* good. The slow-moving Rover. The bumps. The sun moving over her skin through the glass, spotlighting her. Her body sprawled out for his pleasure.

"When a man touches your skin, Cayenne, this is what you do to him. He gets hard. He needs to jack off because it hurts like fucking hell if he doesn't relieve himself. You feel that burn? Put another finger in. Pump a little faster. Harder. I can tell by your breathing you're nearly there. You are, aren't you?"

She couldn't answer. She was close. So close. It felt so good, she was *that* close.

"Stop. Get your hands off your body. Right. Fucking. Now." His voice lashed like a whip again.

She moaned. "Trap." A protest. But she complied.

"Crawl along the seat and feed that honey to me. Are you burning? Does it hurt? Do you need to get off? Tell me how you're feeling right now."

She did what he said, sliding over the seat and the middle console to lift her fingers to his mouth. His tongue curled around them. That simply increased the coiling tension in her, that horrible burn that grew hotter.

"I want your mouth on me. You're going to suck me all the rest of the way home. You keep both hands on me, and you don't touch yourself. I'll touch you when I feel like it, but you don't touch yourself again unless I tell you."

She found that even hotter. She fit her mouth over the wide head of his cock and concentrated on him as best she could. Usually she gave herself over completely to loving him. To giving him the most pleasure she could possibly give him, but her body felt as if it was burning out of control.

She tried to force herself under control, allowing her tongue to stroke and dance, to feel the steel wrapped in velvet of his cock. She tried to take him deeper each time she pushed down on him, tried to tighten her mouth as she drew up. She was just dropping into the zone when his hand landed hard on her buttocks and the nerve endings flared into life, streaking and sizzling straight to her core.

His hand rubbed. Kneaded. His fingers slipped along the cleft of her buttocks, lower still to find her wet and needy. His fingers plunged deep. She gasped. Her channel spasmed hard. Contracted and clamped down like a vise. His thumb brushed her clit. Pressed hard. She moaned around his cock and her hips bucked, trying to ride his hand, trying to gain relief.

He took his hand away, and brought his fingers to his mouth, licking the honey from them. "Keep working. We're almost home. We don't go in until you suck me dry. I have plans, and I can't be feeling like this. You put that there, you take care of it."

She *loved* taking care of his cock. He could sound like he was ordering her to do something she didn't want to do all day, but the fact was, she loved her mouth on him. She loved his reaction. Unfortunately, he had started her body on fire all over again.

She went back to concentrating on him. The shape and feel of him. What he liked best. Taking him deep. Flicking her tongue. Humming. Just suckling turned her on even more. She was dripping wet now and squirming, unconsciously trying to relieve the ache.

As he pulled the Rover into the carport, he caught the back of her head and pressed down, forcing her to take more of him as he threw back his head, groaning. He was big and it wasn't easy, but she managed, breathing through her nose as his shaft swelled and his cock jerked. He pumped his seed down her throat. So much. For a moment she didn't think she could take it all. That was even hotter. The hand at her head, his hips jerking, his shaft stretching her lips. The sound rumbling in his throat, torn from him—by her— by her actions. So hot.

His fist in her hair dragged her head an inch up. "Clean me up. I don't want to get a drop on this suit."

Between her legs only grew scalding. "Trap, I need . . ."

"The sooner you take care of business, the sooner we can get inside."

She bent her head and lapped at him. He spread his legs wider to give her better access. She loved taking care of him because she loved him and wanted him to know she did. She obeyed him because she trusted him. Implicitly. Totally. She'd do anything he said because she believed absolutely he'd take care of her—that he'd always be there for her. There wouldn't be another woman. If he'd wanted one, he would have had one by now. It would always be her.

She gave one last lick and sat up, suddenly realizing what his temper was all about. It wasn't jealousy, although he tried to make it about that. He'd done it before. More than once. This was about fear. Sheer unadulterated terror. Just like when she got shot. Trap reacted badly to fear. He didn't trust fully that she wouldn't leave him. He didn't. Everyone in his life that mattered had left him. She was his world. His entire world. He'd given her that, and it was a precious gift.

Trap opened the door, reached in and pulled her out, setting her on her feet. She was naked and barefoot, but the stairs were right there. She looked around, wrapping her arms around herself as she inhaled to ensure they were entirely alone. The breeze was blowing in their direction and she didn't catch a scent of anyone or anything. Still, walking naked in daylight while he was fully dressed was both frightening and exhilarating.

He caught her hand and tugged, taking her up the stairs. She'd placed alarm lines everywhere. They were thin, nearly invisible. Some were low to the ground, some higher. The entire building was surrounded with them, most attached to the high fence. Along the stairs, several weren't intact anymore. She could see that, because she was looking for it. She was always looking for it.

She took another careful look around and then inhaled again. She drew the perfume of the swamp into her lungs. She didn't feel eyes on her. She didn't even feel uneasy. Whoever or whatever had come, had been there hours ago, probably during the night. They weren't there now.

Trap put the code in for the alarm and placing one hand on her bottom, propelled her inside. He set the alarm again and motioned her forward to the second door. He put in the second code and added his palm print to get them in.

"Get ready for bed, and don't you touch yourself. If you want a canopy tonight, get it done. I'll be a few minutes. I want to take a look at the security footage."

So he'd observed those broken strands as well. She loved that he was using her alarm system as well as his own.

"Cayenne. I'm going to spend hours with you. I'm claiming every fucking inch of your body for my own. You understand me?"

She nodded. Her channel gave another spasm. She wondered if it was possible to have a spontaneous orgasm without him actually touching her. She showered and made certain that she was absolutely clean from her head to her toes. She thought, by taking her time, her body would lose some of the heat, but instead, the anticipation only made her need him all the more.

When Trap entered their bedroom, she was totally aware of him and nothing else. He took up the huge space with his wide shoulders and muscular body. He was fully dressed and she was naked, sitting on the bed, her fingers threaded together to keep from giving into the impulse to relieve herself just a little.

"Come here. I want you to undress me."

Her heart stuttered. She went to him immediately. Her fingers were shaking as she slowly took the jacket from his shoulders and laid it carefully over a chair. She had trouble with the buttons of his shirt, but he didn't help her. He was tall and she had to reach high to get them. She pressed her body against his, feeling his cock, semihard, nearly in her throat. She managed to pull his shirt loose from the waistband and get the buttons open. He held out his arms so she could take out the gold cuff links, at first one wrist and then the other, so she could slip the shirt off. Again she was careful with it, smoothing it over the jacket.

Crouching at his feet, she untied the laces of his shoes. He put one hand on her shoulder as she slipped them off. Her heart beat fast as she looked up at his face. The sensual lines were etched deep. His eyes were dark. Hooded. She almost couldn't breathe with wanting him. She slipped his socks free and then stood to undo his belt and trousers. She let her knuckles slide over his hips and thighs as she took the slacks down the long columns of his legs. Again, she was careful with his clothes, neatly putting them on the chair and then standing in front of him.

"Pull back the covers of the bed and lay in the center. I want you to put your hands above your head."

Her heart began to hammer so loud she was afraid he could hear. Her gaze searched his for a long time. He didn't reissue his order. He just stood there waiting for her to obey him. She took a breath and did what he asked, stretching her arms above her head.

He knelt up on the mattress, leaning over her, sliding his

palm from her armpit to her wrist. Slow. His mouth following. Kissing every inch of her arm. He looped a silk scarf around her wrist and then secured it to the post built into their bed. She kept her gaze glued to his face. The lines there. The heat. The hunger. Most of all, she saw—and felt—that deep-seated need in him to claim every inch of her.

It wasn't about possession. She knew, no matter how long they were together, no matter how often she gave him this, he would always need it, because he would never get over having everything he loved ripped away. The fear would come for whatever reason, and now that she knew what it was, she could be there for him, and if it led to this, she was *so* on board.

His mouth moved over her other arm, following the progression of his palm and then he tied the scarf around her wrist and again secured it to the headboard.

She waited for his touch. For his mouth. He just sat there, his gaze heated. Burning. Moving over every inch of her. Her breasts rose and fell. She couldn't stop her breath from coming so fast. So ragged.

"Trap." She moaned his name.

"Shh, baby." His hand skimmed down her body, from her throat, between the swell of her breasts to her mound. "You're in for a long day. A *very* long day." He bent and gently brushed his lips across her forehead. "Let's turn you over. Relax your arms, there's plenty of play in the scarves."

He caught her easily around the waist and simply rolled her over, crossing her arms above her head. Her breasts pressed deep into the satin sheets. He ran his hand over the left cheek of her buttocks and then down her thigh and along her calf to her ankle, pulling her leg to the edge of the bed. She felt the brush of his hair and then his mouth followed his hand. He secured her ankle with a scarf to a built-in hook beneath the bed and followed suit with her right side so her legs were stretched wide.

She lay quivering. Trying to hold still. Waiting. Needing.

Her breath hitching. She turned her head to the side to try to catch a glimpse of him. "Trap." A plea.

"I know, baby, but you aren't in control this time. Do you remember when you tied me down with your silks? You liked having me at your mercy, didn't you?" He lifted her head very gently with one hand and wrapped a scarf around her eyes. The room went dark.

Fear began to edge into her excitement. "What are you doing?"

"This will heighten your awareness. You'll feel everything. The slightest touch. The slightest breath."

She was so hot. Burning. She wasn't certain she could stand any more awareness. "I need you inside me."

"Like this?" His hand moved between her legs. A whisper. The lightest of touches. Across her wet opening. His finger was gone and then it was back. Gentle. Barely there. Inside her, sliding over her most sensitive spot, and then gone.

She had only thought she was burning. Now the fire was a million times worse. The need was growing every second. She heard him moving, putting something on the side table. And then his hands were on her shoulders. He began to knead the muscles there. His palms were slippery with some kind of ointment. The ointment started off cool but as he worked it into her body, it heated. Every nerve ending began to tingle.

He worked the oil down her back and into the hollow above her buttocks. Her right cheek. Her left. The cleft between her cheeks, paying special attention until she was burning everywhere. Inside. Outside. Then down the backs of her thighs. Her calves. She couldn't stay still. Now every nerve ending burned with need.

"Be good," he cautioned. "I like the way my hand looks on your ass. Especially right now, baby. You weren't very good today on that plane, were you? Flirting. No bra. Nearly giving my silks away. What kind of punishment do you think that should earn you?"

There was a strange roaring in her ears. She pushed into the mattress, desperate to relieve the ache. His hand landed hard, smacking her left cheek and then her right. He'd smacked her before and she'd liked the way her nerve endings leapt to life, but this was different. This time they roared to life. The heat radiated out and around and straight to her core. She couldn't believe it. It should have hurt, but the cinnamon oil seemed to spread the fire through her feminine channel, ratcheting up her need. She couldn't think. She almost couldn't remember her own name.

His hand moved between her legs, fingers still coated in the oil. His fingers worked the oil inside her until there wasn't any part of her lower body that wasn't burning and in desperate need.

"Stay relaxed for me. This isn't very big, but it might feel like it. It's slick and will go in easy if you relax." She felt his fingers between her cheeks and then something pressed into her. Something hard. Stretching her. A bite of pain. Her breath caught. The burn heightened. If she clenched her cheeks it only made it more so.

He rubbed his hand over her bottom and then repeated the smacks. This time a little harder. The flames spread like wildfire. "That's going to feel good in a few minutes."

She wasn't certain what to think. Everything felt good. Everything. Everywhere. Yet at the same time, she was desperate for relief.

Very slowly he released her legs and turned her over, to just as quickly and efficiently retie them. She couldn't see him. She knew he moved because the weight on the bed changed and then he was back. This time his hands went to her breasts, coated in the oil. She wanted to plead with him but it was too late. Her nipples were very sensitive and he worked them, rolling the oil into them, kneading it into her soft, lush curves until her breasts were on fire. The fire streaked straight to her clit.

She couldn't close her legs. Couldn't get relief. She could

only feel, her body so alive and so desperate for his, she could barely catch her breath. "Trap, please. It's too much. It's going to drive me insane."

"We're just getting started," he said. "Have patience. You're always in such a hurry." His hands smoothed down her belly to her hips, and then he plunged his fingers inside her—stretching her with his oiled fingers, stroking the oil onto her clit.

She bucked. Screamed. Tried desperately to ride his fingers. He pulled them away and continued to use the oil on her legs. Rubbing it in deep.

He took his hands away. Then his weight left the bed. It was impossible to hear him move, he was a GhostWalker. He went silent. She lay there writhing—unable to hold still with the oil burning her, keeping her hungry for him.

"Trap?" Fear skittered along the edge of excitement.

"Right here, baby," he said. His voice came from across the room, reassuring her immediately.

"What are you doing?" His presence steadied her.

"Sitting here having a Scotch. Watching you. Deciding what I'm going to do next. You look beautiful squirming around, all that cinnamon honey spilling out. I have to let you cool down some before I eat you. I have a few toys I ordered a week or so ago, and this seems like the perfect time to try them out."

"Toys?" There was trepidation in her voice. She couldn't hold still. She couldn't imagine being any more desperate than she already was and just the way he said the word made her hotter, if that was even possible.

"I like toys. I like seeing you come apart for me." He moved then. She heard the tinkling of ice in his glass. "I see that excites you. You just got wetter for me, didn't you?" He put the glass down on the table and reached for one of the toys he'd purchased. "You already like the toy I bought you. It's stretching you, filling you. I want to finish my drink, and I think you want something. Tell me what it is."

"I need you inside me."

"I'm sorry, baby, I can't accommodate you just yet, but maybe this will do in the meantime." She felt him position something soft but hard at her entrance. She was so slick and so in need that she bore down as he pushed it inside her. At once she felt her channel stretch for the toy. "It isn't as big as me, but it will keep you full, especially with that plug in you." He pulled the toy out and then pushed it back in. "I'll set it on low so you won't go too crazy."

The vibration started. No matter how she moved, no matter what she did, she couldn't get the toy to lie against her very inflamed spot. The fullness and vibration only made her hungrier. Needier. More desperate than ever.

"Trap. Oh, God, please. You have to do something."

Trap looked down at her shuddering body. So beautiful all stretched and writhing. So full with the toys he'd bought for her. Her skin glowed from the oil. He padded across the room on bare feet, his cock already as hard as a rock. It was a good thing he had her suck him dry or he wouldn't have been able to take playing like this. She was too responsive.

He took a piece of ice from his glass and rubbed it on her right nipple. She screamed and arched into his hand. He did the same to the left one. Then he placed an ice cube in his mouth and pulled out the vibrator.

"Do you belong to me, Cayenne?" he asked, his voice casual. He lay belly down on the bed, between her legs. He stroked a finger down her mound, right over the hourglass he loved.

"Yes." She answered without hesitation.

"Belonging to me, being my wife, means you don't crawl into another man's lap without your fucking bra on." He flicked her slit with his tongue. "You don't ever, unless you're using silk as a defense, give that to another man." His tongue, ice cold, plunged deep into her scalding heat.

She screamed. Writhed. He pinned her hips down with his hands. "Do you understand me? Say you understand, because if you don't, I can keep this up all day. I might anyway, just to prove a point."

Her head thrashed and she yanked at the scarves, trying to reach him. Reach between her legs. She couldn't talk anymore. She couldn't think, her mind in complete chaos. There was a roaring in her ears.

He shifted slightly, cupped her bottom and brought her mound to his mouth. She screamed again as he did exactly what he'd been wanting to do since he saw her in that silken dress. He ate her. Devoured her. His tongue removed honey, now flavored with cinnamon, and he drank it down like a starving man. He used his teeth. He used his tongue. He suckled on her clit and then stroked it with the edge of his teeth.

He bit the inside of her thigh and suckled. Then the other thigh. Using his fingers, he stroked the plug in and out while his tongue danced and she writhed.

Please. Please. Please. Please.

Her chant was music in his ears. He loved the way her body responded to him. He felt the coiling and pushed her higher, wanting to give this to her. He reached down with one hand and slipped her ankle out of the loop in the scarf, guiding it around his shoulders. He did the same to the other. Last, he removed her blindfold. He needed to look into her green eyes when she came.

There's nothing more beautiful than seeing you giving me that gift. That perfect, beautiful moment between my woman and me when I'm loving you, and make no mistake, Cayenne, I'm loving you.

He watched her as she came apart. As her body nearly convulsed, rippling with strong shocks, a tidal wave of pure pleasure that *he* gave her. It lasted a long time, the waves rolling through her. He felt it in her thighs, saw it in her belly and breasts. Her beautiful face, the dazed shock in her eyes and the way her mouth formed his name as she screamed out, unable to stay silent.

He took one last swipe of her honey and was up on his

knees, dragging her closer, pulling each leg around his hips, slamming into her, driving through those rolling waves, *feeling* the powerful surge, the contractions of those tight, tight muscles. She was scorching hot, surrounding him with fiery, living silk that gripped him and squeezed with a beauty he'd never known before.

He could live there. In her. In her mind. In her body. Sometimes, looking at her, when he was inside her, love for her overwhelmed him. The emotion was so strong, so foreign to him, it brought him to his knees.

I love you, baby. More than life. More than anything.

From the moment he'd removed the scarf from her eyes, her gaze had never left his. Not once. She gave him that, knew instinctively he needed it. He moved in her, hard, brutal strokes, surging in and out of that scalding tight tunnel of pure silk. He loved the feel of her surrounding him like that, gripping and milking. He stroked the plug in and out of her as a counterpoint to his cock, watching her face as one orgasm rolled into another, even more powerful one.

So beautiful. He breathed the truth into her mind. *My world. My incredible wife.*

He hammered into her, taking her through another powerful climax and straight into a third. He loved watching her face. He couldn't get enough of that look, or the indescribable feeling of pure bliss being inside her body in that tunnel of living silk.

I can't again.

Her voice was breathless. She was already there, clamping down on him with fiery friction, flames dancing as she drew his seed from him, forcing an explosion that left him wrung out, floating with her in some place he'd never been before. If there was ecstasy on earth, right in those moments, he was there.

The emotion for her was so overwhelming he trembled with it as carefully, his body shuddering right along with hers, he began to glide gently in her, bringing her back down with tenderness, as he removed the plug and held her hips to him, still locked together, still moving.

"Unloop the scarves from your wrists, baby."

She lay looking up at him with that wide, dazed expression he loved so much. "I don't think I can. I can't move. I really can't." The aftershocks were strong, her body still rippling with life around his.

Her breasts heaved with every ragged breath she drew into her lungs. Her gaze, so green, like two gems, moved over his face. There was stark love on her soft, beautiful features. Stark. Raw. Certain. The expression ripped into his heart, shredded his soul and put him back together again.

"I love you, baby," he whispered. "So damn much I don't know how to show you."

"You showed me," she whispered.

"Did I scare you?"

She shook her head, her green gaze moving over his face, still claiming him, still loving him. His heart stuttered in his chest. He'd never felt more vulnerable in his life.

"I trust you, Trap. It was exciting. The most exhilarating, beautiful experience of my life. I felt your love surrounding me."

He'd wanted her to feel it. Wanted her to understand that no matter how much of an ass he was, how foul his mood, how vulgar he sounded, he loved her and he would never harm her. He'd cut out his own heart before he harmed her.

"You knew you could get loose, right? Anytime you wanted?"

She nodded. "Not at first, but later when I had to grip the scarves."

"And you know, all you have to do if you don't like something is to say no and I'll stop. Immediately. That's all it takes. We can talk about it and how it made you feel. Always, baby, no matter what I'm saying, what's coming out of my mouth, when I touch you, you should feel love. You don't, you don't feel safe, you say so and we stop. That's a promise."

"You don't have to tell me that, Trap. I know."

"I can't ever let you go. I don't want you to be my fucking prisoner, Cayenne, but I can't ever let you go."

"Come here," she whispered softly in her voice. The one that crept into a man's head. Into his soul. "Come here to me. I want to feel your weight."

He slowly lowered her legs to the mattress from around his waist where he'd drawn them as he'd hammered into her. She seemed far too small and fragile for the rough sex they'd shared. She'd loved it. She pleaded with him for harder. For more. She'd sobbed for relief, but she'd never once stopped him.

He gently stretched out over the top of her, feeling his cock jerk, pulsate with the friction his action caused, but for once in his life he was going soft. Not semisoft, but actually fully relaxed. He kissed her eyes, brushed kisses along her cheekbone and down to the corner of her mouth.

"I love your mouth. Did you know that? I can't ever get enough of kissing you. Or your taste."

She wrapped her arms around his neck, hands sliding into his hair. The action lifted her breasts, pushing them tight into his chest. "I don't ever want you to let me go, Trap. You have to understand something about me. I want you to listen and hear me. Really hear me."

He propped himself up on one elbow to take his weight, allowing his body to release hers, his cock sliding across her hip to rest there while he shifted so he was partially off of her. "I can do that."

"You're uncomfortable around people, Trap, even, sometimes, the ones you know and care for. You have affection for them and a fierce loyalty. I feel that loyalty toward them because they make you happy. I like that. I hope to establish friendships with them because of you. Maybe with Nonny, Pepper and Flame for myself. But regardless, I'll always be uncomfortable around people, just as you are. I spent my life alone. I've let you in. I'll let our children in. Deep. Somewhere deep. But I'm not built for large crowds. Maybe it's the spider in me. I don't know. Whatever it is, I spend my time with you, and if we have children, them, and I'll be content."

He was silent, aware of his heart pounding hard. She meant that. The money. The fame. The cameras and society trappings meant nothing at all to her. Living there in the swamp, she was most comfortable.

"I'll give you whatever fucking thing you want, Cayenne," he promised, meaning it. "I'll keep you happy, right here in this crazy place that we're turning into a home. Just say the word and it's yours."

Cayenne studied his face. One hand brushed along his jaw and then her fingers slid over his lips. Her hand dropped to his chest to press him back onto the bed. "I take it you're finished being a world-class bastard for the day?" she asked, turning in his arms to slide one thigh over his. She straddled him, her legs spread wide over his hips, the pads of her fingers stroking his belly.

He nodded. "You tamed the beast as usual, Cayenne." He was silent for a long moment, watching her face closely.

She could feel him moving in her mind. Moody. Brooding even. Sated. Loving her. She stretched out on top of him, just as sated. "You know why you were upset, don't you, Trap? It had nothing to do with me not wearing a bra or Malichai. You know that, right?"

She laid her head over his heart, listening to it beat. So strong. Steady. Her Trap, loving her so much. She slid one hand up to his shoulder, the other curled around the nape of his neck. Even stretched out, she couldn't cover his broad chest. But she was where it counted, right over his heart.

"I know." The admission was low.

"I'm not going anywhere." She kept her voice just as low, searching for the right words. She knew he would always have that fear of losing her. She just hoped it would lessen over time. "There will never be another man for me, Trap.

I'm not helpless or vulnerable, except to you. Not another human being. Not even Nonny, and I like her. A lot. When you get like that, it can't be about you being jealous because, deep down, you know you have no reason to be. I'll *never* give you a reason to be. You have to recognize that what you're feeling is fear—fear of losing me in some way."

He rubbed his palm along her thigh to the crease just under her buttock. He liked that soft crease and massaged there before moving his palm over her bottom. He liked that her rounded cheeks, silk over sleek, firm muscle, fit into his hand. He felt absolutely at peace. Content.

"They're out there. The uncles." He said it matter-of-factly. He never thought, in a million years, that he would feel so calm thinking about facing the men who had destroyed his family. They'd taken something from him he could never get back. He would always have a deep-seated fear that something would rip Cayenne away from him. "They came at night while we were gone, and they'll be back, maybe tonight. I saw them on the security tapes."

"I know," she said with equal calm. "They don't matter to us, Trap. They can't hurt you. Not anymore. They may want to, but they can't."

"They came for the money." His hand smoothed over the curve of her left cheek and up into the hollow of her spine. "It's really about money, not revenge. Not because of my father. They left him there. They didn't even try to save him. They didn't care about him. I paid the ransom for my aunt, and they've used the money to hide. To disappear. They want more money."

"Does it really matter?" She yawned, kissed his chest right over his beating heart. "We're going to kill them. Both of them. You know that." She stated it just as matter-of-factly as if they were discussing the weather. "Right now, I need to sleep, but before I do, we need to finish our discussion. It hurt today. On the plane. The things you accused me of. Trap, I didn't like it. I know when you get afraid, you get ugly. I get that. I do. It's okay with me if you have to withdraw. It's even okay if you have to be rude and ugly, but not with me. Not *at* me."

She nuzzled him with her chin, her green eyes on his face. "That hurt a lot, honey."

His hand moved up her spine, taking in the silken perfection of her skin. "I don't know how to stop myself when I'm like that. I try, baby, but I've been using that rudeness to push people away for so long, I'm not certain I can stop."

"I'm not asking you to stop, Trap, I'm asking you to have a care about what you say to me. Swear. Be an ass. Be remote. But don't make it so personal that you accuse me of wanting to be with someone else."

"I didn't like seeing him touch you. I didn't like the thought of you giving him your silk. You want to tie someone up, babe, that someone is me."

She nodded. "I understand that, but I didn't want to tie him up, and you should have known that. You need to come to my rescue when your friends are pushing me to do something that makes not only you, but me, uncomfortable. They're *your* friends. It's your brotherhood. I'm trying to fit in and follow your lead. I don't know how to have friends. I don't know how to work with a team. If you don't have my back, I'm floundering and will most likely make mistakes neither of us want."

His hands smoothed back down her spine to that hollow just above her buttocks and then lower to slide over the swell of both cheeks again. Soothing her. Soothing him. He held her to him, savoring the feel of her there.

"That's what I'm asking for, Trap. You have a care when you feel jealous or fearful of losing me and you take my back. I don't need diamonds or beautiful dresses, I need that from you."

He took a breath. Let it out. Searched her face. She meant that. The only thing she asked of him. Not his money. Not what he could get her. Just this. "Then it's yours, Cayenne.

Understand I'm going to fall down a few more times before I get it right, but I'll be trying my best to give you what you need." He locked his arms around her, holding her to him. "Sleep there. Right there. I'm going to be waking you up in a couple of hours again. You know that, don't you?"

She nuzzled his chest and flicked his flat nipple with her tongue. "I expect you to wake me up, and I'll be very disappointed if you don't. I should go get cleaned up though."

He heard the exhaustion in her voice and kept his arms locked tight around her. "Sleep with my seed deep inside you baby. If I'm lucky, you'll get pregnant."

She closed her eyes. He felt the drift of her lashes against his skin. "I already am," she whispered against his heart, and then her breathing evened out.

He lay there just holding her. His heart pounding. His mind shocked at the happiness flooding him when he knew his uncles were coming for him. No, coming for her. For Cayenne. His pregnant wife. He should have been reaching out to his fellow GhostWalkers to help him dispose of his uncles, but he had her. His very lethal, pregnant wife.

CHAPTER 22

Trap woke Cayenne two hours later and made love to her. Gentle, tender love. He was careful of her, each stroke almost lazy. Languid. As if they had all the time in the world. It was still light out, and he ran her a bath, carried her to the bathtub and sat in it with her so he could wash her body with just as much care and tenderness. After checking the security tapes and seeing no action, he tucked her back in bed, tight against him, his arm around her waist, her breast cupped in his palm and they fell asleep like that, close, his body around hers protectively.

Cayenne woke him not more than an hour later, her mouth working his cock. Taking him deep, so that he was already hard and ready before he opened his eyes. Groaning with pleasure, he watched her, appreciating the sight of her, loving that she derived so much enjoyment from the act. She loved him with every stroke of her tongue. Every tight pull of her mouth. When she took him deep or brought him shallow. When she hollowed her cheeks, hummed and flattened her tongue or sent it dancing.

She straddled him and rode him rough. He used the strength of his hips to surge into her while his hands at her waist brought her down with firm, intense strokes. He loved watching her breasts jolt and sway each time he slammed her down on his cock. She changed the pace repeatedly, spiraling her hips down, working his cock the way she would a pole. Impaling herself over and over until her entire body was flushed a beautiful rose. Until her breath came in ragged pants.

He watched her face as the powerful orgasm swept her away, and her body took his with it. She merely slumped over him, right there, with his cock deep inside of her.

"Lift up a little, honey," she murmured. She sounded sated and happy. "Put space between your hips and back and the mattress."

He obeyed without question. Her body still sheathed his cock in her tight, scorching tunnel and that was all that mattered to him. She slid one hand under him and silk began to enclose them both, wrapping them in a tight weave, a cocoon of sheer silk, tying them together, her body over his, her head on his chest. His thighs and lower legs were free as were his arms and head, but they were locked together, woven in silk. He knew, had he asked, she would have suspended them from the ceiling so they could rock together in a cradle. He knew he'd suggest that one day soon.

She murmured something soft against his chest, mostly breath. Mostly air. He knew it was love. She fell back asleep. Trap lay awake for a long time, savoring the feeling of her there, locked to him even in her sleep. She wrapped him up with her arms and legs so that she surrounded him, and they were locked in her silk together, his cock deep inside her, so that he breathed her in with every breath he drew.

He fantasized about all sorts of things she could make from her silk. Various swings, from bondage to double swings to spinning ones. So many possibilities. A sex stool with maybe a vibrating dildo she could impale herself on while she sucked him off. A sling. One that he could restrain her in, keeping her wide open to him. One she could restrain him in. Definitely endless possibilities.

Go to sleep, crazy man.

I'm working here. For us. I'm an idea man.

For yourself. And you lack imagination when it comes to silk. I already have thought of several really great ideas. Of course, since I'll have you at my mercy, I don't know how great you'll think they are until after. Then I know you'll love them.

As long as turnabout is fair play, I'm in. All the way.

I'm holding you to that. Now go to sleep. I'm exhausted. Thinking about those various swings and slings has me all hot and bothered.

I can feel you, already hard as a rock. Seriously, Trap. I think you could go all night. There was amusement in her voice. Drowsy. Sexy. She wasn't saying no, but she was amused. Her hips moved subtly, locked in place by the silk.

Of course I can go all night. He could prove it to her. *All day and night.*

He moved with her. Gently. Barely. A whisper of movement. So sexy his heart jerked in his chest in time to his cock jerking and swelling more. Still, she was exhausted, and he liked the idea of her sleeping just like this. With him filling her. Stretching her. He brushed a kiss on top of her head. "Go back to sleep, baby. I will too."

"*Mmm.* Nice." Her voice was drowsy. Sexy. Filled with love. He felt the brush of her mouth over his heart.

He drifted off that way, surrounded by her body and her love.

Trap woke to the sound of Cayenne's voice. *Come here to me, my love. I want to show you what silks can do.* Her voice whispered over his skin. Filled his mind with infinite possibilities and fantasies.

He sat up alone in the bed. Looking around, his tuxedo was hung up and the room was immaculate. He smelled her fragrance drifting from the master bathroom and immediately went to find her. She wasn't there so he took care of business, took a very fast shower and wandered out into the great room totally naked, following the soft sound of music playing.

Darkness had fallen and the night shades had come down, locking the world out. Through the cleverly designed shades he could see the swamp, but anyone outside couldn't see in, even if they had lights on. Cayenne hadn't turned on any lights, but the flames of many candles danced from a large semicircle on the floor. From the ceiling hung two long drapes of intricate silks. Music filled the room, but so soft and sensuous he felt the stirring on his body before he even looked up and saw her.

Cayenne was stark naked, her long hair flowing around her like a cape. One foot was wrapped in the silk, one hand as well. She began to move, a sexy, sensual undulation, her body swaying with the music, always moving but going from one position to the next almost in slow motion.

The silks wrapped her up, let her fall, her foot wrapped in one silk while the other was in the second one so she did the splits and then moved into a sexy pose with the silk between her legs while the other wrapped one foot so her leg was stretched behind her. She moved from that position to one upside down, her body arched, stretched, hair falling in a long black waterfall.

He found himself mesmerized. One hand fisted his cock while he watched her, unable to look away from what he had to call art, yet was the most sinfully sensual thing he'd ever seen.

She did the splits upside down, and he stared in wonder at the red hourglass in the black patch of curls at the junction of her legs. When she turned and he stared up into her opening flower, dewy wet, like the plants in early morning, he found himself fisting his cock harder.

"Lower yourself down here," he ordered, his voice almost hoarse.

She complied, but she did it slowly, sensuously, like a

spider might, nearly crawling to him on the silken streamers, upside down, her hands finding his shoulders and then sliding down his chest, her arms wrapped around his belly, breasts pressed tight against his waist, mouth engulfing his cock while her feet remained wrapped in silk.

This is imagination with silks, my love.

He threw back his head and had to agree with her earlier assessment. He had a great imagination when it came to inventing things, but she definitely had him beat when it came to silks.

He wrapped his arms around her, taking her weight so that she released him, inverted, and he carried her to the wall. "Wrap your legs around me, baby."

She did, spreading her legs, and he found her slick and hot and welcoming. He took her against the wall and then again on the floor with the flames of the candles dancing all around them. She'd prepared a picnic, and they ate together on the thick rug near the fireplace, laughing together and just touching occasionally.

"You think we've given them enough time to realize we're here?" Cayenne asked. "I looked at the screens earlier, and they weren't here yet, but about half an hour ago, the alarm silks were tripped."

"They had to see the Rover," he said, leaning over to brush her mouth with his.

She stretched and stood up. "Let's get this over. All this sex is making me sleepy, and really, honey, they're more trouble than they're worth. I could take care of them for you if you wanted me to."

He shook his head. "I have a very deep-seated fear of losing you, remember? Just the thought of you close to those two sets my teeth on edge. I don't like you being involved at all, Cayenne."

She sent him a quelling look. "Seriously, Trap? Are we going to argue over this? I'm involved. If these men think they can take away your life again, honey, they are sadly mistaken. If you think I'm going to stand by while they try, then *you* are sadly mistaken. I'm going out there first. You go up to the roof and cover me."

He pinned her with glacier-cold eyes. "You are getting very bossy, woman."

She *loved* that he called her *woman*. She was a woman. His. But he had to understand, he was her man and she had his back. The danger didn't matter.

"Honey, you're every bit as important to me as I am to you. I'm not going to sit on a shelf while you go out and face Whitney's supersoldiers or one of Violet's hit squads. And I'm certainly not going to let you face those despicable uncles of yours."

She leaned over and brushed his mouth with hers. He sat on the floor, the remnants of their picnic all around him. "Do you have any idea how much I love you? Whatever you feel for me, I feel for you. This is a partnership, Trap. You and me. Together. That's how it has to be."

He leaned into her, burying his face against that red hourglass, one arm slung around her hips, locking her to him. He held her for a long time. She let him. She gave him the time he needed to come to the right decision—her decision—because this wasn't going any other way.

Trap was arrogant, rude and bossy. She was okay with that. But he had to know when she put her foot down, she meant what she said. This was a line he wasn't going to cross.

"All right, baby," he agreed softly, lifting his head to look up at her. "But you don't get one fucking scratch on you. Not one. You do, and you're going to pay."

She smiled at him, her fingers tunneling into his thick mass of blond hair. "I can live with that. Get dressed and let's do this." His little declaration was intriguing. It might just be worth it to get a scratch on her.

Hiding a smile, she hurried. She knew letting her go out to face his uncles was difficult for him, but for her, his worry was absolutely absurd. She would never let him face them alone, no matter what he said or decreed. She dressed in her vintage blue jeans, the soft ones that clung to her body but allowed her to move easily and fast in them.

She donned a turtleneck shirt, one of the few she had from her stay in the cell. She'd made it herself, spinning the silk for several years, weaving it together and then sewing it. It fit tightly on her, and came up her throat and down past her waist. Extra armor. She was already spinning the silk to weave a similar shirt for Trap, hoping to have it ready by his next birthday. It was months away and she had plenty of time to work during the times without him around to get enough silk to weave into such a large piece of material.

She slid on soft shoes, ones that allowed traction in the marshier areas of the swamp. She was light and could skim the ground or use the trees and her silk to move fast. The uncles weren't going to be so lucky. Cayenne braided her hair and smiled at her reflection on their mirror.

Trap had dressed beside her, and he caught her small smile. "What?"

"I like the idea of hunting tonight. I know exactly where I'm going to lead them."

"You stay where I can cover you, Cayenne," he cautioned. "And don't get cocky. They may be civilians, but they're dangerous. They are sociopaths, and they'll kill you just for fun."

She tilted her head to one side, her gaze meeting his in the mirror. She could see her eyes had gone multifaceted, a signal that the spider in her was rising. "Hunting them is going to be fun. Does that make me a sociopath?"

"That makes you my woman." Trap suddenly reached out and dragged her into his arms. "Giving you this isn't easy, Cayenne. I don't like it. My stomach is in fucking knots."

She was relaxed. She wasn't in the least afraid, but she rarely was when she went into combat. She had confidence in herself. She wanted Trap to have that same confidence in her but she knew that had to come with time. Maybe it never fully would sink in that she was as lethal as he was in a battle, but as long as he treated her as his equal, she could deal with his fears.

"Watch and learn, husband." She slid her hands up his chest and wrapped her arms around his neck, lacing her fingers at his nape. She kissed him. Hard. Wet. Pouring love into him. "I've got this." Her whisper was against his lips.

He swallowed hard. "All right, baby. Do your thing. No venom if you can help it. If the bodies are discovered, we don't want anything that might trace their deaths back to us. Accidents happen in the marsh and that's what we want it to look like, although I'd like to put a bullet in their fucking brains and maybe set them on fire like they did my family. Peel their skin off a little at a time like they did my aunt."

She pressed closer to him, feeling the rage buried beneath the ice start to erupt. "This will be worse. They'll die slow, Trap. Knowing it was coming. Seeing it come." She kissed him again, and this time he took over, just like she knew he would. He needed her in that moment, needed her steady, calm confidence. Needed to know she was there, with him, not appalled at the extent of his rage or his need for equal justice.

Cayenne held him for a few more minutes, waiting until the ice was back in his veins, and then she stepped away, turning, squaring her shoulders and sauntering out of their bedroom, past the silks hanging from the ceiling in the great room, to their front door. She flipped on the light switch to illuminate the room so that when she pulled open the outer door she was framed there, the light behind her.

She faced the swamp, looking to the south, where Nonny's pharmaceutical plants had been cultivated. A good acre of them. All different kinds. Just to the edge of the acre the marsh crept in, fueled by the water continually battering and eroding the land mass. In that marsh were places the ground was so thin even she couldn't tread lightly without falling through. Cypress trees threw out knobby knees in an effort for survival, one of the few trees that could thrive in standing water.

She turned her head back to face inside the house to start their charade. "I can't sleep, honey. I'm going to take a look at the night-flowering plant Nonny asked me to check on before we left. I won't be long. You stay in bed."

She waited a heartbeat or two as if listening to his answer, and then she stepped onto the raised porch and closed the door. As soon as she turned back, she let her senses expand. Paid attention to all the feelers and alarm triggers she had strung around their home. In the last month she'd managed to add long and short lines. She had every inch of the yard surrounding the house inside the fence line rigged with feelers. Outside the fence and in the trees and brush, she had more.

It wasn't difficult to locate the hiding place of the uncles. They hadn't let something like a few spiderwebs deter them from hiding at the western corner of the fence. From where they were, she knew they could see her perfectly. She hurried down the stairs as if she didn't have a care in the world and headed toward the marsh, skirting around the plants Nonny had spent so many years transplanting into one large area for the people in the swamp. When they needed medicine and had no money, they went to Nonny to have her mix one of her concoctions.

Cayenne didn't use a flashlight. She didn't need one. She knew exactly where she was going and where to step. She came up to the darker grove of cypress trees, the ones she'd mentally marked just in case she needed a disposal site. Beneath two of them was particularly thin ground. She knew, because weeks earlier, when she'd examined it, she'd nearly fallen through. There was still a divot in the ground where her foot had sunk into water.

She sauntered as if she were entirely at ease or didn't suspect she wasn't alone. She even hummed. Still, over her humming, she heard them. Twigs snapped. Leaves crackled.

Twice, someone stumbled and muffled a curse. Sound carried at night, especially in the stillness of the swamp.

An alligator bellowed somewhere close by. A barred owl sounded an eerie two-toned hoot, the last note drawn out like a Cajun accent. She crouched down abruptly in the higher grasses, looking as if she was inspecting a plant. She turned slightly to watch the two men split up and come at her from either side. Both held an object in their hands. Not guns, but Tasers. She suspected that was how they'd managed to subdue Trap's aunt and take her from the house.

As the one to her left closed in on her, she stood up fluidly and lifted one hand toward the cypress branch sweeping over the marsh. As the man triggered the Taser, she flew upward, on the thicker anchored silk. Using momentum, she shot out more silk, wrapping him thoroughly and efficiently, so fast, his body spun as the thick, sticky silk wrapped him up like a spider's midnight snack. She kept climbing, out of reach of the second Taser and into the higher branches where the second man would have a difficult time shooting her, even if he had a real gun.

She anchored her lines, added several more for structural strength and yanked the body up off the ground so he swung in the air from the branch she'd carefully chosen. All the while she continued to spin the cocoon around him. Her spinet glands were located in her palms, something she was grateful for. She could produce various types of silk when needed. Each was from a different gland. She used her strongest silk for her anchor lines and her stickiest for wrapping her prey.

"Bobby!"

"Get me out of this, Richard," Bobby shouted hoarsely.

His brother rushed to help him, and the moment Richard was out in the open, Cayenne dropped a woven web around his neck like a noose, pulling him up short. She quickly began to bundle Trap's uncle up. He tore at the silk, but the strands stuck to him like glue. She was fast. She'd been practicing from the time she was a toddler, and she took particular delight in speed. She wrapped him in thick, sticky silk until only his head showed above the cocoon and he was suspended from a second tree, facing his brother.

Cayenne lowered herself from her anchor thread and stood on the outer edges of the marsh. "I guess you came looking for me. Did you have something you wanted to say?" She studied their faces. "You both clearly drink a lot. You lived well on Trap's ransom money. I guess you had to pay someone a lot of money for new identities."

Richard spat at her. "You bitch. Get us down."

She ignored his command, wondering if he believed anyone would be stupid enough to obey him when he'd come to kill them.

"Trap's on his way. He was covering you the entire time with his rifle. One wrong move and he'd have splattered you all over the swamp, and we'd roll you into a gator hole, but you were easy. Too easy." Contempt edged her tone. "You got lazy on that money, thinking you could do the same thing you did the last time."

Again it was Richard. "You can smirk all you like, but we've done it dozens of times, collecting ransoms from rich fucks like Trap," he boasted. "All brains, no brawn, that's my weak nephew. Scared shitless and willing to pay anything to get his whore back." He fought the restraint of the silk, wiggling, cursing and swinging his weight in an effort to dislodge himself from the tree. The more he fought, the tighter the loops bound him until he was nearly completely enshrouded.

"I'm going to tear out your heart, bitch," Bobby screamed, bucking wildly. The branch creaked ominously. "What the hell are you anyway?"

She smiled up at him. "In some circles I'm known as the black widow."

The two men gasped and rocked hard, bundled in their cocoons.

Trap came up behind her, his eyes as cold as ice as he surveyed her handiwork. He loomed over her, close. The heat of his body warmed her cool skin. She leaned back into him as his arms came around her.

"They like to kidnap people, honey," she said softly. "Apparently your aunt wasn't their only victim. They were easy though. Really easy. Made noise, weren't in the least bit stealthy. Wyatt's girls could have taken them." She raised her eyes to the wriggling bodies. "The girls are toddlers, and they would have killed you both." There was contempt in her voice and no mercy. She had none for them.

Trap was silent, staring at the two men who had helped to change the course of his life. He didn't say a word to them because he had nothing to say. His uncles cursed and demanded, but as time stretched out and he continued to remain silent, their fear began to mount to terror—so much so that it was tangible.

"Drop the first one, baby," he said, after watching the two men wear themselves out with struggling against their bonds. "Just looking at them makes me sick."

She didn't hesitate, but yanked Bobby's anchor line. He fell hard, feet first, to the ground, broke through the thin crust, the force of his fall taking him all the way to his chest. Mud covered the silk and splashed up, thick and nasty, smearing his face. Water leached to the surface, and his eyes widened with terror.

"Trap. Get me out of this." Bobby didn't have the use of his hands. Entirely helpless, the water and mud sucked at his body, slowly pulling him deeper. "Trap. Come on, get me out."

Richard had stopped moving, staring at his brother with horrified eyes as more water seeped to the surface and Bobby slipped deeper until his shoulders were mostly in the mud and the water splashed up his neck and into his mouth.

"Richard," he called. "Do something."

"Richard has a little problem of his own," Cayenne said.

"I don't think he's going to be thinking too much about helping you, Bobby."

She cut the anchor on Richard's silk casing, and he dropped like a stone, much as his brother had. He went into the thick, greedy mud up to his waist. Water leaked all around and took him down at a much more rapid speed than his brother. The two men stared at each other in utter horror. Helpless. Like their victims. They were unable to do anything at all—the water kept rising, and the mud continued to suck them deeper.

Trap watched without changing expression as first their chins went under and then their mouths. Noses went next. Eyes disappeared. Eventually even the top of their heads vanished beneath the surface. An alligator bellowed again, and another one answered. The barred owl gave its low, mournful hoot.

"Funny to think, after all this time, they're really gone out of my life and with no real fuss. Just gone. Done." Trap tightened his arms around her and kissed the top of her head. "I expected to feel something."

"Like what?"

"Remorse. Triumph. I don't know. That what we were doing was wrong, but I was going to do it anyway." He nuzzled his chin through the silk of her hair. "I don't feel it was wrong. I feel good. Like I can breathe easy for the first time in years."

She tipped her head up and looked at him over her shoulder. "Let's go home, honey. I want a bath. A long one. Maybe a soak in the hot tub with you. I haven't tried that yet."

He dropped his arms from around her waist so he could thread his fingers through hers. They turned back to their house, walking close, hand in hand. Neither looked back. Neither thought about the two men who had died hard, sucking mud and water into their lungs.

"I'm all for that, baby, but I would like a repeat performance with those silks of yours. That was so fucking hot."

She laughed softly. "I told you you'd like my ideas."

"You were right." Trap brought his wife's hand up to his mouth, turned it over and kissed her wrist. "I'm man enough to admit that, babe."

"Oh, no, look." She held out her arm—the one she deliberately snagged on brush. There was a faint red line about two inches long. "I got a scratch. I'm in so much trouble, aren't I?"

She laughed again, the sound like music, mingling with the rhythm of the swamp at night. Trap's heart jerked hard in his chest. His cock did the same. He found himself smiling and happy—actually at peace—contented as they made their way home.

Keep reading for an excerpt from
the next exciting Carpathian novel
by Christine Feehan

DARK
PROMISES

Available March 2016
from Berkley Books!

"Joie, can you believe this night?" Gabrielle Sanders stared out the window at the stars scattered across the sky. The night was almost a navy blue with so many stars overhead it would be impossible to count them. The moon was rising, a beautiful half crescent of shining light. "It's perfection. Everything I dreamt of."

Her wedding night. She'd dreamt of it for so long. At last, this was the evening she'd waited for and the weather was cooperating, just as if it knew she was marrying the man of her dreams.

"We've got to get you ready, Gabby," Joie answered. "Come back here. I need to make certain you have everything you need and give you the 'talk.'"

Gabrielle turned back with a short laugh. "I'm marrying Gary, Joie, the love of my life. I certainly don't need the 'talk.' I love Gary Jansen with every breath in my body," Gabrielle Sanders whispered as her sister smoothed a hand down the filmy ivory and lace gown and stepped back to survey her handiwork.

"Daratrazanoff," Joie corrected, a hint of worry in her voice. "You still persist in acting as if you're human, Gabrielle. You aren't. Neither is Gary. Both of you are fully Carpathian. When Gary rose Carpathian, he rose as a true Daratrazanoff. He's from one of the most powerful lineages the Carpathian people have. You can't pretend he isn't."

"He's still Gary," Gabrielle protested gently. She took both of her sister's hands in hers. "Be happy for me. Truly, I've never been happier than this night. We've waited so long to be together."

"I am happy for you," Joie said immediately, smiling at her sister. "You look so beautiful. Like a princess."

Gabrielle looked at herself in the mirror. Her dress was exactly right. The perfect fit, a lovely fall to her ankles, swirling around her so that she appeared to be ethereal. She loved the square lace neckline and the fitted bodice showing off her small waist. She was tall enough to pull off elegant, and the gown did just that.

Joie didn't understand. None of them did. Only Gary. He knew. He saw inside of her. Way down deep where no one else had ever looked.

"Joie, I'm not like you or Jubal," she admitted, referring to her brother. "I'm not a woman who craves adventure. I'm not a warrior who wants to go fight the injustices of the world. I'm just Gabrielle. No one special, but I like my life simple. Peaceful. I like to sing when I wake up and hum all day long. I like picnics. Horses. Galloping across the fields and jumping over tree trunks and streams. I love sitting on a porch swing and talking quietly with someone I love. That someone is Gary."

"Oh, Gabby." Joie put her arms around Gabrielle. "I didn't realize you've been so unhappy. You have, haven't you?"

Gabrielle hugged Joie back, feeling lucky to have a sister and brother who loved her so much. She felt their love at all times. Their support. More than anything, she wanted Joie's support now in the biggest moment of her life.

"I don't fit in this world, Joie," she said gently, trying to find a way to carefully explain. Joie pulled back and looked at her with liquid eyes. Gabrielle's heart beat louder. She didn't want to hurt her sister, but she wanted to be honest. "I like to observe people from a distance, not be in the middle of some kind of crazy battle between vampires and shifters. I didn't even know there were such things as shifters or vampires in the world. Carpathians. Lycans. Mages. Jaguars. It's all crazy, like a mad nightmare, Joie. Violence and war aren't big on my agenda. In fact, the entire Carpathian way of life is totally foreign to my nature."

She had, thankfully, never heard of Carpathians when she was growing up. And she'd always thought vampires were a myth. She still wished she thought that. Carpathians never killed for blood, but they slept in the rejuvenating ground, couldn't be in the sunlight and existed on blood. They hunted the vampire who lived to kill their victims.

Gabrielle gave a little shiver. She'd had enough of battles. Of wars. Of seeing someone she loved—such as Gary— nearly lose his life when it wasn't even his fight. She had nearly lost him. Gregori had converted him, bringing him fully into the Carpathian world—as if they hadn't already brought him there.

Gary had somehow become an integral part of Carpathian life, so essential to them that even the prince sought his opinion on matters Carpathian. Gregori, second to the prince, was always with Gary now. It wasn't as if Gary was born a Daratrazanoff. He was born Gary Jansen, a genius, off-the-charts intelligent; a tall, thin reed of a man with glasses and a thirst for knowledge. A geek. Like her.

Now he was a tall, completely filled-out, walking warrior. He went into battles without flinching. Even before Gregori had converted, he had. She'd watched him slowly change from her nerdy geek to a completely different man as the Carpathians put more and more demands on him.

Joie moved to a chair as if Gabrielle were delivering a

terrible blow, and she probably was. She hadn't told anyone but Gary her true feelings. Her beloved Gary. He was quiet and solid. He could always, *always* be counted on. Everyone counted on him, but especially Gabrielle.

She kept trying to make her sister understand. "Joie, you and Jubal belong in the Carpathian world. I don't. I don't even want to be here. Not anymore."

Joie inhaled sharply. "Gabby . . ."

Gabrielle shook her head. This had to be said. She wanted Joie to understand just what Gary meant to her. What he'd been for her in the past and what he would be in her future. "I hope, after tonight, after I marry Gary, we'll go away together and live in a beautiful little house. Nothing big. Nothing fancy. Just small and snug and filled with love. That's it. That's my dream. Gary and my little house tucked away someplace where there are no such things as vampires, and women carry their children to full term and give birth to healthy, happy babies. No wars. Just peace and happiness."

There, she'd said it. That was the strict truth and Joie needed to know how she truly felt.

Joie's eyebrows came together as she frowned. "You mean you want to move away from here? Where your laboratory is set up? You love working here. You want to move away from the Carpathian Mountains? From the prince? From Gregori?"

Gabrielle straightened her shoulders and lifted her chin. "*Especially* away from the prince and Gregori."

Joie shook her head, looking shocked.

"I don't belong in the Carpathian world, I just don't. Only Gary seems to understand that about me. He doesn't mind that I'm not a fierce warrior woman. The thing is, Joie, I don't *want* to be different. I'm a book person. I like to live quietly."

"Gabrielle, you are so far off track about yourself and Gary. Where is this coming from? You love adventures. You've gone ice climbing with me and Jubal a million times. You've gone caving. Hiking in remote countries."

Gabrielle nodded. "I went caving because you and Jubal did, and I enjoy spending time with you, but I don't live for adventures in the way you do. I'm really a homebody."

"Are you crazy, Gabby? You're a genius who thrives on studying hot viruses. Newsflash, sister. Studying that kind of virus without a way to fight it can get you killed. If you didn't like adventure you would never, under any circumstances, study them."

"You fight the world's injustices your way, and I fight them mine. Viruses make sense to me. I can solve the puzzle and try to help with things like finding a way to stop the Ebola virus from being let loose on the world. Vampires make no sense. None." She gave a little shudder. Joie would never understand that she escaped into a lab, that once she focused on whatever she was studying, everything around her disappeared and she didn't have to think about anything else at all.

"You have crazy, mad skills in a lab, Gabby," Joie said. "You're a genius, it isn't just Gary. He isn't smarter than you."

"Actually he is. Most men bore me silly after two minutes alone in their company. I can talk to Gary for hours. More, I can just listen to him when he talks to others. He's brilliant. He's also the kindest, sweetest man I know."

Joie shook her head. "He's a Daratrazanoff. Every bit of power, of knowledge, their blood, their ancestors, all of it was given to him in the cave of warriors. You know that. You were there. He was powerful before, Gabby. He's even more so now."

Gary always took the backs of the hunters and he'd never let any of them down during a battle, not once. Gabrielle knew it because when he'd nearly died, their best hunters came in to give blood and to pay their respects. She knew it because Gregori Daratrazanoff had made him his brother, his own flesh and blood. The power of the Daratrazanoff family ran in his veins. Was in his heart and soul. Was there, in his mind.

Okay, she had to admit to herself she shied away from

the sheer power there at times, but still, he was always her Gary. Gentle and kind with her. Seeing her when others couldn't—or wouldn't. She'd tried to tell Joie and Jubal that she was different, not at all wild or willful, but they laughed and said she didn't know herself very well.

Maybe she didn't. But she knew what she wanted—what she'd always wanted—and that was Gary. "I don't care what his last name is, or whose blood runs in his veins, he's *mine*," she declared firmly. "He's always been mine and I want him back. His life shouldn't be fighting vampires. He's such a genius and I miss him in the laboratory. I want him back there. Once we're married and we find a home, we can set up a lab and he can research solutions to all the Carpathians' problems *away* from the Carpathian Mountains and vampires and anything else that is monstrous."

Joie cleared her throat and Gabrielle's gaze jumped to her younger sister.

"Just tell me, Joie," she said. "We've always talked straight with one another."

"You can't change him, Gabby. Gary is a man who will put himself in harm's way over and over if it comes to his sense of right or wrong. He has a clear sense of honor, of duty, and that's why Gregori accepted him from the start— from the very beginning when he first met Gary. Gregori didn't associate with humans, but Gary already had the same values. He was willing to put himself on the line. Like Gregori, he's a man of action, and he's decisive about it."

Gabrielle shook her head. "They've forced him to become like them. He belongs in a laboratory. He loves research and he's got the mind for it, Joie. You know he does, but more and more they're pulling him off that work to go hunt the vampire with them. He's with the Prince and Gregori all the time."

"Because they value his advice, Gabby," Joie said gently. "You should be proud of him."

"I am, super proud," Gabrielle assured her sister, and she *was* proud of Gary. "He's a brain. *Gregori* changed him."

Joie bit down on her lip, her eyes shadowed. "He didn't, Gabby. Gregori wouldn't have changed him—he couldn't. Fundamentally, Gary is the same man he always was. Gregori looked into his mind and he saw a brother—a man who thinks as he thinks. Gregori accepted Gary because Gary is exactly like he is. Of course Gary didn't have the skills or knowledge to fight the undead, but he does now. He is Carpathian through and through. You have to be very sure you know him and you accept who he is, not just a small part of him."

"They almost got him killed. In a way they *did* get him killed." She ducked her head and twisted her fingers together. "I was there when he was dying. I was *right* there. Do you know what he said when Gregori told him he was going to convert him? Gregori explained that Gary was *dying*. We all knew."

She pressed a trembling hand to her mouth as the memories flooded in, the ones she tried so hard to keep at bay. She actually felt sick to her stomach. Her lungs refused air and her heart accelerated to the point where she was afraid she might have a heart attack. She would never forget the sight of Gary, torn and bloody in so many places. He'd saved the life of Zev Hunter, lifemate to Branislava of the Dragonseekers. Zev was *Hän ku pesäk kaikak*, guardian of all, and a very needed member of their people. But in saving Zev's life, Gary nearly died. So close. It had been a terrible few hours. The worst. She never wanted to go through that again.

She wasn't a healer like some of the women. That wasn't her gift. She didn't even know what her gift was other than a party trick or two. So she could look at a map and locate things. What good was that? Her family—and the Carpathians—said she was psychic, but she wasn't. Not like Joie, not like Jubal. She was just plain Gabrielle. No one special. But Gary was a gift and he saw her that way as well. She'd nearly lost him to the madness of Carpathian life.

"He said he could better serve the people as human," she whispered, her fingers covering her mouth as if she couldn't say the words aloud. "He was ready to die for them. He didn't make the decision to become Carpathian. Gregori made it for him."

There was hurt in her voice. She knew Joie heard it. The Carpathian people had been put above her. Everything in her life had changed when she'd nearly been killed. A member of a human society of vampire killers had stabbed her repeatedly, a vicious, brutal attack. She still had nightmares, although she didn't share that with anyone, not even Gary. She had been brought into the Carpathian world in order to save her life.

Had it not been for Gary, she would have wished they hadn't saved her. She didn't belong. It was that simple. Mikhail, the prince of the Carpathian people, had given her the choice. Live or die. Of course, it had been her own decision to be converted, but Gary was a huge part of that. She'd never had regrets because of him. At the time, terrified and in pain, she had been happy for the chance. Mostly because she knew *this* day would come. Her day. The day she married Gary.

"Gabby," Joie said. Her tone said it all. Compassionate. Sympathetic.

Gabrielle blinked back tears. "I know he has a sense of duty. I know that. I love that about him. When we're bound together as lifemates, my soul to his, that sense of absolute duty and honor and love will be for me. I'll be first. Traian puts you first. Even Gregori puts Savannah first. Lifemates are always first."

"You're absolutely certain that Gary is the one for you, Gabrielle?" Joie asked.

Gabrielle had always chosen to think before she spoke, especially to her sister and brother. She loved them both fiercely. She turned what Joie said over and over in her mind. Was she fooling herself? Was her love for Gary real? Did she see him the way he saw her? Because she knew, without a doubt, Gary saw her. Inside of her. He knew her better than anyone else had ever known her.

She moistened her lips. She had never really used her

abilities as a Carpathian to look into Gary's mind. That was true. She could. He would have allowed it, but she wanted that human aspect of finding out slowly about her partner. She even needed it. She was lost in the mountains, amid the wars going on, wars she didn't understand and wanted nothing to do with.

"I love Gary, Joie. I always have. His mind is so incredible. He starts working on something and it's breathtaking to watch him. He gets a scent and he's like a bloodhound. It's such a beautiful and mind-blowing thing to see. He's always going in the right direction. I love that about him. I love that I don't have to talk down to him. Or dumb it down. When I talk, he listens to me and he believes I'm intelligent. Together we can accomplish so much."

"You already have," Joie said gently. "Give yourself credit. You and Shea were right there with Gary, trying to find solutions and coming up with all sorts of things."

"But it was really Gary who pointed us in the right direction. It could have taken years or longer to figure things out," Gabrielle said. "I love his mind. I love how it works. I love how gentle he is and how kind. I love how sweet he is."

"What about his sense of duty," Joie said. "That's a *huge* part of him. His sense of honor. His integrity. Those things make up his character. He'll put others before his own life. He'll put himself in a dangerous situation in order to protect others. He, like Gregori, is a shield."

Gabrielle felt her stomach settle. Her heart slowed to normal. The breath moved in and out of her body naturally. "Once we're lifemates, that shield is mine, Joie." She knew that was the absolute truth. She'd known it practically since the moment she'd laid eyes on him. He was hers. After tonight, she would be forever grateful she was Carpathian. Tonight was her night. The wait was finally over.

Joie smiled at her. "I can see you're absolutely certain. I can tell Dad and Mom I had the 'talk' with you and you passed with flying colors."

"I'm so in love with him I can barely breathe sometimes when he's around," Gabrielle admitted.

"You really are breathtaking," Joie reiterated. "I've always thought you were beautiful, but the way you look tonight, Gabrielle . . . Gary is a lucky man."

Gabrielle smiled. Her heart leapt. *She* was the lucky one. She and Gary would exchange their vows and go away, far from the mountains where every single night Gary was asked by the Prince, or Gregori or someone, to perform some monumental task that no one else could possibly do but him. Some terrible thing that put his life in jeopardy. She couldn't bear that, not ever again. Being proud of your partner was just fine until they died in your arms, then pride wasn't all that great anymore.

Gabrielle smoothed her hands down the line of her filmy gown and took a deep breath, pushing her fears away. Nothing was going to mar this special night. Nothing at all. Tonight was hers. Once more she glanced out the window up at the night sky where the stars glittered like a ceiling of diamonds. The rest of the tension coiled in her stomach slid away.

There wasn't a single cloud. Not one. Just a beautiful blanket of stars, and she knew why: Gary. That was the reason. Carpathians created storms easily. They could also bring beautiful, perfect weather when they needed it. Gary had brought her this night. She didn't feel the subtle pull of power, but she knew it was there.

"He's waiting for me."

"He can wait. You need something borrowed," Joie said. She pulled a necklace from around her neck. A small pendant hung from a thin chain. "I keep this with me most of the time." Her fingers wrapped around the pendant. "Well, *all* of the time. I found Traian in that cave and when we were escaping, I found this embedded in the ice. I think it belonged to one of the mages. Maybe even Dad. I've never showed it to him because I love it and feel very drawn to it and I really don't want to lose it. It feels as if it should be mine."

Gabrielle understood that her sister was giving her something that was important to her. She took the pendant and chain on her open palm, studying it from every angle. It was made of rock. It looked like quartz to her, but it was shaped into four circular corners with lines in the middle of each circle. It was highly polished, but still appeared crude. Gabrielle closed her fingers around it and felt warmth instantly. More, she felt her sister's presence—as if she held a small bit of her in her hand.

"I can't take this," she whispered, her heart fluttering as love for her sister overwhelmed her. "This is meant for you. I feel you in it." She could feel the way Joie loved her. Fiercely. Protectively. Unconditionally. She had that. Tears filled her eyes. Joie gave her that.

Joie reached out and gently put her hand over Gabrielle's. "Just for this night. For *your* night. I want to be there with you in some way. I can't go to the field of fertility with you, but I can give you something that matters to me so I can travel with you and know how happy you are. And you deserve to be happy, Gabby."

"Thank you, Joie. I'll wear it, then." Gabrielle carefully slipped the chain over her intricate hairdo and let the pendant rest between her breasts.

"Something blue," Joie said, and grinning, fashioned a lacy garter to slip under the wedding gown and onto Gabrielle's thigh. "Gary will be happy to discover that."

Gabrielle blushed. "Lovely. He will."

"Something old," Joie said, sobering a little. "Jubal gave me this for you. He said it was Dad's, an ancient bracelet from an ancestor we've never heard of."

"Dad gave this to Jubal? It's for a woman," Gabrielle said, her eyes on the delicate links, all fashioned by a brilliant ancient jeweler. The bracelet was made from a material she was unsure of, but the links were locked together and couldn't come apart. She couldn't see the clasp.

She wanted it instantly. It was beautiful. Primal. It held power. She felt it in the delicate links. "Why would Dad give this to Jubal?"

"He said Jubal would know who it belonged to and when to give it to her. Jubal says it belongs to you and now is the time," Joie said.

Gabrielle bit her lip and took the links from Joie's palm. Instantly the bracelet felt alive. Warm, like Joie's pendant, but there was a surge of power, almost like an electrical current. The links moved, snakelike, in her palm. She should have been afraid, but she wasn't. Her heart beat faster, but only in anticipation.

This was hers. Just as the pendant was Joie's and her brother had a bracelet that was really a weapon, this delicate piece from ancient times was meant to be part of her.

She closed her fingers around it, accepting it. Accepting that it held power and would somehow become a part of her. She felt the ancient links move again, slipping out the side of her fist to curl around her wrist. For one moment the links blazed hot, changing color from that strange metallic to a glowing red. Her wrist felt hot, but not burning, just the sensation of heat—a *lot* of it. Then the bracelet was there. Closed. No clasp. No way to take it off. It was as if the links surrounding her wrist were a part of her.

Joie caught her hand. "It's beautiful, but, Gabby, it's some kind of weapon like Jubal's is. I believe my pendant is for protection, but I think this is a weapon."

"I don't know what this is or who it was made for," Gabrielle said softly, stroking the links with the pads of her fingers. "But I know it belongs to me. It's *supposed* to be mine. I love this, Joie. It feels right on my wrist, almost as if it's part of my skin." She lifted the bracelet to admire it in the moonlight.

As soon as the beams of light hit it, the bracelet lit up,

moving of its own accord, a glittering warmth that surrounded her wrist, snug but not at all tight. She loved it. More, she loved the fact that it had belonged to an ancestor before her and that Jubal had been the one to pass it on to her.

"You have something old. Something borrowed and something blue. You still need something new. You said you wanted to blend traditional with human, so we need to cover all four bases," Joie said.

"Everything is perfect, Joie. I couldn't ask for anything more."

"Shea, Savannah and Raven had something made for you. Something brand-new. Byron made it. Do you remember him at all? He lives in Italy with his lifemate, but he's a gem caller and they asked him to make you something special for your wedding."

Tears clogged Gabrielle's throat. She knew she'd become bitter toward the Carpathians ever since Gary had nearly died—ever since Gregori had brought him fully into their world. She felt like she'd lost him twice. First in death, and then to the Prince and his second-in-command. Gary was fully a Daratrazanoff, and with that name came the power and responsibilities given—and those were huge. Still, she'd pushed aside the friendships she'd forged with some of the women and that had been wrong. Very wrong.

"I don't deserve anything from them, Joie," she admitted in a low voice. "I've been standoffish."

More than that, she'd been restless and irritable, as if something deep inside her called to her. Wanted. No, even needed and recognized that time was growing short. She'd pushed for the marriage because she knew if she didn't do this now, something terrible was going to happen.

She pressed both hands to her churning stomach. She'd woken up from her sleep—the terrible paralysis of the Carpathian people—deep beneath the earth. She could hear her heart thudding dangerously loud. She felt the echo of the nightmare, the vicious stabbing as the knife blade penetrated her body, slicing deep over and over. She relived it, but the moment she woke, there was an echo of something else. Something she couldn't quite catch. So elusive, but so important. The feeling of dread built in her until every rising she wanted to run away and hide.

She still couldn't tell Joie, as much as she wanted to. She could only tell Gary. He didn't look at her as if she weren't quite up to the standards of the Sanders family. Joie and Jubal could kick serious butt. Gabrielle stood over Gary's broken, wounded body and cried her eyes out. She had nightmares when other Carpathians said they didn't dream—as in ever. She was growing afraid as each rising passed. She had to be somewhere and the need in her was so strong, she feared she would take off on her own soon. She didn't make sense. The Carpathian way of life was definitely not good for her and she had to find a balance before she went crazy. Gary was her balance.

"Shea, Raven and Savannah love you, Gabrielle. All of us noticed you've been withdrawn, but it's entirely permissible and even understandable, after what happened to Gary. Everyone knows you love him. How could that not affect you? Of course you've been moody and withdrawn."

"Don't make excuses for me," Gabrielle said. "They're my friends. You're my sister and I shut all of you out."

Joie hugged her tight. "I'm the queen of shutting people out, Gabby. You're a Sanders. When we have problems, we tend to keep them to ourselves until we figure out a solution. It isn't possible with your lifemate. I'm warning you right now. He'll know when you're upset and he won't mind in the least getting into your head and reading what the problem is. Males want to fix everything."

Gabrielle smiled. She couldn't help it. It was the truth. The good thing was, Gary knew her. He knew how to fix her. He didn't have to invade her personal space and she liked it like that. Although, since he'd risen as a Daratraza-noff, she'd noticed he was far quieter, and he'd always been quiet. Much more serious, and he'd always been serious. He had the same look that Gregori sometimes got, or Darius—Gregori's younger brother—one bordering on command, as if everyone had better do as he said when he said it. Still, he never looked at *her* that way.

Joie showed her the ring. It was beautiful. Elegant. Breathtaking even. It was to be worn on her right hand, the ring finger, and the moment Joie slipped it on, Gabrielle knew there was more to the ring than platinum and gemstones. She loved it just like she loved the bracelet, the pendant, and her blue garter. Perfection for her wedding. She knew each of the gems set in her ring were power gems and each would have a purpose. She'd learn about them later. For now, she could enjoy the fact that her sister and her three best friends were sharing this monumental event with her.

She stood there for a moment, feeling radiant and lucky. She actually felt beautiful, like a princess about to meet her prince. She'd never been happier than at that moment, knowing he was waiting right outside for her. She felt him. She always knew when he was close to her.

"He's here," she said softly to Joie. "He's waiting for me."

Joie hugged her again and kissed her cheek. "You've never been more beautiful than you are at this moment, Gabrielle. I hope you always stay this happy."

"I'll be with Gary. How can I not be happy?" Gabrielle asked, and hugged Joie back.

She turned toward the door, a lump in her throat. She wanted to see his face when she stepped through. That would tell her everything. She would know if he felt the same way. Joie, staying to one side of the door, pulled it open for her and Gabrielle picked up the sides of her dress and stepped outside. Her crystal shoes and ivory gown were all lace and crystals, so that the moment the beams of light from the moon hit her, she sparkled like the stars overhead.

Gary turned toward her and she drew in her breath. He was gorgeous. Every time she looked at him, she felt as if she were seeing him for the first time. He looked older than when she'd first met him, but it suited him. He had a few scars, but they suited him as well. His hair was long and thick, growing like the Carpathian's hair seemed to do. That gave him a more primitive, ancient look, but she found she liked it. There were a few streaks of gray spun into his dark hair.

Gary was a few inches shorter than Gregori, but no less commanding. She'd never seen that in him before. He'd always been a man to slip into the shadows and let others take the spotlight. She couldn't imagine him in the shadows now. His eyes were glued to her. He no longer wore his glasses. In any case, because he was so often in battle, defending the children against vampire puppets, he'd long since settled for the contacts Gregori manufactured for him. Now he was fully Carpathian and didn't need glasses or contacts, and she could see the amazing green of his eyes.

She loved the expression on his face. She couldn't have asked for a better manifestation of his love. His entire face lit up. His mouth went soft. His face went warm and his eyes went hot. *Really* hot. A million butterflies took wing in her stomach. Her lungs felt a little as if they couldn't quite get enough air. She moistened her lips with the tip of her tongue. He was so beautiful to her. Inside and out. Everything about him. Especially his mind. She loved his mind, although, right at that moment, when he was looking so handsome in a dark suit, so appropriate for a wedding, she thought maybe she could love his body even more. Well. Equally.

He held out his hand to her. "You look beautiful, princess."

He always called her princess when they were alone. Never in front of others. He made her feel like a princess in a fairy tale. Always. No other person in the world was so gentle with her in the way that he was. When violence swirled around them, Gary was always her rock.

"Thank you. I think you're quite handsome tonight as well," she said a little shyly. She felt shy with him. She didn't know why. Gary knew her better than anyone else did, but still, it was their wedding, and after tonight, they would be bound together in the Carpathian way. Not just in their hearts, but in their very souls. She secretly loved that idea. Being his other half. She *loved* it, knowing it was better than any fairy tale.

Gary drew her to him, his eyes still drifting over her face. Over her body. Slowly. Taking her in. Appreciating the time she'd spent getting ready. Human time. Not Carpathian. She had carefully put on every article of clothing manually. Taking her time, making it right. Wanting this night to be a mixture of both cultures, human and Carpathian.

Her hand was trembling and he knew it. He immediately enveloped her hand in both of his.

"You're safe with me, Gabrielle. Always."

She knew that. She had always known it. She loved the timbre of his voice. So gentle, like a caress. He was such a good man. As much as Gregori intimidated her and she didn't want Gary to be *anything* like him, she couldn't help but admire the flashes of Daratrazanoff in Gary. The confidence. The ability to keep her safe.

Maybe it wasn't so bad that he was a Daratrazanoff, especially if they could move away from the Prince. Always Mikhail Dubrinsky and his family would draw vampires and now, rogue Lycans. To eliminate the Prince was to eliminate the Carpathian people. Mikhail now had a daughter and a son. Both were threats to the vampires and rogues.

The attacks would never stop and Daratrazanoffs protected the Prince. If they remained, no matter that she was his lifemate, even putting her first, Gary's life would always be in danger, and she didn't want that. She couldn't have that. And that made her *so* not a Carpathian. It was ingrained in every man, woman and child to protect the Prince and his heirs. Even she felt it. Gary, as a human, had always taken on the protection of all the Carpathians, from unborn children to the Prince himself. Now, as a member of one of the most powerful families of Carpathians, he would be twice as much in demand.

"Gabrielle?" Gary prompted softly. He didn't tug on her hand or try to hurry her in the least. He never did. He was never impatient with her. She knew he was capable of impatience because she'd seen him giving orders to some of the other males and he did it in a voice that meant business—and they obeyed him.

"I'm ready." She lifted her chin, pushing aside the weird urge to run that kept getting in the way of her happiness. Run where? To what? Everything she wanted or needed was standing right in front of her. She just had the vague, persistent feeling of dread, as if something terrible was going to happen any minute. The feeling was growing stronger every day. Another war? Another moment when Gary would save a life at the expense of his own? In saving Zev Hunter, Gary had been eviscerated by the rogue Lycans. He waded in where no other human—well, except her brother—would dare to go.

"Are you ready, Gary?" she asked, needing his reassurance. Needing to know he wanted her with the same urgency that she wanted him. She'd waited so long. Everything Carpathian had gotten between them. They had never had a moment to themselves. It was as if fate had conspired against them.

"More than ready, princess. This is our night. Our time. I want to give you everything you've ever wanted." Gary snapped his fingers and a horse emerged from the trees.

Gabrielle caught her breath. The horse was a good seventeen hands. Pure white. Tail and mane flowed like so much silk with every move the graceful animal made. He came to them, prancing as he did so, his eyes on Gary.

Gary put his hands around her waist and lifted her onto the horse's back, sidesaddle, her dress flowing around her much like the horse's mane. The ivory lace settled in a beautiful drape. Her breath settled in her lungs as Gary took the reins and began to lead the horse through the trees toward the mountain where the fertility flowers grew in abundance—another thing Gary had contributed to their people. He had planted and cultivated the flowers until an entire field grew wild once more up the mountain.

White petals drifted around them and settled on the trail so that there was a carpet of white for the horse to carry her over. Overhead, the leaves rustled as they went under the canopy of trees. She glanced up and swore some of the branches bowed toward them as they passed, setting the leaves swaying so that they appeared a beautiful silver in the moonlight.

Wolves began a serenade, and she knew they sang to them. She loved that. She loved that nature surrounded them and seemed to bless their joining. The horse's gait was so smooth she didn't even have to hold on, and could balance without effort. She felt as if she were floating through the air toward their ultimate destination.

The hooves made a light sound on the rock as they started up the mountain, adding to the beauty of the moment. She couldn't have asked for a more perfect way to make the ascent. Her man—no, her lifemate—leading her to an incredible field of flowers on the back of a white stallion. Who had a man like that? Only Gabrielle Sanders, soon to be Daratrazanoff. Only she did.

*The sisters of Sea Haven are bound by the heart and
the magical power of the elements.*

FROM #1 *NEW YORK TIMES* BESTSELLING AUTHOR
CHRISTINE FEEHAN

THE SEA HAVEN NOVELS

*In the swirling tides of the ocean,
she found a handsome stranger...*
WATER BOUND

She was the obsession of two men...
SPIRIT BOUND

Her only choice was to trust him...
AIR BOUND

*Can she find happiness with a man
steeped in secrets and shadows?*
EARTH BOUND

PRAISE FOR CHRISTINE FEEHAN'S
SEA HAVEN NOVELS

"Characters as heartwarmingly interesting as those in
her Drake Sisters novels and as steamy as those in her
Dark novels."   —Fresh Fiction

christinefeehan.com
facebook.com/christinefeehanauthor
penguin.com

M1425AS0715

Can't get enough paranormal romance?

Looking for a place to get the latest information and connect with fellow fans?

"Like" Project Paranormal on Facebook!

- Participate in author chats
- Enter book giveaways
- Learn about the latest releases
- Get book recommendations and more!

facebook.com/ProjectParanormalBooks